ALWAYS ANI

Siân O'Gorman

About *Always and Forever*

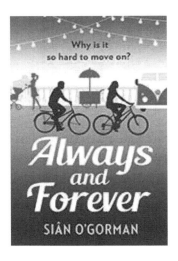

How can you find yourself again, when you can't face what you've lost?

Joanna Woulfe is looking to get her life back on track after her husband John leaves their family home. Once a high-flying PR Director, Jo now looks after her son Harry and seeks support only from her mother Marietta and her best friend Nicole. But Nicole's own marriage is facing its greatest ever crisis, and Marietta, too, is distracted by the reappearance of an old flame, ex-Showband-singer and lothario Patrick Realta.

Soon Jo enrols with a colourful local amateur dramatics group and begins a flirtation with the handsome young Ronan Forest. But is she really ready to move on from her old life –

and from her years of marriage to John? And what was it that happened three years ago that sent the couple into free-fall?

Before long Jo will realise that is only by looking back that she will ever truly be able to move forward…

For Zoë

Way back in the mists of time…

It was dusk, the strings of fairy lights hung around the cricket pavilion, the band playing 'Besame Mucho', the singing, the slightly drunken dancing, the long black dress I wore trailing behind me, my friends and I drinking rosé on the grass. We had reached the dying-days of college, exams dispensed with; all we wanted was to suspend time. And it was such a beautiful night, the perfect summer's evening. For a moment, it seemed, the world did stop, and it was as though this feeling of balancing between two worlds would last forever. And it was at this moment, I stood up, gathered my bag, found my shoes and was about to slip away.

'You're not leaving, are you Joanna?' John Beckett was standing in front of me and I was surprised he even knew my name. He was wearing jeans, sandals and a loose shirt, unbuttoned, half-untucked. There was something so gloriously young about him; he had an energy, an excitement, a brilliance that burned brighter than in anyone I had ever met.

'I'm not… well, I might… I don't know what to do exactly.' I *was* hoping to leave, something to do with not wanting the evening to end in disarray, as it always did once the mojitos and gin and tonics took their effect. 'I was—'

'Don't,' he said.

'What?'

'Leave.'

The name John Beckett was known to me way before I actually met him. Both of us were at Trinity College, me doing English, him, history. In our third year, he was president of the students' union and always about, megaphone in hand or ripping sellotape with his teeth to put up another poster on another lamppost. He was an organiser of things, protests, events, concerts, and the life and soul of the college. He had to be, I surmised in my arrogant, youthful way, full of himself.

I always had half an eye on John but had dismissed him, rashly, as not my type. We'd nod to each other but he always had some blonde posh-type hanging off him and I was too busy lusting after inappropriate men with long hair and skinny jeans.

John hung out with the poshos of Trinity, so I sort of assumed he was one, too. You know the type, from one of the rugby-playing schools of South Dublin. Little did I realise that he couldn't have been more different. John went to a normal school and lived with his Dad, Jack, in a tiny house in Sallynoggin.

'Don't leave?' I said. 'Why?'

'Because I've never talked to you and I don't want to miss my final chance to get to know the most intriguing girl on campus.'

'Intriguing?'

He grinned. 'Yes. You just are.'

I'd never thought of myself as intriguing before. It was something to savour, something to think about. Intriguing. I liked it. I smiled back at him.

'And beautiful,' he added.

That was it. Our perfect beginning. The night we found each other and held on tight.

John and I were married five years later, in the Trinity Church, the reception in the cricket pavilion, the same Cuban band playing. Honeymoon in a campervan driving around the south of France.

And then, of course, reality slowly seeped its way into our so-called perfect life. Maybe it's not good to begin with perfection, because then, surely, the only way is down. Was the turning point when I decided I wanted a child? Was it all my fault?

John found a job at the *Irish Times*, working evening shifts and weekends. Anything to get started. Meanwhile, I was employed at Declan Connolly PR, a small but exclusive company which gave me great experience but also required huge personal commitment and enthusiasm. Both of which ran out when I decided I wanted a baby. Suddenly, I was fixed with a desire stronger than anything I had ever felt for anything or anyone. My job, which I had once loved, was now far less important than my as-yet unfertilised, unrealised, child. The Blackberry and briefcase were never going to compete with my baby.

But getting pregnant didn't happen the first year, or the second. By the third I had become rather desperate and, by the fourth, more than slightly crazed. And so our IVF years began. John, being John, was as kind and supportive as he possibly could be. I had gone ahead with it without really consulting him and each time he dutifully turned up at the clinic, before racing back to file his copy.

But even *I* was slightly scared of the person I was rapidly metamorphosing into, someone single-mindedly determined, ruthless even, all softness replaced by steel. But a baby wasn't just going to magically appear. *Someone* had to make it happen. And that someone was me.

At work, I managed to hide my IVF struggle from Decco – my manager – and everyone else, fooling them all into thinking that all I cared about was work. I remember one particular meeting with some potential clients, a start-up for a new cycling-taxi service (slower than walking as it turned out, which was not, I realised, the point). They had a large budget and I was to pitch for the ad campaign, the whole branding of the service.

Fuelled by fertility drugs and gingernuts, crammed into my mouth moments before entering the room, I was ready for them. The presentation was like an out-of-body experience. I felt invincible, suddenly imbued with an energy and a conviction that I knew it all, I was the answer to their prayers. Even Decco noticed. 'Joanna,' he said, 'you were amazing in there.' He grinned at me. 'What are you on? Because whatever it is, I want some.'

'Clomid,' I said, but he didn't really know what that was and just laughed and slapped me on the back.

'You're on fire,' he said. 'Come on, I'll buy you lunch.' And I went, because a) I like Decco and b) I couldn't think of an excuse, when really I was feeling so incredibly nauseous that I thought I would throw up. Watching Decco tuck into his rare steak and posh chips, I strained every fibre of my being to ensure I didn't vomit into his miniature jug of Béarnaise. And we won the contract; another gust for my Clomid-blown sails.

Nicole, my best friend, was the only person who knew I had ovulation and pregnancy tests in my handbag. The only one who knew the whole truth about my increasing hysteria.

Three failed attempts over five years. And then, God, Allah, Daniel O'Donnell (delete as applicable) be praised, because on my fourth round, just when I was emotionally scraping myself off the ground and trying to imagine a child-free life, I took one more test.

Nicole had called round to see me after work. 'I think,' she said, peering at the stick, 'I think…' She stopped and spread out the leaflet from the box, examining the diagrams.

'I think,' she said, laughing now, 'I think you might be pregnant!'

We danced around and around the room, both of us crying.

'Is this really happening, Nic?' I said, not daring to believe it.

'I think so,' said Nicole, grinning at me. 'You better start taking it easy. Crack open the Dairy Milk and take root on the sofa.'

'It's too much to take in.'

Nicole shrugged. 'You'll be fine. You always cope. You'll be amazing.'

She always had so much faith in me. I wish I'd been able to live up to it, but now the stuffing had been well and truly knocked out of me. Where is that woman, that other Jo? Nowhere, that's where. No wonder John eventually had enough of me.

Chapter one

Our marriage had screeched to a halt a long time ago but it was John who finally called time. I'd stopped bothering with him, focussing entirely on our three year old, Harry, but still sometimes – ever so rarely, but sometimes – I'd get a glimpse of the old John. He might say something funny and I'd feel my mouth want to twitch into a smile, or I might spot him through the window as he cycled into the drive, trousers tucked into his socks, wearing the slight frown he had when he was thinking. We used to be happy but not anymore. 'I'm going to move in with my Dad for a while. Get some space.' John's mouth was dry and I could see him trying to swallow. 'Just for a bit.'

This particular bombshell was dropped on a Friday evening, the time of year when spring has not yet sprung and the cold and dark has become an unrelenting slog. Irish winters tend to take their toll, in all sorts of ways.

Anyway, I'd just put Harry to bed, clutching his grey rabbit, when I heard the rattle of John's key at the door. We'd been together for fifteen years by then, both of us older and more careworn than when we had met as students. He was now standing there, just inside the door, looking frozen through, his clothes all bunched underneath his luminous cycling jacket.

'What do you mean you're moving in with your Dad?' My voice was this new one I had developed, which sounded strange and unreal to me. Before everything that happened I always sounded so confident, but these days I wasn't myself at all. Or rather this *was* the new me and I just had to get used to feeling like this, permanently petrified that life would deal a new blow.

John had tears in his eyes and I thought, why is *he* crying? John never cried, never in all the years since I met him and now tears were rolling down his face. He stepped forward and tried to take my hand with his damp, cold one but I flung it away. Please, I thought, not now. Staring at him, I searched his face for clues, trying to work out what he was trying to say. Was he leaving for ever? Was this the end of me and John?

'It's just…' he said. He pushed his hands through his hair. 'I can't…' He still held his helmet. Put it down, I thought. Put it down and stay. But he didn't. 'I have to,' he continued. 'For my own sanity. I've tried. I've tried everything. I know it makes me sound like a coward and perhaps I am, but I wish you would understand.' As he spoke his jacket rustled along, accompanying his words. 'I'm just not coping well,' rustle-rustle. 'I've got to get my head together, some space… oh, I don't know… I just can't breathe sometimes.' Rustle-rustle. 'I'm in a shop, or on the train to work and I feel that if I don't get some fresh air I'm going to stop breathing in front of everyone and… and…' Rustle-rustle. 'I need a rest.'

'Me too. I'd like a rest!' I found myself shouting. I quietened down, thinking of Harry upstairs and thanking God that my mother, Marietta, was at the golf club's Friday night drinks.

'That's not what I meant. I just need to get away. Sort my head out, that's all. I think…' There were more tears in his eyes now. 'I think I'm going to go mad if I don't.

We were both exhausted. The past few years had taken their toll. Who knew life and happiness could plummet so rapidly? Now, the thought of putting on a suit and heels and spending my days trying to please clients makes my blood run cold. Before Harry and everything else, my career in PR had been my life and if someone had asked me then if I ever saw myself as a stay-at-home mother, I would have laughed in their faces before taking a sip of my double-shot cappuccino. I was happy to allow John to go out to work, as long as I got to stay at home, where I felt safe and where I could keep Harry safe. Marietta had only just convinced me to let Harry sleep in his own room, something I resisted, until I tried it and he loved it. We all slept better now but I still carried the baby monitor around the house and checked on him several times in the evening.

'John...'

'It's like there's this cliff,' he went on, determined to speak, to try to make himself understood, 'and I'm walking along the edge and earth keeps falling away and it's dark and my foot is going to slip any moment. It's terrifying.'

I knew how he felt, all too clearly. But being terrified was just something I had learned to live with. While I retreated into motherhood and dealing with my own grief, John went another way. Far away from me. But he could have come home with a tattoo of Ozzy Osbourne, or announced he was transitioning and I wouldn't have noticed. Or cared. I was just surviving. And Harry. Harry had to come first. John and I had separated a long time ago, only now he was moving out.

I looked away but really all I wanted to do was to put my arms around him, to hear him whisper into my ear how much he loved me, like he used to do. To remember that feeling of invincibility between us. But we weren't invincible. We were broken; only he had realised it before me.

At the front door, he hesitated. 'So, I'm going.' I refused to meet his eye. 'Goodbye Jo.' He swung his bag across his shoulders and I watched him wobble off on his bike and out of our marriage.

Soul-sappers

- Running out of milk, so no tea

- Watching Mastermind on your own

- The pointlessness of cooking when a) Harry doesn't eat much and b) biscuits are plentiful and easy to open

- The ensuing weight-gain

Chapter two

After a sleepless night, I broke the news to my mother, Marietta. She was always most receptive after her daily power-walk as she, like us all, responds well to sea-spray and ozone. Aged 62, fit as the proverbial fiddle (because of the golf and the arm-pumping walks and all that) Marietta's brain was still as sharp as the tacks she used to sell when she ran Hardman's Hardware. Despite this, recently her behaviour was becoming slightly odd. She was often somewhat distracted, lost in thought, and she kept disappearing and never really answering where she had been. She'd also run off to take calls and return looking flushed and preoccupied.

'Mam,' I said, 'John has… John's gone…'

'John's gone?' She was stirring porridge for herself and Harry's second breakfast (his first had been Nutella on toast with me at 6.30am). 'He's gone? John?' She balanced the wooden spoon across the pot.

I nodded. 'Gone.'

'John?'

'Yes! For God's sake, Mam! He left last night, said he had to get his head together.'

'Where's he gone?'

'His Dad's. Jack's.'

Her lips tightened. 'I thought this would happen.'

'You thought this would happen?' I rasped. 'What do you mean, you *thought* this would happen. And if you were so sure, Mystic Meg, why didn't you tell me and save me from the shock?'

'Well,' she said, filling the kettle and clicking it on. 'He's depressed, isn't he?'

'You think he's depressed?'

She shrugged. 'I guessed he wasn't coping. He's a bottler.'

'Bolter more like.'

'He bottles things up. Not one to talk about his feelings. Not one to want to worry you.'

'Bit late for that. But depressed? Really?'

I was getting the distinct impression she was on his side and not mine and I was outraged. 'How are you so sure? How do you know he hasn't met someone?'

'I'm not; I don't,' she said. 'But he's a good person is John… he's obviously very unhappy.'

'Unhappy?' I was suddenly painfully aware that I hadn't given John's mental well-being one thought over the last few years. He had become unimportant. I had needed him to be alright, to be the one thing I didn't have to worry about. But maybe he *had* met someone nicer than me (not difficult to do under the circumstances). Someone who doesn't have bags under her eyes or think that cereal for dinner is perfectly acceptable. Someone *fun*. I was ballooning in front of his very eyes, too… it all made sense.

'So, what am I going to do?' I said, eating Harry's cold, leftover toast, daubing extra Nutella on the slices. (Butter *and* Nutella. Was that wrong?). I felt as though my insides were being clenched and twisted by some invisible force. I couldn't breathe. 'What am I going to do?'

'Harry!' she called. 'Porridge!' And then, turning back to me: 'You're going to carry on,' she said. 'That's what you are going to do. One foot in front of the other.' Her phone beeped. She grabbed it and checked the text and then popped it back onto the work surface. She then slid it into the pocket of her trousers.

'But how can I do that?' There was no answer. Marietta was back to stirring the porridge, mind utterly absent.

Harry came over and crawled onto my lap, tucking his head against my neck. I rubbed my face in his thick, brown hair. He smelled of shampoo and Playdoh. In one hand he had a plastic lion and I could feel the Lego in the pockets of his corduroys. 'Hello Harry, my sweet. Are you ready for your porridge?'

'Granny's porridge?'

'Yes, Granny made it.'

'I only like hers. Yours is lumpy.'

'That may well be but I make the best toast, isn't that right?'

'And the best pasta and the best fish fingers.'

'And you are the best eater.' I kissed his cheek. 'Isn't he Mam? Harry, the best eater?' She didn't answer. 'Mam?' What was this? Always so switched on and focussed, she was now scatty and preoccupied. Mam?' I said again.

'What?' At least her hearing was working.

'What's your mother's maiden name?'

'What are you on about?'

'What colour are my eyes?' I said, closing them.

'Haven't the foggiest,' she said. 'Have you taken leave of your senses?'

'What's my name?' I said.

'Sweet Mary and Joseph!'

'It's Jo!' I said. 'My name's Jo! Not Mary *or* Joseph.'

'I don't know what you are talking about.' She began serving Harry's porridge and I saw her take the salt from the counter and sprinkle it on.

'That's salt!'

'No it isn't,' she said. She tasted it. 'Yes it is,' she smiled at Harry. 'Silly Granny.' She took out a new bowl and served him again, this time using sugar.

'By the way, Mam. Where were you last night?' I gave Harry a spoon and he started feeding himself. He was due to start attending a crèche five mornings a week. He was growing up but he was still my little boy. If only, there was some way of trimming his roots and making him into a bonsai boy but every time I dressed him, I could see the ascent of his pyjamas as they became smaller and smaller, nanometre by nanometre. 'I was awake gone 3am and you weren't home,' I said. 'I didn't know that Friday nights at the golf club were so hedonistic.

'Didn't you?' she said vaguely.

'You were out all night!'

'Not really! Honestly Joanna, you'd think you were my own father. I was in the golf club and we all got talking and there was some dancing. We're not old fogies you know. There is life in the old dogs yet. Nothing for you to worry about.'

And then she laughed a strange tinkly little laugh that didn't sound like her at all. This was all I needed, my mother going strange just when the rest of my life was heading south.

Once Harry had finished his porridge and I was clearing up, I delved in the fridge for the secret stash of chocolate I kept for emergencies. If this wasn't a situation – husband gone, a long and lonely life of single parenthood stretching ahead - which called for the magical properties of Lindt then I didn't know what was.

Chapter three

My best friend Nicole was more conventionally sympathetic than Marietta regarding my new John-less state. She kept up the calls and texts, sending me various cuttings from *Psychologies* magazine or sending me daily aphorisms such as 'dare to live the life of which you dream' or simply 'get up, get out and get on' which, although less flowery, I appreciated for its simplicity. She let me do a lot of crying and had a constant supply of tea bags, boiled water and biscuits. I don't know what I would have done without her.

The first few weeks post-separation I spent in my pyjamas. It didn't seem to bother Harry and the two of us watched a lot of children's television, so much so that Peppa Pig began to infiltrate my dreams. In one, she cooked a huge meal for Fireman Sam which he said he didn't like and she became unfeasibly annoyed and threw the lasagne (I think it was) at the wall.

Somehow Marietta refrained from tutting when she would return from her power walk or golf outing or lunch with friends and we'd be on the rug, building something indiscernible from Lego. For some reason she wasn't as harsh as I thought she might be. In the mornings, she'd even bring me up a cup of tea and leave it beside my bed.

'How do you feel today?' she would ask.

'Same.' And I would close my eyes and let the tea get cold until Harry snuggled in beside me. His stomach beginning to rumble, we'd then get up for breakfast.

After far too long of this self-indulgent indolence, I had a reason to get up. Harry was starting his crèche sessions and although I hated that our time alone was coming to an end, I knew rationally that it would be good for him. Part of me (actually quite a big part) wanted us to live together for the rest of our lives, watching television, eating toast and playing. But I was aware that this was not a sensible plan and poor Harry would have to spend thousands on therapy when he was grown up. And that I did not want on my conscience, along with his certain obesity and stunted language skills.

So, one Monday morning, I showered and dressed, put on some make-up and came down stairs. John had arrived already so we could both take Harry to crèche. He and Marietta were looking very cosy together, drinking tea. Harry was wearing his new dinosaur hoodie.

'You look smart, Harry,' said Marietta. 'Doesn't he John?'

'He looks brilliant,' said John. 'Like a big boy.'

Big boy? Harry? I didn't want him to be a big boy. I felt pangs at the thought of saying goodbye to him at the crèche. But Harry looked so delighted, sitting there on John's lap, proudly showing his daddy his new lunch box and juice bottle, and the secret pocket in his bag where he was hiding his plastic lion. At that moment I knew all I wanted was for him to be happy. And I would just have to suck it up.

'Yes, he does look like a big boy, all ready for school,' I said and I noticed Marietta looking approvingly at me. 'Shall we go?' I said. 'Ready John?' And the three of us, Harry in the middle, John wheeling his bike, the three of us holding hands, walked to the crèche. If anyone saw us they would have thought we were the perfect set-up. Handsome dad, cute kid and mother with slightly too much make-up on in an attempt to look less tired. We were playing at being a family.

'Alright?' said John, once we'd dropped Harry off. He'd seen me wiping away a tear.

I nodded. I didn't want him to think that I wasn't coping or that he'd been right to leave mad, crazy me. I wanted him to think that I still retained a semblance of dignity, even if inside I wanted to howl. 'You?'

'Not really.'

'Harry? Growing up?'

'Not just Harry,' he said. 'Other things as well.' He looked as if he might cry again. I was just going to see if he wanted to go for a cuppa at Brian's Café when he looked at his watch and his expression changed. 'Better go. Already late for the editorial meeting.'

'Yes of course.' And I looked away to show him I didn't care. 'I've got a meeting myself. Decco wants to pick my brain about something.' I was so out of it all I doubted my old boss would want to pick my brains about anything, unless it involved *Iggle Piggle* or *Upsy Daisy*.

'Going back to work?' He looked interested for a moment.

'Maybe. Just thinking about a few options.'

'Right.' He stood there for a moment too long. 'See you Jo. Good luck with Decco.'

'You too.'

He swung his leg over his bike and cycled off.

I didn't always cry in those first few weeks of Harry starting crèche but sometimes after dropping him off, I'd come home and slip back into bed. But those times became less and less and soon I began to go for walks, not as arm-pumping as Marietta's, but more meditative. And Harry enjoyed crèche and made a best friend that first day. He and Xavier fell in love and eventually all I could see were the good things about it.

The friends, the independence, the learning to read and write and tie shoelaces and the delights of papier maché.

He was growing up, he was moving on. I knew I had some catching up to do. I'd get there... eventually.

Chapter four

Nicole was tiny, with black curls endlessly bobbing around her face, which was like a little doll's – rosebud mouth, rosy cheeks. I always felt like her ungainly, inelegant older sister, even though she was actually six months older. She always dressed in flat shoes and neat trousers, there was a touch of the Parisienne about her, her attractiveness only enhanced by her Ballinrobe accent and her ability to see the ridiculous in everything. One eventful weekend away, when we eventually re-found civilisation after losing our bearings on the Wicklow Mountains, it was she who downed a glass of whiskey in the local pub and saw the funny side, while I was still shaking with fear about the night we nearly spent being eaten by sheep.

We had lived together at university and had seen a lot of life together. Drunken holidays in various Greek islands, our two marriages, my futile fertility fandango, the death of both our fathers… well, just everything, really. She was now a primary school teacher, surrounded by tiny children all day long, and was endlessly kind and patient with them. Children were something she and her husband, the charismatic, undeniably attractive, gallery-owning Pole, Kristof Gold, had decided against. Theirs was a marriage that would never have to take the strain of children. Was this, I wondered the secret of its success?

One morning, after dropping Harry to crèche, I went to meet Nicole at Brian's Café, round the corner from my house. It was run by the eponymous Brian, who wore Buddhist prayer beads and burned incense while he made pots of tea and mugs of instant coffee. The KitKats and the Buddhist prayer flags were unlikely bedfellows but, somehow, it worked. Alongside the cheese rolls, he also had a range of alternative food, which, after all these years, I had never seen anyone actually order. Today's special was Tibetan tea-cake which, to my eyes, looked like an ordinary tea-cake scattered with potpourri.

Nicole was already there, milky tea in front of her, a copy of *Embrace Pain and Hug Yourself* on the table. Her eyes were closed.

'Meditating or sleeping?' I said into her ear.

'Neither,' she said, opening her eyes and standing to hug me hello. 'Thinking.'

I sat down, signalling to Brian.

'Tibetan tea-cake?' he suggested hopefully, after shuffling over in his Buddhist shoes (turquoise with little bells).

'I don't think so,' I said. 'Maybe next time. But more tea, please, and toast. Butter. Strawberry jam.' Brian nodded and shuffled off. 'Sugar,' I confided to Nicole, 'is the only thing keeping me going these days. Biscuits *and* cakes. Comfort eating, Marietta calls it. She's worried I'm going to balloon.'

'Balloon away!' said Nicole, who, I noticed, was even thinner than usual. 'I think I might try it too.'

'What?' I said.

'Ballooning,' she said. 'It looks so nice, just to take the foot off the gas, stick your head in a bag of cream cakes and not come up for air, you know?'

'Oh yes,' I agreed. 'To just go on eating and not worry about the side effects.' Although Nicole didn't look as though a cream cake or even a stick of celery had passed her lips in quite some time. She was worryingly thin. And pale. 'That's the only thing that stops me. The side effects.'

15

But however much Nicole thought about ballooning, she pushed away the Tibetan tea cake that Brian brought over 'on the house'.

'Sorry Brian,' she said. 'I'm just not hungry. Anyway what makes the tea cakes Tibetan?'

'They are blessed by the Dalai Lama,' he said.

'Personally?' I said, impressed.

'No, not quite personally, but by Skype,' he said. 'Not by *him*. But by one of his representatives. Someone who works very closely with him. Close enough anyway. There's a Buddhist nun on Achill Island who will bless anything you wish. She'll bless you, your baby, your teacakes, anything. And all by Skype.'

'How much does she charge?'

'It's very reasonable,' he said. '20 cents a blessing. Cheaper than a KitKat.'

'I think I might try it,' mused Nicole. 'I wouldn't mind being blessed by the Dalai Lama. It can't hurt, can it? It's got to be less traumatic than a Catholic blessing, all that holy water thrown at you. Having to confess non-existent sins. This sounds a lot less involved. Just a quick Skype. I'd give anything a go.'

She suddenly looked gloomy and picked up the copy of *Embrace Pain and Hug Yourself.*

'Nic?' I asked. 'Is anything wrong? What's with the self-help book? You do know it's a slippery slope, don't you? Next up are *Ted Talks*, subscription to '*O*' Magazine, veganism…'

'Don't knock it,' she said. 'It's the only thing keeping me sane at the moment.' There was something about the way she spoke that made me think this didn't seem like the ordinary, every-day, recreational use of the self-help genre.

'We have a dog!' she said, suddenly brightening. 'We couldn't say no to taking him and he's incredibly sweet. Quiet and fluffy.'

'I thought you two were cat people?'

'Mrs Fitzgerald, from next door,' Nicole continued. 'Remember her? Such a nice woman. Well, she had to go into a nursing home. On the orders of her son, apparently. And he chose one which wouldn't let her bring Puffball. She was in tears when she asked me and of course I couldn't say no.'

'Nice son. But *Puffball*? What kind of dignity does that give him? Wouldn't he prefer to be called Rex or Rover?'

'The name is a bit unfortunate, I must admit,' she said. 'He was Mrs Fitzgerald's pride and joy and I've already brought him in to see her twice.' Nicole showed me an image on her phone. I could just make out two brown eyes in the midst of a fluffy white cloud. She rested her face in her hands. 'It's just that…'

'What?'

'Could you…' she said. 'Would you… you probably won't feel like it…'

'What?'

'You're probably not in the mood, not after John. You said you thought you'd never want to socialise again.'

'I said there was no point leaving the house. Except Harry needs fresh air. I can't deprive *him* of Vitamin D. Social services might have a word.' I looked closely at her. 'Why, what's going on?'

'Will you come to dinner?'

'Eating is something I am still able to do. Unfortunately. My appetite was not affected by John's departure. When do you want me?'

'Tonight,' Nicole said. She was looking burdened, somehow. Not herself. Something was bothering her. 'It's just that I need you... your company. It's me and Kristof and someone else. An artist. She's... his colleague... a friend. So, can you come?'

'Of course. I'll ask Marietta to look after Harry. Unless she's gallivanting.'

'Thank you.' Relief flooded her face.

'Nic, what's going on?'

'Things... you know.' As she lifted up her cup, I could see her hand was trembling. 'It'll just be nice to have a friendly face there.'

'You're not ill or anything?' I was starting to get worried now. 'Kristof's okay?'

'He,' she said, grimacing, 'is hunky-fucking-dory. So, you'll come to dinner? I really need you. I'm dreading it. I need somebody there just for me.'

'Who's the other woman?'

'That's exactly what she is. Coco Crawley.'

'Coco Crawley? The performance artist?'

'And every woman's living nightmare. She's what could be called irresistible.'

'So, *she's* not mainlining biscuits and cakes, then.' Sometimes I cursed my insatiable need for jokes and flippancy.

'No, just men.' She picked up her phone and book. 'And especially Kristof.'

'Kristof?' I was confused. 'What do you mean?'

Nicole looked me squarely in the eyes. 'They are shagging. The two of them.' She spoke so loudly that some of the other customers looked up.

'Shagging? Are you sure?'

''Course I'm sure. It's common bloody knowledge. Well, that's what you get for marrying an artist, I suppose. I should have married someone nice and normal. A postman. Or a newsagent.'

'Free magazines.' I shook my head. 'What do you mean exactly?' Nicole was standing up to leave. 'Don't go! You can't leave me hanging.'

'I've got to. Puffball doesn't like being alone in the house for too long. He gets lonely. And anyway, I've got to get things ready for tonight.'

'But you are not seriously inviting her round if… you know.'

'Welcome to my world, Jo,' she said. 'This is what I have to do in order to remain married. Monogamy, according to Kristof, is overrated and the sooner I get over it the better.'

'Nicole—'

'Listen, I've got to go but I'll see you later, alright?' She came over and hugged me goodbye. 'Listen, Joanna. We can get through all of this, okay? We've survived life so far and I don't see why we won't get through this, too.'

And she left, leaving me utterly stunned. The supposedly doting Kristof was, in fact, a philandering fool.

Chapter five

It was Nicole who alerted me to the supposed miraculous qualities of a 'gratitude list'. She had torn out an article which extolled its benefits from some magazine. The idea is that it helps you remember the good things in your life. It makes you pay attention to the tiny, nice things that happen every day and not just the huge, horrible emotional tsunamis that can swoosh in at any moment.

Nicole bought me a lovely Moleskine notebook to start me off so I had no choice but to begin. I didn't want to let her down, not after she had listened to me so patiently, for so long.

Life-lifters, I call them, dutifully writing down anything remotely pleasant from the highs of holding Harry's lovely hand, to simply hearing my favourite song on the radio.

And they do work. Sometimes I think that life isn't too bad when the sun is shining and Harry is drawing away beside me and I'm looking forward to *Poldark* that night, but then I feel that tug inside me and suddenly I don't feel like writing life-lifters anymore. Instead, I find myself writing soul-sappers, my *in*gratitude lists.

I know everyone wants me to move on and that's what I should be doing, but going forwards means that I have to leave something behind and I am just not ready. Moving on seems so brutal.

'Did you ever watch the Crystal Maze?' I said to Marietta, when we were sitting down in the early evening before I went to Nicole's. 'There was this one part where you had to cross this special floor. You had to get to the other side to safety but you could only step on certain squares. Except you didn't know which were safe and which weren't. And if you stepped on the wrong square, you would be zapped, eviscerated, beamed away to nothingness…'

There was no sign from my mother that she knew what on earth I was talking about. Instead she carried on sending a text.

'That's what life feels like to me,' I said, continuing on, slightly desperately. 'As though at any moment I am going to step on the wrong square and it's all over. It's terrifying. Everything's terrifying. Like I can't move in case something goes wrong… because it has and it will…'

She put down her phone. 'Have you thought about doing something out of your comfort zone?' she said. 'When your father died, it was quite the change. There was I, wondering what to do with myself. I mean, he wasn't exactly the most dynamic of men… but it was strange coming home from the shop and him not sitting in the armchair watching *Columbo*.'

'He loved that programme.'

'So, that's when the golf got going…'

'But I hate golf.'

'I am not suggesting you play golf. You'd need good hand-eye co-ordination for one thing—'

'Just what are you suggesting?'

'I mean get out of your comfort zone. Do something you would never do. Break the mould. Like me, with golf. I had never held a club in my life before Fionnuala encouraged me to give it a try… and look at me now.' She presented her whole self with a flourish. And she did look the picture of golfing-health, glowing with later-life happiness. I felt pale and pasty in comparison.

'I'll think about it…' I said, wondering if she was right. 'But one thing's for sure, I'm really not playing golf. Argyle socks and sun-visors aren't my thing.'

'You're my comfort zone, Harry,' I said to my little boy that night, after I had read him *Thomas the Tank Engine*, a book that invariably sends me (and never him) to sleep. He was so tiny lying in his bed, blanket tucked in, grey rabbit under his arm, big eyes looking at me intently. It was so much to live up to, his trust in me. And immediately, I felt that fear, that stab of pain again, as I thought about how fragile he was and how much he meant to me. It was over-whelming sometimes. 'I don't want to do anything like paragliding or tag rugby or learning how to tango. Or play golf. I like being here with you.'

But first, anyway, I had Nicole's mysterious dinner party so, after checking and re-checking Harry's baby monitor and ensuring that Marietta had her phone charged, just in case there was a problem, and opening Harry's window a notch, so he had fresh air, I drove to Nicole's, ready to meet Coco Crawley.

Life-lifters

- First cup of tea in the morning

- Harry playing in the sandpit in the park

- Seeing Harry with his arm around Xavier at playgroup

- *Poldark* – it can only be watched alone

Chapter six

Nicole opened the door, a wine glass in her hand, a small ball of fluff – Puffball presumably –peering around her ankles. Tiny and sweet, a walking albino afro, Puffball was looking at me with sad, brown eyes.

'Vino?' Nicole said. 'I'm on the Rioja. It's very good. *Too good.*' She cackled in the way she only did when she was on the wine. 'You must have one. Or four. This is my third, or is it fifth?' She laughed again and then took a sip which slipped into a good glug. 'God, this stuff is delicious. It's the alcohol, you see, that makes all the difference. You know what I mean?'

'All too well,' I laughed. 'And you must be Puffball,' I said, picking him up. 'He's adorable, like a fluffy baby.' He licked my hand and, like all people who need only the slightest encouragement, I felt myself falling in love. 'He's gorgeous.'

Dogs, I had always believed, were so much better than medicine, way more effective than any self-help book. Maybe I should get one to fill the void of masculinity in the house? A bouncy labradoodle, perhaps, or an ever-so loving lurcher?

Nicole and Kristof's house was more like an art gallery than a home, I often thought, not without a smidgeon of envy. The hall, as you entered, contained two vast canvasses, which looked as though they had been attacked with a few cans of Dulux by somebody who'd consumed a few cans of Dutch Gold. Hanging from the ceiling in their living room was a large object that looked not dissimilar to a penis. I had never plucked up the courage to quite ascertain its identity as I thought that maybe it obviously was, or obviously wasn't. Either way, I would just expose my blatant philistinism.

Nicole always seemed a little out of place in this white-walled, dark-floored space. She was smart, rather than bohemian, cashmere separates rather than wool-mix, and looked, slightly, as though she had walked into the wrong house or indeed the wrong life. Kristof, however, was in his element.

He was very attractive, slightly exciting and slightly scary. He was only handsome if you liked men with a strong jaw, ice-blue eyes, a mean lip and a body that owed much to the shipyards of Warsaw. But while he looked as though he could throw a grown man across his shoulders, Kristof was where Kristof's heart lay. And bare-knuckle, soul-stripping human interaction. He wasn't one for light chit-chat. He wouldn't have suited me, for example, sometimes you might just want to eat your cornflakes in peace, but his intensity seemed to work for Nicole.

John always thought him a little over the top and was never quite as impressed with him as I was. Kristof sometimes said things that were wildly insensitive, but, as I explained countless times to John, they were what he *thought.* He didn't save your feelings, because it was the truth as he saw it. That was just the way he was. He was an artist, in touch with his opinions and not at all concerned with how people might react.

John was never swayed by my PR for Kristof. There was no particular love-lost between them. They happily tolerated each other, but I felt I had to make the effort for Nicole's sake. Being impressed by Kristof was essential to being her friend.

'Come on.' Nicole was already moving towards the kitchen. 'I need another glass of this. It's essential to my survival at the moment.' She kept her voice low, so Kristof who was in there, banging pans and listening to loud classical music, wouldn't hear.

'So…' I asked, pulling on her sleeve until she paused just outside. 'Is she here yet?'

'Not yet,' she whispered.

'But were you serious? She and Kristof aren't… you know… surely?'

'They are.' Her eyes narrowed, her fingers white around the glass. 'She's one of the fucking artists from the gallery. Swanned into town at the end of last year and has been causing mayhem ever since.'

'Wasn't she the one who lay on the steps of the Central Bank singing Famine laments or tucking herself into a ball and rolling around in front of the main door?' The entire nation had found her performance highly amusing, especially the bankers who had to step over her. When the IMF came to town, she sang 'The Fields of Athenry' in a loud voice, a one-woman response to the financial crisis.

'That's the one. Caitriona 'Coco' Crawley. She's amazing,' said Nicole, flatly. 'According to everyone. Beautiful, exciting, talented etcetera. Everything, it seems, I'm not. After the Central Bank thing, she went off to Goldsmiths and won the Constable Prize for her menstruation piece. You must have heard about it…'

'No, I can't remember that.' I had been in my own little bubble for the last few years.

'She collected her menstruation blood,' whispered Nicole, 'and poured it into moulds of patriarchal objects, such as a crucifixes or penises. And she saturated a copy of the Irish constitution with it. Then, when she was in London, she watered the hanging baskets outside the House of Commons with it as a symbol of female empowerment.'

'Good God.'

'And she won the Constable Prize as a result. Kristof's what you might call *much* taken with her. And…' she paused and took a breath, '…he wants us all to be friends.' She mimed quotation marks around the word 'friends'.

'But surely they're not shagging… I mean, he's married. To you.'

'Thank you for remembering. But monogamy is meaningless, apparently. You're setting yourself up for failure.'

All this was quite a bit for me to take in. 'Kristof? I thought the two of you were happy?'

'We are… if I accept his stance on fidelity. Which I have up to now. It's just that Coco isn't just a casual thing. She's—'

'It's serious?'

She nodded.

'Oh Nicole.'

She drained the contents of her glass. '*This* is helping. Come on and I'll get you a glass.'

Re-tucking Puffball under my arm, I followed her into the kitchen where Kristof was standing, be-aproned, amongst steaming pots of food. He turned down the music before bear-hugging me (and, as a consequence, Puffball) while Nicole poured herself another brimming glass and me a smaller one, as I was driving. He liked a good hug, did Kristof, but he always pressed himself against you just a little too hard, often inadvertently squashing your breasts as he did so. He was just that European touchy-feely sort, that hand on your waist band would always find its way onto your bare flesh. He was just so friendly. And arty.

I could feel the bear-hug relaxing, it was nearly over. 'How are you, Joanna?' Kristof said, releasing me finally. He looked at me in that intense way which we Irish are not quite used to, as though he really actually wanted to know. But right now I was feeling rather disgusted by him. That over-friendliness which I had put down to an artistic temperament was, in fact, decidedly creepy.

'Great,' I said, trying to maintain eye contact. 'All well, you know.'

'Is it? Really?' His arctic eyes bored into me, a technique he used on everyone, men, women, dogs, performance artists, and which had the immediate effect of sucking one into Kristof's aura. 'And John,' he said, the two of us eyeball to eyeball, me desperately trying not to let mine swivel away. It was a battle of wills. 'How is he? Nicole told me of his absence.'

I could feel the tears rush into my eyes. 'Yeah, you know… well…' I had to work hard on thinking of something else before I began to blub. Nicole needed me for moral support. I could not lose it now. I dug deep.

'Men aren't like women,' said Kristof, breaking our gaze to open a bottle of white wine, splashing most of it into the pot. 'They are the cats of the world. Women are the dogs.' I wondered where he was going with this. 'Cats,' he went on, 'want to be stalking the alleys at night, yowling and scrapping and tom-catting. Women like be at home by the fire, being stroked. Men,' Kristof was on a roll. 'We are a species apart. It's hard for women to understand us. We are ruled by our genitalia. Much to women's horror.' He shrugged again but looked delighted at the thought.

'No…' I tried to protest. 'I don't think it's John's genitals that made him leave.' I couldn't quite believe I was saying this. 'It was…' What was it again? '*Life* happened…'

Kristof just smiled the smile of a man who is going to let me believe what I want to believe and turned back to the stove. Nicole pulled a face at me.

'Anyway,' I said, trying to change the subject. 'Talking of dogs. I think I may have fallen in love with Puffball, here.'

Kristof shrugged his huge shoulders. 'It's a dog,' he said. 'Nic wants him to be a house dog but dogs should be outside.'

'Outside?' I yelped, rather dog-like myself. 'He's too small for outside.'

'It's not like I want him in bed with us,' insisted Nicole. 'He's only sleeping in the kitchen.'

The doorbell rang and we both jumped.

'Aha!' said Kristof. 'Coco arrives!'

Chapter seven

Suddenly a tall, gorgeous woman, dark hair cascading over her bare shoulders, scarlet lipstick, black, strapless dress paired with Doc Marten boots and a cape – which she swirled in the manner of a magician – was in the room, clutching Nicole's hands and kissing them, as though paying homage. Nicole stood there, trying to smile but, really, rigor mortis had set in.

'Nicky!' said Coco. 'It's so lovely to see you and thank you, thank you for inviting me. Such a treat! I am so, so delighted to be here.' It all came out in a rush and it was as if she were Nicole's long-lost friend, not her sworn enemy. 'You know, Nicks, I feel so inadequate when I see you. You do it all so perfectly!' She now had a little girl face on, looking as irresistible as Puffball.

'You're welcome,' said Nicole, who had managed to get her hands back. 'This is my friend, Jo.'

Coco turned to me and clasped *my* hands to her bountiful bosom. 'Any friend of Nicky's is a friend of mine,' she said breathily. 'I've already heard a great deal about you and now you can tell me all the rest. You must tell me *ev-er-y-thing*.'

'Well, we won't have time for *everything*,' I said. 'You know, I might leave out my star sign or the exact details of my menstrual cycle.'

I thought she might laugh, even just to be polite. 'No,' she said, with an intensity equalling Kristof's. 'I want to know those as well.'

Oh Jesus, I thought. She's a maniac.

'And where's my greeting?' Kristof was standing there, arms outstretched. 'I didn't get one yet.'

'I'm too busy, Kristof,' she said, airily. 'Saying hello to your gorgeous wife and her fabulous friend.'

Kristof pouted like a little boy. Coco went over to him and kissed him on the lips. Just once, but it felt so wrong and strange. It was all too intimate, so out-there. I mean, I know artists are all about being free and all that but most people, me included, find societal constraints quite reassuring. Here, they had been kicked away. No wonder Nicole had hit the bottle.

'You look beautiful,' said Kristof lasciviously while Coco laughed, trotting around in a circle and ending with a curtsey, looking at him from under her thick, dark lashes. She seemed certifiable, to me. But then who was I to judge? Me, who was border-line mad quite often these days and very aware that one never knew when the cold hand of crazy would tap you on the shoulder.

Coco winked at us. 'Men,' she said, as though she wasn't talking to the man in question's wife, 'are so simple. Not like us girls, are they? Putty, they are, in our hands.'

Kristof looked like he would happily be moulded by her. I felt like throwing up.

'Dinner?' Nicole's voice cracked. 'Is it ready? I was just wondering because…' she looked at me for help.

'Moules marinière,' said Kristof. 'Is that okay for you?' He spoke to all of us but he was looking at Coco. 'How are you with shellfish?'

'Well, as someone who grew up picking them from the rocks near Cleggan,' she said, 'I would say I'm pretty okay with them. We would steam them with the heat of a fire made from dried seaweed and suck them from their shells as though we were mermaids. Salt water runs in my veins,' she continued.

'My spirit is imbued with the ghosts of my ancestors, those who survived on the fruits of the sea during the Famine.' Coco looked entirely serious, Kristof raptly attentive.

Maybe, I thought, she *is* joking, and this is part of her performance. The role of an unhinged Kate-Bush-alike. Out of the corner of my eye, I saw Nicole reach out for the wine bottle and I wished to God I wasn't driving. Wine suddenly seemed like a very good idea.

Over dinner, Coco did indeed suck each shell of the mussels, drinking the juice, then running her fingers over the plate and licking each in turn. Kristof was transfixed by her, offering more bread and refilling her wine glass. I felt I needed somehow to try to make everything normal.

'Sharks,' I said, out of nowhere.

'What's that?' said Nicole.

'Well,' I said, immediately wishing that I hadn't allowed my subconscious to bubble forth. 'It's just a new theory I'm working on.'

'About sharks?' said Coco, leaning in. All six eyes (eight including Puffball, who was on my lap) were on me. I had to plough on.

'It's a metaphor,' I said. 'That we are just all bobbing around in the sea and everything seems alright but, because you are in the sea, you don't hear the music. You know, the one that warns the cinema audience that you are about to be attacked...' This normal conversation of mine was anything but. I looked around desperately.

'What music?' said Kristof. He was smoking a cigarette and blew a perfect smoke ring, which curled up to the ceiling.

'You know,' said Nicole, saving me. 'As in Jaws. Duh-ne, durrr-ne, duh-duh-duh...'

'Dun-dun-dun-dun…' I joined in. 'Exactly.' We looked at each other. We both knew I was failing in normal social discourse but she could tell that I was trying for her sake. 'And so,' I carried on gamely, 'everyone else is prepared for the fact that there is a shark circling below you, ready to grab your ankles, but you're not. You're on your own. And it could happen any moment, at any time.'

'So,' said Kristof, leaning in, 'stop swimming. Get out of the water.'

'No, Kristy,' said Coco. 'Life is water and water is life. We can't get out and we can't stop swimming.' She leaned in towards me, hands on her chin, a smile playing on her lips. 'I understand exactly what you are saying. I feel like I could do something with that. A tank of sharks…'

'It's already been done,' said Nicole, a withering note in her voice which was most unlike her. 'Damien Hirst, remember?'

'He's a charlatan,' said Coco. 'He was all about the effect. There was nothing there about the lives of women, the true life-force, the *givers* of life. I'm not interested in *men*.' She laughed disparagingly, fully aware that Kristof was watching her, mesmerised. She leaned across the table and popped a cigarette from Kristof's packet into her mouth. He immediately leaned across, lighter in hand, the three of us watching her inhale deeply and then blow her own perfect smoke ring. 'I'm about meaning, about the emotional connection, the mess, the blood, the sweat and tears we shed, the cries we make during child-birth on behalf of our menfolk… The pain of being a woman,' she said. '*That's* what I connect with.' Making eye-contact with Nicole was now impossible.

'Wearing a bra,' I said. 'That's the biggest pain of being a woman. The only time I am happy is when I take mine off.' I wasn't going to let Coco dominate the proceedings, not in Nicole's house. It just wasn't fair.

But Coco laughed. 'Men,' she said archly, looking at Kristof, 'have *no* idea what we go through.' She lingered over each word. Kristof was enjoying her performance immensely. It seemed it was for his benefit entirely. Then Coco fiddled behind her back, reaching up one arm and then the other and plonked her bra on the table. It wasn't from M&S, *that* much was obvious.

'So, Jo,' she said. 'I hear your husband has left.'

'Yes…' I said, looking wildly at Nicole.

'I told her,' said Kristof. 'If you don't mind. Coco likes to get to the essence of who we are.'

'I don't do small-talk, you see,' she said. 'When Kristy said Nicole's friend would be here, I asked him all about you. He mentioned it.'

'Well, there are more interesting things about me, Kristof.' I said, trying to pretend that I didn't mind that my marital woes were now dinner party fodder.

'Of course, it's just that heartbreak is one of my specialisms,' Coco said. 'That's why Kristy told me. I worked on this piece where I lay in the foetal position for days at a time. It was called *My Heart You Have Taken from Me*. I lay in MOMA for a month like that.'

'Wow.'

'It was my breakthrough. I was only 23 – a child. My heart in pieces after a relationship had ended; but after MOMA I stood up and I felt re-born.'

'And stiff…' I couldn't help myself.

'What do you mean?'

'After lying in the foetal position for a month.'

'Yes, there's that as well. I went straight to this tiny Thai woman I know in New York. She walked up and down my back for a few hours, cracking my spine with her heels. *Then*, I was re-born.'

Nicole filled up her own wine glass without bothering to check anyone else's, then glugged it back in one.

'Anyway,' she said. 'My point is heartbreak is just love by another name. Sometimes I enjoy having my heart broken more than the wild passion before that. I like the agony. It reminds me I'm alive. You know? Life is for living,' explained Coco. 'We're dead for a long time. To live full-frontal, to expose one's breasts to the winds of life…' None of us could help glancing at her breasts when she mentioned them. 'Sometimes the winds are warm and caressing, sometimes they buffet you so you think you might be blown away. But at least you have been touched by passion, by love. It's the only reason we are here and we would be fools to deny ourselves the pleasures of love and of flesh.'

'Tart?' said Nicole. 'Anyone for tart?'

Chapter eight

Leaving Nicole in that situation was very difficult. I wished I could take her and Puffball away with me. We could live in an all-female commune. Apart from Harry, of course. And Puffball. There'd be a touch of the Greenham Common's about it. Even the thought of it seemed cheering. But at the door, when she was seeing me off, quite drunk now and leaning against the wall for support, she tried to reassure me.

'Iss fine,' she said. 'Iss all fine. Grand. I can deal with it. Don't you worry 'bout me. Iss all fine. Iss juss different, that's all. Juss different.'

'If you're sure…'

We hugged goodbye and I drove away, not remotely reassured and more worried about her than ever. Before I went to bed I checked on Harry, fast asleep in his bed, clutching his grey rabbit, his little face peaceful and quite beautiful. Sometimes he took my breath away with how innocent and lovely he was. I had made him and I had to keep him safe. The responsibility felt almost over-whelming.

'Jo,' said Marietta, the next morning at breakfast. 'I was wondering if you might… well, join me in a spot of shopping. I'm after a bit of a makeover.'

'A makeover? Why? Have you been at the woman's magazines again?'

'Joanna, please.'

'Why do you want a makeover, for God's sake? You've never changed. You've never wanted to. You can keep borrowing my old work clothes. I'm not going to wear them again. And you've got that new jacket. The sequiny one.'

'That was borrowed. And the dress. From Fionnuala. She has some lovely pieces. But I need a few things for me. I can't always be wearing the same things… or borrowing them.'

I decided not to be insulted by the fact that my own mother had chosen not to borrow from my un-extensive wardrobe. At least she was asking for my help with her makeover.

'So, you want fashion advice from me?'

'Well, more of a shopping partner, actually. Just someone who can…'

'Hold the bags. I get it.'

'Will you come?' she said. 'I need a few jackets, some nice trousers and a couple of dresses. You know, spruce myself up a bit.'

'You're 62… you look great. You never look scruffy. Unlike me.'

'Yes, but you're young… you can get away with bird's nest hair and yesterday's make-up. Clothes have never been important to me. I was busy running the business for so long but now I'm out of it, I thought I might experiment a bit.'

'Mam,' I said suspiciously. 'Are you looking for pizzazz?'

'Pizzazz?' she mused. 'Yes, that's what it is. Pizzazz. I want some pizzazz, like Joan Collins. You said I look like her. And she always looks good. She's got buckets of pizzazz.' She gazed pointedly at my own attire. 'Joan wouldn't be caught dead in a pair of tracksuit bottoms.'

'Well, maybe when she's hanging around the villa in St Tropez, she might wear a pair of these,' I said. 'We just don't know. She can't wear sequins *all* the time.'

We both knew this wasn't true.

Marietta shook her head. 'Anyway, I've got to go. So, will you help me or not?'

'I will.'

'When?'

'What about this morning, when Harry's in crèche?'

'We'll go into town, so.'

'Okay.' I paused. 'And is there any other reason you want to do this?'

She pursed her lips. 'Well,' she said. 'I didn't tell you, I'm going away for the weekend. Just with friends, you know how it is. And I'd like a few nice things to wear.'

*

Later, after an exhausting morning of shopping, where Marietta bought several beautiful outfits, she appeared downstairs, wearing her new black slim-fitting dress, a small bouclé jacket and high heels.

'You look amazing!' I said, causing her to blush. But it wasn't just the clothes. She had a glow of happiness around her.

I went upstairs and watched her through my bedroom window. She was standing on the pavement looking out for something, or somebody, and there was a forlorn expression on her face. But then a gold Porsche hove into view, sliding effortlessly down the road, like Gatsby's Rolls Royce. Marietta twitched into life again, her shoulders back, springing towards the car like she was 18 again. I could see the gleam of the man's white hair, as he leaned across to open the passenger door.

And then inside, she leaned over to him and the two of them kissed. Passionately. Her hands deep within his white bouffant. Eventually, they separated and she took out a handkerchief and wiped her lipstick off his mouth. And then the car glided away.

I remained transfixed at the window, trying to take it all in. Holy Christ.

So my wildest suspicions were correct. She was in love. My mother was cavorting like a teenager.

Soul-sappers

- Soft-play places

- Cleaning (constantly)

- Coco and Kristof

- My mother and her new romance, while I watch TV alone. Again

Chapter nine

Nicole had been such an amazing friend to me over the years and now, when she needed me, I was feeling useless. What could I do except phone or text? She wasn't answering my calls so I wondered about calling round... bashing the door down, police-style, shoulder first. Shouting at Kristof, booting Coco out and trying to make everything normal again.

I sent her another text. 'Just tell me you're still alive xxx'

And this time she answered. 'All fine! Self-help books kicking in. Will update soon. Hope you are okay too xxx'

I wasn't doing too badly, truth be told. I was happily in my comfort zone, only venturing forth to take Harry to crèche. But comfort zones are misleading. Because despite their innate cosiness you can't, it seems, stay in them forever. Life always conspires to shake you out.

And so, it was that I found the Seaside Players. Harry and I were in the supermarket and, after paying for our shopping, I lingered at the notices wall. There was a jumble sale next weekend, people offering things: dog-walking, shirt-ironing, and guitar lessons. A lost cat, a man interested in a 'lady for conversation and maybe more', a woman searching for a room in which to write. But it was something else which caught my eye...

Thwarted thespian?

'To live is the rarest thing in the world. Most people exist, that is all' – so said Oscar Wilde, author of The Seaside Players' next production of

The Importance of Being Earnest. T.S.P. is on the look-out for a Gwendolen. Are you her? Declare your genius and try out at an audition at St Anne's Hall, Marine Road.

The date of the audition was today. I had an hour to go. I felt something stir within me, a feeling of terror and excitement, something I hadn't experienced for years. Not since… yes, that was it, since drama club at school and it was first night. The smell of grease paint (or rather our mum's make-up), the sound of the audience taking their seats and the sight of Sarah Peters snogging creepy Anthony Foley, from the local boys' school. I could feel the ghost of my inner-thespian rising up. Or more likely, my inner drama queen. And checking my phone, the date of the audition was today. The stars, at which, as we know, we are gazing from the gutter, were indeed aligned.

I took down the details, feeling my synapses fizzle into life. If I didn't want to move forwards, maybe going backwards to the days when I trod boards with the blitheness of a teenager would be good for me. It wouldn't be too much of an ask. I could do this.

Turning the car right around, I drove straight to St Anne's Hall and parked in the car park behind the building. 'Come on, Harry,' I said. 'I just want to see something.'

St Anne's was an old, forgotten church hall. It was quite staggering that it had escaped the beady eye of a developer and survived the Celtic Tiger untouched. Holding Harry's little hand, I pushed open the creaky door and stepped into a large, gloomy room with piles of stackable chairs on both sides and a stage at the far end, framed by raggedy black curtains. In the dim light, I could just make out a group of people sitting in a circle, each holding a sheaf of paper.

Harry wrinkled his nose. 'Smells, Mummy,' he said. 'Smells horrible.'

It was the scent of dust and years and years of bodies. The unmistakable fragrance of church halls, the world over.

'Actually, Harry,' I whispered. 'I think we'll just go straight home. This wasn't a good idea. Not one of Mummy's best.' I turned to shuffle us both out quickly, before anyone saw us.

'Gwendolen!' said a voice. 'Is that you Gwendolen?'

I stopped and turned back. 'No,' I said. 'I'm not Gwendolen.'

'Oh but you are,' the voice again, and the man, who was small in stature, stood up and began walking towards me.

'I'm not Gwendolen,' I repeated, suddenly panicking, feeling as though I had entered some awful reality television show where anything could happen. This was terrifying. 'I'm Joanna,' I said, my voice breaking. Harry and I were walking backwards now and as fast as we could.

'I know you are,' he said, even more terrifyingly. 'You're Joanna Woulfe.'

'Yes,' I said, squinting now. My eyesight isn't the best, even with my contacts in. Since Harry was born, it seems to be on a steady decline. Wait a minute. I knew this man. 'Mr Donnelly?' I ventured. 'Is it you?'

'It is indeed, it is indeed,' he said. He had now reached us and was looking up at me and clasping my hand with both of his, shaking it hard. 'Well if it isn't my Lady Macbeth or my Miss Jean Brodie.'

Mr Donnelly had been my teacher, back in the day, the one who ran the drama club. He still had the grey beard and cord jacket and that slightly chalky, dusty air of an old-school teacher. He was such a nice man and would find roles for all of us, even if it was just 'person sweeping floor' or 'unspeaking maid'. Over the six years I was in the school, I played everything from Lady Macbeth in an over-long version of the play (by the end, there were just a few stalwart parents left, some of whom were actively drunk as one had nipped out in Act III to buy some wine). I was also Nancy in *Oliver!* Where I sang so enthusiastically I may have lost some of the character's subtlety. 'It was a long time ago,' I said. 'I can't believe you remember.'

He tapped the side of his shiny forehead. 'They're all up here,' he said. 'Every single one. You don't forget a production. Or your star. *Mon etoile!* And who is this little chap?' He bent down to Harry, took his tiny hand and shook it gently.

Harry looked up at him. 'My nose is full of smell,' he said.

'Harry!'

But Mr Donnelly laughed. 'History,' he said. 'That's what you are smelling, young Harry. And greasepaint. That's the smell that gets into your nostrils once you plump for an actor's life – or once it, more likely, chooses you. And maybe the aroma of our spirit guide, Oscar Wilde?'

Harry sniffed obediently and nodded.

'It's the scent of incense and earl grey tea and the smoke of drawing room fires. I can sense him with us. Whenever I say a special prayer to Mr Wilde, I can smell it and I know he is with us, in spirit.'

At that moment, I wasn't quite sure if I was shirking my parental duty by allowing Harry to listen to all this, but Mr Donnelly straightened up and winked at me.

'Do you know, you might just be the answer to our prayers? I said a small incantation to Mr Wilde last night and… my wish has been granted.'

'I shouldn't have come.' I found myself saying out loud. A school production was one thing but being in a show with grown-ups was quite another.

'Oh yes you should,' he said. 'Because, as you will have gleaned, our Gwendolen has gone. Milton Keynes I think.' He turned to the group near the stage who had been listening to every word. 'Is that right, my dear Ms De Courcey? Is was Milton Keynes, wasn't it?'

'That's right, Mr Donnelly,' came a voice, poshness oozing from every cadence. 'Milton Keynes.'

'And so,' he turned back to me, 'we have a Gwendolen shaped hole into which you will fit perfectly. It's like the Fates have been at work,' he beamed. 'I am pleased. Very pleased indeed.'

'Ladies and gentlemen,' he called to the group. 'I think we may have found our Gwendolen. And there we were, losing hope. You see, the god of theatre always prevails.'

He may have been pleased but I *couldn't* be Gwendolen. Damn the other Gwendolen and her flit to Milton Keynes.

Harry was pulling on my hand. It was time to get him home for tea.

'But I haven't done any acting since school,' I said, panicking. I had been rash in the extreme thinking acting would be good for me, all my initial thespian fervour leeching out of me faster than you could say 'the Scottish Play'. 'I don't really want to do much, you know, with Harry and everything.' I was flailing. 'I don't know if I'd have the time to learn lines and things.'

'Well, I think you are going to be just fine,' he said placidly, ignoring my protestations. 'Why don't you just come to the first rehearsal and we'll see how we get on.'

'Okay, so.' God, I am such a people-pleaser. 'Okay,' I said, 'yes I will, Mr Donnelly.'

'Call me David,' he smiled. 'First rehearsal is tomorrow night,' He dug inside his jacket pocket and pulled out a small book. 'Take this, *The Importance of Being Earnest*,' he said. 'By our very own Mr Wilde. Read it tonight my dear, and begin to *feel* the role. And remember, young Harry, keep sniffing the air. See if you can smell Mr Oscar Wilde.'

Harry nodded dutifully, wide-eyed, leaving me to curse my mother and her prescription for leaving my comfort zone. Sweet Jesus, what had I got myself into?

Life-lifters

- Harry's feet – so small

- Thinking about Harry's future and imagining all the things that might happen, such as girl (boy?) friend, university, a wedding

- Not commuting

- Listening to the radio all day long. I am now an expert in all sorts of things

Chapter ten

The following day, the Marietta mystery was finally cleared up once and for all. I was dragging the wheelie bin from the road to the side of the house, Harry helping (or rather hindering) me, when the gold Porsche turned onto our road. And there was Marietta in the passenger seat.

We latched eyes as we both, for a split second, wondered what to do.

'Stay there Harry! Don't move!' I ordered and I began running towards the car, Usain Bolt-style. 'Mam,' I shrieked, unbecomingly. 'Mam! Hold on a moment!' Marietta was frozen to her seat while Mr Bouffant eyed me coolly. There was something familiar about him. Had we met before?

'There you are Mam!' I said, unnecessarily loudly. I opened the Porsche's passenger door and poked my head right in. 'I was wondering when you'd be home!' I stuck out my hand to Bouffant-man, a big smile plastered on my face (my PR face, as John used to call it). 'I'm Jo,' I said. 'The daughter.'

He reached out for my hand and shook it, smiling smoothly and confidently, the kind of smile practiced in front of a million mirrors. I took him in: hair not unlike Puffball's, a large reddish nose and matching cheeks and ears, and tiny, black eyes sizing me up under tufts of eyebrows. He grinned at me, a big, toothy, showbiz smile. 'Patrick,' he said. 'Patrick Realta.' God, the teeth! He bared a row of large yellowing gnashers which contrasted badly with the blinding white hair. He looked half-horse, half-Barbara Cartland.

Patrick Realta. As soon as he said his name, I knew where I recognised him from. Patrick Realta was an ex-showband singer from the late sixties. Once upon a time, when Ireland was a cultural wilderness where excitement was at an all-time low, where your only chance of adventure lay in emigration, the beating heart of young people was the showband scene, where musicians would tour the church halls and ballrooms of the land, bringing rock'n'roll to the kids. Think *Footloose*, set in Ireland, with nuns and priests, and you're nearly there.

Patrick Realta, along with his band, the All-Stars, strutted the stages of the ballrooms and town halls of the land, whipping impressionable teenagers up into a frenzy of frustrated sexual desire, with songs such as *Let's Skip Mass*, *All Alone in Athlone*, *Rockin' Rockall*, *They Can Have Paris We'll Take Kilbeggan* and – their biggest hit – *The Cow Shed of Romance*. He had been *huge*. His fame was petering out when I was growing up, but he hung round on the fringes of celebrity and some RTÉ producer would book him for a quiz show here, a judge for Eurovision there. He was the last of a dying breed, one that represented an Ireland that didn't exist any longer; one that involved wholesomeness and being happy with one's lot, where travel meant emigration and Sundays meant eating hot food at 12p.m. Patrick and his kind were always popping up on nostalgia programmes and TV tributes to other legends of the scene.

I do remember him being on TV once and Dad snapping the machine off, a decisive move which shocked and surprised me, as normally he was a passive consumer. But the moment stayed with me and it suddenly flashed back to me now.

'*The* Patrick Realta?' I said.

'Is there another one?' He couldn't help looking pleased, obviously a man who liked to be recognised. I thought for a moment he was going to offer me an autograph but Marietta began to climb out of the car and push me out of the way.

'Thank you ever so much, Mr Realta. For the lift. It was most kind of you.' She spoke in a queenly way. 'Give my regards to… the other members of the business group. Goodbye.'

As we reached the cherry blossom tree, the two of us practically fell onto the grass verge. Marietta righted herself and managed to give the car a regal wave goodbye to match Patrick's suave one and then she began hot-footing it back to the house. There was nothing for me to do except chase after her and we trotted all the way to our house. We didn't speak until we were in the kitchen.

'He seems nice, Mam,' I said, pointedly. 'Your *friend*.'

'Oh, Patrick?' she said, as though she had to remind herself who I was referring to. 'Yes… yes he is a nice *friend*.' She was acting as though she had never given it any thought before.

'Mam,' I said, carefully. 'Were you… were you on a *date*?' We really had to stop speaking in italics.

'A date?' She managed to laugh. 'A *date*! The very idea!'

'But were you?' I said.

'Joanna!'

'I just want to know, that's all,' I said. 'Just tell me. Please?' I was begging now. 'Are you…' I searched for the right word. 'You know. *Going out* with Patrick Realta?'

She blushed beetroot, which made me realise that this was no ordinary later-life fling, frolicking of the no-commitment generation. This was something more. She was unsteadied and unnerved by it. What exactly did he mean to her?

She cleared her throat. 'Patrick and I are old friends,' she said. 'We go back a long way.'

'But you've never mentioned him to me,' I said, puzzled, trying to get to the root of it. 'In all the years I've known you, you've never mentioned your friend the Showband star, Patrick Realta. I would have thought that it might have been casually dropped into conversation.'

'Will you... will you just leave it, Joanna?' She snapped.

'Sorry... I—'

'No, I'm sorry... I'm just tired,' she said. 'I didn't mention it because... well, I... it didn't seem important.' She walked to the kitchen door. 'He's just an old, old friend...' She stopped. 'Actually,' she said. 'We knew each other as teenagers.'

'Really?'

'Yes,' she said, a small smile beginning to play on her lips. 'He grew up in Dún Laoghaire and was always around the town, playing music. Paddy he was then. Paddy Ryan. He became Patrick Realta when he joined the All-Stars. He seemed so grown-up, so sophisticated. Sheila and I used to go and see them whenever they were playing in the St Francis Xavier Hall. That was before they got really big.'

'Right...'

'Yes. Anyway...' she said casually. 'So that's that.'

'No, it's not... there's more... what are you not telling me?'

'Well, I didn't see much of him after that. He got married and moved to Foxrock and he was touring all the time and he lost touch with us, the old crowd. He began moving in different circles. Posher. Monied, you know?'

'And he left you behind?'

'Something like that.' Marietta's smile didn't seem quite true somehow. 'He's actually a very successful business man now,' she said. 'When he gave up show business he got into property.'

She had been in love with him. It was so clear. I wished I could put my arms around her.

'And now?'

'It's like the last forty years hadn't happened.' Her cheeks were red. 'It's funny, you know, but we've picked up where we left off.'

'That's lovely, Mam.'

'It's like the world has stopped,' Marietta went on, a faraway look in her eyes. 'As though everything has stood still and there we are, boy and girl, all over again.' Her voice cracked in a most un-Marietta kind of way. '*The world is full of magic things…*'

'You and Patrick?' It wasn't like Marietta to find poetry in everyday life.

'Nothing, nothing,' she said, recovering herself and her voice.

'What are you thinking, Mam?'

'Just that I was practically a child,' she said. 'Someone who didn't know anything about life.'

'Well,' I said, trying to be reassuring. 'You do now.'

'Not really,' she said. 'Sometimes I feel like I haven't learned a thing.'

Later, I went to take her a cup of tea, with a peace offering of two shortbreads on the saucer. I knocked gently on her door. But she didn't need much in the way of sugary solace. She was on her phone and all I could hear was laughing. 'I didn't!' she giggled. '*You* did!' And then more laughing. 'Really? Well, we'll have to find out… You know something, Patrick, you are a terror.' She sounded so happy. 'Are you now?' she went on coquettishly. 'I might be… okay so, I am, *terribly*… No, I can't either. I know it's only been four hours but…' She laughed again. 'You're a devil you are! I'll see you later,' she purred. 'Six it is. Well, you'll have to find out. Yes you will!'

I tiptoed back downstairs and drank the tea myself, snaffling the biscuits. It was like living with a teenager, life full of exciting and terrifying opportunities, hormones all over the place, and there was me, feeling as though, if it weren't for Harry, my life may as well be over.

Chapter eleven

Sometimes, however, it felt as though nothing much had changed. When John would call round to pick Harry up, he'd chat away to Marietta as though he still lived there, while I scurried around to find Harry's coat, his plastic lion or his string collection or whatever.

'How are you?' he'd say, looking sheepish and sorry (too late for that, John, I would think).

'Grand,' I would say. 'Just fine and dandy. You?'

'Yeah, you know…' He'd trail off then and would look away and I would pretend not to notice how sad he looked and resist going over and putting my arms around him. I couldn't remember when I had last put my arms around him anyway, even when he had lived with us and we were a so-called 'normal couple'. To the outside world at least.

I knew I would have to start moving on but sometimes, early in the morning, even before Harry was awake, I'd lie under the duvet and just wish the sun wouldn't rise, or my little Braun alarm clock beside me would stop ticking, and I could just remain there, alone with my thoughts, peaceful and free from all the pressure of getting over things and leaving the past behind. Moving on, in other words.

I had no choice though but to press on regardless and when John dropped Harry back one Sunday afternoon, I thought of doing something that everyone else seemed to take in their stride. Something normal. A walk on the pier in Dun Laoghaire.

'Would you like to go for a walk on the pier Harry? You could bring your scooter?'

'I'll go, Mummy,' he said, seriously. 'But only if Mr Icy is there.' Mr Icy was the grumpy man who sold rather fake and rather sickly cones from a van parked halfway down.

'We'll see, Harry,' I said, employing the only tried and tested technique in a parent's armour that actually works: bribery. 'Only if you're good.'

'I good, Mummy, he assured me confidently. 'I very good.'

And doing something so normal rubbed off on me. For the first time, I could imagine that maybe being a single mother wouldn't be so bad and that Harry and I were going to be alright. We saw some people we knew there and I waved, almost cheerily. I am doing this, I thought to myself, and there was Harry scooting alongside me. I would normally be frantically worried that he was about to scoot wildly into the sea, but I remained calm and refused to think about how I'd rescue him once he plunged in.

We both deserved an ice cream, I thought, almost smugly.

'Mr Icy gone, Mummy!' said Harry, real shock in his voice. And he was right. Mr Icy, who was always there, even on Christmas Day, was gone.

Instead, in his pitch, there was a new van, a lovely blue vintage Citroen, and on the side was painted:

'FroRo – magic ices made from the creamiest milk
from happy Wexford cows'

We ventured forth. Harry more reluctantly because we had no idea if FroRo – whatever that was – could compete with Mr Icy. Was it even ice cream?

'What do you say, Harry?' I said. 'Would you like to try something new?' He didn't look like he was feeling particularly adventurous and nor was I. Both of us inched, slightly reluctantly, towards the van.

'Hello,' said a smiling, handsome man, poking his head out to us. 'And what can I get for you today? Ice cream?' He looked down at Harry. 'I'll bet you like ice cream, don't you?'

Harry nodded. 'It's my favourite thing in the world.'

The man laughed.

'I have it for breakfast and sometimes for dinner as well.'

'No you don't, Harry,' I said hastily. 'That's not true.'

The man laughed again.

'It is true Mummy,' said Harry earnestly. 'I had it this morning.'

'Well, you had a taste,' I admitted. 'Not a bowl. It was a tiny spoonful. And after your porridge.'

I wasn't coming across as mother of the year and for some reason, standing in front of this handsome and rather attractive man, I wanted to. Dark hair and bright blue eyes, with the prerequisite hipster beard, he looked not unlike most of the younger men I saw around these days. He was in his early 30s, at a guess, and seemed so warm and open. He looked as though he liked people, if that made sense.

'You see?' said Harry, delighted to be proved right.

'So this is your second ice cream of the day,' said the man. 'You are doing well.'

Harry nodded, pleased that success in life was so easy.

'Just one, *very* small ice cream, please,' I said. 'Vanilla. And a flake. What do you say Harry. Please?'

'Please,' he said obediently.

'Coming up!' FroRo said. 'I have special cones for my younger clients.' He spent a moment scooping up an ice cream, and then poked in a flake with a practised flourish. 'Organic ice cream,' he said. 'Milk and cream and eggs from back home in Wexford. I make it myself. Well, not the milk,' he said. 'I rely on others to make that for me.' His smile made my knees buckle slightly.

'And are they really happy?' I said. 'The cows? How can you tell? Do they sing? Tell jokes?'

He laughed.

'No,' he admitted. 'It's just my hunch... based on many years of observing them. This particular herd seem more frolicky than your usual cows. They have a spring in their hoof.'

Now I laughed, a bit too hard. Handsome and able to make ice cream, what wasn't there to like?

'And what can I get you?' FroRo turned to me.

'I wasn't going to have one. I don't normally...' Mr Icy's were whippy, sickly and made from everything but milk.

He nodded, understanding what I was getting at. 'Mr Icy's are a bit different to mine... they have their fans but I'm trying to change the whole ice cream van world. Ireland makes the best milk, ergo we should be making the best ice cream. Taking on the Italians. We tried taking them on at football and failed. Miserably. But I say, beat them on gelato.' I smiled. His rallying call for ice cream was hugely attractive. A rebel with a cause.

'Chocolate,' I said, sold. 'Do you have chocolate?'

'Of course! I'd be lynched if I tried not to serve my chocolate. It won first prize at the Irish Food Awards last year. My strawberry was highly commended. One moment...' He pressed a mound of chocolate ice cream into one of those posh wafer cones. On the very top he placed a real cherry and a tiny paper flag with the purple and gold colours of Wexford.

'It's beautiful,' I said, going for a lick. The flavours and creaminess and sweetness dissolved on my tongue and was whisked throughout my body. 'No, it really is.' I was surprised how good it was. 'Oh my God, it's amazing.' It was the best ice cream I had ever had. 'How much do I owe you?'

'Nothing,' he said. They're on the house. I mean van. I'm calling it market research. Two happy customers.' We both looked at Harry who busily working his way through his own cone.

'Thanks so much,' I said, smiling back. 'That's so kind of you.'

'I'm here most days.' He reached behind him. 'Here's my card.'

Ronan Forest. FroRo.
Organic and fresh ice cream, from farm to cone, to
you.
Three Oaks Farm, Middleton, Co Wexford.

'Thank you, Ronan. Say thanks, Harry.'

'Fanx,' he managed through a mouthful of ice cream.

'My pleasure,' Ronan said.

I felt myself hovering slightly, not wanting to leave. It must have been a combination of the sugar rush and my knees buckling, but I knew I should sit down.

'He was nice, wasn't he Harry?' I said, when we had reached a bench. '*Very* nice.'

'Nice,' said Harry.

'Who the man or the ice cream?'

'Ice cream.'

'Yes, it is good,' I said, craning my neck to see Ronan aka FroRo, but he was busy serving new customers. I was just being silly. There was I trying to be normal and I had ended up fancying an ice cream man. 'Now, sweetheart,' I said. 'Daddy is babysitting you tonight because I've got my first rehearsal for the Seaside Players.'

Harry carried on licking his ice cream.

'And I'm feeling a bit nervous, because I haven't acted for so long. I wish I hadn't got myself involved now,' I continued. 'I wish I was staying in with you.' I heard a splat. 'Oh Harry. Don't worry. You can finish mine.' I grabbed some tissues, fruitlessly dabbing away at his clothes while giving him my ice cream before any tears began.

Life-lifters

- Ice cream, in all its myriad flavours

- Parks, the very civic-mindedness of them

- Amateur dramatics

- The humble Twix

- Mastermind: the life of Boy George came up, got 15 points (fist pump)

Chapter twelve

Marietta *always* had a hug for John whenever he turned up to collect Harry. He was still her favourite (and only) son in law. My mother, the turn-coat, embracing the man who had walked out on her daughter and grandchild. This evening he had brought two boxes of posh chocolates when he came round, straight from work, to babysit Harry. I had to pretend not to be remotely pleased about the chocolates. Harry was upstairs, all tucked in and kissed goodnight.

'Oh, thanks.' Nonchalant politeness was my modus operandi. Marietta was far more gracious. 'How do you always remember?' she twinkled. 'You are too good.' Scowling at her from behind my almond-crunch, which I had already begun, I realised that I had never known she was so *good* with men. Must have been how she managed the hardware shop for all those years.

Isn't it just incredible, I thought, how the two of them can act like nothing has happened? How John, who only weeks ago was saying he couldn't *do* family life and was about to fall off a cliff or whatever it was, could now be all smiles and chocolates. He was probably loved up with some woman. Just like Paul McCartney and Heather Mills in their early days as a couple. Well, not them, actually. I really wouldn't wish *that* union on anyone.

'I'll save mine, John,' said Marietta, patting the box. 'I'm off out with a friend tonight.'

'Mam's boyfriend,' I said. 'Patrick Realta.'

'*The* Patrick Realta?' He let out a whistle.

'The Patrick Realta,' I confirmed.

'He's a very old friend of mine,' explained Marietta, shooting me a look. 'We are having a very nice time together.'

'I'm glad for you Marietta,' said John.

'I'm just going to get ready. Won't be long.' She gave me another glare as she left the room.

'So,' said John, 'how're things?' He looked at me and he wasn't the avuncular, smiling ex-son-in-law he was with Marietta, he looked worried and scared again. Maybe it was me who had that effect on him. No wonder he wanted to get away.

'Harry's in bed,' I said. 'With his new spider.'

'Spider?'

'He's been sleeping with it every night,' I explained. 'We bought it in the newsagents. Loves it. Name of Webby.'

John laughed. 'Webby?'

I shrugged. 'I'm running out of ideas.'

He laughed again. 'So, you're going literal. Always the first sign of a parent who's had to name too many toys.'

His laugh was always so infectious, but I managed to remain straight-faced. I realised that I didn't *want* to make him laugh. It wasn't right. We were a separated couple and should be rowing, throwing horrible looks at each other and hissing expletives under our breath. It would be so easy just to try to make each other laugh, like we used to. But things weren't the same. John had *left*. I refused to be drawn into the kind of repartee that we used to engage in, before Harry, even when I was secretly pleased to feel that it was still there, that pleasure we used to have in each other, the fun we used to have. Being at his Dad's was obviously doing him good.

'Yes,' I said. 'It would make life so much easier if we just had names that describe us, like they did in olden days, like

Smith, for the blacksmith, or Carter for the cart maker, um…'
I desperately tried to think of more examples.

'Winterbottom?'

'It was,' I said, valiantly ensuring that this conversation
would not be derailed by John's insistence on finding most
things amusing. The old John seemed to be reappearing, his
mouth twitching, eyebrows raised. The old Jo, however,
remained humourless and determined to drone on. 'The name
Winterbottom was for those who felt the cold very badly.
People with particularly bad circulation,' I said. 'They were
called Winterbottom.'

John laughed. 'Pratt? Explain Pratt.'

'Well,' I began, clearing my throat. Where was Marietta? I
couldn't be *this* utterly tedious for much longer. I was actually
boring myself. 'That was a special name for someone in the
village. The Pratt was the joker, the funny person, often the
idiot…' Where was I getting this from? 'So, for example, if you
looked back in your family tree, I'd bet you'd find quite a few
Pratts in there.'

'Really?' he said, raising an eyebrow in that way which once
would have had me weak at the knees. 'I'm from a long-line of
Pratts?'

'Yes,' I said, looking him straight in the eye. 'A very long-
line.' *That* knocked the smile off his face.

There was a knock on the door. 'Ah, that's Dad,' said John.
'He's going to have a look at the guttering.'

'But you don't live here,' I said, as sweetly as possible.
'Anyway, I've got someone coming round to look at it,' I lied.

'Jo,' he said. 'I just moved out, okay? It doesn't stop me
doing things for the house. I'm not going to leave you in the
lurch. I'm not that much of a tool.'

I kept my face neutral which I hoped he would translate as 'yes you are, you really are'. We went outside and, in the gloaming, I could just about make out the silhouette of a figure up a ladder; John's sixty-nine-year-old father was rattling the guttering.

'Got it!' he said. 'Ah, hello Joanna.' He waved at me causing the ladder to wobble dangerously. 'Down in a mo!' We watched as he worked on the guttering for a few minutes and then he precariously made his way back down to us.

'Some solder is in order. I was right. I'll have done tomorrow if that's okay with you, Joanna.' He hugged me hello. The scent of Imperial Leather soap hung in the air, along with a tinge of Vosene shampoo.

'Thanks Jack, that'd be great.'

'That's the girl,' he said. He took my hand. 'If you need anything doing,' he said, 'call me. Anytime. I'm still here. Well, for as long as the good Lord allows.'

'And I'll be over to do the grass on Saturday,' said John. 'Needs the first cut. And a prune of the hedge as well.'

'Okay,' I said, not sure if I should accept this. I felt uncertain about what the protocol was in such a situation but made a mental to google it later. Should you let your estranged husband fix your guttering and mow your lawn? Someone, somewhere *had* to know the answer.

'Is your Mam inside, love?' said Jack. 'I won't be a tick but I'll just say hello.'

We moved inside to the kitchen where Marietta was, dressed in one of her new outfits, a floral jacket and smart jeans. She was checking her phone.

'Oh, Marietta,' said Jack, admiringly. 'Now you're a sight for my old eyes.'

'Thank you, Jack,' she said, smiling.

'Marietta's got a whole new wardrobe. Impressing her new fancy man,' I teased. 'Another date tonight, Mam?'

'Well, now,' said Jack, looking interested. 'Who's the lucky fella?'

'Patrick Realta!' I said, triumphantly.

Marietta glared at me. 'He's an old friend,' she explained to Jack, who was smiling at her. 'We knew each other as youngsters.'

'Ah, yes, he grew up round here, didn't he? Dun Laoghaire was his patch. But didn't he go to Foxrock? He went up in the world.'

Marietta coloured a little at this.

'But he was a star,' continued Jack. 'Paddy Realta.' He whistled. 'Well, I never. I remember seeing him once,' he said. 'At the St Francis Xavier. He was some mover, wasn't he? Didn't they call him Paddy the Pelvis?'

We all took a moment to imagine the old days when Patrick Realta and his pelvis were quite the sight.

There was a beep on Marietta's phone. She picked it up. 'He's outside!' she half-shrieked, the fever gripping her again.

'Where're you off to? You and Patrick?'

'Dinner,' she said over her shoulder. 'Dancing.'

And she was gone, tapping out of the kitchen as though she was Ginger Rogers on her way to her lover. Jack went back outside to pack up his tools and put down the ladder.

'So.' I said to John. 'My turn to go now.'

'Right. So where are you going?'

'The Seaside Players,' I mumbled. *Not* that it was any of his business.

'The what?'

'You know, the am-dram group. The Seaside Players.'

He raised his eyebrows. For a moment I thought he was going to laugh but then he put on his interested face.

'Don't look so surprised,' I said. 'Remember I was in lots of plays at school. I told you. I was Lady Macbeth! I was Nancy!'

Now he did laugh. And I felt my mouth twitching despite myself.

'The man running The Players is my old drama teacher, David Donnelly.' I continued. 'Anyway, he used to say I could have gone all the way.'

John laughed even more.

'I mean,' I said, hastily. 'I could have been a professional.'

'Like Judi Dench?'

'Well,' I said, 'maybe a *younger* version of Dame Judi.'

'Like who?'

'I don't know,' I said, racking my brain. 'Kate Winslet or someone.'

He laughed again.

'It's actually not funny, John,' I said, trying to look unamused but thinking how I had forgotten what a lovely smile he had. I still wanted to touch him, to put my arms around him and hold him close. And then we'd go and drink some tea and eat some biscuits and talk about our days but there was so much unspoken between us that hung in the air. I couldn't forgive him for leaving me. He should have stayed. We could have worked it out.

We waved Jack off and stood there, slightly awkwardly.

'So,' I ventured. 'How's life in Champneys?'

'Jo.' He rolled his eyes. 'It's not a health farm. I am living with my Dad. Never ideal under any circumstances.'

'Sorry,' I said. 'I mean Bachelor Towers.'

'You mean me and Dad?' he said.

'Yes, you and your Dad. The Bachelor Boys.'

'You know, Jo,' he said, defensively. 'Living with Dad is not exactly like being in the Rolling Stones or whatever you are imagining.'

'Status Quo then? Or Bucks Fizz?'

He sighed heavily. 'We watch history documentaries and *Who Do You Think You Are* and programmes featuring Dan Snow,' he said. 'And I listen to his theories of what is happening to the country and why there are no decent socialists left. That kind of thing.' He stopped. 'You know, Jo, what happened, happened to me too.'

I didn't answer him.

'I'm just going to check on Harry, okay?' He said and left me wondering who was in the right. Was it fair to lob barbs and jibes in his direction? And was it right for me to inhabit the moral high ground?

On the kitchen table, John's phone beeped and a message flashed up. Of course I didn't *mean* to read it but mobile phone screens are just so bright these days that even with my mole-like sight, I can read them from across the kitchen.

'Good luck tonight,' said the message. 'I'll be thinking of you.'

What the bloody hell was this? I snatched up the phone.

Sender's name: Liz.

Elizabeth Eagers was an old friend of John's from college. They'd done history together at Trinity and they'd even had a thing going before John met me. Casual hook-ups after too much to drink, that kind of thing. But they'd remained friends and were both now working at the *Irish Times*. And we were all ridiculously mature about it. She'd even been a bridesmaid at our wedding. Yes, she'd even caught the fecking bouquet!

Liz had split from her husband about two years ago. She'd found him crawling around in his underpants in the street at

5am, having consumed two nostrils' worth of cocaine and enough Jack Daniels to kill off his remaining six brain cells and sink his marriage. I remember John telling me that he'd had a problem with addictive substances all their married life, but when their friends eased off on the old narcotics, Knobby Neil kept on going, having to find younger and younger friends to keep his partying to the levels he required.

Blood boiling, I expertly scrolled through Liz's texts and John's answers, while listening out for his returning footsteps. I was looking for mutual declarations of love. Bastard! I thought. He needed time away, was it? A little space from family life? He wanted to shag Liz senseless and obviously couldn't do it while he was still married to me. It would have been better had he just had an affair instead of lying about needing space, moving out. It was, in some way, far more duplicitous. Why had he bothered with me for all these years then? Was I just some beard while she made up her mind and now Knobby Neil was off the scene, John was on it?

What did she mean, 'good luck tonight'? Was she talking about him dropping in on us? What had he told her? That I was some kind of gorgon, the cliché of a vengeful soon-to-be-ex-wife? I focussed in on some of the texts. 'Thanks for letting me talk', he had written a few days ago. 'I can really open up to you. You are an amazing listener.' Was that a reference to me? I thought. Was I not a good listener?

'I'm here anytime,' she wrote. 'Call me. You are such a special person, you know?'(I nearly vomited at this.)

Thanks Liz, he wrote. 'You've been a great friend.'

John had turned to Liz Eagers instead of me. Me, who'd made an entire career from communicating ideas. I was the queen of talk, the princess of mutually beneficial chat. The high priestess of exchanging ideas. Yet he preferred to talk to Liz Eagers.

'Sound asleep,' he said, when he came back downstairs. I hastily put his phone back onto the table, tears in my eyes.

'Good, that's good,' I muttered.

'Break a leg,' called John as I ran out of the house.

Chapter thirteen

Over at St Anne's Hall, I was at a rehearsal for The Importance of Being Earnest with my fellow Seaside Players. How had I got myself into this mess? I could have been planning a nice quiet evening in, just me and the new Boden catalogue, but my rash enthusiasm had landed me months of work and then having to perform in front of a real, live audience. I felt sick at the thought but I really couldn't let Mr Donnelly – I mean, David – down, not now I'd willingly joined them.

'What do you think?' I said to myself out loud, as I summoned up the courage to push open the big door of the church hall. 'I'm going to do this. Are you proud of me?'

There was no answer. But I didn't mind. One-way conversations are remarkably satisfying.

I stepped inside tentatively. 'Joanna!' David saw me and scuttled over. 'We're going to do a run-through in a few minutes.'

My hands were actually shaking. The moment had come. I had thrust myself into this position and now I was stuck. I looked to David for support, but I realised there was no one who could save me now. I had to read these lines and face the humiliation of this whole sorry escapade. I only had myself to blame.

'This is Connemara De Courcey,' he said, 'our esteemed assistant director. Connie, you remember Joanna Woulfe, our Gwendolen.' Connie was the posh woman from the other night and we shook hands. She was wearing a big green farmer's fleece, a tweed skirt and lace-ups. Her grey hair was cut short and she smiled at me over her spectacles.

'How d'you do?' she said, sounding like the Queen.

'Fine…' I wobbled. 'I think.'

'Don't you worry,' she said, taking my right hand on both of hers. 'At the end of the day, we are here to have fun. We are amateurs and proud of it. You enjoy yourself and you are very welcome in our small company.'

I smiled and tried to look normal, but I could still feel myself trembling.

David was looking around. 'Fergal,' he muttered. 'Where is he? Ah! Here he is! Now, Joanna, this is Fergal Forest. He's one of our greatest stars. Been with us for the last four years, isn't that right, Fergal?'

I couldn't tell if David was being facetious but then when I looked at the man who had joined us, he *was* dressed like a star. Even if we were meant to be humble amateurs, he was dressed for Broadway. He was tall, with dark hair, tight jeans, a paisley shirt half-tucked in and a little scarf around his neck. There was something of Daniel Day Lewis about him, utterly pretentious but rather sexy at the same time.

He kissed my hand. 'Delighted you've joined us,' he said. 'I was worried that Frederick was going to be my love interest which would have been beyond my acting talents. Thankfully, with someone like you, it won't be too much of a stretch.' And he winked at me, making me like him immediately. He was a bit of an idiot, that was clear, but despite the silly scarf and the shaggy hair which kept falling (accidentally on purpose) into his eyes, there was something rather attractive about him. I found myself grinning back at him.

'Now, you must meet our other stars,' said Connie. 'The two playing Cecily and Algernon. Robert! Siobhan! Come and join us!' Under her breath, Connie said. 'Siobhan is quite the actress. A real talent. We are very lucky to have her.' They came up towards us. 'This is Jo Woulfe, who will be playing Gwendolen,' she said.

Robert was around 30, Siobhan perhaps younger and disarmingly pretty, that second-look kind of pretty. Her blonde hair was pulled over her shoulder in a long plait; she had perfect features and beautiful green eyes. She tugged at a long strand of hair that had come loose and bit her lip. She looked nervous. That made two of us. 'Pleased to meet you,' she said.

We shook hands. 'I hear you're brilliant,' I said. 'You'll have to show me what to do.'

She blushed and smiled the sweetest smile. 'Oh no,' she said. 'The others are. Especially Piers... and Fergal.'

Robert thrust his hand towards me. 'Robert Burke,' he said. 'You're very welcome.' He was dressed in a blazer with a badge on the pocket. Beneath his name it said: SUPERBUY. 'Just come from work,' he explained. 'I'm the day manager, just been promoted from night.'

'Congratulations,' I said.

'Every penny counts,' he said, taking Siobhan's hand. 'You see, we're saving for a deposit. Trying to buy a house. Getting married in a few months, as soon as the show is over. Living with my Mam at the moment. We have been for the last two years. That's been brilliant, though. I wouldn't mind staying there for the rest of my life. Me and Siobhan with Mam. I know Mam would be... Siobhan doesn't seem so keen, are you love?'

'Do you have your script, Jo?' said Siobhan, obviously trying to change the subject.

'Excuse me a minute,' Robert said, producing a sandwich box and taking out something wrapped in foil. 'Egg and cress,' he explained. 'And a Trio. The dinner of champions. We always do this when we are out for the evening.'

He passed a sandwich over to Siobhan, who took it, looking slightly embarrassed.

'A takeaway pizza,' he said, chewing away, 'costs six euro. Our dinner of egg and cress and a trio costs one forty-seven each.' He looked triumphant. 'I've got water too,' he said. 'Filled up from the taps at work.' He proffered it to Siobhan. 'Here we go, take a good gulp of that.'

Siobhan did as she was told.

'We haven't bought anything new for two years,' he went on. 'Mam makes all our food and we give her 50 euro a week for board and lodging.'

I glanced at Siobhan who was trying to eat her egg and cress, but she was looking at something else in the room.

'Robert,' said Connie. 'Your economising is a lesson to us all. Now, Joanna, let me introduce you to the others. They are a far more frivolous lot.'

'Frivolous?' said a voice. 'How very dare you.'

'This is Piers Byrne,' said Connie. 'Our resident... now, how shall we describe you?'

'Resident curmudgeon? Resident pain in the arse?' said the man, holding out his hand to me. 'Delighted to make your acquaintance. I'm Lady Bracknell. My fifth time playing her would you believe.'

And then I met George and Frederick, who were to be playing the manservant and the butler and who also designed and sewed all the costumes. George was ancient. He had bright red hair, wore a cap and walked with a slight stoop. I wondered for a moment if he, like his actorly-doppelganger,

Daniel D-L, remained in character permanently. And then he shook my hand, 'Good day, missus,' he said. He was like something out of *The Quiet Man*.

'Good to meet you, George.' I said.

He lifted his cap. 'To be sure,' he said. 'Blessings on your noble brow.'

I turned my attention to Frederick who was to play the butler, Merriman. 'Delighted,' he said in a plummy voice, 'I'm sure.'

'English are you?' I was trying to be friendly but the look he gave me made me wish I hadn't probed. Sometimes people really don't want to disclose anything about themselves. Sometimes histories and routes through life are so complicated that it is exhausting to keep having to explain yourself. I knew the feeling.

He gazed at me with disdain. 'Born and bred, but the salty spray from the Irish Sea is what I breathe now,' he said, rolling his r's theatrically. 'Came over on the boat as far as Dun Laoghaire. I was heading west but went no further as I found there was no need. I had found my spiritual home. Isn't that right, Connie darling?'

'Dun Laoghaire isn't everyone's idea of the Promised Land, but it obviously suits you.' She smiled at him and then turned to me: 'I met him on his very first day here,' she said.

'I was what you might call down and very nearly out. But, my dear,' he said, 'you are very welcome to our little troupe. And after what happened to poor Alexandra.'

'Our former leading lady,' explained Connie. 'The *previous* Gwendolen.'

'It's a tragedy. One which would not look out of place in the pages of the great bard,' said Frederick. 'She had to flee…'

he confided. 'Gone to mend her broken heart. Last heard of in Milton Keynes, I think.'

'Now, Frederick…' said Connie. 'I don't think it was a broken heart that took her to Milton Keynes but more of a job offer. She's happily working for a medical research company there. She sent me a postcard wishing us all luck with the new production.'

But Frederick was undeterred and, while Connie looked around for David, he mouthed, with big sad eyes, 'broken heart,' while miming a heart breaking in two.

'I've got to go,' said Rob. 'The new night manager needs some keys. Still hasn't quite got to grip with things.' He left, quickly, anorak zipped up tightly over his blazer. 'Work sleeps for no man,' he said. 'Oscar Wilde said that. Or was it something to do with all work and no play makes Jack a dull boy. He definitely said that. So witty, wasn't he?'

I had to agree with the last bit, anyway. Rob kissed Siobhan chastely on the cheek. 'See you at Mam's,' he said. 'She's taped *Coronation Street* for us to watch with her when we get in.'

'That's nice,' said Siobhan faintly. We watched him leave.

David came over. 'This is for you, Jo,' he said. 'It's the script.'

'Okay…' I grappled with the document. 'I thought we were doing *The Importance of Being Earnest*. Not *War and Peace* or the *Mahabharata*.'

He smiled. 'Ha-ha! No, Jo. It looks like it's a lot of work, but it's just Gwendolen you have to learn. You know how to learn lines… you were Lady Macbeth once upon a time, remember? And very good you were too. As was Bernadette Coughlan as Macbeth himself.'

'Yes, she loved the beard she had to wear. Didn't take it off for the whole week of the production. Said she had to stay in character. Drove the nuns mad. You had to write a letter explaining why it was essential she remained true to the role.'

'Oh yes!' He seemed quite tickled by the memory. 'The nuns weren't immensely pleased, I do remember that much. But, to be fair, they acquiesced and Bernadette triumphed. Such a talented young actor.'

'What is she doing now? Have you heard from her?'

'Yes, last seen in Galway in one of the parades, with an outsized papier maché head of Bono on her. I was down there for the festival and this figure danced towards me on Shop Street. I used to teach the real Bono but it was the first time I was ever hugged by him. Now, are you set? Learn your lines and we will rehearse properly next Friday. For now we'll do a bit of a read through.'

'Right. Gwendolen and Jack... positions please!' said David. He turned to me. 'Joanna, you are there and Fergal, there. Right, everyone in their placing.'

Fergal was up first. 'My own darling!' he began, reading from the script.

'Earnest,' I said, hearing my voice shake, 'we may never be married. From the expression on mamma's face I fear we never shall. Few parents nowadays pay any regard to what their children say to them. The old-fashioned respect for the young is fast dying out. Whatever influence I ever had over mamma, I lost at the age of three. But although she may prevent us from becoming man and wife, and I may marry someone else, and marry often, nothing that she can possibly do can alter my eternal devotion to you.'

I couldn't believe I had managed to get all of that out. I looked to see what David was thinking, half-hoping he liked it and half-hoping it was awful and I could go home.

'Dear Gwendolen!' said Fergal, taking my hand, and holding lightly.

I had another big speech to come. Fergal was getting off lightly. I swallowed and began again. I managed to get through it without my cheeks burning and without, I hope, making a complete fool of myself.

'Well, well, well!' said David, clapping along with the little crowd around us. 'So, Connie, have we found our Gwendolen? Was I right?' he asked.

Connie was on her feet, smiling. 'We may very well have,' she said. 'Are we agreed?'

David nodded. 'One Gwendolen goes and another arrives. It's like a revolving door of Gwendolens. I really do believe that Mr Wilde is looking down on our little production and giving us his blessing. We won't let him down, I know it. We will do our great friend and countryman a real service, I feel so sure.'

Fergal kissed my hand. 'Brava,' he said. 'Brava.'

Connie was watching him. 'I think, Mr Forest,' she said witheringly, 'that it is better that we keep our exuberance to the stage, and we keep sexual harassment where it belongs. In the Dark Ages.'

He grinned winningly at her, unabashed by her put-down and even she smiled back at him. 'Incorrigible you are, Mr Forest. Utterly incorrigible.'

Chapter fourteen

When I got back to the house, John was sitting in the kitchen, a mug of tea in his hand, watching *Primetime* on his iPad.

'So!' I said, trying out a smile.

'So.' He sounded flat, deflated.

'How's Harry? Did he wake up?'

'He's fine. I've just checked on him.'

'Right.'

'Jo…?' He stood up and leaned against the kitchen table, watching me.

'Yes?'

'Were you going through my phone?'

'No! How could you say such a thing?' He carried on looking at me. 'Yes,' I admitted. 'Yes, I did. But not for long.'

'Why?'

'I don't know…'

'You saw a text from Liz.'

'Yes.'

'And did you draw any conclusions?'

'No… none whatsoever. Okay, yes I did. I concluded that you two were a thing, an item… and that's why you left.'

'That's not why I left,' he said. 'And we aren't a thing. An item.'

'You're not?'

He shook his head.

I didn't know what to believe or what I *wanted* to believe; that they were an item and that's why he left which, although painful, was at least an explanation. I didn't want to think about Marietta's theory, that he was depressed. That was too much to take on board. If it were true I didn't know if I could help him. I wasn't sure I had it in me and that appalled me. So, in a perverse way, if he *was* seeing Liz, it made things a little easier to deal with.

'We've been friends for a long time. It's nice to have a friend, wouldn't you agree?'

'Yes, John, I'd agree.'

'Right, so we're clear so?'

'Totally clear,' I said. 'So there's nothing going on with you and Liz? And when you say you are friends, you mean you are friends, not *friends*?'

'Jesus, Jo!' He pushed back his hair with both hands. 'There's nothing going on! Liz and I are friends. We're just good friends. Like we've always been. Jo, I know this is difficult for both of us but it really doesn't help you thinking that I am seeing someone else. That is not why I left. It really...' He stopped. 'It really takes away from my feelings. It really makes me think that what I feel, what I go through, is not remotely of interest or importance to you. You are just obsessed with what you are going through. Your husband moves out – for very good reasons – and you reduce it to the fact that he must be seeing another woman. Like I am just another middle-aged cliché. Like I am just someone who can be dismissed as a one of those guys who can't be trusted.'

I stood there, thinking that this was exactly what I had been thinking. It was so much easier to think that. And he was right. I was self-obsessed.

'No!' I said. '*Of course* I wasn't thinking that. How can you say such a thing? Now if you will excuse me, I need to get to bed because I will be up early with *your son*.'

John looked at me and almost imperceptibly shook his head. 'See you Jo,' he said, wearily. He began to slip on his coat and scoop up his newspaper, IPad and phone. At the doorway, he stood for a moment. 'I'm still your friend too, you know,' he said, tiredness, sadness and defeat etched on his face.

'That's nice,' I said. 'You can't have enough friends. You've quite the collection.'

He let out a sigh of exasperation and left the house.

As soon as the door closed behind him, I burst into tears. Why was I so horrible to him? Why was I so angry with him? It wasn't his fault really, I knew that deep down, but I needed someone to blame and he had been the nearest person. It was unfair... but then he had compounded it by leaving and therefore giving me a real reason to be angry. I didn't know how to make it okay, how to stop feeling so enraged and how I could handle the fact that he had left. It was all too much. All I wanted to do was reach out and hold his hand, to comfort him. But something was stopping me. It was as though my heart had shrunk.

Life-lifters

- No rain today. Second day in a row. Yay!

- My cup of tea at breakfast was one of those perfect ones. The one in ten kind

- Harry ate all his cottage pie (Thank you, Delia!) which is good because it took precisely 113 minutes to make from start to finish. Was exhausting

- The new Lakeland catalogue has arrived. Presently lying next to me in bed, looking enticing

Chapter fifteen

'What about a walk on the pier?' I suggested to Harry. 'We could have an ice cream?'

Harry needed little persuasion. And neither did I, to be honest. 'Maybe that man, FroRo, will be there,' I said. 'Remember? That nice ice cream?'

'Mr Icy!' shouted Harry from the back of the car. 'Mr Icy! Mr Icy!'

'Definitely *not* Mr Icy,' I said. 'Someone far nicer.'

'Mr Nicey!'

'Yes, sweetheart.' I approved. 'Mr *Nicey*.'

It was a beautiful late afternoon and the whole of South County Dublin was out, all delighted with this little bit of sunshine. We said hello, Harry waving from his pushchair, to a few people we knew, families that were in the same crèche, a neighbour from three houses up, Rav from the DIY shop, the eponymous Brian from Brian's sitting on a bench motionless, eyes closed, unaware of the seagull pecking at his sandwiches which were slightly open beside him. The gull flew off as Harry and I went by.

And then I heard a whistle, the kind a farmer might use to call his dog, and I immediately looked up, never realising until that moment how trainable and obedient I was. FroRo was waving to us from the van. 'Hello!' he said. 'Lovely afternoon!' I hadn't spotted him because he was now parked between the crepe seller and the scampi and chips van.

'Hello,' I said. 'How's it going? Say hello, Harry.'

Harry waved and began to get excited, knowing an ice cream was but a short conversation away. Ronan smiled at me. 'In the mood for an ice cream?'

'Definitely.'

Ronan stretched out of the hatch to hand a tiny ice cream to Harry, with extra napkins, and then passed me a huge chocolate one. There were a couple of stripy canvas deckchairs set up outside the van. 'Sit down,' he said, nodding towards them. 'And I'll come and join you.'

He reappeared from the side of the van holding another chocolate cone and sat himself down on the other deckchair. Harry stayed in his pushchair, licking away.

'It's delicious,' I said. 'How's business going?'

'Great! Here on the pier every afternoon, weddings and corporate events keeping things ticking over and orders from cafes and restaurants picking up.'

'But why are you in Dublin if your heart is so obviously in Wexford?' I motioned towards the little Wexford flag in the top of my ice cream.

'It's still available in Gorey,' he said, 'don't you worry. It's just that I thought the people of Dublin should realise what a superior county Wexford was. We don't want to keep all the good things for ourselves. Be generous, spread them around.'

I laughed and licked my ice cream. There was a light breeze off the sea, which glinted in the sunlight. Everyone was in Sunday mode, either walking off large lunches or getting their ozone fix before office life in the morning. This place was magical.

'My brother lives here so I have somewhere to stay. I'd sleep in the van if I had my way, but health and safety have other ideas. But Fergal's place is alright. He's decided to put up with me for a bit.'

'Fergal?' I looked at him, studied his face and then recalled his business card. 'Ronan Forest.'

'How may I be of service?'

'Your brother,' I said. 'He isn't an actor is he?'

'He acts a lot of shite, if that's what you mean? He does amdram, but his real job is working in a cash and carry, warehouse manager. But that's not for ever. He's always on the go. How do you know him?'

'Fergal Forest!' I laughed. 'We are in The Seaside Players together. Well, I've just joined. He's much better than me.'

Ronan looked at me, a smile spreading over his face. 'You're not the fair Joanna, are you?'

'Well, my name *is* Joanna.'

'He was singing your praises the other night, saying what a great actress you are. And how you have transformed the group into something quite different.'

'Really?' I was dying to know exactly what he meant, but I tried to sound casual. 'What did he say?'

'That the troupe was getting a little claustrophobic. There was a lot of squabbling before you turned up and now everyone is on their best behaviour.' He grinned again. The same grin as Fergal's I could see now, but without that edge of lasciviousness, that constant flirtation that was fine in small doses but could be exhausting after a while. Ronan was a better-looking version of Fergal too, who was attractive but with a slightly scrawny edge. Ronan was just deeply handsome.

'That's good to know,' I said, wondering who was squabbling. 'I'm only doing it for a little while. Someone recommended that I get out of my comfort zone.'

'And are you?'

'Totally,' I admitted. 'I'm already petrified and I've only had one rehearsal. I did some acting in school but since then, nothing. I can't believe you two are brothers,' I said. 'But there is a resemblance.'

'He wouldn't thank you for mentioning it,' said Ronan. 'I'm not one of Fergal's favourite people. He's a fine fella, but it's complicated. Most sibling relationships are though, aren't they?'

'I wouldn't know. Only child.'

'And Harry?' He said. 'Has he got a brother or sister?'

'No,' I said. 'No he hasn't. He's on his own.'

'Joanna,' he said. 'Are you alright?'

I swallowed. 'Absolutely fine! Great ice cream, by the way. Even better than last time.'

'I can't take any credit for the ice cream, really,' he said. 'It's the cows. Really lovely, gentle girls they are, from the neighbour's farm. Their milk makes the best ice cream. I just do the odd bit of stirring.'

I watched him as he spoke, this tall, slim, broad shouldered man, with his happy and open face. Someone unburdened by life, or maybe just someone who could surf the waves of life, rather than letting them crash over him. Unlike John, I thought. And unlike me.

'I like the van,' I said, changing the subject.

'I bought it for nothing, from this guy in Tramore. He imports them from France and this one was proving unsellable. Too small for a food van, too big for a coffee van. He was only too glad for me to take it off his hands.' Ronan leaned back, hands behind his head. 'So,' he said casually, 'where's Harry's daddy?'

'He's gone. We're separated.'

'Really?' He looked surprised. 'Why?'

'Oh…' I looked away at the sea, thinking of all the times me and John walked this pier and looked out at the icy-grey water. 'It's complicated. Life is… very complicated.'

He nodded. 'It can be, yes.'

'A rug was pulled out from under us. I don't know… I'm not making any sense.'

'It's okay,' he said. 'I shouldn't have pried. It's just that… I was curious.' He smiled at me.

'We'd better go.' I stood up, hanging my bag over the pushchair handles.

He stood up and, taking a napkin, wiped Harry's face clean of ice cream. 'That's better little fella,' he said. 'Good as new.'

'Thanks Ronan.'

Harry and I waved goodbye and I began to walk away, feeling something I couldn't quite articulate. He was lovely, was Ronan. Really lovely. Someone I could have chatted to for much longer. Someone I could start being me again with. Someone who didn't know anything about the old me. I could start all over again.

Chapter sixteen

Two nights later, when Harry and I were walking through Dun Laoghaire on our way home from shopping, there was a beep from the Citroen van at the traffic lights. Ronan.

'Get in,' he said. 'I'll give you a lift home.'

It had started to spot with rain. I wasn't in the habit of getting into vans with strange men but when a large raindrop landed on my nose, I found myself nodding. 'Alright then.' I smiled back. 'Thank you.'

'I have a booster seat somewhere, it's been here since I bought the van, left over from the guy who had it before. I'll dig it out of the back. Give me a moment.'

So, Harry on a booster next to me, pushchair folded in the back, looked at me, delighted at this exciting new mode of transport. 'What do you think?' I said to Harry who was wide-eyed with wonder. 'This is pretty cool, isn't it?' He'd never been in the front of a van and couldn't quite believe his luck. Ronan let Harry press the button to play the music. 'Popeye the Sailor Man'.

'Again!' said Harry, clapping his hands. 'Again!' His little fingers pressed the button.

'How've you been?' I said to Ronan, after I'd given him directions home.

'Just back from Wexford,' he said. 'Making ice cream, dealing with suppliers, that kind of thing. It went really well.'

'Beats working in an office. Ice cream making – that's not a job, surely, it's a leisure activity.'

'Too right,' he grinned. 'I've done my share of office jobs but just realised I needed to do something that made me happy. Wexford strawberries and cream from the farm… it was a no brainer. And I get to grow a beard and wear jeans every day. What's not to like?'

'You're just another hipster.'

He laughed. 'Please, no!'

'What's wrong with that?'

'I may have a beard but that does not make me a hipster.'

'Protesting much?'

He laughed again. 'Yeah, I admit it. But what the hell. I'm happy.'

I couldn't argue with that.

'I don't know if I'm cut out for Dublin, though,' he said, as we turned into our road. We had turned into our road. 'I was involved in my very first road rage incident today. Wouldn't happen in Wexford.'

'Don't you have road rage in Wexford?'

'No,' he laughed. 'We have nice people who are nice to each other. They don't mind if you do something wrong, like drive too slowly or chat to someone you know on the pavement. People are happy to *wait*.'

'You didn't end up shouting at someone, did you?' I laughed, not quite believing it from this gentle soul. 'Just over there on the left,' I added.

'No, but they shouted at me. I was coming up a tight road in the van, just off the motorway, and suddenly we all got stuck and no one could move and this one fella wouldn't move back. And he was the only one who could have. It was a mess!' He laughed again. 'And then he got out of the car and came right up to me. He was furious and told me to roll down my window and then proceeded to eff and blind me. I told him to chill his boots and that made it worse, I'm afraid. I could see a blood vessel popping on the side of his head. And I was afraid he was going to collapse or something.'

'Oh God…'

'I know,' he said. 'And then he clutched his chest. And at this point we had quite an audience, everyone watching this man shouting at me. Jayze, I was thinking. How do I get out of this? At this point, I would have been happy to lift his car with my own hands to untangle us all. But there was an old lady in a Fiat Panda who was the one who had blocked us all in the first place, so at least he didn't shout at her. She just locked herself in her car looking terrified. There was a Jack Russell on her passenger seat going wild, too. I could see him springing about barking.'

'So what happened then?'

'So, he's clutching his chest and his whole face flashes from bright red to total white and then back to red again and then white. Like a barbershop sign. And before I can get out of the van, he's on his knees. Having a heart attack.'

'Jesus Christ!'

'So, I get on the ground with him, massage his heart, and stay with him until the ambulance arrives.'

'And what happened then?'

We were parked outside our house now.

'Well, we managed to move all the cars. Got his parked up on a verge. I rang his wife on his phone and told her where he was. And then I followed the ambulance to hospital just to make sure.'

'And did you hear about the guy? Is he alright?'

'He's as grand as they come,' he said. 'His wife just texted. She says he promises not to lose his temper again and is going on the muesli, that kind of thing. I'm going in later with the football scores. He's a Bohemians fan.'

'But how did you know how to massage his heart, or whatever you did?'

'St John's Ambulance. I was in it as a kid. Something to do, like a club. That and Gaelic football. We didn't realise that it might actually come in *use* one day. Well, except there was this one time…' I noticed that his face had clouded over.

'What do you mean?'

'Ah, it's just my Dad, you know?' he said. 'He had a heart problem. He was a farmer and one day he collapsed while we were out on the fields.'

'Oh, I'm sorry to hear that.'

'He died straight away. And I tried to do what I could… but there was no way. The guy today, it obviously wasn't that serious. It might have looked like I was helping him but it wasn't a heart attack that was going to kill him. I just kept him company. I was nigh on useless with my Dad, though.'

'That's awful.'

'It's okay. He was a lovely man, a great man. We were close. His time was up, that's all.'

'How old were you?'

'15. He'd had a great life, though. It was worse for our dog, Flash.' He laughed. 'I know it sounds mental but *we* could process it, we knew what was going on… Mam, myself, Fergal. But the dogs, especially Flash, couldn't work out why Dad's boots were still empty outside the back door, why he wasn't appearing from round the corner of the house. We had the wake in the house and let them see him. *That* was what killed me. Seeing Flash nudging Dad, tugging at his sleeve from inside the coffin. *That* started me off and once I started, I couldn't stop. Eventually we had to go to the church and to the graveyard and all the time Flash was glued to the coffin. We were all in bits.'

'Poor Flash.'

'He died himself two months after that. He was never the same once Dad was gone. Moped around, never ran for a thrown stick, or ate much food. That was pretty heartbreaking I can tell you. And then when *he* went – just laid down one night and didn't wake up – It brought it all back to us, Dad's death, you know… tipped Fergal over the edge.'

'Why? How was he?'

'Fergal?' He shrugged. 'Still blames me. Blames me for Dad.'

'Blames you? Whatever for?'

'It was me who made Dad come up the fields that day. He hadn't been feeling well but I'd been ploughing and I insisted on him seeing what I'd done. I feel awful about it, terrible, and I wish to God that I hadn't.'

'But it wasn't your fault. It could have happened anytime.'

'Of course it could have, but sometimes you need someone to blame. It helps, you know?'

'I know.'

'Fergs was in agricultural college at the time, was going to be a farmer just like Dad, but he dropped out after that. Never quite found his way back.'

'Fergal a farmer… I can't imagine it.'

'There's many ways to be a farmer, you know? We're not all flat-cap wearing and *Farming Journal* reading… well, we are, but we can do other things too. One farmer I know is a Musical Theatre buff. Goes to New York every year. Leaves the cows and lives it up on Broadway. Last month it was *Hamilton*. The year before *The Lion King*. Another guy, name of Wilkie Thomas, is a marathon runner. Once he's milked the cows, off he goes, down the lanes and boreens. Came fifth in the Dublin marathon last year. We had a party to celebrate. So, Fergal isn't a fish out of water. In small places you have to accept differences. It's the only way. But I think he's left farming behind now. Has his sights set on London, I think.'

'So the two of you lost your Dad.'

'Ah, we're grand,' said Ronan, pushing back his hair and shrugging. 'We had a great dad and role model. We'll get ourselves sorted. It's just not easy to bounce back after something like that. You just learn to live with it, don't you?'

'Yes,' I said, 'I suppose that's what you do.' I unstrapped Harry and pulled him onto my knee, giving him a kiss. 'Okay, little sweetheart?' I whispered. 'Ready to go inside?'

'I'm building a house on the land at home,' Ronan said. 'We don't farm anymore, just lease the fields. It's a timber house. I do bits when I'm at home. Get the lads involved, cook up a huge barbecue at the end of the day. That's what I want. The simple life.'

'And what about your ice creams?'

'My van is mobile,' he said. 'I can go anywhere. But where I want to live more than anywhere is in my wooden house, overlooking the hills and fields and hearing the song thrushes and the blackbirds singing all day long.'

'Sounds beautiful.' I began to open the door. 'Thanks so much for the lift.'

'You're welcome. My pleasure. What are you up to this evening?'

'I'm going to get started on assembling some wardrobes and bookshelves. I made the mistake of going to Ikea.' I laughed. 'They've been sitting in the hall for the last three days. I'd better get going on them as soon as Harry goes to sleep.'

'I'll do them for you,' he said immediately. 'You've enough to be thinking of. I'm a dab hand at that kind of thing. Why don't I come round tomorrow and put them up for you?'

'No, it's fine…'

'Please. I want to.'

'Yes,' I found myself saying. 'That would be great.'

'I'll be there at eight. Is that too early?' He pushed his hair out of his eyes.

'Early? That's half the morning gone for me.'

He laughed.

And then Harry pressed the music button again and the whole neighbourhood was regaled with 'Popeye the Sailor Man'.

We clambered out of the van, into the soft rain, said our goodbyes, and once I had Harry by the hand and the pushchair in the other, we walked to the house, my mind full of the conversation we'd just had. The loss of Ronan's father; poor Flash; Fergal. At the door, I turned and watched the van disappear around the corner. There was a man, I thought, who understood loss, who wasn't scared and timid about facing it all. I wondered if his attitude would rub off on me. I hoped it would.

Chapter seventeen

Ronan arrived bright and early with a large wooden box. 'My tools,' he explained, setting them down in the hall. 'Like a good hipster.'

'First things first, tea. It's Barry's. Nothing artisan. Would that offend you?'

He laughed. 'Anything other than Barry's would offend me.'

We went into the kitchen where Harry was eating his toast. 'Ronan's here, Harry. He's going to make your wardrobe for your room.'

'Mr Nicey!' said Harry.

Ronan ruffled his hair. 'Hello Harry. How's the toast?'

'Burnt,' said Harry. 'Exactly the way I like it.'

'He likes it really well done,' I explained. 'But it's not actually burnt.' Harry just shrugged as though I was wrong and carried on eating.

While I filled the kettle and began making the tea, Ronan looked around the room. 'This is cosy,' he said, standing by the stove. On the wall was a photo of Harry, John and me, taken last year on holiday in West Cork. We were all smiling in the photo, though, which is why I framed it. A stab at preserving a moment.

'Is that your ex?'

My *ex*? I hadn't thought of John as my 'ex'. He had once been my everything and the thought of him being my 'ex'... it was horrible. 'Yup,' I admitted, realising that he was indeed my 'ex'. 'That's him.'

'How do you find being on your own, with parenting?'

'Grand. I'm beginning to like it actually.' My own words surprised me. But having singleness thrust upon me had given me the opportunity to claw some of its distinct benefits: reading in bed in the middle of the night, light on; being able to flick through catalogues without anyone raising a quizzical eyebrow at their intellectual deficit; eating jam with a spoon, that kind of thing. 'Anyway my mother lives with us and she's like an uber au pair. Which I know is too many European words but there you go. Anyway, she was uber and an au pair…'

'What happened?'

'She seems to have fallen in love. She's rarely around lately.'

He laughed. 'Good on her. Life is for living. My brother has fallen hard for someone, too.' He added. 'He seems almost love-sick, though, can't eat, doesn't have much to say. Just says it's complicated and goes back to mooning about and staring out the window. Flings is all he has had up till now. Apart from one notable exception when he was still living at home. But this seems to be the real deal.'

'So how complicated is it?'

'I think, and I could be wrong, that she might have a boyfriend already.'

'Oh dear. That is complicated.'

'I hope he doesn't get hurt. He's a sensitive soul really.'

'But what about the other man? Shouldn't Fergal back off until she's free, until she disengages herself?'

'Of course. But then it wouldn't be complicated. And not so dramatic. Fergs loves the drama too, I imagine.'

'What do you think will happen?'

'I have no idea. I just hope he's going to be okay.'

'So you do care about him?'

'Yes, of course. Most of the time.' He smiled. 'He has a self-destructive streak. He'll push and push at things until everything falls down around him. He's always been like it. A free spirit. Gave my Mam most of her grey hairs, worrying about him. To be fair, I was the cause of some of them too but Fergal… well, he ran away for the first time when he was five. Hid between the wheels of the dairy tanker. Could have died, but instead he was found fifteen miles away at the next stop. Mick, the driver, brought him back. He and Fergs were friends for life.'

I laughed.

'And then, when he was 17, he ran off to live with this woman, Roisin Houlihan. She was 32 or thereabouts. Seemed ancient at the time. God, he was so in love with her, looked after her kids and everything, taught them how to play the melodeon. But her ex-husband returned one day and Fergal… he returned home, broken-hearted. He sat at the kitchen table and cried and cried. Mam was so upset for him and let him pour out his heart to her. How much he loved her, that he'd have done anything for her. And then Dad died later that year.'

'Why don't the two of you get on better?'

'Brothers.' He grinned. 'He claims I always had the best bedroom and I claim he was Mam's favourite.'

'Which is true?'

'Both and neither.' He shrugged. 'The way of the world, I suppose. Love and hate are too close. So, enough about my brother. What did you do before Harry?'

'PR,' I said. 'It was my life. Wearing a suit every day, flying here, there and everywhere. Sandwich at my desk. Meetings, deadlines, a boss who believed red wine was acceptable after 11am, that kind of thing. Watching cat videos with the girls in the office. The usual desk-bound chaos. And now my life is a very different kind of chaos.'

'Good morning.' It was Marietta, all ready to go on her walk. Ronan stood up, ready to shake hands and say hello.

'Mam, this is Ronan. He sells ice cream. FroRo ice cream,' I said. 'You might have seen his van on the pier, when you're doing your walks. Ronan, my mother, Marietta.'

'Ice cream, is it?' she said, taking his outstretched hand, 'and what are you doing here at this hour in the morning, FroRo?'

'I'm putting together some flat pack,' he said. 'I hope it isn't too complicated.'

She eyed him suspiciously. 'You remind me of someone,' she said, narrowing her eyes. 'Who's that actor? The one with the hair.'

'Haven't a clue,' I said. 'Ronan?'

He shook his head.

'The thin one, you know. German.'

'Michael Fassbender?' How is it that on the paltriest of evidence we often know what our mothers are thinking?

'That's the one. Michael Fast-bender.'

'What about him?'

'You look like him, she said to Ronan. 'The very spit. You're not related to the Fast-benders of Killarney are you?'

'Not that I know of,' he said.

'Ah well,' she said. 'You might be and might not know it.' She popped her ear buds in, ready for her walk. 'I'll see you later. Good to meet you Fronan.'

'You too,' he said. 'Now, I'd better get on with the wardrobes. If I was a proper hipster, I would be whittling them with my own hands, not ripping open cartons from Ikea.'

'You'll have to give your beard back,' I said. 'You're wearing it under false pretences.'

Soul-sappers

- Never having a lie-in

- Sugar highs (and lows) – both me and Harry

- Wondering if I'll ever get over what happened

- Not wanting to get over what happened

- When your mother is the only adult you see all day and it doesn't bother you

Chapter eighteen

'How did you manage that?' I asked, sincerely, as though Ronan had built the Taj Mahal. 'It's incredible.' And the wardrobe *was* perfect. Straight and unwobbly, the doors hung properly, the drawers at the bottom sliding in and out smoothly.

'Calm down,' he said, laughing. 'It's just flat pack.'

'Yes,' I said. 'But you did it on your own. And you didn't cry, or start banging in nails just trying to keep it together. Just you and a tiny little Allen key.'

'You're making me blush, now,' he said, smiling. 'If it makes you feel any better, I did go wrong at one point and had to undo a section.'

'You're human,' I said, breathing out a sigh of relief. 'Phew. I was beginning to think we were blessed with some kind of immortal being, some kind of God-like creature. The Allen Key Achilles.'

But the way he looked at me at that very moment made me blush and look away. I busied myself clearing up the vast sheets of cardboard packaging.

'Here, Harry,' he said. 'This is for all your clothes and the book case is for your toys and your books.' And they began filling the shelves with the piles of books I had placed on the floor as I loaded it up with his toy baskets filled with teddies and blocks. John and I should have done this ages ago and there was Harry living in a room which was disorganised and crowded.

'What do you think Jo?' Ronan said.

'What's that?'

'Do you think Harry deserves a ride in the ice cream van, just round the block? I've got to get going, go to the pier before the lunchtime walkers appear. But I said to Harry that maybe, *maybe*, he could press the Popeye button again.'

'Oh yes,' I said, 'now *that* sounds like an idea.'

'Well, then,' said Ronan, 'let's go!' He turned to me. 'Do you want a ride too?'

'In the van?' I said.

'In the van,' he said. 'Or…'

He was flirting with me. With *me*. It felt scary and terrifying and nice… incredibly and brilliantly *nice*. But more than that, I felt as though I had known this man for years and years. It was good to make a new friend. It was exactly what I needed. That he happened to be rather attractive was just a bonus.

'A ride in the van sounds great,' I coughed.

And that's what we did. The three of us sat in the front and he drove me and Harry around the block, up the hill a bit, past the playground where we waved to strangers and Harry pressed the Popeye button.

Eventually, he drove us back home. 'I'd better get going,' he said. 'Ice creams to sell and orders to sort out. Make sure everyone gets their deliveries. I'll be working late, I'd say. I've got a food festival in Stoneybatter tomorrow. I want the van looking good and I'm going to try out a few new flavours for the hipsters. I was thinking of basil and tomato. What do you think? Would you try it?'

'I'll stick with chocolate,' I said. 'Pizza flavoured ice cream isn't my thing.'

'Well, how about bacon and cabbage? One for the patriots?'

'I hope you're joking,' I said.

'Of course!' he laughed. 'I'm sticking to chocolate, strawberry and vanilla.'

'You can't go wrong with them. My best friend lives in Stoneybatter,' I added. 'I'll text her and tell her to come down and ask for potato flavour.'

'You do that.' And he paused, for an instant too long. As though he didn't want to leave. Christ alive. This brought me back, to when men actually wanted to be with me and I had all the time in the world to linger. When there wasn't a toddler to be looked after, or the laundry to put away, the sitting room to tidy and the weight of a lifetime of baggage hanging albatross-like round my neck.

'Okay, then,' I said, opening the door and beginning to get down. 'Well, thank you for a lovely morning. And for the wardrobe. What can I say? The work of a genius. What do you say Harry?'

'Fank-oo,' said Harry, obediently and I lifted him from the van. But we both still continued to hover.

'Right,' I said determinedly. 'Right, we're going.' I looked at Ronan and he looked back clearly and confidently, and this time we didn't smile but held each other's gaze. I had an instinct that he was exactly what I needed.

Chapter nineteen

That evening there was another rehearsal for The Seaside Players and when I stepped inside the hall, everyone was busy. David was on the stage, deep in conversation with Piers Byrne who was wearing a huge hat. Fergal was talking to Siobhan, Connie was pulling clothes out of bags and checking them, while Frederick and George wallpapered a large screen. Robert was sitting on one of the wooden chairs, on his own.

'How're things, Robert?' I said. 'All well? How was your day?'

'Well,' he pondered. 'The cherry tomatoes didn't arrive and we had several customers asking for them so that was difficult. And there was a complaint about the chicken wings. Too spicy apparently. Brought one of our customers out in a rash. And someone spilt three litres of milk on the floor and I skidded in it and landed in the cheeses.'

'Not a good day, then.'

'That's a normal day,' he said. 'We are kept on our toes in Superbuy.'

'Except when someone spills milk.' He looked at me blankly. 'Have you learned your lines yet?' I said quickly.

'Nearly,' he said and then, in a quieter voice, 'I'm only here for Siobhan, really. I get through it. I'm not talented like she is. But David is only too keen to have her at the Players, so he allows me to come along as well. He knows that my heart isn't in it. Or my brain. They belong to Superbuy. But you know what they say?'

'What?'

'Keep your friends close, your enemies closer.'

'Siobhan's your enemy?'

'No!' He laughed. 'She's my fiancée. But enemies are everywhere. Especially with a girl like Siobhan. She's too pretty to be allowed out alone.'

I couldn't work out if he was joking or not.

'It's just that I just want to keep her company,' he went on. 'That's what married couples do, don't they. I'm trying to get her a job at Superbuy but she doesn't want it. Being the boss's wife, you know. And I can understand that. People might think she'd get preferential treatment, like I wouldn't mind if she lifted a can of beans or came late in every morning or stacked the shelves wrongly. Like the Weetabix before the Cornflakes, when obviously it's the other way round.'

'Is it?'

He looked at me as though I was mad. 'Course it is. Have you ever seen it the other way? Have you?'

I couldn't think straight.

'You see?' He looked triumphant. 'There's rules you see, in supermarkets. Little secrets. We know them, those of us in the inner circle. And we are on pain of death not to reveal them to those who aren't.'

'But you just have?'

'Have I?'

'The Weetabix and the Cornflakes one.'

The colour drained from his face. He looked around furtively. 'Don't tell a soul, right? It's classified, that one.'

'What about the milk being at the far end?'

He looked panicked. 'How'd you know that?'

I tapped my nose mysteriously.

'Bit of good news, Joanna,' he said, changing the subject. 'Mam has managed to track down a lovely wedding dress in the charity shop today that she says would be perfect for Siobhan.'

'And has Siobhan seen it?'

'Not yet, but Mam said she had to buy it there and then as it would have been gone in a flash. It's gorgeous, she says, like a less flouncy version of Princess Diana's but still all puffy and everything. Cost fifteen euro, so that's a dint in the wedding budget, but we can always try to sell it again afterwards.'

'Wise, very wise.' I stopped. Across the room, we heard Fergal and Siobhan laugh.

'Mr Show-off,' said Robert, glaring at Fergal. 'God, he really fancies himself, doesn't he?

I shrugged non-committedly.

'Luckily,' he went on, 'Siobhan's far too sensible to take any notice of *him*. Anyway,' he returned to our conversation. 'Siobhan will have gone off acting by then, I know it. I mean, my Mam was just saying that girls these days don't know if they're coming or going, jeans one day and skirts the next, or if they want men to open doors for them, or if they don't. It's a lot simpler if one person makes all the decisions. And I'm the sensible one. Everyone knows that.' He looked pleased with himself. 'Mam always says I was born with a notebook in my hand. While all the other kids were playing football in the street, I was on Litter Watch. If anyone dropped so much as a sweet wrapper, I'd be over to their parents in a flash. Mam always said that you don't win friends doing the right thing. That's how I met Siobhan, actually.'

'Doing the right thing?'

'Litter Watch. She dropped a crisp packet. Flew out of her pocket, she said. Likely story. And I was all for doing what I called my citizen's on-the-spot fine—'

'Is that legal?'

'It should be. But she was mitching from school. And dropping crisp packets. So we got talking and, that was it, really.'

'She went *out* with you? After you arrested her for dropping a crisp packet.'

'I dropped my citizen's on-the-spot fine. We went to the cinema and she said she thought I was funny. I never did understand that one because I didn't mean to be. But we were meant to be.' He stopped and laughed. 'Get it? Didn't mean to be? We were meant to be? Maybe I am funny. But I didn't *mean* to be then. There I go again!' He chuckled away and then rooted around in his shoulder bag. 'Would you like an apple? I bought them from Superbuy this evening. About to be thrown out they were but with my staff discount, they were one cent per one apple. Only a little bruised. Look.'

And then Fergal spotted me. 'Gwendolen! Our Gwendolen has arrived!'

'Mr Up-Himself,' said Robert to me as Fergal jumped off the stage, coat flying, Siobhan and Connie having gone. 'This one's got an eye for the ladies, so a bit of advice, from me to you, watch this one. I certainly am.'

Fergal fell to his knees and skidded towards me, landing at my feet, and looked up grinning, making me laugh. Robert, behind him, gave me an I-told-you-so look and pointed two fingers at his own eyes and then at Fergal.

'Nice entrance,' I said, laughing.

'You know me,' Fergal said, getting to his feet. 'Evening *Bob*.'

'*Robert*.'

'Sorry, *Bobert*,' apologised Fergal unapologetically. 'My word, you *are* looking handsome tonight. What is it? New anorak? New perm done by your mother at the kitchen table?

The electricity from your polyester work uniform is creating some kind of halo around you. It's all most becoming.'

Robert stood there, accepting it all.

'And your scarf, Fergal,' he retorted. 'Did you *steal* it from an old lady?'

'Ah this?' Fergal fingered his silk paisley. 'Well, I wouldn't call Fiona Shaw *old*. And she gave it to me, I didn't steal it, when we worked together on a production of Mother Courage. *Darling* Fiona. She said it brought her luck and wanted the same for me. And it seems to have worked. I *am* feeling lucky.' He eyeballed Robert. 'What about you, Bob? Feeling lucky?'

'Well…'

'What's in your packed dinner tonight?' Fergal went on, refusing to stop baiting him.

'Cheese and pickle,' answered Robert. 'And a flask of tea. And a Wagon Wheel. And a one-cent apple. Anything wrong with that? All the food groups taken care of. And money saved.'

'Sounds lip-smacking,' said Fergal, losing interest and putting his arm around me.

'Anyway,' said Robert. 'I've got to go. Mam's been locked out of the house and she needs me to get the door open. I'm the only one with arms skinny enough to slip through the letter box and open the latch.'

'Your talents,' said Fergal, 'show no end. Anyway, Gwendolen,' he said, turning to me, let's go through our big scene. The kissing one!' He said, loudly. He linked arms with me and marched me to the stage. 'I *had* to rescue you,' he whispered into my ear. 'Let's leave Bobbity to his Wagon Wheel and his Mam. Christ, he's boring. Dull as ditch water.

Like a priest crossed with an accountant, crossed with my brother. But a million times worse.'

'Did you really work with Fiona Shaw?'

'No, of course not. But I was in the audience for her production of Mother Courage. I am but a poor amateur and she the queen.'

Just as I was laughing, David walked over. 'Ah! Joanna,' he said. 'Thank you for coming... we are going to run through your first scene in fifteen minutes but maybe you could go over it first with Mr Byrne, our Lady Bracknell, and with Fergal, our Jack.'

And we did, and it was wonderful. I don't mean *I* was wonderful or we did anything brilliant or that we were any good (well, Piers was amazing and Fergal was pretty good, actually) but it was fun. As I started speaking the lines (script in one hand), I remembered how much I enjoyed being someone else. *Playing*. And having fun.

And then we had to perform in front of David and all the cast and I suddenly felt nervous again as they all gathered around. But when our scene was over, there was a round of applause and Siobhan whispered to me. 'That was great! You're a natural.'

'Oh no,' I said. '*You* are.'

'Thanks Jo,' she said. 'I'm not great, but it's my passion. I love being on stage, it's the most exciting thing I've ever done.' She lowered her voice which I thought was strange, considering we were among thespians. 'It really is my passion,' she confided. 'It's all I think about.'

'Well, you're in the right place.'

'I've been accepted at Drama College. Rada,' she whispered. 'I just heard today. No one knows. But...' there were tears in her eyes, 'I'm not going to be able to go. Robert would kill me.

His *Mam* would kill me. And she's not someone you want wanting to kill you, if you know what I mean. And there's the wedding and everything. So… so, I can't go.'

'But you must! Robert would understand, of course he would. You've the rest of your life to be grown up and sensible and get married. You've got to go to Rada.'

'Just the idea of it…' Her eyes shone. 'Can you imagine? Acting all day long, with all those teachers and other students and being in London… I feel giddy at the thought. But,' she shook her head, 'Robert always says you can't always get what you want. That's true, isn't it?'

'Yes, it's true,' I agreed. 'But opportunities like this don't come very often. You've been offered a place at Rada. Rada! The best drama school in the world. I mean, come on! You have to follow your dreams… you really do.'

'I wish it was that easy,' she said, sadly. 'Life can get very complicated sometimes. Robert makes everything easy. Everything is jotted down in his notebook: shopping lists, spending lists, what we watch on television, what underpants to wear on what days.'

I laughed.

'I'm not joking.' Even Siobhan smiled. 'He's just him. He's a good person. He was so good to me when I wanted to leave school. I didn't get on with my parents and didn't really have anyone. All he tries to do is simplify everything, but I just seem to end up complicating things.' She took my hand and squeezed it. 'I'm so glad you've joined us. It's nice to have another female around. Me and Connie were feeling out-numbered.'

'What's that you're saying?' Fergal had sidled up beside us.

Siobhan blushed. 'I was just saying to Jo that I was so glad she's joined us.'

'And so am I,' he declared. 'She's just what we need, someone beautiful and intelligent.' And then he turned to Siobhan. 'And, as for our ingénue,' he said. 'Well, be still my beating heart.'

For a moment, they looked at each other and I could have sworn electricity crackled over their heads, but it was time to go home and so everyone began packing up, finding coats and pushing scripts into bags.

I said my goodbyes and went out to the carpark and sat in my dark car for a moment, texting Nicole, to make sure she was alright. And then, out of the corner of my eye, I saw two figures moving behind the hall where the bins were kept. They were locked into some kind of embrace. The girl in jeans and with a long blonde plait, the man wearing a waistcoat and scarf.

Siobhan and Fergal.

I slunk down in my seat, peering out over the dashboard. They had pulled apart now and I could see she was crying and saying something to him. And then he was saying something to her and she tried to leave but he pulled her back.

Oh my good Lord.

I couldn't help but watch for a while longer, now trapped in the car, but eventually, Siobhan walked away and, I presume, into the hall, at the front. While Fergal lit one of his roll-ups and stood there for a moment, smoking it. In a few minutes, he flicked the stub away and walked, ever so nonchalantly, round to the front too.

What had I just seen? Fergal and Siobhan together. Had they been having an affair? Was Siobhan the girl Fergal had been mooning after? The one that Ronan had mentioned? What was going on?

Now, I would have to pretend I hadn't seen a thing.

Life-lifters

- The track pant (note singular). What else would I wear every day?

- Pasta (esp. spirals). What else would we eat?

- Theatrical troupes! It's like playing, but being grown up

- Brian from Brian's. He is going to ask that woman to bless me by Skype tonight at 6 p.m.

- Being lactose-tolerant. Otherwise I wouldn't have met FroRo God, these are paltry.

Chapter twenty

On the main street in Dalkey, my eye was caught by the sight of a man swanning along, coat flapping, stubble bristling, scarf nattily tied, long hair flowing. Oscar Wilde himself had been reincarnated. It was Fergal Forest, Ronan's big brother, my co-star.

He looked over and saw me.

'Jo!' he shouted and ran across the road, dodging cars and bicycles. He leaned in to kiss me on *both* cheeks and I was again struck by how handsome he was.

'Hello Fergal,' I said, wondering if anyone I knew could see me. Here I was being embraced by an unconventional bohemian, a devilishly good-looking one at that.

He took my hand and gazed into my eyes.

'She walks in beauty, like the night
Of cloudless climes and starry skies;
And all that's best of dark and bright
Meet in her aspect and her eyes…'

I laughed, in spite of myself. 'Idiot.'

'But a *nice* idiot?' He raised an eyebrow. 'Please say I'm at least *nice*.'

'Perhaps. That's all you're getting.'

'I think,' he said, grandly, 'that I might die without Byron.' He grinned, diluting his incredible pretentiousness with his rather beguiling and cheeky charm. I wondered about him and

Siobhan. He couldn't be more different to Robert if he lived on another planet.

'Coffee,' he announced. 'I am going to expire if I don't have coffee!' He shouted this out a bit too loudly, so that some people glanced our way. 'And you need one too, I can tell. You are looking rather peaky. Let's de-peak you!' he said. 'With coffee. And cake. Do you know of an establishment?'

'Brian's? It has a Tibetan vibe. You'd like it.'

'Lead on!'

We ducked inside the café and settled ourselves in the corner as we waited for Brian to come and take our orders.

'The strongest coffee possible, please,' said Fergal. 'And the sweetest cake imaginable.'

'Two cappuccinos and two slices of Victoria sponge please, Brian,' I translated. 'Thank you.'

Fergal settled back in his chair, flicking back his long hair and looking at me through narrowed eyes, as though he was sizing me up.

'Apparently you and my brother are acquainted.'

'We are, yes. And very nice he is too. A credit to you.'

He pulled a face. 'They always say that.'

'Who?'

'Women.'

I laughed. 'Sounds like you might be slightly envious of your charming brother.'

'Not at all,' he said. 'He's a pain the hole. Just warning you.'

I laughed again. 'I rest my case.'

'The bearded wonder gets around. Always popular with the ladies. I didn't know you were a Hipster Hugger, Joanna? Anyway, let's not talk about him, any longer. So,' he said, changing the subject, 'have you read the play? Do you know your lines, Gwendolen?'

'Not at all!' I said. 'I mean, I've read it and everything but I haven't started to learn it. I will get down to it very soon.'

'Next rehearsal is Tuesday,' he said. 'We can start working on it then. We'll learn them together. Maybe,' he said, sitting back, 'I should come round to yours some evening?'

Brian brought over our coffees and cakes. Neither looked as though they quite fulfilled Fergal's order. The coffee looked like dishwater and the cake dry and unappetising. However they both totally did the job.

'So, what about you Fergal?' I said. 'What's your story? You're from a farm, isn't that right?'

'What else did he tell you?' he said, as though bored with the subject. 'He really must get himself a more interesting life instead of always looking to me.'

Ronan? How could he say that about Ronan? They looked alike but they seemed very different people.

'I don't think he's looking to you... he's got his own business, hasn't he?'

Fergal shrugged. 'Anyway, let's not waste time on him... he is nothing but an embossed carbuncle in my corrupted blood.' He flashed his large smile. 'I was telling you about me.'

'Okay,' I said. 'How did you get involved in the Players?'

'Well,' he said. 'I've always been good at acting the maggot and acting the fool. I auditioned just like everyone else. *Pride and Prejudice*. Siobhan was Elizabeth Bennet and I was Darcy.'

'Of course.'

He tried a smouldering look on me. 'And I've never looked back. I work in a cash and carry and every day I wonder why I didn't stay on the farm. I'm thinking about going back actually. Leaving the big smoke, getting a couple of cows – the good life. Or the bad life. Depending on your point of view. Or I might go to London. I can't decide.'

'So what's keeping you here?'

'There's a girl,' he said. 'I can't do anything until she makes up her mind.'

'Sounds complicated.'

'It is and it isn't. She has me right here.' He prodded his palm. 'Putty I am. Helpless. A fool.'

'Aw…' He had me feeling sorry for him.

'Don't worry about me,' he said, eyes big and helpless. 'I'll survive. Don't waste your tears on me.'

'I wasn't going to.'

He smiled. 'This is good,' he said, taking a big sip of his coffee and hacking at the cake with a fork. 'Feeling better now. Human again. Heartbeat back to normal.'

'Why don't you go into business with Ronan? He seems to have quite a good thing going. He's got contracts with restaurants and cafes now, too. I should ask Brian if he would stock some FroRo.'

'And I thought you weren't going to worry about me,' Fergal laughed.

'I wasn't! I meant—'

'Anyway, never gonna happen.'

'What?'

'Me and Little Ro-ro. We. Don't. Get. On.'

'But you're brothers. And it's Ronan. Who's lovely, despite what you say.'

'So? Your point being?' he said. 'Listen. He's a goody-goody. The baby. Everyone else is on at *me* to get a proper job but as soon as Ronan says he'll be selling ice creams, everyone's delighted.'

'But you live together,' I protested. Were all brothers like this, I wondered, oscillating between being mortal enemies and best friends.

'Under duress. And only to keep my dear old Mam happy. She thinks the sun shines out of his backside. Now, don't get me wrong. We get on *sometimes* but we're nothing alike. I mean, he's Mr Boring and I'm Mr Interesting.'

I laughed, despite myself. 'I don't think he's boring,' I said. 'He's very nice.'

'Not you as well. It's those eyes of his, isn't it? Like a puppy dog he is. And that ridiculous beard. God, it works every time. Women are so shallow.' He sighed, theatrically. 'Now, don't you be falling under his spell right? All the girls do. You can fall in love with me.'

I laughed again. He was impossible. 'Let's just fall in love on stage, okay?'

'As long as we get to kiss in the final scene,' he said. 'I want a full-on snog.'

'Oh God! Please don't.'

I realised I was enjoying myself. Next thing, I was telling him all about Marietta and her mysterious man-friend turning out to be Patrick Realta.

'That old ham,' said Fergal. 'I thought he'd died years ago. Oh God. What was that infernal racket?' Fergal starting singing. 'It's Sunday morning, the sky is blue, the birds are singing just for you. Let's make each moment last... no one needs to know, let's skip mass...'

We started laughing then. 'That is gas!' he said. 'Does he look embalmed? I imagine he would look barely alive these days. Dead but tanned.'

'Well, hello you two.' We looked up to see Ronan standing there. 'So this is where you're hiding, Fergal. I saw you from outside. Hello Jo, sorry about this. But this fella here has let me down for the last time.'

'Listen, Ro-ro, you are disturbing us. I am currently in conference with my beautiful co-star,' said Fergal. 'So it was impossible for me to mind the van for you today. Anyway, I'm just no good at serving ice cream. My fingers are too expressive.'

'Too expressive?' Ronan was looking coolly at his brother. 'I won't even get into that. But you promised. You said you would do the morning shift, while I was in the wholesalers. I paid you, remember? Fifty quid upfront.'

'Time and ice cream waits for no man,' said Fergal. 'I was on my way but then I met the lovely Joanna and she was in need of a chat – an intellectual one, about life and existence, nothing you'd be interested in, of course – and how could I say no? To a woman in need?'

'Fergal,' I interrupted. 'I wasn't in need. And you gave me the impression that you had nothing to do. I'm so sorry,' I said to Ronan.

'Well,' Fergal said. 'I sensed *something*. Ro-ro, how could I refuse? You would have done the same.'

'Would I?' He was still frowning but I could see that he wasn't angry.

'You would, but you do have a greater sense of duty than I; duty to the call of commerce and industry. I, on the other hand, feel the call of the human soul in need.'

'Fergal—' I had to object to him using my soul as an excuse for letting his brother down.

'I'm never going to ask you to fill in for me again,' said Ronan. 'And I want my fifty euro back, as well. Okay?'

'I've spent it,' said Fergal, quickly. 'Well, not spent it. Given it away, actually… to someone in need. Someone I know, a friend, needed it for something.'

'Fergal, I have no idea what's going on, but just pay me back. Okay?'

'Yes, little brother.'

'Sooner rather than later. Okay?'

'Yes, Ro-ro.'

'And don't call me Ro-ro.'

'No-no.'

And finally Ronan smiled. 'You idiot. You are a fecking unreliable, useless idiot. You know that, don't you?'

'Yes, yes of course I know it. But it's exactly why I am so lovable, isn't it?'

Ronan rolled his eyes. 'I'll see you soon, Jo,' he said to me. 'I'm off to the food festival in Stoneybatter. I'm already late. But I'll call you. Okay?'

I nodded. 'Okay.' I was surprised about how pleased I felt at the anticipation of a phone call from Ronan. He winked at me.

I stood up. 'I've got to go as well,' I said to Fergal. 'Got to pick Harry up from crèche.'

'Goodbye, sweet Gwendolen. Till Tuesday!' He shouted this out in a loud thespian manner, causing people to look up from their frothy coffees. He kissed my hand but I found I didn't mind. I was starting to find a bit of fun in life again. Something I thought had gone forever.

Chapter twenty-one

At first, I wasn't quite sure it was Nicole standing on the road, across from my house. She looked wholly unlike herself, pale, hesitant, almost unreal. I hadn't seen her since the dinner party and despite my numerous texts and phone calls, we hadn't actually spoken.

'Nicole!' I shouted. I began to walk towards her, Harry on my hip. 'What's wrong?' I broke into a trot. 'Come on…' I called again. She didn't move. It was as though she wasn't sure what to do. Had she stabbed Coco and Kristof? Was she on the run?

'Nicole—' we were now only feet apart. 'Nicole.' I said again, gently. 'Are you okay? Sweetheart… what's going on?'

She was just looking at me, her eyes wide with fear, or something else. She looked tired, drawn, and pale. Her normally swishy hair, grey and greasy; she was wearing a man's coat and tracksuit bottoms.

'Nic,' I said. 'What's happened? Has anything happened?'

'Just…' Her voice was tiny, hesitant, like it belonged to someone else, a smaller person, someone entirely unrelated to the Nicole I knew and loved. 'Just everything.'

'Come inside, will you? Come on.'

'I thought I could deal with it,' she said, shakily. 'I thought that I could absorb it. You know, I always do… But I didn't want to tell you, burden you; you know, after everything…'

I took her hand, cold and slight and soft and gentle.

'Absorb what?' I asked. 'What did you think you could deal with?'

'Him,' she said. 'Her. Them. I thought I could do it, read some self-help books, take it all on board. But I can't. I've realised I can't. Not now.'

Her face suddenly crumpled, her mouth torn as though she had been physically hurt.

Harry was watching her, fascinated. Sorry, Harry, I wanted to say. I didn't want you to find out quite yet. I was hoping you'd get another few years out of your innocence but this is life. This is what life actually looks like, all heartbreak and hurt. It's not just fun, games and vanilla ice cream. Well, only some of the time. This is what humans do, they hurt each other and they get hurt. And there is nothing that can protect us, apart from living in a cave for the rest of your life or never feeling anything ever again. This is life in all its glory.

'Oh, Nic... Come on inside.'

She allowed me to lead her across the road and I noticed she was limping.

'What's wrong with your foot?'

'Blisters.'

'How did you get here?'

'I walked.'

'Walked? It's got to be 12 miles, at least.'

'I just started walking and crossed the river and then followed the coast.' She looked at me. 'Sorry. Stupid thing to do. I think I'm going mad.'

'Oh Nicole.' Her hand was shaking; I could just feel the tension in her whole body, her energy coiled so tightly it was as though she might burst. 'I know that feeling. Staying still is maddening. Sometimes I used to push the pushchair to the park and then go round the block again because I didn't want to go indoors.'

'Nearly there,' I said, as we walked up our drive. 'Nearly there… nearly there.'

Once inside, leaving Nicole in the kitchen, I quickly put Harry in front of the television, refusing to allow maternal guilt to kick in. I gave him a few jelly tots as well.

'Don't worry, Harry,' I said, although he didn't look too worried, digging his hand into the sweets. 'We'll be back on the hummus and rice cakes and tap water tomorrow. Normal life will resume.'

When I went back into the kitchen, Nicole hadn't moved. I boiled a kettle, thinking that she could soak her feet.

'Why aren't you at school?' I said.

'Half-term.'

I'd forgotten about that. 'What's going on?' I said. 'Are you alright? Tell me, let me help you.'

'But you…' she said. 'You've been going through so much, that's why I didn't… I thought I could do this on my own. I didn't want to burden you. You've got your own stuff going on. I'm so sorry.'

'Don't be.' I led her to the armchair and sat myself beside her. 'Please don't be sorry. It's going to be alright.' I stood up again and found the plastic washing-up bowl and filled it up with water and some of my bath salts. I placed the frothy bath at her feet and she began unlacing her trainers.

'Thanks Jo.' She sat there, feet soaking, staring into space, while I boiled the kettle again for tea. Finally she looked at me properly, focussed, for the first time. She was coming back to life. Leaning back in the chair, she sucked in a lungful of air, like she had been diving and had returned to the surface.

'Nicole?' I tried again. 'Where's Kristof? What's happened exactly?'

'He's gone to Kilkenny for the night. He had a meeting about a new gallery there. Well, that's what he said.' Face buried in her hands, she began to cry. 'I think Coco's gone with him.' When she lifted her head up, she looked as though the life had drained from her. There was a glint in her eyes that I had never seen before, a look of madness, of mania.

'I'm making tea,' I said. 'And you're going to tell me what is going on.'

I made Nicole's nice and milky, the way she likes it, and we sat down opposite each other on the two armchairs in front of the stove.

'Tell me,' I commanded.

'Coco is pregnant.'

I gasped and nearly dropped my mug. 'Kristof's?'

She nodded and tried to speak but nothing came out, her face crumpling into sobs.

'But she was smoking and drinking that night… and eating mussels!'

'She had been feeling ill, apparently, but thought it was just a bug, something she thought she had picked up from when she only ate from burger vans around the city. For a piece she did on the price of flesh or something. But it turned out it wasn't the dodgy meat that was making her feel nauseous, it was the fact she is pregnant. With my husband's child.'

'How pregnant is she?'

'Six months.'

'Jesus Christ alive!'

'I know,' she said sadly. 'I know.'

'She didn't look that pregnant at the dinner party…' I tried to think back. She was wearing a dress which skimmed her stomach (and showed her cleavage). Yes, she could have been pregnant. 'How long have you known they have been having this affair?'

'Since it started, I suppose. But it was nothing new. It's what Kristof does. He's always slept with other women,' she shrugged. 'Always. I knew it from the beginning. But I was the only woman he loved. He told me that. They were just flings.' She shook her head. 'You know, I thought you had to accept things about people. Fidelity is over-rated, he thought, and just wasn't important – not when you loved someone – and he said he loved me. And I love him.'

'But sleeping with other women… really? You were okay with that?'

'Not really. But I thought I had to accept it. No one is perfect.'

'True.'

'And that's exactly why I didn't tell you – or anyone. I knew everyone would judge us, judge me. But I love him. Kristof is an amazing man. He makes me so incredibly happy. We have a bond that I've never had with anyone else.'

'Of course,' I nodded, desperately trying to be on the same page as her, see the world through her eyes. 'He's crazy about you. Well…' But I didn't know what else to say, because if you are so crazy about someone, do you sleep with other people?

'But,' she was speaking again, 'I thought I was stronger than this. I thought *we* were stronger than this. But then she gets pregnant. *He* gets her pregnant. And it kind of changes things a little.'

'A lot.'

'Yeah, a lot.' Nicole sighed. 'I knew there was something different about Coco from the moment he first mentioned her. You just know, don't you?'

I nodded.

'He's been bewitched by her, I think. I mean, she's beautiful and gorgeous and everything I'm not.'

'No, you're beautiful and gorgeous and you're not crazy like her.'

'She's an artist, though. She's exactly what he loves and responds to.'

'But he must have met thousands of artists…' And slept with them I thought, grimly.

'But no one like Coco. There's no one like Coco.'

'Thankfully.'

She almost smiled. 'So I've only got myself to blame, haven't I? I went along with it because I thought we were beyond such bourgeois conventions, the petty concerns of ordinary people. I was taken in by it. But you know something, Jo?' She looked right at me. 'You know something? I want to be ordinary, I want to be petty, to be bourgeois, because this bohemian shit pisses me right off.'

'He loves her?'

'He still loves me.' She pulled a face. 'He just loves Coco as well.'

She began to cry again. 'Anyway, wouldn't you? He wants us to get friendlier. He thinks we can all co-exist, that the baby can be born into this wonderful, strange family. The dinner last week was weird enough – sorry about that – but this is something I can't quite get my head around.'

'Right.' I was lost for words. I took a sip of my tea.

'I thought I could deal with it, that it was just the same as with all the other women. But this is different. She's having a child. His child. And *we* didn't have one because he said that we didn't need one. And I went along with that too, for him.'

'Oh Nicole,' I said. 'I can't believe it.'

'Nor can I,' she said quietly. She wiped her eyes with her sleeve.

'When did you first know something was going on between Kristof and Coco?'

'Oh, I don't know. Well, I do actually. As soon as he first mentioned her to me I knew something, I sensed it. It was different. I could just tell. Nothing he said but there was an energy, a charge. Imperceptible, probably. I just knew he was in love with her. It's so weird, isn't it?'

I shrugged. 'Life is weird.'

'And then I met her. And saw them together. At an opening.'

'I hate those things.'

'Me too. And this one was worse than ever. So, there I am, wondering when I can sneak off home. I had books to mark and the kids had their big play the next day, so I wanted an early night, but I spotted Coco coming in and I knew it was her. This woman, that Kristof spoke of so glowingly.'

'Like a 70s Kate Bush crossed with Kim Kardashian. Mannip.'

Nicole looked confused.

'You know, like catnip…' I trailed off, uselessly.

'Anyway, so she's gorgeous and beguiling and has… what is it? Charisma? Energy? The whole room had noticed her. And then Kristof walks over to her and they embrace, no kissing, but there was something so intimate, so familiar about the hug that it was obvious that they were… they were…'

'Shagging?'

She nodded. But her face was set in some kind of agony. 'What am I going to do, Jo? I love him.' She began to cry, huge wet tears. 'I love everything about him. I love the very bones of him, the breath of him, the being of him. It is breaking my heart. I can feel it crumbling inside, like a crack from an earthquake is spreading through me, bit by bit.'

I put my arms around her. 'I know… I know…'

Nicole was going through something I had experienced too, when everything you think is in place, when you have worked so hard and struggled so much to put your world to rights and then a great big trick is pulled on you and everything collapses. You can't make sense of it all or even begin to think things might be alright again. I wished I had some advice for Nicole but I hadn't begun to process my own story yet so I was no use to her.

'Does Kristof know how you're feeling?' I said. 'The stress you are under?'

She nodded. 'He has some idea, yes,' she said. 'Which is why he was desperate to go to Kilkenny. He knows I am struggling. To put it mildly.'

'Right,' I said. 'So you are going to stay here for as long as you need. And we are going to talk about it as much or as little as you like, okay? And I am going to look after you.'

'You don't need to, Jo,' she said. 'I'll be alright.'

'No you bloody won't, okay! And you've just said that trying to cope with this on your own hasn't worked. Please Nicole, stay here, with us. I promise Harry will be like a church mouse, okay? I'll set up the sofa bed in the study.'

'But I love Harry,' she said. 'I'm his godmother, remember?'

'The best,' I said. The best godmother ever.' I hated Kristof for doing this to her. And this ridiculous Coco person. 'The best godmother and the best friend ever,' I said. 'But as for Kristof… and bloody Coco…' I was lost in incoherence.

'Puffball!'

'What?'

'He's on his own. In the house. He'll starve. I'll have to go home.'

'I'll go and get him. Everything'll be fine.' But how on earth was I going to get a fluffy ball of mohair from Stoneybatter to Dalkey during rush hour? It would take hours.

And then I thought of someone. Someone who might be in the area. Someone who was the kind of person who could be relied on in an emergency.

'Is there a spare key?' I said.

'Under the funny stone, amongst the other stones, in the blue pot beside the other pots.'

I knew just the man.

Chapter twenty-two

'Jo!' Ronan sounded delighted to hear from me, making me feel immediately awkward because I've never been good when people are enthusiastic about me. I find it easier when any regard is imperceptible. 'How's it going?' he said. 'I was just thinking about you.'

'You were?'

'Yes,' he continued. 'I was planning to ask you something.' As he spoke, I knew why I'd phoned him. It wasn't just because he was in the area and could rescue Puffball, it was because I *liked* relying on him. He was safe and kind and dependable. He was someone easy, so different from the emotional livewires I was surrounded by. But back to the plight of Puffball.

'I was going to ask *you* something!' I said.

'You go first.'

'Okay… it's a favour. Quite a big one. But I thought you might still be at the food thing in Stoneybatter? Are you? Say if you're not, it's grand. I just… you know…'

'I am, as it happens. Just packing up now. The cheese and onion flavour went down well, as did the smoked salmon and brown bread.'

I laughed.

'So,' he went on. 'I'm utterly at your service. How may I be of assistance?'

Over on the chair, Nicole's tea was on the arm beside her, undrunk. Sometimes in life, I was beginning to realise, you just had to hold steady and see it through. Don't fight it, just accept it, and stay in the moment, however much you want to rail. But I was still in the wobbling stages, with the tilting and the terrifying lurches. Ronan was a man who knew how to stay steady. I liked that about him.

'Ronan, I really need your help. It's about a dog called Puffball.' Briefly and breathlessly I explained the situation, saying that my best friend was in trouble and her dog was stranded but that there was a key hidden.

'Consider it done,' he said immediately, and ninety minutes later, he was at my door, Puffball under his arm.

'Delivery of one dog!' He announced, as Nicole rushed over and buried her face into Puffy's fur.

'Thank you!' I said, feeling enormously grateful. 'Will you stay for dinner? Cheese on toast?' I wished it was something a little more impressive, but I have never met anyone who didn't like cheese on toast and Ronan was no exception.

'Now you're talking,' he said, grinning at me. 'I'll give you a hand.'

He grated the cheese while I toasted and buttered the bread. Puffball snoozing on Nicole's lap, Nicole still gazing into space. Ronan and I moved around the kitchen seamlessly, him laying the table, me filling up a jug of water and finding glasses. I was beginning to really like the way I felt around him. It made me feel as though I had nothing to fear, that life wasn't about to bite me on the behind. For too long now, I had been living with fear, trepidation and terror and Ronan made everything – life – feel doable and unfrightening. He caught me looking at him and winked. He seemed to like me too.

Nicole didn't eat much and pretended to listen to the conversation but she was miles and miles away, consumed, I imagined, with thoughts of Kristof and Coco. When we'd finished, Ronan piled up the plates and began slipping them into the dishwasher, while I got Harry ready for bed.

'I think I'll sleep as well,' said Nicole. 'I feel wiped out.'

When I was tucking Harry in and kissing him gently, I said, 'I'm so sorry I've been so distracted, Harry. It was an emergency. Sometimes life has emergencies but it doesn't stop me loving you.' He nodded at me, as though all was forgiven. And, as I tiptoed out of his dimly-lit room, his eyelids were closing. His grey rabbit was tucked up under one arm, his spider under the other. Life was so simple for him, unperilous, drama-free (as far as he knew). For adults, however, it was a different story. Peril at every turn.

'Are you okay?' Ronan said quietly, when I came downstairs after making sure Nicole was settled and comfortable on the sofa bed. I had lit my posh lavender candle for her and collected some of my catalogues from around the house – Lakeland, The White Company, Ikea. There was nothing like a bit of soothing catalogue-flicking after a horrendous shock. I left out my cashmere socks that I had never worn as they were too nice and my best pyjamas.

'Great, thanks,' I said to him. 'And I don't know how to thank you for rescuing Puffball.'

'I'm a dog person,' he explained. 'I wouldn't have done it for a cat.'

'I wouldn't be talking to you if you weren't,' I said. 'I could tell you were a dog person the first moment I met you.'

'Really?' he said. 'And what else could you tell?'

'Oh I don't know… that you were an Aries and your favourite colour was taupe.'

'Wrong on both counts,' he laughed. 'But I made my own assumptions about you.'

'Really? What were they?'

'That you liked ice cream—'

'That is true.'

'And that you were beautiful.'

Oh God. 'Thank you…'

He smiled. 'I was brought up to tell the truth and it's so blindingly obvious that I had to tell you.'

It wasn't blindingly obvious and I feared for his sanity, but I felt my face getting hot.

'Can I do anything else?' he said. 'Any other canines to rescue? Or cows? I'm good with cows.'

'No, you've been so amazing,' I said, hoping he would go now so I could try to return to normal again. 'I didn't know who else to ask.'

'It's no bother. I'm only too glad to help. Got a wedding afters for 9p.m. tonight over in Bray… so…'

'You'd better be off,' I finished.

'Yeah,' he said, reluctantly, as though he didn't want to go. 'But call me at any time, okay? I'll be back from the wedding by midnight. So…'

'Thanks Ronan, but I'm sure we will be okay.'

He turned at the door. 'If you ever need to talk to someone, I'm a good listener.'

I believed him. 'Thanks Ronan,' I said. 'But I think I'll be alright. It's Nicole, she's the one who needs to talk.'

'Yeah,' he said. 'But what about you? You know, if you want someone to unburden to… someone who you—'

'— can bore the arse off?' I suggested.

He laughed and shrugged. 'I can't imagine you'd ever be boring.'

He knew me so little, I thought. 'You'll regret you offered,' I said, not wanting him to go now. He was so easy, so uncritical, someone who fitted into the world as smoothly as a Chippendale joist. I liked him, I realised, very much.

He put his arms out for a hug. 'Take care, okay?' he said.

'Yes,' I said, muffled by his strong arms, the closeness, the warmth from him, the kindness of a virtual stranger. Human contact. And I could feel the old me growing like a tiny seedling, pushing its way through the soil, towards the light. We didn't move, lingering a moment too long.

'Okay?' he said, looking into my eyes, concern in his.

'Yes, why?' My eyes were wet but I had hoped he hadn't noticed.

'Nothing,' he said. 'Just that—'

'So, thanks again for delivering Puffball,' I said, briskly. 'Above and beyond the call of duty.'

'I like being dutiful,' he said. 'It suits me.' He smiled. 'See you soon, Jo.'

'See you Ronan.'

And I closed the door, feeling suddenly alive, as though I could do this thing called life. I could even do this thing called romance. And while I thought all the fires had been put out, they had been glowing all along.

But there was Nicole, all alone. She had an impossible decision to make. The man she loved and who claimed to love her, loved another. What a tangled web of emotions. Where do you even start with that one?

Soul-sappers

- Love and relationships. Why were they invented?

- Am now officially plump (putting it kindly)

- Immersion isn't working, so had to take cold shower this morning. Too freezing to wash hair so now have horrible, greasy mop

- Talking of greasy mop. Made dinner tonight, took ages and was horrible. Sweet potato chips are not chips

Chapter twenty-three

Puffball was still curled up on Nicole's lap very early the next morning, when Harry and I went downstairs at the crack of dawn. She stood up, disturbing Puffball's slumbers. 'Tea?' she said, looking brighter and more like herself.

'Yes please,' I said, popping bread in the toaster and rootling around for the butter, ready for Harry's breakfast. 'Was the sofa bed okay? Did you sleep at all?'

'A little. But I feel so much better. It was just good to get away from the house.'

I nodded. 'Well, what about getting away for the day? Going for a drive later when Harry's in crèche. We could go to Wicklow. Fresh air, a sandwich or two. What do you think?'

She nodded. 'That sounds lovely.'

*

Harry ran shrieking with delight into his room at his crèche, seeing his pal Xavier, a small, silent child who would just look at you under his thick, dark eyelashes. God knows what they talked about all day, but theirs was a true love, one filled with passion and the simplicity of a shared love of dinosaurs. Harry was my happy little boy, I thought, as he and Xavier hugged each other tightly. If I have nothing else in my life, I have Harry.

Outside, Nicole (along with Puffball) was waiting for me in the car, parked under a cherry tree, which was scattering its pink blossom over the windshield like confetti.

'Alright?' I said, pointlessly, when I climbed in.

'You know something?' she said. 'I am. It's going be alright. I know it. I've just to find my way through it. It'll all work out in the end, for the better. Kristof and I are going to be absolutely fine.'

'We're all fine, I suppose. Eventually,' I said, reversing and pointing the car in the direction of the Wicklow hills. 'It's the waiting for the eventual to kick in, though.'

'Do you think,' she said, after a while, 'that it would have been better if I'd never met Kristof and lived my life single but unbothered by life's chaos. Or is this better – what we had, I mean, have? Is this what you get for falling in love? Some kind of karmic redressing?'

'I'm not sure,' I said. 'I don't think that if you are happy, then you have to be made unhappy as a matter of course. Life just *is*. Good and bad, boring and interesting – you just have to keep on keeping on.' I really should take my own advice, I thought, but then it was always so easy to dispense it, never to act on it.

'And that's exactly what I'm doing,' she said, brightly. 'Keeping on.'

We were leaving the city now, the fields beginning to open out, the ewes with their offspring tucked in close, the meadowsweet along the road blending with buttercups, the blue sky filled with bouncy clouds.

'I suppose,' she mused, 'I have to decide if Kristof's worth it. If the pleasure outweighs the pain?'

'Don't ask me, I said. 'I haven't a clue. There has to be someone who does know, though. Some old, wizened lady who has lived to tell a few tales.'

'Kristof has life sorted.'

Too bloody right he has, I thought, but just let out a neutral 'oh yes?'

'He's asks for what he wants, he's upfront with his needs. He doesn't pussyfoot around and hope people will guess what he desires. He goes for it. And Coco too. Apparently she's flying through her pregnancy. Glowing, she is.'

'How do you know?'

Kristof told me.'

'Nice of him.'

'Wants me to be fully involved, he says. Says I'm part of this… this situation.'

'Nicole, I have to say, I had no idea how utterly selfish he is. I thought he was just—'

'Just what?'

'Arty.'

She actually laughed. 'No, he's just selfish. And arty. They are not necessarily mutually exclusive.'

'How did he first tell you?' I overtook an old car which was being driven at creeping speed by a man who could barely see over the steering wheel. 'About the other women?'

'From the off, really. He didn't believe in monogamy. Thinks it's unnatural and that you are just setting yourself up for hurt and disappointment if you try it. And I went along with it. You know, he had a point. And I was so in love with him – and him with me – that it didn't seem to matter. *I* was the woman he wanted to marry. I was, he said, the love of his life. Until now.'

'Right.' I gripped the steering wheel so hard my knuckles turned white.

'He's discreet, you see,' she said, defending him, justifying his actions while I felt nauseous at the strain of remaining non-committal. 'And this is the way we are. Not to everyone's taste, but when you love someone you start to question if the conventional way of doing things is the right way. We are not biologically programmed to just have one partner for the rest of our lives. It's an entirely social construct. Also, he is a highly sexual person and he needs sex more than most other people.'

'And do you think you can change him?' I asked. 'Is that your aim?'

She shrugged. 'Maybe? Who knows?' But I had the distinct impression she felt she could. 'He loves me,' she continued. 'He doesn't want to lose me but he understands that if it is difficult for me then I can leave, and he will accept that.'

I wondered how on earth Kristof had managed to get Nicole to swallow that, making her feel as though she had any control in this situation. It was, if you looked at it, quite an impressive feat.

'So,' I prompted, 'how did he tell you that she was pregnant?'

'The morning after that dinner. He just came out with it, like he was telling me about work or what shoes he was going to buy.'

'Oh God. And what did you say?'

'I was in shock, really. Kind of a stunned silence. I've remained like that ever since. Until last night, actually, when I was able to start considering my options.'

We had been driving through the low-ish lands of Wicklow at this point, sheep in fields, stone walls, the greens of fields and trees, the farmhouse with the 'duck eggs for sale' sign, the old abandoned petrol pump, the rabbit which ran in front of the car as though its life depended on it. Which, I suppose, it did.

'It's beautiful here, isn't it?' Nicole said.

'Yes, it is,' I said.

She rolled down her window and we heard birdsong as the fresh mountain air flooded the car. 'I used to come here when I first moved to Dublin. I was in a walking group, you know. I always loved it.'

The car began climbing up to the mountains and the trees and greenery gave way to the russets, pinks and browns of bracken and heather; driving on, on, as the mountains gave way to valleys, and streams sneaked their way along valley floors and sheep roamed freely, unfenced and scraggly. We reached the brow of the hill, looking down into the Powerscourt valley, the huge house in the distance, the fields and trees.

Eventually we were at the top of Wicklow, at the Sally Gap, the crossroads at the end of the world. I parked in a lay-by and dug out the flask and we drank our tea and ate our brownies looking at the view. Puffball gambolled in the gorse and heather.

'Remember when we got lost?' I said. 'We went off on a hike at 3 p.m. on a November afternoon.'

'It was actually beginning to get dark when we left Dublin,' she laughed. 'But we survived, didn't we? We made it.'

'Yes, we did.'

'We always do, you and me,' she said. 'We always find a way.'

'Do we?'

'We do.' She seemed so certain. 'It's just a question of finding the right path.'

'Will you stop reading those self-help books? Please?'

She laughed. 'You're responsible for me and Kristoff meeting actually,' she said. 'Do you remember? You invited me along?'

'That do at the Guinness Storehouse? When some bright spark thought it would be a good idea for Guinness to support the local artist community.' I remembered it alright. My boss Decco and I were doing the PR for the event and I spent the evening trying to stop one of the flamethrowers from climbing up the rigging. All I could see was a towering inferno in waiting. 300 years of the Guinness brewery in Dublin, destroyed in one evening by over-enthusiastic corporate entertainment. And then all the artists and musicians and cultural types from the area drank as much as was bodily possible.

'I'd been teaching all day,' she said, 'and it was just the boring speeches bit with someone droning on about how delighted the firm was to support the local community and blah blah blah and my shoes were hurting me, so – without anyone noticing – I slipped them off and was thinking of going home. But I was too tired and sat down at the back, wondering where I would get the energy to get myself into a taxi. And then I saw this man looking at me. He was big, huge. Not the kind I'd ever been out with before. Not spotty or weedy or boring but powerful and interesting and exciting. And beautiful. He had this energy which was palpable, I could almost touch it. So I ignore him, as you do...'

'Of course.'

'But then he was standing in front of me and offering to massage my feet. Which normally would freak me out but he held up these huge hands, both palms. I'm very good, he said, at massaging feet.'

'Oh Jesus. I did not know this!'

'I know,' she said. 'The mortification. So I was probably a bit drunk, but I let him take one of my feet and massage it.' She shrugged. 'And it was amazing. I was kind of hooked from that moment. Still hooked now. Don't think I'll ever been unhooked.'

'Despite… despite all the extra-curriculars?'

'Despite them.' She shrugged. 'I know, I know. Nothing is perfect. There is no happy ever after, and this is my life. This is what it looks like and it's complicated and crazy but it's real. This is what we, as humans, have to deal with. And we do. All of us get through things.' She looked at me. 'Don't we?'

'Well…' I didn't really want to go there. 'So… what happened then, that first night with Kristoff?'

'We left, me barefoot. And there was a little Asian shop on Meath Street and I bought some flip flops. One euro or something.'

'And that was it?'

'And that was it.' She was smiling at the memory. 'That was on the Friday. He'd moved in by the Tuesday.' She looked out of the window. 'Listen, I've been thinking. You know I could deal with him sleeping with other women…'

'Yes…'

'So, I think I've just got to get used to this… this latest development. You see, last night I was awake and thinking – it could be a good thing. I mean, it seems awful now, but… A baby! I have to see the positive. What do you think?'

I think you should run for the hills, I thought. But I kept my mouth shut and just nodded.

'You know, perhaps we could adopt the baby. I am sure Coco is too busy to look after a child and I could… I could…'

'Adopt? Is she likely to put the child up for adoption?'

'Kristof's the baby's father. That counts for something.' She shrugged. 'No, I don't know, but all I'm saying is that there are options. You know, creative solutions. Kristof and I will get through this. We will.' She suddenly smiled, a beautiful, happy expression slipping over her face. She looked like a Nicole I had forgotten about. 'We're both going to be alright,' she said. 'Things will get better for both of us. I know it.'

'Nicole…'

'Yes?'

'Are you sure this is okay with you,' I said, 'him sleeping with other women? Is that good enough for you? Do you think you might deserve more?'

'I love him, Jo,' she said. 'I love him. Flaws and all. I can't sit in judgment of him, or make demands, that isn't the way life works. You make decisions and you stick with them. I've just got to get over my shock, readjust, and everything will be okay. Different, but okay.'

We sat there for a moment in silence.

'I'm going to get some fresh air,' she said.

Taking Puffball, she walked up the mountain a bit and stood there in the windswept near-wilderness of Wicklow, letting the wind blow through her hair, like she was Cathy from *Wuthering Heights*. And then she returned to the car, opened the back door for the dog, we clicked ourselves back in and began the descent back to civilisation and to our lives.

Chapter twenty-four

After I'd dropped Nicole back in Stoneybatter, I made my way home to Harry who'd been picked up by Marietta. But outside my house was a gold Porsche. Bracing myself for an encounter with Mr Showband himself, the bouffant of hair, the breaker of hearts, I opened the front door.

Harry was in the hall, playing with his matchbox cars, zooming them around. Scooping him up, I pressed my face into his neck and squeezed him tight, his little body, his ribs, his small legs and arms, his curly hair. I was so grateful for him, so happy that he was my little boy. My Harry.

'I love you, my lovely boy,' I said. 'I am so lucky to be your mummy.' And I did love him, like all mothers love their child - but at the same time as I breathed him in, I had that stab, that wrenching feeling, as though I shouldn't love him as much as I did.

'Cars,' he said, wriggling and wanting to get back to his fascinating game. 'Cars!'

'Come into the kitchen and I'll make some tea,' I said, 'and meet Mr Patrick Realta, your granny's *boyfriend*.'

And there sitting in my house, in the arm chair, was Paddy Ryan, aka Mr Showband. Formerly of the All-Stars and every ballroom in the land, and now here, sitting in my kitchen, looking very at home indeed. He had a tea towel tucked into his collar, shoes off and feet on my posh Swedish cushion.

And there was Marietta, never the most domestic type, fussing around and placing a vast sandwich on his lap. This was a woman who had single-handedly run a hardware shop for more than three decades. As South County Dublin's premier purveyor of hammers, joists and joints, she ran a team of burly and often surly men but I had never, ever seen her place a sandwich in front of someone with so much deference, so much delight. She had transmogrified into a Surrendered Wife. But what did I know? She was obviously far better at relationships than me.

'Aha!' said Patrick, noticing Harry and me. 'Well, if it isn't Marietta Junior.'

'Hello,' I said, smiling. 'Joanna.'

'Patrick's just popped in for a bite to eat,' Mam said. 'Would you like a rasher and egg toastie?'

'Maybe,' I said.

'You should,' said Patrick. He took a bite. 'These sangiches,' he said, his mouth full, 'are feckin' fantastic, that's what.' He wiped the mayonnaise from his lips with the tea towel. 'Hit the spot, so they do. Hit the spot.' He stood up and clasped my hand in both of his, a Bill Clinton move, the power shake. 'Especially,' he said, 'when I've had a headache all day.' He winked. 'Too many whiskies last night, but these have put me right.'

'That's what you need,' I said. 'Comfort food.'

'Your Mam is a treasure,' said Patrick, sitting back down. 'She said she was minding the little fella so I thought I might pop in for a cuppa. And look at this! It's a Full Irish Breakfast Bap.'

'But it's the evening,' said Marietta. 'It's supper you're having.'

'Jaysus,' he said. 'It may be supper I'm having now but we'll be having breakfast together before we know it. Ha?' He winked at her while she blushed red, delighted rather than embarrassed. They seemed happy and relaxed with each other.

'So,' said Patrick, putting down his bap for a moment. 'This is a nice house. Small, cosy... but a good area. How much did it cost you?'

'Well,' I said. 'We—'

'It's just that I do a little property development myself,' said Patrick. 'You know, speculation, that kind of thing.' He smiled. 'That's what's kept me busy since I left show business. Isn't that right, Mar?' he said.

'That's right Patrick,' she said, proudly. 'Patrick,' she turned to me, 'is a very successful businessman.'

He nodded. 'I do my best. Beats having to do summers in Tramore or Ballybunion.'

'Patrick,' said Marietta, 'have you finished? Shall we go?'

'Delicious, Mar,' he said, pushing away his plate, patting his stomach and swallowing a burp.

She smiled at him, a full, happy, giddy smile. And her hand went to her wrist, something glinting there, where her Swatch used to be.

'What's that, Mam?'

'Oh this?' She blushed again, delighted. 'Just a watch that Patrick gave me.' She bared her wrist and there was a gold watch, the hands with little diamonds on their tips, pink and white diamonds studded around the face. And the words *Rollex* written in the middle.

'Swiss engineering,' said Patrick. 'Nothing like it. Works perfectly. Like clockwork.' He laughed hysterically at his own joke. I thought I was going to have to pass the tissues.

'It's beautiful, Mam. What a lovely present.'

'I'm so lucky,' she said. 'Thank you again, Patrick.'

'Anything to stop you being late for me. Precision Swiss engineering. Finest in the world. Comes with a price tag,' he patted his wallet which was sticking out of his jacket pocket, 'but nothing but the best for my Mar.'

'Where are you off to?' I asked.

'The pictures.' said Marietta. 'There's a new Meryl Streep.'

'Or the Catherine Zeta-Jones,' said Patrick, winking. 'I can't decide which I'd prefer. Brains or beauty? Ha.'

'We can decide when we get there,' she said briskly, and I was relieved to see a glimpse of the old Marietta. She wasn't total putty in his hands. Unlike her bottom. As they trotted out, I saw his hand grab her rear, giving it a big squeeze. I looked away, quickly, trying to convince my brain I hadn't seen such a thing. Too late. It was tattooed to my inner cortex. Brain bleach in the form of thousands of pounds of psychotherapy would be the only answer.

'Be seein' ya!' Patrick said to me. 'Be seein' ya.' And he gave me another huge showbiz wink.

Soul-sappers

- Having a crap memory. Learning lines impossible

- When there is no food in cupboards except baked beans and you can't remedy this without rigmarole of getting you and a small child out of house

- When Cadbury's changed recipe of Dairy Milk

- *Poldark* is now over. Miserable Sunday nights stretch into the distance

Chapter twenty-five

The next morning, there Marietta was looking happier than ever. Flush of face, bright of eye, spring in step. Bottom squeezing had brought colour to her cheeks. Literally. She kept looking at her diamond-encrusted watch, studying it, flashing it about.

'How was the cinema, Mam? What did you go and see in the end?'

'It was about a woman,' she said. 'And she was... something or other.' I wondered just how much of the film she had actually watched. 'I'll baby-sit Harry tonight,' she said, quickly changing the subject. 'You've your rehearsal, don't you?'

At least she was still able to remember *some* things. 'Are you sure?' I said. 'That would be brilliant. I was going to ask John as I thought you might be going out with Patrick again.' I didn't want to tell her that I wasn't quite in the mood to see John. I was just so confused about everything. Some space would be welcome.

'It'll do me good to stay at home for once,' she said. 'And you to go out... Get you out of yourself.'

'Why does everyone say that?' I said. 'Why do I have to get out of myself? I like being *in* myself. Well, staying in, watching television. *Poldark*, that kind of thing.'

Before Harry was born, John and I used to love staying in, eating chocolate and drinking tea on the sofa watching Scandi-noir. John does a brilliant Scandinavian accent, all monosyllabic and moody. He would chase me up the stairs being quite frightening and realistic while I shrieked. It wasn't the same watching them on my own, now they were just very serious detective programmes. With no laughs. John always made everything fun. Even Wallander.

'I've invited Fionnuala and Joan around,' Marietta said. 'Katie's wedding is only six months away and Joan is up to ninety with all the plans. We've said we'll give her a hand. Katie's asked her to look after the venue and the flowers and the invitations. And Katie's quite the control freak. She has Joan petrified she'll ruin everything with a spelling mistake or the wrong kind of flower. *And* Joan's to look after the religious element. Subtle is what Katie has requested.'

'Subtle? What does that mean?'

'It means, Joan thinks that you'd barely notice it, but it's there in case anyone wonders. Everyone's happy that way.'

'Very diplomatic.'

'Pity the Showband All-Stars are all retired now,' went on Marietta. 'They'd be a great wedding band, so they would. They'd have everyone jiving and jitterbugging in no time.'

'Shame.'

I busied myself throughout the day achieving very little. I had just finished getting ready to go to the rehearsal, having put Harry to bed, when the doorbell rang.

'That'll be the girls.' Called Marietta.

And in moments, Joan and Fionnuala, Marietta's friends for the last forty years were in the house, the three of them settled at the kitchen table with a pot of tea and a pile of wedding magazines, talking nineteen to the dozen.

'Your outfit,' I overheard Fionnuala saying as I passed by the door, on my way out. 'I was thinking of French navy for you. Eminently flattering with your silver hair.'

'My convent uniform was navy. I just can't go there.'

'That was half a century ago!'

'I can't... brings back terrible memories. The nuns you see...'

They all understood immediately.

'The Queen tends to go for bright colours,' said Marietta. 'Stands out apparently. Mother of the bride, you don't want to be fading into the background. What about tangerine?'

Whatever Joan's response was, it made them all laugh. It was so lovely, I thought, to listen to how happy my mother sounded, with her oldest and best friends, planning a wedding and having rekindled the love of her life. I was so happy for her but sometimes if felt like I was the only one who had to force myself out of bed every morning, the only person feeling utterly alone. It was a soul-sapper of a day, I knew that. Maybe tomorrow would be filled with life-lifters. But first I had to drag myself to rehearsal. Maybe pretending to be someone other than me was exactly what I needed.

Chapter twenty-six

'Wonderful, absolutely wonderful, Gwendolen.' David had taken to calling us by our stage names. 'You have substance beneath your froth, wisdom belying your wit. You truly understand the words of our dear Oscar Wilde.'

We were having a cup of tea, during a break in rehearsals. I had been feeling low since the morning and the day had been full of soul sappers

'Really?' I said, reaching for one of the biscuits which Connie had brought. (Everyone was passing on Robert's fruit cake which he had retrieved from the bin behind Superbuy. 'Perfectly good,' he'd said. 'Only four days past the sell-by but still perfect. If,' he admitted, 'a little dry.')

'But,' I went on, 'I thought Oscar was all fripperies and frothiness.'

'Oh no, dear,' he said. 'The underlying complexities expose the realities of such a constraining society, which then, as we know, had terrible consequences for Mr Wilde.' He shook his head. 'It doesn't bear thinking of, does it? Oscar in Reading Gaol, serving hard labour. It gives new meaning to the phrase 'crimes of passion'. Such a deep, clever, compassionate man who lost everything for love. There was nothing superficial about him. Toast of London, the talk of the town, maybe, but a man whose rivers ran deep.'

I nodded. 'Of course,' I said, my eye suddenly spying long, multi-stranded turquoise beads wound round Siobhan's neck which were catching the light, shimmering in the dim aspect of the hall. 'That's beautiful, Siobhan. Present from Robert?'

'Looks like it's from a cracker,' said Fergal, jumping in. 'Or was it a Kinder Surprise?'

'A cracker,' she said, smiling at us, fingering the necklace. 'Last year's.'

'It's lovely, that's what it is,' said Connie, admiring it and even David forgot about Oscar Wilde for a moment to nod kindly at her, it was clear that none of us believed the cracker story. We weren't, it had to be said, born yesterday.

'Crackers aren't what they used to be, are they?' I said, going along with it. 'You used to always get one of those fortune-telling fish which always curled up completely, whoever was holding it.' The origins of the necklace would remain a mystery. Or if it had come out of a cracker, I would have to get myself some when I was next feeling festive. Whenever that would be.

Robert was sitting in the corner, bent over the table, writing something. He looked up. 'We don't believe in wasting money,' he said. 'It's very nice and all that, but a few plastic beads do not a successful or happy life make. A nest egg does. Not a chocolate egg. Those Kinder Surprises are a total waste of money.'

'It was a cracker,' we all said in unison.

'Same thing. Waste. Of. Money.' He bent his head again and went back to writing. 'Siobhan, could you join me please, love? I need your help here.'

Siobhan was still fingering the necklace and I saw Fergal glance at her, his face totally impassive, as she stood up to join her betrothed.

'I've played Lady Bracknell five times before,' Piers Byrne said, changing the subject. 'Three times at the Abbey, twice in London. And now here with the Seaside Players of Dun Laoghaire. How the mighty have risen,' he said. Piers had taken me under his wing, saving me chairs and biscuits and telling me long and involved anecdotes about his time on the stage at the Abbey Theatre before his 'health issues' took over. These days, he jogged every morning, ate granola for breakfast and ended the day with camomile tea. His Lady Bracknell was a study in a tightly controlled hysteria, never tipping into pantomime. 'But I have no idea why I'm always Lady B. It must be the nose. Aristocratic, wouldn't you say?'

'Ideal for sniffing, too,' said Fergal. 'Or is it snorting?'

'Off you fuck, little Fergal,' said Piers, without breaking his smile. 'I don't know what is wrong with you tonight. You are like a little boy who didn't get enough huggles from mammy. Would you like one from me? To make up for it?'

'It was a joke, Piers,' said Fergal. 'Just a leg-pull. I thought you were up for those?'

'I am, *normally*,' said Piers. 'When it's funny and not a reference to the fact that I'm in recovery. Nothing to be ashamed of. But there's something off with you tonight. Did something happen to put you in a bad mood?'

'No,' said Fergal shortly, but he managed to recapture some of his gallant self. 'And I most humbly apologise if I have offended your person. I beg your forgiveness.' He glanced over at Siobhan and Robert who were talking together. Anyone would think, looking at them, that they were love's young dream.

'I am not offended,' said Piers. 'So forgiveness doesn't need to be dispensed. How's work going?'

'Dispiriting,' answered Fergal.

'Love life?'

'Messy.' Fergal glanced quickly and imperceptibly at Siobhan.

'Aha!' said Piers. 'Now, we're getting somewhere. Been dumped have you?'

'It's complicated.'

Piers nodded. 'The ones that are worth it usually are. Don't you agree Jo?'

'Not really,' I said. 'I'm over having complications and an interesting life. I'm quite happy to settle for boring now.'

'Jo's become friends with my brother, did you know that Piers,' said Fergal. 'They've become quite pals of the bosom. Makes sense now. There was I thinking Joanna here was a woman of the world who enjoyed the company of exciting and sophisticated men. And then she says she likes the boring ones. Like Ro-Ro. He's quite the charmer my little brother,' Fergal continued. 'I can see Jo might be quite susceptible to it.'

'I think I can look after myself but thanks for your concern, Fergal.'

'I don't think it's appropriate to talk about Jo's bosom,' said Piers, again deftly deflecting Fergal's rising bile. 'We should talk about mine, instead. I am rather proud of it.'

'I'm just jealous, that's all,' he said, smiling at me. 'Forgive me. Sometimes I'm in a mean mood. No wonder no one wants to love me.'

'You star-crossed lovers will work it out,' said Piers, kindly. 'It'll all end happily. Love always finds a way. Have faith, my friend. Who could resist that face?'

We both looked at Fergal who had the most winning expression on his face now.

'I have no idea,' I said.

'I do,' said Fergal gloomily. 'All too well.' He glanced again at Siobhan and Robert. Had they heard everything? It looked like they were going over some kind of list. We heard Siobhan say: 'But I've never even met them. They're bingo friends of your Mam's!'

'What are you two up to?' said Piers.

'Our wedding list,' said Robert. 'Who we're going to invite. We only want something small. Just 15, we were thinking. There's my Mam and Dad, Siobhan's Mam, obviously.' He stopped to smile at her. 'And Mam has a couple of pals she has to invite. And then there's Mr Emmanuel, my manager from Superbuy – have to invite him, don't I, if I want to progress up the Superbuy ladder? And *Mrs* Emmanuel.' He looked to us all for support and we tried to nod back, Connie was even smiling kindly at him, but there was no missing Siobhan who seemed utterly defeated by the plans. She hung her head, as though she was surrendering. Robert went on blithely.

'Mam can do the catering,' he said. 'She does a very nice coddle. I can get a deal on some sparkling vino from Superbuy. And a few boxes of crisps. Sorted. Should be in and out for under twenty five euro. I mean, you don't want to *throw* money away. Not when Mam is such a great cook and crisps being the perfect party food. Isn't that right, love?' He nodded at Siobhan, ensuring her only response was to nod mutely back. 'I mean, Siobhan wants her Nanna to come along. But I say, she's 95 and needs a lot of minding. It's not the greatest idea you've ever had, love. It'd be better to leave her in the home and go and see her later. Bring her some cake. Mam's fruit cake. We'd better cut off the icing though. It can be a bit denture-unfriendly. Actually, I'll tell Mam not to ice it all. That's another unnecessary.'

'But Nanna isn't an unnecessary. She never had a nice do for her wedding and I always said she could come to mine; always, from when I was little.'

'And she will, love. In spirit.' He explained. 'She's got, you know, the old, what-you-call-it, Alzheimer's. She won't miss a thing. Anyway, we've got to keep numbers down.' He looked up at us. We were all mesmerised by this lesson in killing romance stone dead. 'I mean,' he appealed, 'you can't invite *everyone*, can you?'

But none of us knew quite what to say; our supportive nodding had come to an abrupt end. Even Connie's kind smile had died on her face.

'But she's my grandmother!' broke in Siobhan.

'It'd mean more to her to see you later. When you can concentrate just on her. I'm not inviting my grandmother. *Or* my grandfather.'

'They're dead!'

'Exactly.' He looked almost triumphant while Siobhan flushed bright red, with either frustration or fury. I couldn't quite tell.

'You're not actually going to get married?' Fergal jutted in, laughing but really looking at Siobhan. He, I could tell, was trying to change the subject for her. Deflecting attention and giving her space to collect herself. 'You're not going to actually *do it*, are you?'

'And what's wrong with marriage?' Robert demanded, turning hotly to Fergal. 'Mr Perennial Bachelor.'

Fergal curled a lip, his coolness in stark contrast to Robert's irritation. 'It's just something that boring people do, that's all,' he said, languidly. 'It's a pointless and expensive exercise. Anyway, don't most marriages end in divorce? Is that not the truest of truisms, *Bobble*?'

'Not *all* marriages,' insisted Robert. 'Not ours. My Mam and Dad's marriage has lasted for more than 50 years now. That's what I want for me and Siobhan, something real and long-lasting.' He looked at her. 'If I am as lucky as my Dad was marrying my Mam, then I'll be a very happy man.'

Fergal laughed again but both he and Robert swung their eyes to Siobhan, gauging her reaction. She, however, preferred studying her toes. And then she looked up, her voice quiet.

'Come on Rob,' she said. 'We should go over our lines.' And they moved off, Robert muttering and throwing daggers at Fergal, who affected nonchalance and put his feet up, grabbing a copy of the play. But I noticed that from the corner of his eye, Fergal was staring at their retreating figures and his script was upside down. The rest of us tried to affect normality by finding something to do.

But it was Frederick who really took our minds off the brewing tensions. He and George kept to themselves but I was growing rather fond of them both. George was in permanent Quiet Man mode, cap on head. Perhaps, I was beginning to believe, he was really like that, a bog body preserved since the 1950s (or rather a Hollywood idea of 1950s Ireland). He called me Miss Joanna and bowed every time we met. Along with the cap, he wore the full Donegal tweed, waistcoat and all, and big hand-knitted socks.

Frederick, however, was rather more experimental with his clothes. This evening he was wearing jeans. 'What thinks one?' he said, standing up and giving us a twirl. 'Fifty cent from the charity shop,' he said. 'In what is alliteratively known as the bargain bin.'

To my trained eye, they looked like a pair of women's boot-cut jeans circa 2006. 'Oh,' he said, pulling out a cardigan, a little on the bobbly side, 'and this little beauty.'

No one seemed to be able to break it to him that he was entirely dressed in women's clothes and, to my dawning horror, I recognised the cardigan as once belonging to me.

'Lovely, Frederick,' said Connie. 'You look very good indeed.'

'How much was the cardigan, Frederick?' I asked, casually. It was one I had bought in Brown Thomas for an embarrassing amount of money.

'Oh, I think 50 cent as well. It too was in the refuge receptacle. I've never worn jeans before,' he said. 'Far more comfortable than I would have guessed. I'm now thinking John Wayne, Gary Cooper. Calamity Jane.'

We all agreed he looked splendid and even Fergal put his glowering mood to one side to help him to tie a scarf. Frederick looked very pleased. 'I haven't had new clothes in years,' he said. 'It's true what they say, clothes maketh the man. Isn't that right, George?'

'I couldn't be sure at all, at all, at all,' said George. ''Tis not something I would know, now, you know.'

'My dear,' said Connie, peering at my face through her over-large round glasses, 'you do look rather pale. Are you eating properly?'

It was unfortunate that, at that particular moment, my mouth was all Hobnob. 'Grand, thanks,' I managed through the biscuit.

'I don't know how you women do it these days,' she said. 'Doing it all.'

'*Eating* it all,' I said, but she was smiling at me so kindly that I felt tears prickle the back of my eyeballs. Swallow, I ordered myself. Focus. God, I was truly pathetic. One kind smile and I was in danger of losing it. Normally I was better at keeping it all together. Kindness and compassion, especially when I wasn't expecting them, always shot straight into my heart, before I remembered to armour myself. Connie noticed my face and took my hand for a moment and looked straight into my eyes, searching to see if I was alright.

'Anything I can do?' she asked quietly.

'Nothing, I'm fine, long day, that's all.'

She nodded, wisely – and thankfully - allowing me the space to recover and she deftly changed the subject. 'Did you hear the rain last night?' she asked. 'It was just like the hoses from Ealing studios pointed straight at my roof. My word, they are powerful and last night brought back all those memories.'

'You were in films?' I asked, feeling grateful to hear my voice sounding normal and sure of itself again.

'Briefly,' she said. 'I had neither the face for leading lady nor the talent for character actress but I loved acting and being around actors. The Seaside Players is Ealing Studios in microcosm for me these days. There are a handful of films where you will see a younger version of myself walking in the background, serving tea to Basil Rathbone or lady's maid to Greer Garson. And then I became an assistant to Miss Margaret Rutherford. Marvellous lady. It was my job to ensure she always had a cup of tea waiting as she came off set. She used to say, make it stronger than Hercules and hotter than the Devil. I've never forgotten it. Such a wonderful actor she was. I was also assistant to a certain J. Arthur Rank. Quite a formidable gentleman. He knew my father, you see. Old school friends. I didn't last too long, though. His cigar-smoking wasn't good for my chest. I began to have asthma attacks and, well, I just couldn't continue.'

Instead, she told me, she had moved home to Ireland and, after recovering, went on to start a shelter for those in need; the homeless, the addicts. She was still on the board of the charity. 'It's immigrants now,' she said. 'It never fails to surprise me how many forms trauma can take.'

'Right!' said David. 'Shall we get going again?' And it was time to play again. 'Algernon and Cecily. Positions.' Siobhan and Robert stood up and we all moved stage-side. Robert was wooden as a spoon but he had learned his lines and managed to deliver them without stumbling. And who am I to judge? I was hardly Dame Judi myself. But Siobhan blew all of us out of the water. You *believed* her, she became someone entirely different. We all watched, mesmerised. No wonder RADA had given her the nod. She couldn't *not* go.

Fergal whispered in my ear, making me jump. 'Good, isn't she?'

'Yes,' I whispered back. 'She's amazing.'

'Yeah, she's going to go far, that one. She's got it. The rest of us don't. But she's got something. If only she could rid herself of Mr Limpet, Roberto the Unmagnifico.'

David turned around. 'Fergal, your scene with Siobhan now, please?' He turned back to Siobhan. 'Are you able to keep going?'

She nodded and we all watched as Fergal leapt onto the stage, while Robert took his place beside me in the front row.

'My darling Cecily,' he began, dropping to his knees and taking Siobhan's hand, as though to kiss it. 'Have I ever told you how beautiful you are? How the stars glitter purely for you, how the sun wakes only when your eyes flutter in the morning, for its singular purpose is to light your day and warm your soul? Indeed, as seeing your lovely face and your sweet voice, like a zephyr in my ear, warms my very being.'

There was that crackle of electricity again. But this time, we could all feel it, that energy – two people in love. There was a resonance, a tension that lifted it beyond the guise of mere playacting. Fergal was *living* it. Piers put down the *Irish Times* crossword, Frederick and George looked up from the costumes they were sewing, Connie stopped going over the posters and tickets that were being sent to the printer the next day. Siobhan stood as still as a statue, taking in every word, absorbing the moment with every pore. But, for the rest of us, it was as though we were intruding, that we were witnessing something wholly intimate and private. Robert was sitting on the edge of his seat. 'Is this the actual script?' he said to no one in particular.

'I cannot stand being in the world a moment longer,' continued Fergal, 'where all I have are crumbs of your existence. I am reduced to bringing a cup from which you've drunk to my lips, to feel your fading presence in a room which you have just vacated and to breathe in your scent as you pass. I love you, Cecily… I love you more each passing day, each moment my heart expands exponentially to absorb more of my feelings for you. My magnificent, my wonderful, my own true love.' He kissed her hand as though his words would flow into her through the touch of his lips.

David broke the tension. 'Again, Mr Forest. And this time speak the words of our own dear Mr Wilde, hmm?'

'Of course, David,' said Fergal, flashing a smile and springing to his feet, the energy in the room immediately returning to normal. 'I was just improvising. An old drama school technique. Just to warm up.' But I noticed he still held Siobhan's hand. The rest of us carried on doing what we were doing, Piers sucking his pencil over the crossword, Frederick and George picking up their sewing. But the room was changed. We had witnessed something real.

'He's such a fecking show-off, that one,' said Robert to me. 'Drama school! He wouldn't know hard work if it hit him in the face. Try a complete overnight stock-take. Or keeping the beer shelves filled during the Euros. That's hard.'

Chapter twenty-seven

Going back to work was something which chipped away in the back of my mind. I couldn't stay at home for the rest of my days, but it wasn't until the funny knocking noise in my car became so loud that I just *had* to seek help, that my circuitous route back to professional life began.

Harry was in the crèche when I drove up to the garage I had been going to for years and years, P. J. Murphy, next door to Brian's café. The yard which was normally filled with cars, all fixed up and ready for collection, was quiet, like a ghost garage. The whole place looked closed up.

The office was the nerve centre of the operation and usually (wo)manned by Sheila, P. J.'s wife, who was always there, writing out the invoices, working out the tax on an oil-smudged calculator, putting the cheques into an old cash box. They didn't even have a card reader. She was lovely, Sheila was, just like P. J. Actually, in the olden days, she and Marietta had been friends but now they only chatted on passing, the reason for the cooling off being lost in the mists of time.

'You're quiet, P. J.,' I said, when he shuffled in from the garage. 'It's usually five cars deep in here.'

'Ah, you know…'

'You on your own?'

'Tommy's on holiday and there isn't the work to replace him so…' We walked out to the forecourt together. 'There's a crowd opened up down the road. Fixup.' He flipped up my bonnet and stuck his head under it.

'How could I miss them? Their sign is big enough. What do you call that colour? Acid tangerine?'

He stood up, expertly avoiding banging his head on the open bonnet. 'Just need to tighten the bolts holding the oil tank,' he said. 'You'll be grand for another six months or so. I'll have it done in fifteen minutes.'

'Thanks P. J. So this crowd – they're hoovering up customers?'

'They change your oil for free and do a full service for fifty euro. But I know they are not bothering a tap to do anything, not really. They splash a bit of oil around, blacken their hands and tell you the car is good as new. I can't compete with them.'

'Who told you all that?'

'Tommy was chatting to the lads from Fixup. It's a scam but they are taking all my customers away from me. Just a few regulars left, but no drop-ins. And me and Sheel... well, we've no pension and no choice but to keep going. Tommy'll be working at Fixup soon, I can't keep him.'

P. J. put a hand to his chest, as though he had felt a pain.

'How're you feeling these days?'

'Can't complain,' he said. 'The heart's holding up. So far. But Fixup are giving me a few palpitations, I can tell you.'

'But you and Sheila, what are you going to do? You can't let Fixup just steal all your business. That's not fair.'

'It's life, though, isn't it? They are bigger. Not better, mind, but they are bigger. We're just small fish, me and Sheel. Minnows.'

'It's wrong, though, isn't it?'

'Ah well... I'm too tired to get too exercised by it. Not after the scare last year. Sheila's taking in extra curtains to make ends meet. And me, I'm twiddling my thumbs. Or actually working on that old beauty.' He jerked his head towards a bright yellow and white vintage VW Camper. 'Doesn't bring in any money but it's pure pleasure working on her. Used to belong to Paul Jr but he traded it in for something a bit more practical now he's got young Paulie. It just needs a bit of tinkering with and it'll be as good as new.' P. J. grinned. 'Come on,' he said. 'Before you go, come and have a look at the little beauty.' He brought me to the back of the workshop for a closer look at the van.

'It's gorgeous,' I said. 'Such a cute face. Why can't all cars have smiley faces?'

He looked at the van indulgently, as though it was another grandchild. 'We've got one of these, me and Sheila. We head off all the time, to the coast, to Clifden, to see Paul Jr and Paulie in Lahinch. All over, really. Went to France at Easter. Tea boiling in the back. *Sounds of the Sixties* on the tape player. Heaven, it was.'

'That sounds amazing. The freedom. Where's Sheila now?'

'Her sister's, Brenda the hairdresser. She's trying out a new treatment on Sheila, something Brazilian, I think. Last time it was stripes, the time before hair in mad curls. That's Sheila for you, she'll do anything to help someone out. Even let them mess around with her hair.' He laughed. 'She's always surprising me, is Sheila. Even after 40 years. It's our Ruby Anniversary in a few months. Sheila's taking on lots more curtains to pay for a party. She's wants a get together at the Ham and Hock. I wouldn't mind a takeaway and a night in. Sheila's like that, though. A whirlwind she is.'

He told me to come back in half an hour, but while I was picking up bits and pieces for dinner and a coffee in Brian's, a germ of an idea began to grow. Maybe there was something I could do to help P. J.'s business. Perhaps.

'What about an open day?' I said, when I returned for the car. 'Get people in, sell you and Sheila as your friendly local garage owners, which you are. It's all about customer service you can trust. What do you think?'

'I'm not sure,' he said. 'I don't have a budget for things like that. Fixup won't be happy until they see me out, but I don't have it in me for a fight.'

'Listen,' I said. 'It's possible. We can promote P. J.'s and get people to come here and not Fixup.'

'Yes, but who's going to pay for it?' he said.

'I'll do it free, I promise,' I said. 'I might call in a few favours.'

'I'm not sure about that. It doesn't sound right. Or fair.' He took the stubby pencil from behind his ear and sucked on it ruminatively. 'What about a trade?' His eyes brightened. 'Free services for life?'

I laughed. 'I want to do this. Alright? And there are ways of doing things… you just need to be creative. And, P. J., it's a long time since I've been creative. So you are doing me a favour. Honestly.'

He didn't look convinced.

'Talk to Sheila about it tonight,' I went on. 'I'll come up with a plan, and get back to you. Make a few phone calls. Okay?'

'Okay,' he said, slowly. 'That'd be great.' He held out his hand. 'Thank you Jo.'

'P. J.,' I said, shaking his hand, 'local businesses must be protected and we should do our very best to make sure that their unique selling points don't get forgotten. That's all I'm going to do. Don't worry.'

The plan to help P. J. was forming in my head. I couldn't do much. I couldn't *force* people to have their cars fixed by him but I could remind people that the garage existed. I had been working in PR since graduation. Surely I still had some skills.

Back at home, I fired up my rusty laptop and began bashing out a few ideas. Soon I had a near-completed proposal.

My plan was simple: an open day and a refining of the business. We would be targeting people who were fed up of being ripped off and talked down to by mechanics, we would focus on the local nature of P. J.'s, its trustworthiness and expertise.

Not much had to change, P. J. was lovely, and Sheila lovelier and I didn't want to go in and try and clean the place up. It was a garage. The important thing was to emphasise what it had that Fixup didn't. An open day and the resulting media was the beginning.

Chapter twenty-eight

The next day, Decco and I were standing in a long queue for lunch. I was wondering if he would do me a favour and Decco being Decco, he had promised on the phone to bring me to the trendiest place in town for a bite to eat.

'It's called The Gaeltacht,' he said, stepping aside for some glamorous woman in designer sunglasses, who was picking up a takeaway.

Now, the Gaeltacht is, for anyone not familiar with this right-of-passage, a once-compulsory and now optional part of the Irish childhood. You spend three weeks in a sparsely populated part of the country, where only Irish is spoken. In my day, you were sent home if you uttered a single word in English. We survived there on ketchup sandwiches and Curly Wurlys bought from the one shop. It was an evil experience but, such is the resilience of youth, we loved it and went back every year. However, our Irish remained mysteriously unimproved.

'What do they do here that's so good that it has people queueing round the corner?'

'Panwiches.'

'*Panwiches*? Is that some kind of Panini?'

'Not at all!' he scoffed. 'Only old-fashioned, proper Irish foods are served here, none of your foreign inventions. A panwich is a sandwich made from "plastic" sliced pan. And it *only* comes in ham or cheese. Like Mams used to make. Bad sandwiches, basically. And crisps come in one flavour only: cheese and onion.'

'Of course.'

'Cans of drink are served warm,' he continued. 'Chocolate Snack bars slightly melted. The woman shouts at you if you speak English. By the way, how's your Irish?'

'Terrible.'

He looked delighted. 'Then she'll give out to you. Great!' He rubbed his hands. 'It's like some kind of recession regression, you know? The anti-Celtic Tiger, the Neo-Irish Revival. It's where it's at these days.'

'But I thought,' I said, 'the Celtic Tiger freed us from bad food and that was the only good thing about it? And now you're saying we want to return to it? Powdered soup, soft biscuits, fizzy pop that made you crazy before it was remarketed as energy drinks?'

'It's good for the soul,' he said. 'We all ate the Italian sandwiches and the croque monsieurs and now it's time to get back to guaranteed Irish.' He laughed. 'Us next, come on...' And he ushered me inside.

After ordering in (near-forgotten) Irish, we were given our sandwiches, which were roughly cut, bread slapped around with butter and cheese and pushed into a paper bag. A bag of crisps and a warm can of red lemonade and we were done.

'How is it?' said Decco, watching me as I layered my crisps into my sandwiches and gulped down the lemonade.

'Like being 15 again,' I said. It was like being in Willy Wonka's factory, eating one's past. It was profoundly satisfying. 'I love it.'

'I knew you would,' he said, munching on his.

'I'm glad you called me, Joanna,' he said, filling the poky space with his boomy voice. His stomach expanded by years of expense-account lunches. 'I assume this is because you want your old job back?' He took another slurp of red lemonade. Decco was usually strictly Cabernet.

I shook my head. 'Not exactly.'

'Time, Joanna, if you will forgive me the inelegance of the sentiment, is not on your side. There are whippersnappers out there hungry for success,' he said. 'And I am surrounded by them. Born in the 1980s and clueless as to what's what, but more ruthless than any I've ever seen.' He lowered his voice. 'I read a CV the other day from a *child*. Just graduated. Born the year of my hip op.' He shook his head in shock, as though the world was under threat by zombie invasion.

'Who are these guys and how do we stop them?' I asked.

'We can't. They're too powerful for us,' he said, laughing. 'We just don't have the strength.'

'I don't think I can get back into it. I'm not ready. I'm not sure I'm ever going to be ready.'

'Joanna,' he said, pushing his chair back to give his stomach some breathing space. 'What's this about you not coming back? The child is three. That's practically full grown.'

'Decco, I'm not that person I used to be. I can't do it.'

'Hormones,' he said, sagely. 'Hormones. Women have them and it makes them go crazy...' I glared at him. 'I'm joking!' he said, laughing and then suddenly turning serious again. 'No, I'm not. Are you quite sure it's not your hormones?'

'Quite sure.'

'Totally, 100 per cent sure?'

'Totally100 per cent.'

He studied me. 'I'll leave the door open.'

'Decco—'

'Ajar. I'll leave it ajar. I'm not pressurising.'

'Decco, I just—'

'Unlocked. Final offer. On the latch.'

I laughed. 'On the latch. Thanks Decco.'

'But you were good for the company, Jo,' Decco said. 'Your clients miss you.'

I shrugged, because I no longer cared about my clients. Once upon a time, I would have done anything for them; fly to New York with half an hour's notice, go straight to some anonymous office and talk, pitch, scream, whatever was required and then turn right round again and be back in Dublin eight hours later, for my other clients. I became expert in existing on power naps: in taxis, in my office and, when things were bad, while sitting on the loo. Even those 30 seconds would give me enough pep to get through the rest of the day. But now that didn't inspire me. The thought of P. J. and Sheila and their garage did.

'So,' said Decco, crumpling up his paper bag, 'what is it then that you want to talk to me about?'

'Okay,' I said, wiping my face with the back of my hand. It seemed right and proper. 'You know your friend Bono?'

Well, he's not my *friend*,' said Decco, hastily. 'I've just met him a couple of times at Paul McGuinness' house.'

'Well, you know your *acquaintance* Bono?'

'Yes, what about him?'

'Would he like to be involved in a bit of local promotion? He lives yards away from this garage I'm working with, well, helping out. I wonder would he like to get involved? Support local all that. Good PR for him as man of the people. He can turn up sunglasses on, shake a few hands and job done. No one could ever say he forgot where he came from. Not that they do.'

I filled Decco in with my plan and pitched, passionately, my call for support-local, the need for friendlier garages, to make it easier to look after your car. He listened intently. I could practically hear his brain whirring with thought.

'I'll see what I can do, Jo,' he said. 'No promises, but there might be a favour or two I can pull in.'

At the door, saying goodbye, he hugged me. 'Take care of yourself, Jo,' he said. 'Let me know if I can do anything. And let me know when you want to re-join the beleaguered and demoralised workforce.'

'Will do. Thanks Decco.'

'And let me know if I can do anything else. Call me. Whatever you decide, if you need advice, a drink, come and find me.'

'Thanks Decco.'

He smiled and then released a huge red lemonade burp.

'Decco!'

'I'm sorry,' he said, but didn't look sorry at all. He looked delighted. 'That was a pre-Celtic Tiger burp. You don't get many of those these days.'

Life-lifters

- Cheese and onion crisps

- Plastic bread sandwiches

- Red lemonade

Chapter twenty-nine

Fergal was due later to go through lines, and just as I had changed after putting Harry down and was turning on the kettle for tea, there was a knock on the door. Fergal was early, I thought, running to answer it.

But it was John. He looked strange, as though he was forcing his smile.

'I'm sorry for calling round, Jo,' he said. 'It's just that…' He faltered.

'Are you alright?'

'No,' he said, his smile dying on his face. 'Not really. I just needed someone to talk to. And not Dad. Someone who understands.'

'Come in, come on.' Taking his arm, I gently pulled him into the house. 'Cup of tea?'

I quickly texted Fergal and put him off. John hovered in the kitchen, not knowing whether to stand or sit. This used to be his home and now it wasn't. We both could feel the sadness of that; the gulf that separated us from what we once were.

'I am sorry, Jo,' he said. 'I have no right to be here. I was just driving past and I saw the lights on and—'

'I know… it's okay. Do you want to sit down?'

He half shrugged, half nodded but sat on one of the wooden chairs at the table while I made tea. The kitchen was utterly silent, neither of us speaking, our sadness, our emptiness, our loss filling the room. How could a void feel so full?

I made his tea, exactly the way he liked it (milk in first, not too strong and in his nice Amnesty mug). 'There we go…' But his eyes were brimming with tears.

'It's lonely, isn't it?'

He nodded. 'I didn't realise it would hit me so hard,' he said. 'I thought I was getting on with it, I thought leaving was a step forward but it was a million steps backwards, because I have that to deal with, not being here with you and with Harry… And then this morning, I felt like someone had sledgehammered my stomach. I had meetings all day. I haven't eaten and… and… I wish…' he began saying, when he was stopped by a loud rap on the door.

Suddenly I didn't want him to leave. I wished we were who we used to be, that we could stay talking, that later we would go upstairs and brush our teeth together, jostling for space at the sink, and then read side by side and chat about things and *know* a whole life stretched ahead, one of ups and downs, adventures and worries, peaks and troughs, a life watching Harry grow up. A life of cups of tea and making love. A life being married.

'Open up!' A man's voice from outside shouted. 'Open up so I can ravish you!' Fergal.

'I'm so sorry,' I said to John. 'I texted him…'

John stood up. 'Ravish you?' he said, eyebrow cocked but face utterly neutral.

'It's Fergal, from the Players. He's just an idiot,' I said. 'He's trying to be funny.'

There was an even louder rap on the door.

'Coming!' I turned to John. 'I'm so sorry.'

'I'll leave you to it,' said John, standing up. 'To your actor *friend*.'

'John,' I began. 'I can see who I like. *You* see who *you* like.'

'What's taking you so long?' said Fergal from outside.

There was no delaying any longer and I went to open the door, Fergal almost tumbling inside. 'You are looking nice,' he said, sweeping in and giving me an over-friendly, actorly hug. 'Especially in those rather fetching jogging trouser things. Give us a spin.'

'Fergal, shut up,' I said. 'Didn't you get my text?'

'No, why?' He delved into the pocket of his paisley trousers and retrieved his phone. 'Ah, yes.'

'It's just that—'

At that moment, John came into the hall.

'Oh, I didn't realise you had company.' Fergal eyed John who was looking furious, all signs of his outpouring gone.

'John, this is my friend Fergal,' I said. 'And Fergal, this is my… my husband, John.'

Fergal immediately dropped the actorly-affection and transformed into something far blokier. 'Good to meet you, mate,' he said, shaking John's hand hard. He *was* a good actor. 'Everything all right?'

John grunted and stood there, glowering. This is what separation is, I supposed, a mixture of confusion and mess until you finally know where you are. Neither of us knew how to behave in this situation.

'Fergal's playing Jack in *The Importance of Being Earnest*,' I explained, recovering myself. 'He's here to run through our lines.'

'It's okay,' said John, curtly. 'I was just leaving anyway.' He put his hand on the door. 'Thanks for the tea, Jo. Good to meet you, Fergus.'

'You too.' Fergal didn't correct him and stood, sensitively, obviously picking up that there was something going on. I thanked him for that. He's a *nice* idiot, I thought. In many ways he was not so dissimilar to Ronan.

John moved towards me and, for a moment, I thought he was going to hug me, to hold me again, like we used to do so easily, so naturally. And I braced myself because I knew exactly what it would feel like, the way his arms would wrap themselves around me, and how I would feel inside. I realised, in that instant, that I wanted him to.

But he didn't. He turned and left, leaving my arms hanging, my body unwarmed by his, the smell of him, the feel of him, gone out of the door and away into the night.

Fergal looked at me. 'Everything alright?'

'Yes… yes, of course. Now, are you ready? Got your script?' But all I could hear was John's fading footsteps. It was like he was leaving all over again. We had missed our moment and might never find our way back to each other.

Chapter thirty

Falling in love was simple. You just gave in. But falling *out* of love was something very different. You had to give up and none of us are hardwired to do that. We all keep going, it's what we do. Looking at Nicole, across the Formica of Brian's, I could see that she too was still in the eye of the storm, still clinging to the wreckage as the wind whirled and raged.

'I might have been wrong,' she said, stirring and stirring her coffee.

'What do you mean?'

'Handling this, taking it on board, in my stride. You know, that nonsense I spouted.' She put the spoon down and placed both hands flat on the table. 'She wants Kristof to go for her next scan with her.'

'But I thought you knew he was going to be involved?'

'I didn't think it would be like this, going to scans, being a father… I mean, it's like he's her partner or something.'

'You thought he would just be told things, not actually do anything.'

'Yes.' She paused. 'Christ. I didn't think that it would be them and me,' she said, trying to keep her voice low. 'I thought it was us – and her. But it's not. It's me on the edge, the outsider. The one who doesn't know what is going on. I have to wait to be told, like I'm nothing.'

'What are you going to do? What *can* you do?'

'This.' She rootled around in the bag at her feet and placed a book on the table. *Love Rivals: How To Win When He's*

Found Someone Else and *When Rolling Over and Playing Dead Is For Losers.*

'Is this wise?'

'What?'

'Reading those things.'

She placed her hand over the cover. 'These things are keeping me sane at the moment.' She delved into the bag again and starting piling books onto the table. I've done *Men Who Love Other Women.* This one was good: *The Predatory Female.* Coco to a T, that. A few home truths in this: *Why Does He Do That When He Says He Loves Me.* Men and addiction,' she explained. 'In Kristof's case, sexual addiction. Aha, this one was good: *Women Who Bark at the Moon,* all about the inner primal being.' She pulled out another. '*I'm So Angry So Why Can't I Scream?* That helped me through a particularly sleepless night. Um… what else? Oh this. *Staying Calm When Everything's Shit.* Really helpful. Mind focussing, you know?'

'What about *Married to an Arsehole?* You should get that one. Or *He's a Loser, Dump Him.*'

She almost laughed. But not quite. 'I've nearly finished *Love Rivals,* though, and there's a whole chapter that is my life exactly. Look…' She flicked through it and pressed down on the spine at an open page. 'Chapter six, "Losing your grip? Dig in your heels." You see? Genius! That's exactly what I need to hear. I don't want people to say to me that I should just move on. I am going to get through this. You're always going on about staying in the moment… Well, *that's* exactly what I am doing.'

She gripped the table. 'You see?' she said. 'This is me staying in the moment. This is a table. I am here. *I* exist.'

'Nic…'

'Isn't this right? Aren't I doing brilliantly, coping marvellously. Trouper, that's me.' She had tears in her eyes now. I unpeeled one of her hands and transferred the grip to mine.

'Nicole. Don't be a trouper. Nobody likes a trouper.'

'But they do!' The whites of her eyes were shining. 'You see, no one wants women to fall apart. All these books are about keeping you going, putting on the brave face. Not falling apart.'

'Ignore those stupid books.'

'But I want to fall apart. I wish I could stay in a darkened room all fallen apart. I don't think I can do the brave face thing anymore.'

'I know, I know. I understand.'

'I know you do,' she said. We were gripping each other's hands now, two women on the verge of falling apart.

'I can feel it in my chest,' she said, 'my stomach, everywhere, like this physical pain spreading all over me. I wake up feeling it gnawing away at me and it's there all day. I can't eat because I just feel nauseous all the time. Does that make sense?'

'Yes. Total sense.'

'I'm sorry Jo.'

'Okay,' I said. 'So you can't live like this. Not with this shit going on. You've got to tell those two that this is impossible, okay. Tell Kristof that if he wants to be married to you, he can't play happy families with anyone else.'

'No, no, no!' she said. 'I have to learn to live with it. Don't you see? The pain is something I can get used to. People deal with backache all day, don't they? Or toothache? Or migraines? They get on with life, don't they? I'm going to see this thing through, see it out. I am determined that when I am old and

Kristof is old, we will be together. You know? I've just got to get to a point where this is nothing, or this is my normal. It doesn't have to break us, does it? People can love other people at the same time, can't they?'

'Nicole,' I said, speaking clearly. 'He's been sleeping with other women. Crime number two: he has formed a deeper connection with another woman. Let's call it 'love' for want of a better word. Crime number three: he is having a baby with this woman. Crime number fucking four, he wants you to stick around and carry on being married and for you to absorb Coco and the baby into your lives.' I looked at her. 'Does that sound in any way feasible, manageable, *sustainable* to you? I mean, you are going to make yourself ill. You've already made yourself ill.'

'But I love him,' she said, eyes big, tears forming in the corners. 'I love him.'

'Fuck love,' I said. 'Sometimes life is bigger than love.' What I meant was, you have to look after yourself. You can't just let yourself be swung around by the fact that you love someone. *You* are more important than romantic love. Sometimes you have to rise above it. Easier said than done, but who said life was easy? No one, precisely no one. What are you going to do?'

'I haven't the foggiest fucking clue not the foggiest fucking idea.'

And suddenly we laughed as though all was well with the world and it was the old days when life was simple.

'And I can't read another one of these books,' she said, pushing them away. 'My head is melted.' She paused. 'Listen, I need a favour.'

'Anything.'

'Come to the scan with me next week. Kristof has asked me to go and I stupidly said yes.'

'Are you crazy?'

'I *have* to go. If I don't, they'll think I don't want to be involved.'

'Which you *don't*.'

'Which I do.' She suddenly bashed herself over the head with *Women Who Bark at the Moon*. Luckily it was a paperback. 'I have to go. You don't realise. These people are artists. This is what they do. It's unusual to us, yes—'

'Right-thinking, normal people—'

'But this is what free-love means. Not being governed by rules.'

I shook my head. 'It's not a good idea.' I paused. 'Nic, I don't want to.'

'I know, I'm sorry. I shouldn't have asked. Forget it, please? I'll go on my own.'

'You can't.'

'No, I'll be fine.' But she looked so sorry and so downtrodden that I heard myself agreeing, despite my better instincts, despite the world collectively shouting, 'No! Don't do it! You fool!'.

'Okay then,' I said. 'I will.' I glowered at her. 'For fuck's sake, though, Nic. For fuck's sake.'

'I know,' she said. 'Don't say anymore, because I know.'

Chapter thirty-one

'Why don't we meet up?' Ronan had rung me up. 'A drink, something to eat. A bit of fun?'

I couldn't remember the last time someone had asked me out. It was so long ago that I wasn't sure it had ever happened. I mean, John and I had just talked, got together and then neither of us had ever left until… until one of us did. A date? This was old-fashioned in a post-Tinder world. It was like still writing letters or eating margarine.

'Fun?' I said.

He laughed. 'It's this thing where you do something that you don't usually do and it is enjoyable. And sometimes you even smile while you are doing it and it makes you feel good on the inside.'

'You mean like a date? Going out, going out?'

'Yes. Does that sound so terrible?'

I didn't know. On the one hand, spending time with Ronan wasn't onerous in the slightest and if I was a better, easier person, then it would be a no brainer. I could go out and probably have a lovely time. But I wasn't, I was me. Recently separated, totally confused and the last time I had been on a date was the night I met John. In other words, a lifetime ago.

'No,' I said. 'Not too terrible.'

'Just mildly so?' He didn't wait for my qualification. 'Listen Jo, I'm asking you out because I like you. Because you are interesting and nice and I like spending time with you and I would like to spend more time with you.'

'You would?'

'Don't sound so surprised. Now, what do you think Ms Woulfe?'

And then I remembered my comfort zone conversation. Joining the Seaside Players hadn't been as bad as I expected. Maybe going out with Ronan for an evening wouldn't be the appallingly scary proposition I was imagining.

'Well,' I said. 'I'm usually very risk-averse but I have been advised to leave my comfort zone… so I accept. A drink would be nice.'

He laughed again. 'Well,' he said, 'good. But, you see, I'm not afraid of taking risks or of sounding over-keen, so what about tonight?'

'I can't tonight, no babysitter.' John was working late, I knew, and Marietta was out with Mr Showbiz. 'But…'

'But what?' I could hear him smiling down the phone.

'But maybe you could come round?' My carpe-diem-ness was off the scale. 'I could get a takeaway and open a bottle of wine… or whatever you like. We could talk about ice creams, the price of milk and why vanilla is the most popular flavour. And even the role of the flake – essential component or superfluous condiment?'

'Oh, I'm sure we can think of more interesting things to talk about than ice cream.'

'Okay,' I said, suddenly feeling a quickening of my insides as I realised that, perhaps, maybe, I was back in the game.

'I'll bring a curry. I know a place that does an amazing Massaman.'

'Poppodoms,' I said. 'As long as there are poppodoms.'

'Deal.'

Once we'd said goodbye, I dashed down to the supermarket, with Harry in the pushchair, to buy some wine. There, I ran up and down the aisles in a panicked state throwing random items into my basket, including, inexplicably, a Jamaica Ginger cake, a new toothbrush and a copy of *Good Housekeeping*.

A handsome man was coming round to my house. For a takeaway. And a bottle (or two) of wine. This was a date, an *actual* date. This is good for you, I intoned. You can do this. This is normal and potentially nice. Stay in the moment. But I kept thinking about John. His anguished face the other night when Fergal hammered on the door, kept breaking into my thoughts. Go away John. This is the new, comfortless, me. You left. I'm moving on.

Once Harry was in bed, I began the Herculean task of trying to make myself look vaguely presentable. Attractive even. However the meagre raw ingredients (getting more meagre as the years roll on) and the fact that I did not have two years to dedicate solely to making myself look good, meant that I soon gave up and left it at some smudged mascara and a nice-ish top. My body, which I studied in the mirror, had seen better days. Obviously not the kind seen by Jerry Hall or Gisele or someone, but *my* better days. Clothes would be staying on, I resolved. Anything else was a step too far. I wasn't ready. I would never be ready. Ronan, I told myself, was calling over in the pastoral sense, like care in the community or a visiting priest. No, that wasn't right. I didn't want Ronan to be *anything* like a priest. But I was getting a bit carried away. Why on earth would he be interested in frumpy old, heavily-baggaged me?

However, when the knock on the kitchen door came, it didn't stop me from jumping out of my skin. Standing on the doorstep, huge grin on his handsome face, paper bag in one hand, bottle of wine in the other, was the ever-lovely FroRo. A sight for my very sore eyes. He hugged me and as we embraced, I realised how much I had missed the human touch. Pulling away, he smiled at me and I found myself smiling back. We stood there on the step, not moving, just looking at each other and smiling.

'Sorry,' I said, just before it got awkward. 'Come on in.' I had the distinct impression that Ronan didn't do awkward, though. He was un-embarrassable – and gentle. Two virtues that are much underrated in a man. He walked past me into the kitchen.

'Glass of wine?' I said. 'Red okay?' I motioned for him to sit in one of the chairs by the stove, but I could feel a tremble in my hand which I steadied by gripping it with the other.

It felt like starting life all over again, as though nothing I had ever done before could prepare me for this new situation, having a glass of wine with a man. It was about the potentials in life – romance, new beginnings, and fresh starts. For too long I didn't want a future and now I felt like a runaway train.

'Perfect,' he smiled and I busied myself with the bottle opener, finding two nice glasses and tearing open some pistachios and pouring them into a bowl. But by the time I sat down in front of him, I realised that everything just might work out okay.

Ronan, I was discovering, was that rarest of men, a talker *and* – praise be! – a listener.

'It's such a terrible thing,' I said, swigging back my wine and crunching on nuts. 'I mean, how could he treat Nic like that? She's his wife. He claims to love her. But then he loves someone else. It's just so crazy. Why is he doing it?' I sloshed more wine into our glasses.

'Sláinte,' he said, raising his glass.

'Sláinte.' I waggled my glass at him. 'But what do you think? You know, as a man.' The wine's dizzying effect was taking its delicious hold and I de-shelled a nut, threw it up in the air and pointed my open mouth ceiling-ward. We watched the nut's trajectory like the opening scene of *2001: A Space Odyssey*... and it landed by the fridge.

'I have no idea,' he shrugged. 'I don't understand what his motives are or how his brain works. We are all very different you know.' He threw up a pistachio too, but it bounced off his nose. We both laughed. 'One more!' he insisted and tried again. And this time, it was in. He snapped his mouth shut, a huge crocodile grin on his face, making me laugh again.

'My turn.' I threw a pistachio up and watched as it ricocheted off my cheek and bounced off into the corner of the room, never to be seen again. 'One more!' This time I managed to snatch it between my jaws in mid-air. 'How's about that?' I was elated.

Ronan held up his hand for a high-five and just as we made contact, I felt his fingers curl around mine, the tiny touch rippling through my body. Oh dear, I thought, this was strange... and wonderful... and terrifying. I had forgotten what other people felt like, the feeling of skin on skin. I mean, I had Harry, but it wasn't quite the same as feeling the heat of another adult.

'Curry?' I said, sense kicking in.

'Good idea,' he said. 'We can't live on red wine and pistachios alone.'

And there was me imagining that it might be possible.

We ate on our laps, legs stretched out in front.

'It can't be easy for you,' he said, tearing some of the naan bread. 'You know with John gone and now with Nicole...'

'I haven't told you about my mother yet. She's a beacon of romantic intrigue,' I said, spooning out the lime pickle. 'For years, all of us were very boring romantically and suddenly it's all kicking off in mad ways. My mam, though, is the only one who seems to be any good at it.'

'Good at what?'

'Romance.' I was suddenly aware that we were getting into a conversation that could be construed as flirtatious, so I changed the subject. 'Pickle?'

Ronan shook his head. 'In what ways are you not good at it?

'The fact that my husband upped and left?'

'That must have been tough.'

'I suppose it is, in some ways.' I swigged back some wine. 'But I can see why he did it. Neither of us was coping well with, you know, life and all that. One of us had to pull the plug and he was braver than me. Anyway, life has enough drama without going on about it.'

'Tell that to Fergal. If there's not enough drama in his day-to-day life, he always throws in a firework to liven up proceedings.'

'Well, he is an *actor*, I suppose.' I said.

Ronan laughed. 'He takes after my father. Dad was a very good performer. Was in the local drama group, just like Fergs. And you,' he smiled. 'Great story-teller as well. Dad'd have everyone in the palm of his hands, waiting for the next line. There wouldn't be a sound in the room, except for Dad's voice. He was amazing.'

Later, when we were clearing up and putting plates into the dishwasher, I wondered about Ronan's father. 'You must miss him,' I said.

'Understatement,' he said, simply. 'I miss him every day.' He paused. 'Fergs was hit the hardest, though. He was in quite a vulnerable place after Roisin. And then Dad. He's still angry about it.'

'But it wasn't your fault.'

'Of course not, I don't blame myself, Mam doesn't blame me either. Fergal does a bit… a lot.' He smiled. 'Well, he's becoming less angry now he's in love again. He deserves a bit of luck. We should all get a happy ending.' He was leaning against the work surface, looking at me. 'Shouldn't we?'

'I suppose,' I laughed. 'Happy endings are all very nice and everything but they're not real. Anyway there's no such thing as an "ending", there are just points where you decide to stop telling your story.'

'Even when someone dies, the story continues,' Ronan said then. 'You go on, don't you, in people's memories or in your children or your family. You never just cease to exist.' For a moment I was stopped in my tracks. 'I've never thought about it like that,' I said slowly. 'I always thought death *was* the end. Nothing else. But it's the way you look at things, isn't it? Our lives are never wholly independent of others, we don't live for any amount of time without shaping the world in some way.'

'It's comforting, isn't it?'

'Comforting how?'

'That no one's story is ever really over.' He smiled gently. 'My Dad's isn't,' he said. 'It's a continuum in this soap opera called existence. We're all just a series of overlapping continuous stories, weaving in and out of people's lives. There's never a finale.' He looked at me and smiled. 'This is a deep conversation…'

'Yeah, sorry,' I said. 'Sorry for rambling.'

'No, I've been rambling,' he insisted.

'No, *I* have.

'But it's been nice.' He stood up. 'The rambling. I like rambling with you.' He looked down at me and grinned. 'It's been lovely. Really nice.' He held his hand out to me and as I

187

reached for it, he pulled me towards him. In a moment our faces were inches away from each other. Neither of us moved, as though we didn't dare.

'So, listen,' he said, fixing me with a look. 'I was thinking...'

'Yes?'

'Well, it's just that I wondered if you might be available to go on another date. A proper one. Going out, leaving the house. Being seen in public, that kind of thing.'

This had gone quite well, I was thinking. Not the awkward disaster I might have imagined. Ronan made me feel good. He was so relaxed, so comfortable in his skin, that there was never a moment where I felt that this was strange, or wrong. But then John's face popped into my brain again. Go away John, I thought crossly. Let me enjoy this.

'Yes, I would love to,' I said, firmly, convincing myself. 'That sounds really nice.'

'Good,' he said, looking at me, making my insides go very strange indeed. It was either pleasure or nervousness or terror. I couldn't quite tell. 'Tomorrow? Or is that embarrassingly, ridiculously keen?'

'Tomorrow sounds perfect.' I said, trying to unscramble my thoughts. He took my hand and kissed it.

'Goodbye Jo,' he said, eventually.

'Goodbye Ronan,' I said, my whole being tingling with the thought of a new life, of new possibilities. My world which had once seemed utterly closed and over, now lay stretched ahead of me. I could feel myself smiling. And then he was gone, up the steps and down the driveway, away into the night.

In my silent house, leaning against the door, something stirred within. And it felt amazing. I couldn't remember the last time I had experienced a feeling of such happiness, or of excitement, of anticipation. I was moving on! At long last. Marietta would be delighted.

Chapter thirty-two

But once I unscrambled my thoughts, lying awake, unblinking into the night, I began to have second thoughts. A date. Me. On a date. This was the very essence of moving on. Which, I knew, was A Very Good Thing. But I utterly felt terrified at the thought. And I wasn't quite sure why. And what would it involve? Would we hold hands? Would we kiss? Did I want us to? But if you were going to spend time with anyone, then it would be with Ronan. I felt safe with him. And happy. And that was a very good start. It wasn't as if I had agreed to go out with Donald Trump.

Once up and dressed, I had no time to think about it as I had a business meeting. This was me, working for free, for a small local garage. This was me. And it mattered. I cared about this garage and what it meant to the place I lived, to my neighbours. It was personal. It was funny, but this kind of moving on seemed far less frightening. Tracksuit bottoms swapped for smart jeans, I even went mad and dabbed a bit of mascara on. I was ready. I had begun to think that perhaps this could be the start of something. My own company, perhaps. No more Decco, or big clients, or expensive lunches. Instead, I could just imagine working from my study, eating my lunchtime sandwich in my own kitchen, collecting Harry from school every day. I was daring to dream.

Marietta looked surprised when she saw me. To be fair, she hadn't seen me in anything approximating smartness in three years, so I didn't take offence.

'You look nice, Joanna,' she said. 'Where're you off to?'

'P. J. and Sheila's,' I said. 'The garage. I have an idea, just a PR thing, to boost the business. They need it. They have terrible competition from some tyre-changing crowd.'

'Ah, Sheila,' she said. 'Give her my regards.'

'You two used to be great pals, didn't you? In the old days.'

'We were at school together.'

'But you used to be *best* friends, didn't you?'

'When we were teenagers,' she finally admitted. 'But…'

'But what?'

'We fell out over a man.'

'A man?'

'She didn't like the company I chose to keep. Didn't approve. And I,' she smiled, "*chose* him." She paused. 'It was a long time ago, nearly fifty years. Sheila and I are still friends, just not in the same way.'

This world of dating and jealousies was not something I had ever associated with my mother and her friends and acquaintances. There were so many stories, so much intrigue, that I didn't know about. There was a whole side, an entire universe, to my mother; events, heartbreak, thoughts, feelings and passions, which I had no idea about. It was like discovering a new planet, or a hidden world behind a waterfall.

'By the way, Mam,' I said, hoping she would linger for longer, not feeling quite ready to cut short this moment of confessions and confidences. 'I'm going on a date tonight.'

'With who?' She took out her earbuds.

'FroRo. Remember him?'

'The Michael Fastbender one?'

'The very same.'

'Well, Jo,' she said, looking pleased. 'That is good news. You need to go out and have a bit of fun instead of cooped up here, on your own, watching television.'

'Thanks,' I said. 'I think.'

'But…' she began and stopped.

'But what?'

'It's just…'

'Just what?'

'John.'

'John what?' Why did she have to bring *him* up? Here I was doing what everyone bloody well wanted, that is: moving on, and here she is mentioning my husband, soon to be ex.

'Well, are you saying that it is *officially* over between you? I thought he was just taking a break.'

'No, Mam,' I sighed wearily. 'People don't take breaks from marriage. It is not something you can drop in and out of.'

'But what if he knew about FroRo?'

'He doesn't know. Anyway, it's none of his business.'

'He'd be upset, I know it,' she persisted.

'He wouldn't. He'd probably be relieved. So he wouldn't have to feel guilty that I'm all alone watching television, as you put it.' I stopped. 'By the way,' I said. 'There's nothing wrong with watching television, you know. There's lots of educational documentaries.' I couldn't remember the last time I watched anything remotely educational.

'Well, Jo,' she said, obviously deciding to drop the John thing for now. 'Would you like to borrow anything of mine to wear? One of my new pieces? I have that lovely floral bomber jacket? It would go very well on you, especially now you're out of the baggy trousers.'

'Mam!' I spluttered. 'I think I will be alright without borrowing my *mother's* clothes, thank you very much. And anyway, I will be returning to my tracksuit bottoms as soon as I've met with Sheila and P. J. I'm not giving them up without a fight, now I've discovered them.'

'Well,' she said, 'suit yourself. But I am glad you are going out again, especially with that nice FroRo.'

'So, you'll babysit?' I said.

'I'd be delighted. I've been doing too much gallivanting myself lately. I need a night in. Anyway, Patrick's having a business evening, so he's busy. He's meeting some potential investors.'

'Great.'

'What sort of name is FroRo,' she said, wonderingly. 'Is it old Irish? I'm trying to remember the names of the High Kings, but I've never heard of FroRo.'

'I think it's Icelandic,' I said. 'From the frozen north.'

'Is it indeed. A Viking name?'

'That's right,' I said. 'A Viking name.'

'Well, isn't that grand,' she said.

'Mam,' I said. '*FroRo* isn't his name. How could FroRo even be a name?'

'I don't know. It could be. Not everyone is called the same anymore,' she said. 'Everyone has different names, not just the Johns and the Pauls and the Josephs we had when I was young.'

'His name is *Ronan*.'

'Ronan?'

'And he sells ice creams. Get it?'

No,' she said. 'Not really. Anyway,' the earbuds were popped in again, 'must get going. Do my three miles.'

'Mam?'

'Yes?'

'Could I borrow that nice cardigan of yours? The silky one?'

'My navy?' she said. 'It's hanging up.' I could have sworn she was smirking, pleased to be the fashionable one.

Chapter thirty-three

At the garage, Sheila gave me a big hug when I arrived. Her bobbed hair was white, the ends tinged with pink. Obviously, the work of Brenda Scissorhands.

'Like the hair, Sheila,' I said. 'Very nice.'

'I'm liking it as well, Joanna,' she said, giving it a toss. 'Next time Brenda is going to try blue. Last time it was bleached. You're never too old to begin experimenting. Well, that's what Brenda says. Her hair's shaved at the side.'

'Wow.' I thought of my grown-out layer-y non-style.

'She's always been doing new things but last year she went on this course. She's got all the kids going to her now. And she was sixty last week. Celebrated by going to New York for the weekend to listen to this hair guru give a talk. Said it was the best weekend of her life. Came back with loads of new ideas.'

'That's what I need. A guru.'

'How's your mother?' she said. 'Still golfing?'

'Of course. She's never without a club in her hand. I have to prise it from her at night. Goes to bed dreaming of grassy lawns and Tiger Woods. She still believes he could be number one again.'

She laughed. 'Your Mam was always one of a kind. Never boring. She used to get up to the wildest things.'

'Really?'

'Oh yes. She once swam, fully clothed, off Dun Laoghaire pier. For a dare. We were all mad things in those days, though girls were expected not to be throwing themselves into the sea. But she'd do it.'

'What?' I couldn't imagine Marietta doing anything like that. 'She wasn't… she wasn't *drunk* was she?'

'Oh no! Just wild, she was. Always up to something. Another time, we were at a concert, she was pulled up on stage and she had to dance with the singer. He swung her round and round so fast that both her shoes flew off into the crowd and we never found them. All of us looking and looking for ages. He felt awful about it and carried her home.'

'Who was the singer?'

'Paddy Ryan,' she said, lowering her voice as P. J. came up towards us. 'Patrick Realta he went by later. He was quite something. Well, he thought so anyway.'

P. J. had taken off his boiler suit, normally oil-stained and patched, and was wearing a jacket. He was unrecognisable and I felt touched and slightly overawed by how much this obviously meant to him. He and Sheila were taking me seriously. No one had done that for years.

'What are you ladies talking about?' said P. J., smiling.

'My back,' said Sheila. 'I was just saying to Joanna here that it was playing up again.' I was impressed at her generation's ability to lie so blatantly. It was as though all these years I had been kept in the dark, but now I was being given a glimpse into these secret lives.

'Shall we sit down?' I said. 'And we can talk about my plan.'

We sat behind the counter, drinking instant coffee. 'Now,' I said, 'there's not much I can do, really. But we can create awareness, remind people you are here, and bring in new business. We need to look at what you are offering, maybe you need to modernise.'

Sheila and P. J. exchanged looks. 'We don't have any money,' said Sheila. 'It's just that the garage is everything we have… we don't have a pension. If the garage goes under, so do we.' She shrugged resignedly.

'All the more reason why we should stand up to Fixup,' I said. 'People want small, local businesses. They only go to the big guys because they advertise more, they are more visible. But they are not necessarily cheaper. You need to modernise. Not change, but just modernise a bit. Like Brenda and the salon. And there are a few things that you can do. Packages is something I was going to suggest. Good, simple treatments, so people know what they are getting. Different price levels. First one could be oil change, tyre inflate, water fill-up… whatever.' I realised that I was quickly out of my depth with the things that people needed to get done to their cars. 'And everything else. And move up to a full service.'

Sheila and P.J. looked at each other again. He nodded at her to go on. 'How much would you be charging, Joanna?' she asked. 'We really want to be involved and appreciate your time and enthusiasm and everything but could we be clear about finances before we go any further?'

'Not a penny,' I said firmly. 'This is the kind of thing I do every day. Or I used to, anyway. I want to do this. You're not to worry about money.'

'Right,' said P. J. 'We feel awkward about you not charging us anything.'

'We are going to work with other people,' I said, trying to convince them that it could be done, 'for the open day. Brian from Brian's could provide teas and coffees, I know someone who has an ice cream van. Bouncy castle for the kids, face-painting, candyfloss, that kind of thing.'

'But what about the garage?' said P. J.

Well,' I said, 'we could open it up to free car checks, advice, oil changes, you know… *things*. Just for the day. Bunting everywhere. Give the place a deep clean. Not that it is dirty, but it is a garage. Just a spruce up.' I hoped they wouldn't be offended.

'We can definitely do that,' said Sheila. 'I've been on at P. J. for years to get stuck in with a bucket of soapy water. He's got no excuse now.'

She looked delighted. And so did P. J. My pitch wasn't up to my old standards, it had to be said. I didn't have a digital animation of my idea for an ad, or drawings showing proposed footfall, ideas for new logos or a complete new look for the garage. But what I did have was a strange and lovely feeling spreading though my body. Like the old me was waking up. I felt excited and enthused by this project. It was small and low-calibre but I didn't care. It was the thought of making something happen, about the planning and plotting and the results, the saving (hopefully) of a local business. This is why I went into PR in the first place. I felt now just like I did when I was taken on by Decco, straight out of college and without much of a clue about anything.

'I don't want to frighten away my old customers, the ones who've been coming here for donkeys,' said P. J. 'They might be put off by any razzmatazz.'

'You don't have to change anything for them. Offer them the same service, they won't notice a thing.'

'Except,' said Sheila, who had been reading my printed notes, 'they might like a cup of coffee.'

'Yes,' I said. 'I thought there could be a deal done with Brian from Brian's. They could go in there while they wait, for a free cup of coffee with the price of a bun. He does very nice cakes,' I said.

'Yes he does. I had a lovely Tibetan teacake the other day,' said Sheila, 'and you had that Dharamsala Doorstep. Toast it was, really,' she explained. 'Lots of Yak milk butter. Or so he said. It tasted like Kerrygold, to be honest.'

'So, let's go through my ideas,' I said. 'And if you're happy, we can plan a date for the family open day. That'll kick us off.'

John may be gone and my life may be utterly different in every conceivable and important way from three years ago, but the old Jo was in there. She'd just been hiding. I was kind of pleased to see her.

But first I had to go the hospital for the weirdest scan visit ever. Nicole needed moral support.

Chapter thirty-four

The three of them were standing in a chain, Kristof in the middle, holding hands with Coco on one side and Nicole on the other. She and I made eye contact as I walked towards them, Kristof raising their arms in greeting.

'What a wonderful day!' he shouted. 'A day for happiness, for love!' Coco, I noticed, was dressed, inadvertently or not, as Mary, mother of Jesus. Her long flowing dress was the perfect blue colour of the Madonna's dress seen on a million statues and paintings. She had a long while shawl over her hair. She looked amazing, skin glowing, rosy of cheek, sparkles in her eyes. Fancy dress or not, being the Virgin Mary suited her.

'My girls!' Kristof said, again waggling Coco's and Nicole's arms high in the air. 'We're all here now.'

'Wonderful,' I said, smiling, now standing in front of the trio. And it *was* wonderful, I supposed, and miraculous, as it always is when a baby is on its way. I could still remember my own final scan day so clearly.

Nicole shook her hand out of Kristof's and came over to me for a hug. 'Thanks for coming,' she whispered. 'Are you okay with this?'

'It's fine,' I said, into her ear. 'Weird but fine.'

'Really? Because I was thinking that I shouldn't have asked you to come…'

'It's fine,' I reassured her. 'Honestly.' But before we could say anything else I was being embraced by Coco.

'Thank you for coming,' she said. 'It means a lot to me. To be welcomed by Kristof's family, for us all to share this moment.'

'Family?'

'Yes, family.' She laughed. 'We make our own families these days. Did you not know? We choose who they are. No one bothers with their birth families. It's the truest democracy.' She smiled at me. 'Don't tell me you are still adhering to the old model, the Pater Familias, head of the household, calling your mother every Sunday, turning up at birthdays and anniversaries, still playing the role of the child you once were. Oh Jo!' She took my hand. 'This is so much better. And you can ditch them so much more easily when things get tedious.' She gave Kristof a sexy, admonishing look.

'I can see the benefits,' I said. I thought of Marietta at home and how I would wither without her. 'But maybe I like the old model better.'

'Shall we go?' said Kristof. 'Everyone ready?' He took Coco's hand again and tried to take Nicole's but she ignored him and came by my side and our motley crew walked through the huge doors of the hospital.

It was exactly where John and I had been more than three years ago so I knew the way, though I tried not to think too much about that and instead focussed on Nicole.

'How's it going?' I said, under my breath, as we followed Kristof and the mother of God along the corridor.

'Fine!' she said, a little too brightly. 'Great. Everything's just great. You know, the baby's on its way and Coco hasn't been feeling too ill. She had terrible headaches last week but they've passed now and she says the back pain is much better. And she's even thinking of a new performance piece... called *Mother*, or something. So it's all just... great.'

'Nicole,' I hissed. 'This is too much. This is crazy! You can't… Just walk away.'

'I know it's fucking crazy,' she hissed back. 'But sometimes, Jo, you don't have a fucking choice. It's either be on the inside or on the outside and I can't face being on the fucking outside!' She was red of face, jaw straining, tears in her eyes, the very opposite of the serene Blessed Virgin who was leaning on Kristof's arm.

*

The nurse smeared the jelly on Coco's stomach as we all, breath bated, watched the little screen for signs of life. And there the baby was. I was sure I could see Kristof's huge features on the baby's tiny face, the poor child. And then I could feel tears in my eyes and I tried to think about something else to stop them from falling. I just remembered when John and I were in the same situation and the sweetness of our lives, the hope and happiness we felt. I fixed my gaze on the exit sign above the door, hoping I wouldn't lose it. I felt Nicole's hand find mine and the two of us sat there, tears in both our eyes.

'It's a boy!' said the nurse. 'Isn't that lovely?'

'We like to just say baby,' said Coco, pulling down her robes. 'We don't like labels such as boy or girl. They are so limiting.'

'Right,' said the nurse.

'The baby will decide how it wants to be,' she continued. 'We don't want to force it to adopt anything that would go against its essential nature.'

'Right,' said the nurse again. 'Well, *it* looks healthy and it looks like *it* is going to be a large one.'

'That's my boy!' said Kristof, before catching a furious glance from Coco. 'I mean, that's my… thing!' He went around the room kissing all of us in turn and singing a song in Polish. He was happy. The nurse managed to deflect his lips with a well-timed block.

'So,' said Coco. 'I was thinking we could go for lunch. There's this place called The Gaeltacht where…'

'No,' said Nicole, suddenly. 'Myself and Jo have to go and do something… you have that thing you need to do, don't you?'

'Yes,' I said, following her lead. 'Yes, that thing. I need to go and do it. So I can't stay and Nicole needs to come and do the thing with me. Don't you?'

Nicole nodded. 'Yes.'

Kristof and Coco were looking at us as though we were mad, but I was very clear that the only mad thing we had done was coming along with them in the first place. I should never have let Nicole talk me into it and I should have clung to her ankles to stop her attending, too.

'Come on Nic.' And, before anyone could say anything, I had strong-armed her away from Mary and Joseph.

In the hospital café, we sat down with our teas and two huge slices of black forest gateaux, with extra cream.

'I hate leaving him with her, the two of them together, like they are a couple,' she said. 'If I'm not there, then it's like they can pretend I don't exist.'

I shook my head. 'It's not right, Nic, come on.'

'I know that,' she said. 'Of course it's not right, but what else can I do?'

Tears in her eyes again, she looked defeated and demeaned. Where was the Nicole I knew, the vibrant, confident woman, who had always been there for me? And when she needed me, I felt unable to actually help her while she was stuck in this chaos.

'Kick him out? Change the locks, file for divorce, and move on with your life. You don't need this Nic. You can't live with this. It's intolerable.'

'I know,' she said. 'But I love Kristof and if I don't go along with any of it, then I'm on my own. But…' She took a massive forkful of cake and put it into her mouth, 'I'm getting there,' she said indistinctly, 'I'm making progress.'

Chapter thirty-five

'You look…' Marietta grappled for the right word.

'Awful? Mutton? Plump?' I suggested. It had taken longer than I wanted to try to turn into someone not remotely resembling myself.

'No, not at all. Very nice,' she said, appraising me with the eye of an antiques expert. 'You look lovely. You always do.'

'Thank you.'

She smiled at me. 'It's good to see you out and about again, Joanna. You were always so full of life.'

At 8 p.m. exactly, there was a knock on the kitchen door.

'All set?' said Marietta.

'Think so,' I said, suddenly feeling scared.

'Answer it,' she hissed, 'before he goes away.'

And there he was, wearing jeans and a t-shirt and a broad smile. And holding a box of eggs. 'For you,' he said, giving them to me. 'From my neighbour. She keeps eight hens and brought these round this afternoon. And I said to myself, who would appreciate eggs laid only this morning? And I thought of you. You look like an egg person.' He was grinning.

'I'll take it as a compliment.' I said, inspecting the brown and speckled beauties. 'Beats boring flowers.'

'Oh dear.' From behind his back, he pulled out a small and beautiful bunch of sweet peas, all lilacs and mauves and pinks and blues and whites. 'Sorry to bring boring flowers.'

I laughed. 'No,' I said, 'not these. I love flowers. As well as eggs.'

'I have a few pots in the back of Fergal's house. My mam's a gardener. Always planting things. She says a summer's not a summer without sweet peas.'

'They're my favourite,' I said, and they were. I'd had them in my wedding bouquet and now I breathed them in, the smell of summer and of a day now distant and fading.

Outside, the blue of the sky deepening, the day taking its time to close in, and the trees in full leaf, the sound of after-work lawn mowers, birds chatting to each other and the waft of the obligatory sausage-barbecuing.

And two bicycles. I had expected the ice cream van and had psyched myself up for the potential embarrassment of going on a date in an ice cream van. But bicycles?

'Okay.' I assessed the situation. 'So we're on bikes?'

'Yup.' He walked over to one, which had ribbons tied to the handlebars and a basket on the front. 'I've customised this one,' he said, 'especially for you.' The other front basket held a large bag.

'How did you get them here?'

'Rode one and pulled the other,' he said. 'An old Wexford trick.'

I didn't like to tell him that when John and I hired bikes in Tuscany once, I crashed into a little Piaggio van which was chugging up a hill, just as I was careening down it. The man drove us to Siena where we returned the bikes and went to have a nice glass of wine somewhere. I hadn't dared ride a bike since.

'So,' he said, 'what are you waiting for? Hop on!'

I had no choice except to obey orders and, smiling gamely and wobbling a little, I veered towards the curb, but within seconds I had found my rhythm. 'It's like riding a bike!' I shouted to Ronan, who was just ahead.

'What?'

It wasn't really worth repeating. 'Nothing! Where are we going?'

'What?'

At the traffic lights I was able to quiz him. 'So, where are you taking me?'

'Somewhere clean in this dirty city of yours.'

'I can't think of a single place,' I said, pretending to rack my brains. 'No, not coming up with anywhere.'

'Wait and see then,' he said. And we cycled on, summer breeze in our hair and faces, through Dun Laoghaire, past the pier, the harbour, the throngs of people walking, enjoying the instant carnival atmosphere a warm summer's evening can create. Eventually, we crested the hill and looked down at the beach at Seapoint, the tide was way out, leaving a huge stretch of golden sand and shimmering rock pools. Dog walkers with their charges who shot across the beach chasing imaginary rabbits, the solitary ramblers and the couples promenading, arms linked as one. The sun was beginning to make its way down, the sky taking on a pinky-peach colour.

'Here,' he said, pulling the brakes. 'We're going paddling.'

'Paddling?'

'Yes,' he laughed. 'Paddling.'

We wheeled the bikes down and locked them to the railings. Ronan carried the bag and we walked along the pathway until we found a spot for shaking out the rug and sitting on the grassy edge.

'Ready?' Ronan was unlacing his trainers. He jumped down onto the sand. 'Come on!' He said and, once I had slipped off my sandals, he took my hand and pulled me the length of the beach to the waters' edge, where we splashed in. It was freezing and beautiful, clear as a glass of water, the sand beneath our feet rippling and undulating, sharp shells and smooth pebbles peeking out, the cold seeping into my skin. I could feel it as far as my spine.

'What do you think?' he said.

'I love it,' I said. 'It's amazing.' I let my hand drop from Ronan's and stood, my feet in the water, looking out to sea. If I could swim, I could just keep going. Is it ever possible to escape just for a bit and come home again? Just when you need it? I saw a little open mussel shell, still conjoined to its twin, a little open book of a shell, iridescently violet, and slipped it into my pocket.

Ronan put his arm around my shoulder and pulled me close to him. 'How're you doing?' he said. 'Date going well?'

'So far,' I said. It felt a bit strange to have an arm draped across me that wasn't John's. I wondered what I would do if we met anyone I knew. Was I ready for a new relationship? Was I ready to announce to the world that John and Jo were no more? And now, perhaps, possibly, it was Joanna and Ronan. (We couldn't be Jo and Ro as it made us sound like a Stock, Aitken and Waterman production.)

He turned to look at me.

'Hello you,' he said, gently.

'Hello.' I felt my toes sink into the sand, tiny fish swimming past my ankles.

'You are such a beautiful person,' he said. 'Inside and out.'

'Really?'

'*The* most beautiful,' he said, smiling at me.

'Oh no…' I looked away, thoughts of John yet again crowding my mind. But Ronan dropped his arm and wrapped it around my body, pulling me close to him. He bent down towards me, to kiss me. And, of course, I knew what I should do, I should move on, allow myself to be kissed by Ronan, allow a new relationship to develop. It could be so delightful. Perhaps, this was the new start I needed? Lovely as Ronan was though, I just wasn't ready. I knew it.

'Not yet, Ronan,' I said. 'It's a bit too soon.'

'That's alright. Totally understand.' He smiled at me. 'Sorry.'

'No, *I'm* sorry.'

'I like hanging out with you. That's enough for me and if you want to make it more than hanging out, then let me know. But whatever you want to give me, I'll take it.'

'Thanks Ronan.' I felt so grateful to him for making it so easy for me. Rooting around in my pocket, I found the mussel and held the twin shells inside, gently.

'Hungry?' he said.

'I could be persuaded.' And with the sun setting, children still playing, the world closing down on a summer's day, he took my hand and we began to pad through the water, back to our things.

On the grass, by the edge of the sand, we sat on the rug where Ronan began digging through the bag.

'This should still be cold enough,' he was saying, pulling out a bottle. 'I know nothing about wine. But the man in the shop recommended it.'

'I always think if there is an animal on the label then it tastes good, like a bird or a kangaroo. It works every time. Let's have a look.'

We both peered at it. 'A kiwi!' he said triumphantly. 'It's got to be good so.'

I sat cross-legged on the rug, next to Ronan, while he poured out two plastic cups of wine. We tasted it in the manner of sommeliers, swishing it round, making faces that showed our superlative wine skills.

'Delicious,' I said, swallowing.

'Grassy,' he said, 'which is wine-speak for tastes absolutely fine.'

'Grassy, then,' I said.

He burrowed around in the bag again and produced a roast chicken, a salad in a Tupperware box, an avocado and knife and a large Toblerone. 'And these,' he said, pulling out a bag of pistachios. I know you're partial to these.'

'Partiality bordering on obsession,' I said opening the packet. 'We could do our competition again. I've been practising.' I shelled one and tossed it up. It landed miles away. 'Not quite there yet,' I said. 'My talents obviously lie elsewhere.'

He threw one up and caught it in his mouth.

'You're wasted selling ice creams.'

'Do you think I could make a career of it, pistachio throwing?'

'Definitely. Charge people to see you. You could retire to Monte Carlo.'

He grinned. 'Only if you come with me.'

'Only if you have a massive yacht. And a constant supply of nuts.'

'Deal.' He held out his hand.

'Deal.'

'Is this okay for you?' he said, suddenly, anxiously. 'Just a picnic?'

I opened another pistachio and popped it into my mouth. 'I can't think of anything nicer,' I said. 'Now pass over the knives and forks.'

'We used to drink on Silver Strand, near where we grew up, when we were teenagers,' he said. 'Every weekend we'd get some food and some bottles of beer… a bonfire. We'd sing, you know, everything and anything.'

'What did you used to sing? What was your favourite?'

''Fire and Rain' by James Taylor,' he said. 'Always. God, I still love that song.'

'Me too,' I said. 'Sing some of it.'

'No way!' he laughed. 'I haven't drunk enough of this,' he held up his cup, 'to do anything like singing in public. But what about a toast? What shall we drink to?'

The tide was lazily creeping in, taking its time on this long summer night, as reluctant as the sun was to go down. And I thought, for the first time in three years, I was glad to be alive, sitting here with Ronan.

'To life,' I said.

'To life,' he echoed.

'To new friends.'

'To us.' And we drank our wine and watched the sun make its slow descent. All was well, all was well… except that song that Ronan mentioned. I couldn't stop thinking about it. Fire and Rain… the lyrics kept running through my head, over and over again.

Chapter thirty-six

'Well,' Ronan smiled. We had cycled home in the dark and now the bikes were leaning against the wall of my house. 'Thank you for a lovely evening.'

'It's been wonderful, thank you.' And it had been. 'Cup of tea?'

'Sounds good.'

As I reached for my house key, I could feel the mussel shells in my pocket, the little twins, joined together with that fragile hinge.

In the kitchen, I filled the kettle and gathered two mugs, milk and a bar of chocolate.

'I'm out of biscuits. Sorry.'

'How could you let such a thing happen?'

'They just disappear. I have no idea how.' I was trying to be light and amusing but something was bothering me. I still couldn't stop thinking about the song he had mentioned. For some reason, I wanted to hear it. To hear the words and the music and the sentiment, was something I wanted so desperately, *so badly*, with an urgency I couldn't quite understand. 'You still haven't sung me that James Taylor song.'

'I don't have my guitar,' he protested.

'Go on, will you? Please?'

'Only because you're asking,' he said. 'I find it difficult to say no to you.'

He couldn't see my face because I turned away from him, pretending to not really listen, to make the tea; but I was hearing this song as though I had never heard anything before. He sung it so beautifully.

'*I've seen fire and I've seen rain. I've seen sunny days that I thought would never end. I've seen lonely times when I could not find a friend, but I always thought that I'd see you again.*'

You have to wait, with grief, I have found, you have to wait until you are ready to talk. The words find you, you can never find them. Grief is too deep, too visceral, too scarring for ordinary, everyday words.

In my pocket were my mussel twins but as I fingered them, I felt them fall apart; two separate shells, both exactly alike but no longer together.

Oscar. I always thought I'd see you again. I always thought I'd see you again.

And tears began pouring down my face. Oscar, my Oscar.

'*Won't you look down upon me, Jesus? You've got to help me make a stand. You've just got to see me through another day. My body's aching and my time is at hand, and I won't make it any other way…*'

Ronan kept singing, softly, in the quiet of the kitchen. His voice carrying around the room and me standing stock still, hearing every word, soaking up the meaning and wilting inside, desperately trying not to make a sound. I wanted to listen, to think about Oscar. This song expressed everything I was feeling. My loss. My loneliness, my love.

'*I've seen lonely times when I could not find a friend but I always thought I'd see you baby, one more time again…*'

I suddenly grappled for breath and made a terrible choking sound. Ronan stopped. *Thought I'd see you one more time. Thought I'd see you one more time.*

'Jesus, Jo,' he said, 'are you alright?'

I turned around; realising there was nowhere to hide. I was exposed, vulnerable. My life, my story, now so close to the surface that I felt naked. Oh God. I shouldn't have asked him to sing the song. But I had to, the world had been crushing down upon me, and I knew that I had to hear it. My life, my future, had seemed to depend upon it.

'Listen,' he said, trying to smile. 'I know my singing is bad, but surely not that bad.'

By now I had a tea towel held to both eyes and, from somewhere in the depths of my soul, I let out a cry that would wake the neighbourhood. Ronan got up, pushing back his chair with force, and was by my side, arm around me.

'What's wrong,' he said softly. 'What's wrong, my lovely Joanna?'

Oh God, this was embarrassing. Letting the tea towel soak up my tears, my body wrenched with crying. He pulled me close into his chest and we stood there for as long as it took for me to stop and for my breathing to calm down a little.

'Go and sit down,' he said. '*I'll* make the tea. And I'll stop my awful caterwauling.'

'No… it wasn't that, it…' But I did as I was told and sat at the kitchen table. I put my head in my hands and sobbed like a child, deep cries that came from deep inside, raw, exposed and unprotected.

Oh God. I hadn't spoken about Oscar to anyone, not since it happened. Not even to Nicole, to Marietta, not even to John. They all knew the facts but no one knew how I actually *felt*, the emptiness inside, the ever-present loneliness, the constant feeling that I was about to scream out loud. It was all I could do to pretend to be normal. As long as Harry was alright and I held it all in, I could keep Oscar for myself, bottled inside, where he was safe. I was so scared of letting him out, but that song had released him and suddenly he was all around. I felt bereft and devastated all over again.

'I thought I was doing okay.' I had managed to breathe. The tea towel had reached its absorbency limit, so I used my sleeves.

'What is it?' Ronan scanned my face, his eyes full of kindness and concern.

'I had a son.'

'A son? Do you mean *another* son?'

'Yes,' I said. 'A twin for Harry. Harry's twin.' I placed the two little mussel shells on the table.

'And…' he spoke so softly, so gently, 'what happened?'

'He died. After a day.' A tear fell into one of the shells. 'He died when he was only a day old.'

'Oh, Jo,' he said, covering my hands with his large, warm, smooth ones. 'So this is what you've been going through. I knew there was something. You sometimes look so sad.'

I nodded. 'I wasn't even there when he was ill, because I thought everything was fine. I didn't know he was going to die so I didn't get a chance to say goodbye or tell him how much—' I started sobbing again, 'how much I loved him. And everyone thinks I'm fine and that I'm getting over it but I'm not, not really. And John isn't.'

'That's why he left?'

I nodded. 'Kind of. We just stopped being a team. We were barely speaking at the end. And I can see how much he needed to get away. He was right, you know? He looks better now, like he's beginning to deal with it. But I'm trying to keep everything together, for everyone's sake, especially Harry's. And I can't move on really because I don't want to leave Oscar behind. He's not my past; he should be with me, like Harry is. He should be my future. But if I start dealing with it, then he

214

becomes my past and… and…' I stood up and fumbled for a clean tea towel in the drawer. 'I talk to him, you know?' I said, sitting back down. 'I talk to him all the time. It's like he's with me.' I stopped. 'Does that make me sound mad?'

He shook his head. 'It makes you sound totally sane,' he said. 'It's exactly what sane people would do. You're strong, you are Jo. Brave and brilliant. Like a stone.'

'A stone?' This startled me enough that I stopped crying for a moment. I almost laughed.

'Yes,' he said. 'Have you ever picked up a pebble from a beach? Well, it's only when you take the time to look closely at one that you see how magnificent it is. Smooth and strong. They have endured so much.'

'I'm a pebble?' I laughed, but weirdly I liked being compared to one.

He shrugged. 'Next time you're on a beach, look at one and you'll see what I mean. There are depths there, of colours, of history. A story to tell but no less beautiful for it.'

I started crying all over again.

Chapter thirty-seven

I have a scan picture of the two of them, Oscar and Harry, wrapped around each other, hands touching. We had called them Oscar and Harry as soon as we heard we were having twins and we spent the rest of my pregnancy, John and I, talking about them, using their names. We had two cots, two of everything, all ready for when we came home.

I remember giving birth, or rather lying there after the Caesarean, trying to keep myself calm. Were the babies alright? Had we done it? Was this the end of the years of struggle? Had we finally got our family?

'Two beautiful baby boys, Jo,' said the midwife, 'all perfect.'

She gave me Harry and Oscar, one in either arm, and I began scanning their little faces, all squished and squashed and purple-red. Beautiful in other words. John was quite overcome and was kissing the babies and me in turn and getting jumbled up, trying not to leave anyone out. And it was then that I burst into tears. Happy, excited, relieved tears.

But here they were, gorgeous and lovely and safe and sound. Our crazy little twins. Our perfect family, I thought, as I squeezed John's hand. We were so lucky, so blessed. John saw I was crying and gave himself the permission to. He burrowed his head close to mine and whispered, 'I love you Joanna Woulfe. You are amazing.' I remember laughing, well, laughing as much as you can when you are being stitched up after major surgery, flat on your back and recovering from the shock that your family has just increased two and a half times in one second.

'Oh my God,' I said, trying to be funny, 'there's too many of us now!'

Too many of us. I actually said those words.

There's too many of us now.

I feel so much guilt about everything. Guilt about what I said, guilt about the smug feeling about our perfect little family. Guilt over working too much while I was pregnant, guilt about all that cheese I ate and the glass of wine I had at 40 weeks, guilt about the myriad reasons I could have caused this. And then guilt about the aftermath, guilt about not helping John, not dealing with it all better, being so sad when I should have been so grateful to have Harry.

Guilt and shame, shame and guilt.

Oscar was beautiful. I still have the photo of me holding him in bed. We didn't take one of the boys together, but there is one of me with Oscar and another of me with Harry. John was holding the camera shakily, emotion and stress meaning the resulting image isn't pinpoint clear, but you should see my face. I've looked at it a million times, wondering who that person was, when I thought everything was over. I look happy.

And I examine the picture all the time, wondering am I holding him well enough, did he feel, for the twenty four hours he was alive, he was loved? Did he know his mummy loved him and his brother more than anything in the world? Did he feel my love for him swooshing out from deep within me and soaking into him? Did he know he was going to die?

Life goes on, of course it does, even when you don't want it to, even when you want to just stop and say, hold on a minute, can everything stop rolling, can we take a pause here because I need to take a breath and think about my tiny baby who died, my baby who I didn't get the chance to hold enough, or to kiss enough or to love enough because we didn't have enough time.

Time, please, ladies and gentlemen. Just some time, so I can think about Oscar. My baby who died aged one day old. One day. My mayfly baby. Maybe, I sometimes think, he was only meant to be around for a day, to show his little face, to let me kiss him, to let John kiss him. And to make sure his brother was okay.

Chapter thirty-eight

For the first few hours, I was feeling good. Well, good for someone recovering from a caesarean, but the elation of having my twins was better than any anaesthetic and I was on a high. After everything, the years of trying, John and I finally had our boys. Oscar and Harry. Our family.

Marietta was there within 20 minutes of getting John's text. She must have been walking around close by. We couldn't hold the boys as they were still too tiny but everything, we were told, was fine. She and John hovered between my room and the baby unit.

After what felt like about two seconds of sleep, I woke up to see John and Marietta deep in conversation.

'Your mother has been telling me all about nappies and feeding and…' said John, when he saw me. 'And what else, Mar?'

'I actually don't remember much else,' said Marietta. 'It was, after all, a very long time ago.'

John laughed. 'Oh yes,' he said. 'And Jo is technically a geriatric mother, being over thirty five.'

'It's usually me who's that,' said Marietta. 'So it's nice not to be, for once.' And the two of them laughed away to themselves. They'd always got on so well.

'Let's go and see them,' I said. I wanted to sit there all day, just gazing at them. Maybe even hold them. We were wasting time here in this room. I should be with my boys.

'No,' said John. 'We'll go. You stay and get some sleep. You must be exhausted.' He looked pretty tired too, I remember thinking. He hadn't slept all night. I felt fine though, full of energy, ready for motherhood and for my new life to begin. I'd waited for so long for this and now he was stopping me.

'I want to go, John,' I said. 'I want to see them.'

'Jo, you need to rest. We'll go, check on them and you sleep.'

'But—'

'She needs sleep, doesn't she Marietta.'

And she nodded along, agreeing with him. Two against one and if only, if only, I hadn't been so weak and let them persuade me to stay in the room, If I had gone, then I would have stayed with him. I would have had longer with him. I might have been there… when he died. Oscar would have had his mother with him and he would have known how much I loved him. But I thought I had all the time in the world.

It wasn't John's fault. I know that really, deep down. But why did he choose that moment to be concerned about me needing sleep? I should have gone anyway, ignored the two of them. But I didn't and it rankled, John's insistence on me staying. When it's no one's fault, it helps to find or create a culprit and John was in my firing line.

And I did sleep, for hours I think, but I woke hearing a sound in the room. Nicole was there, smiling. She came over and hugged me. 'I am just so happy for you,' she said, tears in her eyes. 'Two beautiful boys. I bought these for them.' Inside a bag were two tiny, soft rabbits, both grey. 'Twins for your twins,' she said.

'You are going to be their fairy godmother, aren't you?'

'I thought you'd never ask,' she said, smiling. 'But before I say yes, what exactly does it involve? Religious instruction? Having to take them to mind-expanding lectures on existentialism, or taking them to football practice on a winter's weekend morning while you lie in bed? Because if it's the latter, sorry, I don't do cold. Or hanging about.'

'Or football.'

'But the other two would be grand,' she said. 'I'd be honoured.'

'No, I think it's what *they* can do for *you*,' I said. 'I think I have to train the boys to make you cups of tea and bring you biscuits at regular intervals. And to do little jobs such as cleaning out your car or running you baths. That kind of thing.'

'It's a yes,' she said. 'Definitely a yes.'

I was so in love with my new status as mother of twins. It was a glorious feeling. 'Shall we go and see them?'

'Do you need the wheelchair?' she said.

'No, I want to walk. I'm feeling better already.' I heaved myself out of bed, feeling the sharp pain in my lower stomach and began hobbling towards the neo-natal unit. My babies, I remember thinking, I'm going to see my babies. I'd only been away from them for an hour. I'm their mother, I thought. We'll have them home within days and then life proper would begin.

There was a whoosh of air as a nurse pounded past us. And I just knew where she was going and to whom. Oscar. I even knew it was Oscar. I started shuffling and running down the corridor, Nicole behind me.

My body felt so weak and wobbly, there was a wrenching pain from where my skin was still knitting together but I didn't care. I had to get to my baby.

The first face I saw was John's, all colour drained from it. There were four medics around Oscar's cot, the plastic top having been taken off, and them desperately trying to resuscitate him. Harry peacefully asleep in his own bed.

John's arms grabbed me at the last few feet, as though pulling me out of harm's way, and we clutched each other, wide-eyed in terror. Our baby. How could this be happening? We'd been through the drama, the getting pregnant, the pregnancy, even the going into labour six weeks early. I thought we had crossed the finish line. It was all done.

I can't remember what the nurse said to us exactly but I remember latching onto the words 'major surgery' and that was enough.

I found my voice somewhere. 'Stay with Harry,' I said. 'I'll go with Oscar.'

'We'll both go.' It was John. He turned to Nicole. 'Would you stay with Harry?' She nodded and Marietta, John and I followed Oscar.

And with that, our happy family life screeched to a halt.

For three hours we waited in the corridor outside the operating theatre. We didn't speak much. John handed out horrible teas from the machine. Marietta rang John's Dad to tell them what had happened and while she paced around, John was up and down and in and out, trying to see any doctors we recognised. I just sat there, trying not to panic. Everything's going to be okay, I intoned, trying to bring the words deep inside, so they became real and true. We are not going to lose him. That doesn't happen to people like us.

Eventually, the doctor, looking exhausted and drained appeared. 'I don't... I don't have good news.' He spoke clearly, lest we might not understand what he was saying. That we might think there was hope. He wasn't here to give us hope, he was here to signal the beginning of the rest of our new lives, our new identity: the couple who lost the baby. 'Oscar didn't make it. We did everything we could...'

And then I floated away, like a helium balloon, watching and listening, fascinated by this scene which was going on beneath me. Three people, two of them holding hands. A doctor conveying the most awful news, ploughing bravely on despite telling them that their son, their tiny baby son, had died.

And then I was back and John's hand fell limply out of mine and Marietta stood up and all I could think about was Oscar. And there was this hole inside me that is still with me all the time. It has never filled. I don't expect it will.

'His heart,' the doctor was saying. 'Heterotaxy Syndrome. His heart was on the wrong side of his body and his intestines were twisted. It is not something we could have predicted or something that could have been picked up at the scan. We had no idea until he showed signs of not breathing well. I'm sorry,' he said. 'I'm so sorry for your loss.'

'Can we see him?' I asked. 'I need to see him.'

*

Oscar was wrapped in a blanket. He looked as though he was fast asleep and when I kissed him he was warm and smelled so sweet. But it was when I lifted him... he didn't feel real, he felt so light, insubstantial, as though there was no breath, no life, no spirit or soul. Oscar.

My face buried into his tiny body. 'I love you little Oscar, I love you so, so much.' I hoped my words would flow through him and that he would hear me, his mother, and all I wanted to say to him. 'I wish you could have stayed for longer,' I said. 'I wish I could have heard your voice. I wish I could have seen your smile.'

And I never stopped speaking to him.

'Was he in pain?' I asked then, lifting my head. The doctor shook his head. 'No, no pain.'

'You're sure?'

He nodded.

God knows how long we sat there, John, Oscar and I, but eventually we had to say goodbye. Goodbye to our family; doubled in one day and then reduced by a quarter. We would never be the same again.

Being there in the hospital, with all the people, the nurses, the visitors, I felt totally and utterly alone. Along the corridor, unseen, I could hear people laughing. Someone was happy. I saw a man wheeling a woman past the window of the room we were in, him looking more tired and more ill than she.

And it was so scary, being there, when the world was turning and I couldn't quite connect with it all.

'Harry,' I said finally. 'I've got to go to Harry.'

And that was it. Harry had to be my focus, not John, not getting on with things, just Harry. And he, thankfully, was safe and sound, Nicole beside him. He was all I had left.

Chapter thirty-nine

Have you ever held four pounds of something in your hand? Newborn babies are tiny, it's not like holding a person, it's like a holding a tiny jewel. Or something else so precious that you need to wrap it up and hold it close. I hope Oscar knows his Mum loves him, wherever he is.

The hospital wouldn't allow us to bring Harry to Oscar, so poor John wasted twenty minutes of the two hours they let us have with him, trying to persuade them to let us. But they were right, can't take risks with newborn babies. Instead Harry had to say goodbye to his brother in the womb. I hope he did. I hope before they were pulled out that they wished each other luck and that they would see each other again, don't know where, don't know when.

Oscar's funeral was a blur. Nicole and Marietta organised most of it as John and I were zombies, coping with a newborn baby and then having to say goodbye to a child we'd barely had enough time to love. It was all rather unreal. Three days beforehand there was just me and John, and now we were at the funeral of our baby, while holding his twin.

I don't remember getting dressed or brushing my teeth and was still bleeding after the birth, my breasts leaking, but I couldn't concentrate on anything, not even Harry. Marietta held him and looked after him those first few weeks when the shock set in so hard I thought that was it for life. But somehow I carried on and the pain and the horror of what happened became part of me, part of the baggage I carried around every day. I didn't want to touch it to unwrap it because I was so terrified about what would happen to me if I did. Would I cease to function and what would happen to Harry then?

When John took the stand, Nicole budged up to hold my hand. He looked out at the sea of black, a blur of faces, total silence. I wouldn't meet his gaze I remember, because I couldn't stand his grief. If I allowed myself to see how much he was suffering, I knew I wouldn't survive. I wish I could turn back time and go up to him, stand beside him, get through it together. His own father, Jack, was looking back at him though, urging him on and willing him to say what he wanted to say. Thank God for Jack.

John cleared his throat. 'Oscar lived for one day,' he said. 'For one short day. That is the extent of his life. It doesn't sound much, or of any importance. You might think that he didn't do anything, he didn't achieve anything. There are no great obituaries to be written about someone who lives for just 24 hours. But if you think that, you are wrong. It was a lifetime, his lifetime, and he brought love and possibility, he bought life, a beating heart, his tiny fingers and toes, his beautiful face. He brought to this world a brain and a heart and a soul. He was our son. And we loved him.

'Oscar was his own great achievement. He may not have been with us as long as we would have liked. He would have loved, I am sure, to have grown up to play with his brother Harry, to go to school, to become what he was to become. We will never know. Will we watch Harry and wonder would their lives have run in parallel? Or would he be very different? But our conversation with Oscar has not ended. This is not where we say goodbye to Oscar, this is not where we carry on without him. Instead, we take him with us. Oscar will be fully in our hearts and lives.

'My mother died when I was 18 months old,' John went on, 'and it was Dad who brought me up. He was a single father when they were as rare as an Italian try in Lansdowne Road. It was Dad who made sure the tooth fairy came, or that Santa brought me what I wanted, who made me revise. He had dreams for me. He taught me to think big. It was he who told me to get back on my feet, to get back on the rugby pitch. It was he who washed my kit after training, it was Dad who would pick up the fish and chips on his way home every Friday, to eat in front of the TV. And it was Dad who reminded me who I was. And I want to do the same for Oscar. I am here to remind you that Oscar is someone. He matters.'

John took out a crumpled piece of paper.

'You have taken the east from me,' he read, his voice trembling, 'you have taken the west from me; you have taken what is before me and what is behind me; you have taken the moon, you have taken the sun from me; and my fear is great that you have taken God from me.'

All of us in that church, sat there, suspended in time.

'My Dad never gave up on me but today I stand here, our own son in that coffin, our baby son. And I want to say to you Oscar, that we love you. That I love you as much as any father has loved his son and Joanna and I will never give up on you. You will be in our thoughts and in our hearts forever.'

He almost staggered back to the seat next to me and when I took his hand, he squeezed it so tight that I thought my wedding ring was going to sever my finger. But from that moment, we weren't really together anymore. We each took our own paths through grief.

Valium was the thing that got me through that day and Harry got me through the next day, the day after that, and the day after that. John went back to work after a week and that was it. All over. We still had Harry, so we felt we couldn't really complain. Other people lose babies and come home from hospital to an empty cot and no one to wear the baby clothes or to love. We were lucky, we knew that. We couldn't complain. At least I had Harry, I was sure everyone was saying. A real shame, but she's luckier than most. And I knew that, I really did. But I wanted Oscar, too. The little boy I never got to know properly.

So I talk to him. What do you think of that, Oscar? I might say, when another car pulls out in front of me. Or, sometimes, when I am dishing out cereal for Harry, I imagine myself pouring another bowl and handing out another spoon and smiling at another little boy, sitting beside Harry. It stops me going completely mad, this imagining and pretending. It stops Oscar from floating away into nothingness, because I'm just not ready to say goodbye. I wonder if I'll ever stop wondering what he might like, what cartoons and books he would have enjoyed or if he would have been sporty or arty or both. What kind of man he would have become.

Chapter forty

'You see,' I said to Ronan. 'I'm not ready. I'm not ready to say goodbye to Oscar. I don't *want* life to move on. I can't leave him behind. I'm so scared.'

He nodded. 'That's understandable…'

'This is the first time I've talked about what happened,' I said, trying to find yet another clean tea towel. I smiled. 'There's something about you Ronan, you get people to talk. There's a magic about you.'

The hole inside me, the emptiness that was always there; I put my hand to my stomach, it felt different, as though something had changed.

'The power of talking,' said Ronan, simply. 'There's nothing like it.'

Oscar Beckett. Son of John Beckett and Joanna Woulfe, twin of Harry. My little boy. The thing that had frightened me most was him fading away, being forgotten, but now I felt him stronger than ever. He wasn't going anywhere, but it was up to me to talk about him.

Ronan put his arms around me and let me cry some more. And that was it. Life *could* move on and we wouldn't be leaving Oscar behind. He'd be wherever we wanted him to be, tucked in amongst us.

'I don't even have a photo of the two of them together. I have one of Oscar and me and one of Harry and me but not the twins together. I feel terrible about that. I thought there'd be loads of time. I thought we had the rest of our lives. The only thing I have is my scan picture. But you can't frame that, can you. That's just weird. Especially if one of them... died.'

Ronan shrugged. 'I don't think it's weird. Not at all. You should do it.' He kissed the top of my head. 'You're an amazing woman, Joanna Woulfe.' I looked up at him. He nodded. 'You are. It's about time you knew it, too.'

I felt the tears flood my eyes again. I was never good when people were nice to me.

'Thanks,' I managed.

'You get some sleep, okay? I'll check on you tomorrow to see how you are.'

It was very late when he cycled off. I lay in bed thinking and thinking about Oscar and about Harry and about all that had happened to have brought me to this place in my life, so afraid to let go of my son. And then tiredness overtook me, a deep and dreamless sleep, the like of which I hadn't had in years and years.

Chapter forty-one

The next morning, there was a soft knocking on my door.

It was Harry, holding Marietta's hand. It was always me who got up with him and he peeked around the door, his face anxious, wondering if I was alright. It made me feel a stab of love so strong it almost hurt.

'Oh Harry, my sweetheart!' I said, grabbing him and squeezing him. 'I love you so much.'

I hugged him as though I would never let him go. He'd be at nursery school in September and I hadn't, if I was totally honest, been the most present of mothers, or the most fun. It hadn't been fair on Harry. I kissed his face. 'I am so lucky to have you. I love loving you.'

'We thought you'd have a nice lie-in,' said Marietta, putting a mug of tea beside the bed. 'It's ten o'clock.'

'We'll be down in a minute,' I said.

As Marietta shut the door behind her, I brought Harry under the duvet with me. 'Harry,' I said. 'You know Oscar?'

'My brudder Oscar?'

'That's right. You know he'll always be in our hearts, don't you? And that's where he can stay. We can love him, but you are the little boy I can kiss and hold hands with.'

'And play Lego with?'

'And play Lego with. But you can play with Oscar inside your head… does that make sense?'

He nodded.

'I love you Harry.'

'Love you Mummy.'

I looked over at the photo of Harry and John and I in West Cork. It felt as though that was the past and I was moving into a future that until only recently, I never thought could exist.

My phone beeped. A text from Ronan: 'How are you today, you brave and wonderful woman? Thinking of you, Ronan.'

I texted back: 'Thank you for last night. You'll never know what it meant to me. Speak soon.'

*

'So,' Marietta said later when we were sitting down at the table for lunch. She'd made me a bowl of tomato soup and had sprinkled on grated cheese. She'd been making me this for 40 years now and it had lost none of its comforting properties. 'What's going on with you and Fronan?'

'Why?'

'Well, the two of you seem to be very close.'

'We're good friends.'

'Is that what you call it?'

'Yes!'

'But wasn't last night a date?'

'It was, kind of.'

'Was it or wasn't it?'

'It was,' I admitted. 'But it didn't really end that way.'

'What do you mean?'

'I ended up crying and telling him about Oscar.'

'Really?'

I nodded. 'Bit of a passion killer, really, introducing the topic of your son who died.'

'Yes, I suppose it is.'

'I'm not sure I want passion, at the moment, anyway. I think I just want love.'

'Love?'

'And kindness and all the unexciting things like gentleness and sweetness and… well…' I suddenly realised that this wasn't something I wanted to talk to my mother about. But she got it.

'Life can sometimes get too exciting, Joanna. But if you ask me, Ronan is all of those things you are looking for.'

'I know. He's got a good soul.'

'Your tomato soup is getting cold,' said Marietta. 'Aren't you hungry?'

'Not particularly.' I pushed it away. 'Thanks anyway.'

*

'You know I blamed John, don't you?' I said to Marietta later that evening. 'If he hadn't made me sleep that day, if he hadn't chosen that one moment to be the alpha bloody commanding male and tell me what to do, if he hadn't stopped me from being with Oscar then—'

'Then what?'

'Then maybe he wouldn't have…'

'But he was never going to make it, you know that, don't you?'

I shrugged, not wanting to believe it. It was too easy to say it was just going to happen, surely something or someone must be responsible. 'But maybe if I was there, next to him, the doctors would have noticed something earlier and they would have been able to save him.'

'Is that what you think?' She spoke softly to me while a large tear rolled down my cheek. I could feel its full and steady progress, gathering speed as it fell to earth. 'No one's to blame. No one could have saved him. And John was just being kind to you.'

'I wish he hadn't been. Anyway, it wasn't kind when he left, was it?'

'What was he to do?'

'Stay? Or is that too radical a suggestion?'

She shrugged. 'Life is rarely simple,' she said. 'If I know one thing it's that.'

'When I met him everything seemed simple. Like life would always be easy for the rest of our lives.'

'I felt like that once,' she said, smiling at me. 'It never ceases to surprise me how life turns out.'

'Sometimes,' I said, 'I wish that life wasn't so interesting.'

'I've got to go now, Joanna,' she said, looking me in the eyes, studying my face. 'Patrick and I are going out to the golf club for dinner. But I do want to say this. It wasn't John's fault. It wasn't anyone's fault. It just happened and that's the hardest thing to accept. It just happened.'

Life *had* been so simple, loving John had been so easy. As long, I thought, as long as nothing happened to Harry, then everything would be alright. As long as he was safe I could start imagining my new future.

Life-lifters

- My scan picture of my two boys

- My Oscar box – his babygro and grey rabbit, the twin of Harry's, his blanket

- How lucky I am to have Harry

Chapter forty-two

Sheila had been in full flow, galvanising and organising all the other businesses within a stone's throw of the garage. Brian's next door was going to be serving cakes and coffees to everyone all day from a stall. There was to be a magician for the kids, with face painting and balloon animal making, Christopher from the Ham and Hock pub was going to do fire eating. Apparently he had once spent a year at the Lecoq School in Paris and had then travelled the world doing street theatre. Their son Paul Jr was leaving Murph's Surf behind for the day and was going to decorate the whole garage with bunting he'd left over from the last surfing festival. There was to be music from a local band, the lead singer of which lived in the flat above Brian's. They were on the up, apparently, and had just returned from a national tour of church halls and youth clubs.

'It's all coming together,' I said. 'But P. J., have you decided on the service packages?'

'Yes, I have,' he said, slipping me a piece of paper.

The first one was the Mini – a quick once-over, which was priced at twenty five euro, then there was the Hatchback, priced at fifty euro and the top range service was one hundred euro, which he had called the 4x4.

'I like it,' I said, scanning the list and all the other services. 'We need a biog, also,' I said. 'Biography. Everyone knows you, of course, but there's no harm in reminding them. Your story, who you are, you and Sheila, how long you've been in the trade, your favourite cars, what you can do. Experience, trustworthiness, quality, that kind of thing.'

'On it!' said Sheila. 'I'll email it through by close of business today.'

'Who's been to Alicante?' I said, pointing to a slightly faded postcard pinned in pride of place beside the till.

'Ah, Alicante,' P. J. said, shyly. 'I found that earlier when I was looking for something. In a pile of old receipts. A few happy memories there.'

'And?'

'Ah.' was all he said. He and Sheila looked at each other, exchanging a secret smile.

'Yes?'

'This was years ago, now,' said Sheila. 'You see, well… I wasn't sure if I wanted to be married anymore.' She looked at P. J. 'Did I Peej?'

He shook his head, looking down.

'So, me being a flighty type,' said Sheila. 'Well, I went off to Alicante with Brenda.'

'And I didn't know if she was ever coming back,' said P. J. 'I missed her something terrible I did.' His voice cracked. He was looking at Sheila now, and it was though I wasn't in the same room. 'Something terrible.' He stopped to right his voice again. 'And then that postcard arrived.'

'You can read it if you like,' said Sheila. 'Our bump in the road. We all have them. Some people have more than one.' She unpinned the card and handed it to me.

'Coming home. Put the kettle on. Sheila.'

'We always had a cup of tea together in the evenings, you see,' said P. J. 'Still do. It's not the same drinking tea on your own.'

'You know something,' Sheila said, 'it was a wobble, it was, but the single best thing that ever happened to us. We made sure it never happened again. We made a pact, to walk every evening together, like in the old days, and we talk and talk about everything and anything.'

'And I promised myself that I would mind her like she deserved to be minded,' said P. J.

'You had something worth fighting for,' I said.

He nodded. 'We did,' he said. 'She's the light of my life.'

'And P. J. is mine. When he's not getting oil on the new Ikea sofa,' said Sheila. 'Or dismantling engines on the kitchen table.'

Then my phone rang. It was Nicole, in tears.

Chapter forty-three

'Kristof's moved in with Coco. For the baby's sake, he says.' Nicole's voice was breaking on the phone line. 'I've lost him. He says he'll be back once it's born.'

'I'm getting in my car now. I'll be as quick as I can.'

Harry would have to be looked after by Marietta. She could pick him up from crèche. He was being a little neglected these days, what with the open day, Ronan and the Seaside Players. Things would get easier, I promised myself. I would get better at balancing everything. But first I had to see Nicole.

She opened the door, her eyes red-rimmed, wearing one of Kristof's outsized Polski football shirts. I hugged her tightly and she cried in my arms. 'I thought it was going to be okay,' she said. 'I thought that we were managing it.'

'Come on, let's go in,' I said. I could see a few neighbours having a good stare.

'Coco called yesterday and asked him to come over. Said that the baby needed his father. I mean, its father.' She sat on the armchair, hugging her knees.

'That's remarkably conventional.'

'He asked me if it was alright, like, did I mind. And I said no, being magnanimous, doing what I thought was right. You know, going to that scan was so stupid.'

'Tell me about it.'

'No, *really* stupid.'

'Tell me about it!' I almost laughed.

'I'm sorry Jo, for making you go through that… I wasn't thinking.'

'It's okay, really. I understand.'

'Oh God.' Her head sank to her knees again. 'You know something, Jo?' she said. 'I'm starting to like convention. Boring is going to be my thing from now on.'

'Mine too,' I agreed. 'But, it has to be said, there's unconventional and there's unconventional. And this is on the unconventional end of unconventional.'

'So, he goes and he calls me at about 9 p.m. and says he's staying over, so of course, I say yes, by all means, being nice and amazing, like it says in *Bad, Mad and Dangerous to Know, How to Keep a Complicated Male.*'

'I'll put it on my Christmas list.'

'Jo, *please*. It's not helping.'

'Sorry.'

'It's okay. I get it. I'm the one who's mad, anyway.'

'He's bad.'

'And Coco's dangerous to know.' We smiled at each other. 'So he calls again the next morning and says he's moving in with her. For a little while. Until the baby comes. So I ask why and he says he needs to do the right thing and *this* is the right thing, and I say since when has he ever done the right thing and he tells me not to start and why am I not being cool about everything, when we had agreed that I would be cool, and I say that I never tried to be cool, but I was just trying to write a script to a play I never asked to be in. And then he said there's a baby on the way and that is the most important thing and I say I know, but none of this is my fault and he tells me to stop being difficult and that he has to – *he has to* – focus on Coco and the baby and he'd call me soon.'

'Jesus Christ.'

'Oh yes!' she said. 'I knew I'd forgotten something. He says it's his *moral duty* to be there.'

'What the…? *Moral*?'

'So, I've finally seen sense and am going to bin the books. All of them. I think I may have around twenty seven of them now. I really don't want them to fall into another woman's hands because they are full of the worst advice ever. Of all the millions of words I have read in them recently, not one told me that I should leave him and that he wasn't worth it and that it was all playing havoc with my self-esteem.' She stopped. 'I went to school this morning. A class full of eight year olds. Puts things into perspective. Children, being nice and normal and then there's adults behaving abominably.'

'This might be a good thing—' I began.

'We went through two miscarriages together,' she said, while I took her hand. It was the reason why they decided not to try again, but the two of them seemed to have come through that. 'I told him how scared I was about getting pregnant again, the thought of going through that another time was too much. He knew it, he saw me every day having to get on with things. I thought he understood, I thought he cared about me. And I thought we had got to a point where it was just to be the two of us. Other couples do it, make the best of it, and are just as happy.'

I made Nicole some tea and we sat down together at the kitchen table.

'He loves her.' Her voice was flat, deflated. 'I thought he loved *me*. I thought he loved me more than anything and that was the thing that got me through, that helped me rationalise everything and accept it. But he says he loves her.'

'What did he say about you?'

'He loves us both. He still loves me like crazy, he said, but he has strong feelings for Coco and the baby, too.' She placed two hands flat on the table, her fingers spanning out, as

241

though she was trying to allow the strength from the oak rise up into her body. I could see her fingers turning from pink to white before me. 'I can't fight a baby,' she said. 'I can't compete with *that*.' She sighed. 'And I have been so nice, so loving. Biting my tongue about so many things, never complaining about all the cleaning, all the washing, taking out the bins. But it's made not one discernible difference. Coco was always like a spectre. Hovering around.'

'It sounds like this whole thing is one big performance piece for her. I wonder if that's what it is, 'Ménage A Trois' or whatever.'

Nicole suddenly had fire in her eyes. 'If it is, I will bloody kill her. I will! Oh Jo, you don't think it is, do you?'

'I really wouldn't be bloody surprised, Nic, I really wouldn't.'

'You know, I should take her on at her own game. Do my own performance piece. I've got an idea for my own show. It's a bit crazy but just the thought of it is making me ever so slightly happy.'

'What is it?'

'You know my self-help book collection? Oh, I don't know, maybe it's stupid. Anyway I have this idea—'

'You know, Nic,' I interrupted, 'that you're going to be alright, don't you?'

'Am I?'

'I'm convinced of it. Like you were for me.'

'I was and I was right.' She smiled.

The attraction of Coco for Kristof and Kristof for Coco would wear pretty thin, I knew, when sleep deprivation kicked in and they began to argue about such prosaic things as who was going to get up to feed the baby. And Kristof was a man who loved his sleep and always, always, ensured he got his eight hours. It would be something of a shock for both of them.

'So she's won,' she said. 'This is how it ends.'

'He's no prize, Nic,' I ventured, gently.

'He was,' she said. 'He was. I thought he was the greatest prize any woman had ever bagged. I couldn't quite believe my luck. Me, a primary school teacher of average looks, being swept off my feet by this exciting art dealer. It was quite the adventure.' She looked at me. 'I'd still take him back,' she said. 'In a heartbeat. If he was to walk in now and say he was staying, I would be so pleased. Relieved, actually.'

'Nic—'

'But it's not going to happen,' she said. 'I am going to focus on staying strong.'

'Exactly.'

'It's not going to be easy.'

'No, of course not.'

'But then nothing worth it ever is.'

My phone rang. 'It's Harry,' said Marietta, when I answered it. 'He's gone missing.'

Chapter forty-four

On the way to the playground, I tried to keep focussed. Harry was fine, I reasoned. By the time I got there, all would be well and he would have been found, safe and sound and ready for extra ice cream after dinner.

I pulled up and saw the gold Porsche. Standing beyond it was Marietta. 'Mam!' I yelled, breaking into a run. 'Where's Harry?'

'I told you,' she said, looking stricken. 'He's gone. We've searched and searched everywhere, all over the hill, and we can't find him anywhere!'

'What happened? Where were you? How could you let him out of your sight?'

'I don't know!' And it was a different Marietta I saw in front of me, someone who was on the verge of hysterics. 'Patrick and I… we were sitting in the car, talking, and we could see Harry in the playground and then… suddenly we couldn't. I ran into the playground and I was shouting and shouting but no sign… and then we started looking all over, asking people, calling… and that's when I phoned you.'

'Mam!' I said. 'This isn't the 1970s. You have to *mind* kids these days. Not lock them in a car with a bag of crisps or let them loose in a park while you are miles away! Jesus Christ!'

'There's no need to lose your temper, Joanna,' she said. 'Our focus has to be finding him. He can't have gone far. '

'But what if someone has taken him?' My voice quavered. 'You know, *stolen* Harry?'

'Nonsense, Jo,' she said. 'Who would steal a child?'

I gave her a withering look. Didn't she read the papers?

'We need to search the hill. We need to call the police,' I said. 'Where's Patrick?'

'He went up towards the café, thinking he might have gone up there.'

Right, I was thinking. Call the police. Call John. Start searching. I looked up at the sky. It was now after five. Not yet dark, so lots of time to find him. I thought of Harry, all alone. He was such a sweet, loving little boy. He loved hugs and holding my hand and being kissed. He would make towers out of bricks endlessly, he loved drawing and scribbling and baths and being wrapped in a big towel. Oh, Harry!

I dialled John's number. My phone was dangerously low on battery.

'John?'

'Yes?'

'Harry's gone missing. For over an hour now. We're at Killiney Hill playground.' I could feel a cry work its way up from my stomach, and settle in my throat.

'I'll be there as soon as I can.'

'Please John.' I needed him. He understood, he knew. He knew exactly.

'Any luck?' Marietta called hopefully as Patrick appeared, walking back towards us.

'Not a sign!' he said. 'I went all the way to the café and asked everyone, but nothing. No one has seen the little fella'

I dialled 999 straight away.

'There's a missing three-year-old,' I said. My phone beeped to signal the dying battery. 'He's small and was wearing cord trousers. Red ones. He's blond. Blue eyes. Likes dinosaurs. Can't walk very far. He's small, you see. I've said that. Anyway, we're in the park – Killiney Hill playground – and he's been gone for over an hour.'

Luckily the woman on the phone was able to decipher what I was saying.

'Right,' I said, once I'd hung up. 'Marietta, you stay here just in case he comes back. Patrick, you go up that path and I'll take this one.' My voice was shrill.

'I've got a better idea,' he said, smoothly. 'What we should all do is calm down. That's what.' And he made calming motions with his hands. 'You stay here, it can't be easy for a Mammy to lose one of her children, amn't I right? You're in no fit state to go looking. We'll wait for the Guards and they'll sort it out.'

Ignoring him, I headed up the hill, towards the wooded area, calling and calling Harry's name, looking behind the granite rocks, around trees, looking at the ground for hints and clues that a small child might have been there. What did he like? What would have attracted his attention? Flowers, a squirrel? A stick? God, Harry loved sticks.

Just as I looked at my phone, the screen faded to black. Dead. I had meant to charge it at home but had rushed out before I'd had a chance to. I ran back down the hill, praying, hoping – barely breathing – that Harry was alright, that he had been found. And there was John, talking urgently to Marietta. As soon as he saw me the two of us locked eyes and, in a moment, I found myself tightly wrapped in his arms. He whispered in my ear that everything was going to be alright and that we'd find him.

'I haven't been a good enough mum to Harry… not with everything that's happened,' I said. 'He deserves so much more than me… I've let him down.' Tears were coming now. We had to find him. My Harry. Our Harry.

'Shhh, that's not true,' he admonished. 'You've been the best mother to Harry. Don't worry. He hasn't gone far.' But the colour had drained out of him. 'We'll find Harry,' he said firmly. I wondered who he was trying to convince more, him or me.

'What if… what if he went off with someone?'

'Let's wait for the Guards,' John said, jaw clenched. 'It's going to be fine, I promise.'

But Harry was a tiny boy and the world was a vast place.

'Let's go through this again, Marietta. You were sitting in the car… and you thought you could see him…'

'Yes!' she said, 'but it was only a moment. You see, I looked at my watch, my *new* watch, and it was only half-past… and I thought we had loads of time and everything so I didn't think to worry. But it had stopped…' She looked confused. 'And I only looked away for a moment…'

I saw Patrick step in. 'Don't upset yourself, Mar,' he said. 'I'm sure this fella knows the difference between an accident and pure negligence. That watch had nothing to do with it. Kids run away all the time. And, anyway, that watch is grand. Swiss engineering. Best in the world. It's all just an accident. Could've happened to anyone.'

'Yes, of course,' John said. 'We weren't for a moment suggesting that it was Marietta's fault. Anyway, look, the Guards are coming.'

'I'll just get something from the car,' said Patrick, quickly. 'I think I may have left my wallet there.'

We watched as the patrol car began climbing up the hill, John and I still clutching hands, my heart pounding in my chest. But then I heard a sound. A tune. 'Popeye the Sailor Man' was coming from somewhere at the bottom of the hill. And then getting louder and louder. FroRo! Now I could see the van. Ronan himself was honking the born and waving and there on the seat beside him was Harry. I'm Popeye the Sailor Man! I live in a caravan! Toot! Toot!

And I began waving and waving back, so hard that it felt like my arms were about to fly off and my heart was about to burst out of my chest. There was Harry, my beautiful Harry, on the front seat, waving and waving his tiny hands. And I burst into tears.

'Harry!' I screamed as the van got closer and closer.

Ronan pulled up. 'Evening all!' he called, 'Look who I found!' I ran towards Harry, yanking open the door and pulling him out.

'Dog… chasing a dog!' said Harry, looking delighted with his adventure. 'Me and Oscar were running and we saw a dog and Oscar told me to follow him. I always do what my brudder says. We always play together.'

'Harry! You should know to stay with Granny.'

'I looked around for you, Jo,' said Ronan, 'and tried your phone, but it was switched off. But then Harry said he'd been in the park…'

'Oh Ronan,' I said, 'thank you. You're a life-saver. Again,' I hugged him, fully aware of John bristling proprietarily beside me. But I had Harry back and that was all that mattered.

'I'm going to have to give this little fella an ice cream, aren't I?' said Ronan. 'Here we are, Harry, I'll get you your usual, okay?'

I looked over at John and Marietta who were explaining everything to the Guards. John's face, I could see, was tear-streaked too, Marietta was shaking and John had his arm around her. Patrick was nowhere to be seen.

After the Guards left, John ran over and scooped Harry up into a lift normally reserved for *Strictly Come Dancing*. He flung him up high into the air and then hugged him close and kissed him hard. He looked up at us. 'My God… I don't believe it.' He held his hand out to Ronan.

'Thank you so much,' he said, giving Ronan's hand a good, firm shake. 'Thank you for bringing him back to us.' He looked exhausted but he was grinning, his old smile was on his face. He looked happy. 'We are not going to lose you again, Harry,' he laughed. 'Stay with a grown-up, okay?'

'But Oscar keeps me safe. He's my lucky brudder.'

'Well, he did… I suppose.' John looked at me, one eyebrow raised, as if to say, is this a good idea? I shrugged. I had no idea, I was doing my very best and all I could do was hope that one day Harry wouldn't have to endure a very expensive therapy session.

'But,' I insisted to Harry, 'you still need a grown-up, even if you have a lucky brother.'

John and I looked at each other and almost laughed, out of relief and love for this little boy.

'Ronan,' I said, turning to him, 'thank you again.'

'It's okay,' he said. 'Just right place, right time.'

And before we knew it, everyone was licking ice creams, Harry, John, me, even Marietta. Patrick reappeared and had a large one, with *two* flakes, calling it a 199.

'198' suggested John.

'Whatever,' said Patrick, licking his ice cream, not unlike, I imagined, a donkey at the seaside would.

'Sorry Mam,' I said. 'For shouting at you.'

'But it was all my fault,' she said. 'It happened in a moment.'

'You need a whiskey,' said Patrick. 'For the shock.'

She nodded. 'Yes, it might help.'

'We'll go to the golf club for some dinner,' said Patrick. 'Steak and spuds. And whiskey.' He turned to John. 'I'm Red Breast man. Some men,' he said seriously, '*water* their whiskey but I wouldn't call them *men*. Ha!' And he slapped John on the back. 'Ninnies and quares!'

We ignored this political incorrectness for Marietta's sake but John managed to pull a face at me while I remained unmoved and composed. The last thing we needed after our scare was a diplomatic incident and if Marietta liked this unreconstructed male, then we would have to too. As much as possible, anyway.

He and Marietta got into the car. 'Be seein' ya!' said Patrick with a wink from the window as the love birds drove away.

'Be seein' ya!' shouted back John, Harry on his shoulders. He turned to me and we laughed again. It was almost like old times. Except there was Ronan was hovering just beyond, beside his van.

'I'll put Harry in the car,' said John.

'Okay, great.' I walked up to Ronan. He smiled at me.

'Alright?'

I nodded. 'Fine,' I said. 'Thanks to you.' He shrugged modestly. 'You seem to make a habit of this,' I said. 'I'm starting to think you might be my guardian angel.'

'Well, I've got a feeling you might be mine,' he said, smiling. 'Will you be alright?'

'Yes of course,' I said, smiling back. 'You know me, psychologically robust.'

'You don't have to be, you know,' he said, seriously.

I do, though, I thought, I really do. It was so easy to slip into madness, life could have that effect. There was Nicole and how she had been turned demented by Kristof and Coco, there was Marietta and her blind passion for Patrick. And there was me, driven mad by losing Oscar. Sanity was something we were all in danger of losing from time to time. Staying on the right side of crazy was not easy.

'I'll go,' he said, nodding over at John and Harry. 'Leave you guys to it.'

'Thanks Ronan.'

'No bother,' he said, getting into the van and starting the engine. I waved him off down the hill again.

'That was good of him,' said John, who was buckling Harry into the back of my car. 'He seems like a good guy.'

'Yes he is. He's been great friend.'

'That's nice.' John couldn't get the buckle to work and when I looked closely, I could see his hand was trembling.

'Are you alright, John?'

He stood up. 'I think so,' he said. 'I'm wrestling with a few different emotions at the moment. But, generally, I am. More than I used to be, which is good.'

'I'm better than I used to be too,' I said.

'Good.' He stood up. 'That's good. Good that we're both… moving on.'

'I'm hoping for a break from all the drama,' I said. 'Some nice quiet, boring life. A convent, I was thinking. Somewhere dramas can't keep imposing themselves on you.'

John was looking at me as I was speaking. Finally, he took my hand. 'I'd do it all again, all of it, even losing Oscar… just to have Harry. I wouldn't want to change a thing. I would always want him exactly the way he is. Nothing, not a hair, not a freckle different.'

'But Oscar, what about Oscar?'

'It's our life, Jo. It happened. We can't wish we hadn't gone through it. We did and he was our son.'

I felt the tears well up again.

'He wasn't going to survive, Jo,' he went on. 'He wasn't going to live. We had our twenty four hours… I'm so, so grateful for that.'

I didn't speak for a moment. Was this how I felt as well? Would I want anything to be different if it meant Harry wasn't Harry?

'Me too… yes, me too,' I said, tears falling from my eyes.

'I wouldn't change a thing… well, apart from going back to work after a week. What was I thinking? I was in no state to go back and pretend to be normal. My world - *our* world - had just changed utterly and horribly and there was I in work listening to everyone chat about life when mine had stopped. But for too long I wished he hadn't died and I wished that my whole life was different. But he did and however sad that makes me, I realise that I have to own it… that to do Oscar's memory justice, I have to own the past.' He put his hand on the top of the car to steady himself. 'And in there is our other son, Harry. And we need to think about him.'

'I do! All the time.'

'I know, Jo. I know.' He swallowed. 'It's not been easy, has it?'

I shook my head.

'I went to the garden,' he said.

'The garden,' I repeated, trying to keep my voice and thoughts steady. He had never come to the Memory Circle. It was only every Harry and me. I was the one who planted flowers there, tidied it up and then sat there and cried. John had never come with me. Not once.

'Yeah, I just went and sat beside it.'

'Did it… did it help?'

'No,' he almost laughed. 'Nothing *helps*.'

'I know,' I said.

'The thing is Jo,' he said. 'It shouldn't be a problem, and that's what is so difficult. We didn't know him. We never knew him. It's not like someone we knew died. And that's what I find so hard.'

'But we held him John. We held him and kissed him and loved him.'

'Yes,' he said, and his eyes filled with tears. 'We loved him.'

*

'I'd better go,' I said. 'I'm in need of some diabetes-inducing substance. I think I have a bar of Lindt somewhere.'

He smiled and opened the car door and kissed Harry goodbye. 'Look after your mother, Harry,' he said. 'She loves you so much.' He stood back up again. 'See you Jo.'

'See you John.'

Driving away, I felt so sad, but this time my sadness seemed unburdened in some way. I wasn't dragged down by it, defeated, overwhelmed by it. I just felt so sad driving away from John.

Chapter forty-five

An invitation had arrived, on stiffened card.

The Gold Gallery presents

Nicole Kelly

'Self-help no more'

A performance and campaign for real books

Bring your copies of personal development books. Diet manuals also welcome

Sunday from 9am

Intrigued, I called Nicole. 'Can't talk now,' she said. 'But you are coming, aren't you? Bring your self-help books. I need thousands.'

'But what is it?'

'I'll explain everything when you come down.' She sounded excited. 'Just leave that there,' she said to someone in the background. 'Thank you! Sorry, Jo. I've got to go. The pulper's here.'

'Pulper? What's a…?'

'Everything will be revealed!' She rang off with a cackle that could only be described as manic. What on earth was going on?

Meanwhile, the Seaside Players were in rehearsal mode. The first night was only weeks away now. And, from my position on the stage, or at the wings watching, it wasn't too bad. Siobhan was convincing and professional. She more than made up for Robert's lacklustre performance. Piers Byrne was fabulous every time. His utterance of the "a handbag!" line never failed to make me laugh. He had just the right amount of preposterous snobbery about him. He wore a large stiff skirt and a hat over-burdened with fruit and flowers to rehearsal now, which he said helped to channel Lady Bracknell. Fergal was ablaze on stage; as we hastened towards opening night, he seemed to become edgier, like a flea on the back of an old dog, jumpier, more electric than before. Each rehearsal only brought him closer to his glittering inner self. It was the nerves, I thought, he must always be like that, someone for whom adrenaline is a life-force.

Me? I was nervous, increasingly so, learning my lines at night, walking around the kitchen on my own, going through my positions and my words. I thought I had it. Part of me was always buzzing with the idea of it, being on stage. And I was beginning to realise that my old self was still there. She had just hibernated for a while. Harry and I were going to be absolutely fine. But the old me wasn't the same old me, she was the *new* old me.

Chapter forty-five

The next morning, John was standing at the front door with a paper bag.

'Croissants,' he said. 'Almond ones. I just thought—'

'What?'

'I don't know, it's just that I couldn't sleep and I…' He stopped. 'Doesn't matter. I wanted to have breakfast with Harry… and you… if that would be alright? I know I don't have the right…'

'Come on in.'

He smiled shyly at me.

'As long as you have croissants you're always welcome.'

And in a moment, the three of us were sitting down together, like a family and John was telling us about the time when he was an altar boy, when he was 11, and what they used to get up to. They would put the cassocks on over their ordinary clothes, their jeans and runners poking out from beneath their robes. Once they slipped a sherbet rice paper sweet in with the communion wafers and watched as Father Byrne gave it to Mrs O'Neill, one of the holiest of the parishioners. John and his friend, Petey Mathews, watched her face as the sherbet kicked in. They almost died not laughing, but managed to hold it in until they were outside and running home, crying with the hilarity: the shock and then pleasure on Mrs O'Neill's face, as she looked heavenward, as though she had been given a gift from God, the true body of life.

'John!' Marietta appeared. She gave me a funny look and then kissed him hello. 'This looks very nice, I must say.'

'Croissant, Marietta?' said John.

'You know me all too well, John,' she said and sat herself down and reached for one. I noticed that her hands were shaking slightly.

'Everything alright, Mam?' I asked.

'Never better,' she said, breaking off the end of her croissant and popping it in her mouth. 'We do miss you buying these, don't we Joanna. We miss our Saturday morning breakfasts.'

'Do we?'

But we did, because that's what John always used to do. On Saturday mornings, he'd get up and, even though we weren't ever in a particularly good place, go and buy croissants for all of us. He always tried to do things that made us seem like a family. There'd be a bottle of wine on a Friday and a takeaway from the local Balti house. And we'd sit there, watching television, eating our curries. John tried to get us to at least take part in life. But I refused to leave the sidelines.

I reached for a second croissant and glanced at him. He always used to text me 'I love you' every day, without fail, texts that I would ignore, thinking that it was pointless and meaningless. We weren't a family anymore so it didn't matter if he loved me, because we didn't have Oscar. I was angry with John. And I refused to see how much he must have been suffering too.

The texts, the wine, the walks, all seemed pointless as though they were papering over something that was so raw. The Saturday croissants were emblematic of what I thought was John's inability to face the pain. Or, maybe, they were just croissants.

'Nice croissant, Jo?' he said, from across the table.

'Really lovely,' I said, wondering if I had made his suffering worse over the last three years, or if had he made mine worse, as we watched each other behaving so differently. 'Thanks John.' I looked at him, a half-smile on my face, memories of us as a couple, us as a team filtering back.

'You're welcome,' he said, half-smiling back, his eyes full of regret or sadness, or maybe it was relief that he had got away from me. I couldn't quite tell. I glanced at Marietta and saw she was staring into space.

'Have you ever thought about Florida?' she said.

'Not really,' I said. 'Have you?'

'Sometimes,' she said. 'It's has very nice weather. You can play golf all year round.'

'Handy,' I said.

'If you're into golf,' said John.

'Which I am,' she said, firmly. John and I exchanged looks. Something was going on.

'Mam—' I began.

'Jo,' she said, sharply. 'I was not born yesterday, you know? I know what I'm doing.'

'Of course… I didn't suggest otherwise.' She had me totally confused now.

'Are you thinking of going to Florida on holiday?'

'Perhaps,' she said. 'There's a lovely looking place called St Patrick's Condominium. I've got a few things to think about that's all.'

She stood up to leave and when I looked over at John and he looked back at me, his eyebrows lifted imperceptibly. Something was up.

*

Once I'd waved them off, Marietta was sitting at the table eating her croissant.

'Is everything okay?' I said. 'Mam?'

She looked away, the smile dropping from her face as fast as Newton's apple to the ground. Suddenly someone very different was standing in front of me, someone who looked like the legs had been kicked out from under her. Not the Marietta I knew. 'No,' she said. 'I haven't heard from him. For a few days now.'

And for the first time in my life, I realised that Marietta was not invincible. She was the woman who made me who I was today, my mentor, my mother made of iron, but she was, I saw so suddenly, fallible. And she was felled by love. Her hands were trembling a little when she put them to her face. 'He'll be back, Mam,' I said. 'I'm sure he will.'

She nodded but there was fear in her eyes. She fumbled in her bag for her phone and I saw her check it for messages and missed calls before slipping it back again. I saw, with sudden and certain clarity, that she had been through all this before and couldn't bear to go through it again. 'Is it something to do with Florida? The golfing holiday?'

She pressed her lips together and shook her head.

'Or whatever it is.'

'St Patrick's Condominium.'

'Right. That.'

'I think,' she said. 'I think I'm going to scream.'

'What? What did you say?'

'I said,' she didn't speak any louder, 'I said, I think I'm going to scream.'

'Scream?'

'Yes, scream.'

'As in shout very loudly and kind of crazily for a period of seconds?'

'Yes.'

'Why?' I felt lost. I didn't want to see her like this, in such pain and on the verge of losing it. 'What's going on? Please tell me.'

'I've only ever felt like this once before in my life, Joanna,' she said. 'When I was 16. I thought they were gone, those feelings. Once in a lifetime. Being young. I never in a million years thought that someone of my age could feel like this.'

'Like what?' She was acting like a character from a Bronte novel, all passion and feeling, not like Marietta at all. 'Mam?'

'Like I am losing my mind. Over a man. But I am, I'm losing my mind. And I haven't heard from him. I thought yesterday I was going to scream up at the sky, just let it out. The girls were there and I couldn't do it to them, of course. I'd lose my lady captainship for certain. They don't allow that kind of behaviour, quite rightly. But I was so close to howling at the moon. Howling. Braying at the moon.'

'Jesus Christ.'

'Indeed,' she said grimly. 'Jesus Christ.'

'So what did you do?'

'I managed to make it to the ninth hole and then said I wasn't feeling well. I went to the bar, on my own, and ordered a brandy and ginger and drank it in one, so quickly that no one noticed me having a drink in the middle of the morning. And I drove home.'

'Oh. My. God.'

'You're shocked, aren't you?' she said. 'I knew you would be. That's why I didn't tell you any of this. Of course you would disapprove. But this is how I feel, this is me. This is how I feel!' She shouted the last bit.

'I know, Mam, I know, I'm sorry. I don't disapprove. But I love you and I'm worried.'

She didn't say anything, just started fiddling with her gilet, zipping it up and down, up and down.

'Mam! Come on!'

She stopped and looked at me and there were tears in her eyes. She nodded. 'I'm mad about him, mad for him, I've been driven mad by him. And it's terrifying.'

'Wow.'

She shrugged. 'You never get over your first love.'

'That's what they say,' I said, trying desperately to remember mine.

'I thought I had, but it was impossible. It was like a fire was burning in the grate, the embers glowing all those years, and as soon as I saw him again, they burst into flames. I didn't know I still had it in me.'

Neither did I, I thought, but wisely remained schtum on the matter.

'And what about Dad?'

'He knew a little about Patrick. He knew that we had been friends and I think he guessed at some of it, but I never told him. Not really.'

'How old were you?'

'Sixteen. Sweet sixteen.' She smiled to herself, caught up in happy memories. 'Paddy, he was, Paddy Ryan. He only became Patrick Realta when he formed the Showband All-Stars. And he was a star, my star.'

'Go on.'

'We were in love all those years ago,' she said, lost in her thoughts. 'We were just children, looking back, but we felt so grown-up, like no one understood us, like it was only us who existed. The music, the dancing, the holding hands, the being together. It wasn't like the love we'd read about in the books the nuns allowed us to read. This was something else, this was something—'

'Carnal?'

'Passion,' she said. 'No one ever talked about passion. Well, only about Christ and all that that. But this was passion for a *man*. And he for me. It was so exciting. I hadn't been prepared for a world where this existed, I didn't know that you could feel such things, that life could be so joyous, so full.' Her face was lit with the memory, all the colour back in her cheeks.

'We drove all over Ireland, to shows,' she continued. 'I would pretend that I was on retreats. There were plenty of them in those days and everyone thought I was some Holy Josephine. But instead I would wait at the side of the stage and watch him. 'Be seein' ya' he'd say at the end and I'd put my arm through his to show all those other girls that he was mine. And we'd sit in car parks and laneways and...' She drifted away. 'We couldn't help ourselves. It seemed like the most natural thing in the world. But then I thought I was...' there were tears again in her eyes, 'carrying his child.'

'Oh my God...'

'But I wasn't at all. I had just hoped I was. When I was a few days late, I had begun thinking about it, imagining it, its little hands, mine and Paddy's little baby. Ours. Paddy Junior.' The tight look had returned to her face, lips taut, jaw clenched. 'It was just as well I wasn't,' she said. 'Because Patrick found some other girl. Celia. From Foxrock. Posh family. They had two cars *and* a driveway. Her mother had a fur coat. Celia was better than me in every way. Smitten he was, everyone said, and she was paraded around at every concert, round Dun Laoghaire, round everywhere. The Showband All-Stars were really big then, on *The Late Late Show* and everything. And then there was the big wedding, in all the papers, and I had to pretend that everything was all right with me, with Marietta O'Brien, who couldn't hold on to Paddy Ryan and was beaten by a better girl. I was left with nothing.'

'Oh, Mam.' I took her hand and squeezed it.

'They went to Paris on their honeymoon,' she said. 'Paris! Myself and your father had a weekend in Holyhead on the ferry. It rained the entire time.'

'Oh Mam. Why did you let Patrick back into your life again?'

'Because I had never got over him. And Celia died a long time ago. Cancer, poor woman. But as soon as I saw him again, I was sixteen and he was twenty five. Nothing had changed, nothing, and I felt the hole in my heart being mended, as though someone was holding a welding iron against it, sealing it shut. And he said he loved me and wanted to be with me again. And that he'd made a mistake and that he and Celia had never been happy.' She stopped. 'Do you know how much, for my whole life, I wanted to hear those words? That Patrick Realta, my Paddy, loved me and was sorry.'

'You poor, poor thing.'

She shrugged again. 'But the second time around, the heartbreak is worse, because I should have known better.'

I put my arms around her now and kissed the top of her head as though she was my child. 'I'm so sorry Mam,' I said. 'I'm so sorry.'

'What's done is done.'

'You never told me how you met up again?'

'At the golf club away day. We played Foxrock and he'd had been invited with business associates of his. As soon as I walked into the clubhouse, we saw each other.' She smiled. 'It doesn't go away, Joanna, feelings don't die just because you start getting old.'

Suddenly something struck me. 'St Patrick's Condominium. Is it Patrick's development?'

'Might be.'

'Is it?'

She nodded. 'Yes… but…'

'And it's legit is it?'

'Of course it's legitimate!' she said. 'What are you suggesting? That Patrick's a crook?'

'Of course not, it's just…' It's just that something's not right, I wanted to say, and I am worried for you and I don't know what to think. 'No, I'm sorry, Mam.'

'I'm going upstairs,' she said. 'Have a lie down. My head is throbbing.'

Phone her, you bastard, I willed, as she walked out of the kitchen. Phone her. I never realised one could feel heartbreak on behalf of your own mother. That was a new one on me.

Chapter forty-six

There was a queue snaking around the corner, from Talbot Street it disappeared into Mother Teresa Lane. And everywhere there were women, bags of books at their feet, all chanting.

'Real books! Real Books! We want real books, we want real books!'

I had managed to find a few copies of self-help books on my shelves. I had kept one or two, though, there were some which had been actually helpful to me, but the useless ones I had in my bag. And I'd found eight different diet books, all of which involved not eating anything nice and continuing like that for as long as possible; all promising the same thing: slimness is within your grasp, if you just stop eating.

Once the door was open, we surged forwards and there, in the middle of the white space, was Nicole, dressed in a denim boiler suit, calmly shredding books, page by page. Already, a great billowing cloud of shredded paperbacks grew beside the machine.

On the wall, there was an explanation:

> Nicole Kelly invites you to shred your self-help books. This is a response to the way women are encouraged to surrender their own power to so-called gurus. We have no need of them, because all our self-knowledge is within and all we have to do is listen.

The shredded books will be returned to the book manufacturing industry and will eventually become novels. Books to be read for fun, for escapism, for love, for erudition. But never for help.

Brought to you by Kristof Gold at the Gold Gallery.

The women were now coiled around Nicole in a spiral and one by one, they inched forward, ripping pages off their books and feeding them through the machine, Nicole helping them. When they moved on, cloth bags empty, there were cheers and little dances: impromptu pirouettes, twirls, high-fives. A chorus of 'We Shall Overcome' began, thin, wavery voices becoming stronger and stronger until the whole room and the street outside, echoed to the sound of women taking control of their lives. One of Kristof's gallery assistants was videoing it. It was being beamed on social media. The world was watching.

When it was my turn at the pulping machine, Nicole hugged me.

'I know,' she said, before I had a chance to say anything. 'I know.'

'Know what?'

'I've gone mad.'

I laughed. 'I wasn't going to say that, but what do Kristof and Coco think?'

'Coco was entirely encouraged that I have turned my life into performance art. She's got a new show called *Mother* that she's working on.'

'Of course she has.' We smiled at each other. 'Anyway, I've got my diet books and a copy of *So, You're On The Chubby Side! – How To Love Your Ampleness*.'

'Give them here.' She went to grab them off me but I held on.

'I'm not sure,' I said, laughing. 'I might give one or two of them another read. Look at this one, if you just eat a grapefruit for breakfast and then meat only for the rest of the day, you will lost a stone in a fortnight. I didn't do it properly last time.'

'Just drop the book,' she said. 'Come on. Drop it.'

I handed it over as Nicole ripped the covers off and fed them into the machine. 'And the others. Now.'

And soon they were gone, all of them, adding to the huge and wafting pile of shredding paper. And I too left feeling lighter, as though I was ready to float away. On my way past the queue I joined in with 'We Shall Overcome' and high-fived several women who were equally elated. Those books were a millstone around our necks. We just had to trust ourselves.

Outside, Kristof was standing there, smoking. He hugged me in that slightly overfamiliar way. 'Joanna,' he said, gazing right into my eyes in a way that I now found deeply creepy and unsettling, 'so glad you could come.' But he looked unnerved.

'Great show!' I said. 'Nicole's an artistic genius.'

'Yes… is she? I can't tell anymore.' He lowered his voice. 'To be honest Jo, I haven't a clue what's going on in there,' he admitted, 'but it seems to have touched a nerve.' He waved his hand at the women queuing around the block, still more of them joining, talking and laughing. It was a movement, a bandwagon and everyone wanted to get on it. 'This is the first time since I opened the gallery, that I have had queues – queues! – of people to get in.' He shook his head disbelievingly. 'Nicole is a performance artist.'

'She might even win the Constable Prize.'

He shrugged. 'I wouldn't be surprised,' he said. 'I wouldn't be fucking surprised.'

Chapter forty-seven

The Memory Circle was our special place, as it was for so many parents of children who had gone too soon. No headstones or cherubs or statues, but trees and flowers and a simple circle of benches.

It was lovely. Parents would sit on the benches and those who had absorbed their loss, those who were a long way into their journey, might chat away with other regulars, or those, like me, who were still in the foothills, would sit alone. Harry liked it, though, ducking in and out of the benches and swinging off the trees. No one seemed to mind and some of the other mothers would smile at him and me. We all knew why we were there and we all knew how much it hurt. You didn't have to talk to feel a comfort in being understood.

'Do you think Oscar would like your spider?' It was Sunday, our usual day for visiting and Harry and I were walking hand in hand towards the Circle. 'If he was alive?' I always managed not to show any emotion around Harry, just kept things breezy.

'Webby?' He looked at me curiously. 'Why? Are you going to give him to Oscar?'

'Of course not! I meant that if Oscar was able to play with you, he might have enjoyed playing with Webby. With you.'

Harry held Webby close to his chest.

'He would have to ask first, though, wouldn't he?' I said quickly.

Harry nodded. 'Yes. But Oscar isn't a real boy. Not like me. He's not real. Just inside.'

'He is real, sweetheart. He just can't be with us. He died, didn't he? Remember I told you? But we can still love him. He'll always be in our hearts.'

'Okay.' I didn't think he was really listening. He was too busy playing with Webby.

I pressed on, although I'd lost my audience. 'And I'm always, always going to love you, aren't I? And I'm so lucky because I can kiss you and hug you.'

'I am real, that's why, Mummy. I'm real and Oscar isn't.'

I squeezed his hand, and let the subject drop. 'You're my special boy. And Oscar is also my special boy. But I get to hold your hand.'

They would have been great friends, the two of them. Harry wasn't an only child, he was one half of twins. But however much I tried to help him understand, he was too young.

We found our usual bench and I sat down while Harry played his usual game of gravel raking. A little robin bounced alongside me, trying to get close, and I stayed as still as possible, fantasising that he would hop onto my hand.

'Hello!' A voice caused the robin to flee. 'Hello Harry!'

'Daddy!'

John scooped Harry up for a hug and gave me a wave.

'We're talking to Oscar, Daddy,' said Harry. 'He's not real but we pretend he is.'

'Oh really?' said John. 'Well, I've got a ball for you. It's one of those stretchy blobby things and is utterly disgusting. It's the one you were looking at last week. Here it is.' Harry took it with delight. 'I'm kind of jealous,' John said to him. 'I want one of those balls. Maybe I could get one for my birthday? What do you think?'

'Yes Daddy,' said Harry, wide-eyed with sincerity. 'I'll ask Grandad Jack to buy you one. And it will be a secret.' He put his finger to his lips.

'Oh Harry,' said John. 'I love you so much.' He kissed him on the side of his head and then carried him over to me.

'Hello,' he said, smiling.

'Hello,' I said, budging up to make room. 'How come you're here?'

'I knew you and Harry came on a Sunday afternoon and… well, I wanted to join you.' He paused. 'You don't mind, do you?'

Did I mind? I wished he'd started coming years ago, when we first were given the plot. I looked at him, this man I fell in love with so deeply all those years ago, when he was fresh-faced and optimistic; now slightly care-worn, grey around the temples, dark circles under his eyes.

'No,' I said. 'I don't mind at all. I'm glad you're here.' He took my hand then and squeezed it, warm, comforting, and so familiar. 'Thanks Jo,' he said, letting my hand free again. It felt almost lonely after that brief gesture of friendship, and love, long-lost love.

We sat there, the two of us, Harry playing away, the robin slowly returning, John and I saying very little, so as not to frighten her, but also maybe not to frighten each other. Something very powerful was hanging between us and neither of us knew quite what to do about it. It was as though we were in a space of peace, a place of acceptance.

My emotions began to surge, something I was used to because over the last three years, since losing Oscar, I often just had to wait for a moment to regain control, for the moment of grief to pass. But here on the bench, tears flooded my eyes, my loss – our loss – a very real and tangible presence in my chest.

I noticed John also wipe away a tear on his face. His brown eyes were filled with pain, sadness and grief. His jaw set, his mouth closed.

'John?'

It was me who took his hand this time. I held it in both of mine, hoping that I could comfort him. I felt that it was me who had the power to look after him, this time.

'I'm sorry Jo,' he said.

'It's okay,' I said. 'It's okay.' Harry had wandered over to a patch of daisies and had started picking them, making a tiny bouquet.

'But I did it all so wrong,' said John. 'I did it all so badly.'

'You didn't. I did.'

'No, I left, Jo. Just when you needed me, just when we should have been a team. I walked away…'

'I thought we'd get through it.'

'So did I…'

'But you can't take time out from a relationship, not really. Life doesn't stand still, it happens even when you don't want it to.'

'I wish I had known how you were feeling,' he said, suddenly. 'And I wish I had talked to you, that we'd got through it together instead of coping separately.'

'We both retreated.'

He nodded. 'A lesson in how not to deal with grief, I suppose.'

'Yes, but you don't start the process with a plan on how to deal with it. You're just thrown into it.'

John's smile was so full of sadness and so entirely different to the one which belonged to that carefree man on the cricket pitch in Trinity, all those years ago. A lifetime had passed through him – and me. Of course we weren't the same, of course we weren't that couple we once were. He was right to leave really.

'I'm sorry too John,' I said. 'I'm sorry we didn't work it out together.'

'We have Harry,' he said. 'We love Harry.'

Our little boy was now playing with the dream catchers and glass mobiles that someone had hung off a tree, above the grave of their child. He was trying to jump up and make them spin.

'Our beautiful boy,' I said.

John smiled at me. 'I've got to go. I promised Dad I'd pick him up from the garden centre. He can't walk too far these days. And then we said we'd watch *The World at War*.'

'Sounds nice.'

He shrugged. 'I've liked spending this time with him.'

'I've liked being with Marietta.'

'But I know where I'd rather be.'

The implication hung in the air but later when, after strapping Harry into the car, I turned to say goodbye to John, he grabbed me and held me so close and for so long it felt like three years of hugs wrapped up into one. We pulled apart but I could feel my body wanting to seep back into his, tuck myself in under his arm where I've always belonged. Could we ever get it back? I had missed him.

'Okay?' he said gently.

'John...' I had tears in my eyes.

'I know. See you Jo. Look after yourself. Promise me?'

I nodded. 'Promise.'

Chapter forty-eight

The day of the open day began with bright blue skies, and the garage had never looked finer. Bunting criss-crossed the forecourt, the whole place gleamed as much as a garage could gleam. The bouncy castle was lying deflated in one corner, ready to rise into life. Brian was setting up a tea stall and there were others too, including Brenda who was setting up her face paints and hair plaiting stall. The Irish dancing troupe were all in costume, ready to go, on their hardwood, moveable floor. The band were tuning up and checking the mic. One-two, one-two. Mr Balloon, the balloon man, was yet to appear but I was sure all would be ready by the time the journalist from *South Dublin Today* and the reporter from Harbour Radio turned up.

'Are you sure you won't come in?' I said to Marietta, who was dropping me off. Harry was in crèche for the day 'Say hello to Sheila?'

'Maybe I will for a moment. But I'm chairing the golf charity luncheon. I don't want to be late. Patrick's meeting me there.'

'Patrick?'

'He called!' She grinned at me, unable to hide her delight.

'So it's all back on?'

'All back on,' she said. 'Just a misunderstanding.'

'And you're okay about everything?'

'Totally. Everything's grand.'

'Good, that's great Mam.'

She smiled again. 'So, I can't stay long…'

'Come in for a bit, anyway.'

Sheila was outside already, shouting directions to a man up a ladder hanging more bunting. He turned and waved, showing us his Murph's Surf, Lahinch t-shirt. Ah, Paul Jr.

Sheila waved at us and came over and gave Marietta a hug. Paulie, Paul Jr's little lad, began running around the forecourt looking at everything. All he had to do was wait for the bouncy castle and he would be in heaven.

'Now, you're looking well,' Sheila said. 'But then again you always do. *Like* the jacket. Very nice.' She felt the cuff. '*Someone's* been splashing the cash.' And then she spotted the watch, diamond glinting, on Marietta's wrist. She took a closer look but said nothing. 'You look fabulous Mar.'

'As do you, Sheel,' said Marietta. 'The hair is eye-catching. I didn't realise that was the point of hair, to be eye-catching, but it's always nice to have one's preconceptions challenged.'

Sheila laughed. 'Oh, it's good to see you, Marietta. You're the same as always.'

Marietta smiled. 'You too,' she said. 'Pink hair and all. I don't think I'll swap my ash-blonde for pink tips. It's too visible for me.'

'I don't think Patrick would be so keen,' I said, joining in, nudging Marietta.

'Patrick?' said Sheila, ears prickling.

'Mam's new man,' I said, impetuously. 'Patrick Realta. Do you know him?' I felt Marietta's eye bore into me.

Sheila looked from me to Marietta and back again. 'Not… you don't mean… not… *Himself*?'

'Yes,' she said quietly. 'Himself. The very same.'

'Paddy Ryan… back from the dead.' Sheila wasn't smiling now. 'Well, I hope that particular leopard has changed his spots.' She stopped when she saw Marietta's face change, from blush to beetroot. 'Well,' said Sheila, quickly. 'I'm sure he has, after all, we have all grown up a bit, haven't we. It must be over forty years since I last saw him. He was on *The Late Late Show* a few years back. Ageing well, I thought. Face hadn't fallen in. Still a good head of hair on him.'

Marietta was now smiling, although it was a slightly tight-lipped one. 'We're all older and wiser, these days. And we're all allowed to forget our early misdemeanours, are we not?'

'Of course we are.' Sheila was in enthusiastic agreement. 'Do you remember the time he took all the money Father Brendan Duff raised for Africa from the sponsored hurling match and he went and bought a new suit with it?'

Marietta nodded briefly and tried to change the subject. 'So, the bunting looks—'

'Glittery it was,' Sheila explained to me. 'Sequins and everything. It rustled when he walked, like wearing a plastic bag.'

'He paid it all back,' insisted Marietta.

'With money from his own Mam's purse!' Sheila laughed. 'And what about the time he rigged up a big screen in the St Francis Xavier Hall and charged everyone to watch the Pope's visit? Everyone paid though because no one wanted to make a fuss that week. It was like God himself was in town.'

Marietta had stopped smiling. 'It was a long time ago, Sheila,' she said curtly. 'We were all of us young in those days. Don't I recall you drinking too much of that sherry and pulling up your skirt for when the five fifteen from Rosslare went past? Everyone saw your smalls that day. And, if I remember rightly, they were very small indeed.'

'Well, well,' said Sheila. 'I daresay we were all young and foolish. And isn't that one of the nicest things about getting old, not being so foolish. Well, how's he keeping?'

'He is keeping grand, so he is,' said Marietta, primly. 'I reminded him about you, but he couldn't remember you. I said you were the one with the nose, he recalled you right enough.'

'I've grown into it,' said Sheila. 'Now, Marietta, let's forget the old days and have a cup of tea before the day gets going.'

'I can't stay too long,' said Marietta. 'I've a golf charity luncheon. I don't want to be late.' And the two of them slipped into the office, both diplomatically ensuring the past was just a distant memory.

And then I heard 'Popeye the Sailor Man'. Ronan. The van pulled into the forecourt beside the bouncy castle, which was now inflating. He waved to me. But then, within minutes, the whole thing took off, the place flooded with locals, P. J. and Tommy in the garage checking under bonnets, refilling oil, and taking money, Ronan dishing out ice creams and the sound of the Irish dancers' feet, the smell of candyfloss and Tibetan tea cakes filling the air.

Chapter forty-nine

The day was a success. Most of the gang from The Seaside Players turned up. Fergal was on the bouncy castle, his long paisley scarf flying out behind him, George and Fred in long conversations with the mechanics. I saw George under the bonnet of a car. Piers wandered around eating a large FroRo ice cream.

By the time Decco turned up in his Jaguar, things were going well. He drove it straight to the workshop and asked P. J. and Tommy to take a look at it.

'Needs an oil change,' he said. 'And a new timing belt. Could you help?'

P. J. and Tommy got to work. Some of the lads from Fixup had come down on their lunchbreak and they all gathered around the car. Decco stood back and grinned at me. 'Should be about now. Ready for the big guest, Jo?'

'Did you manage it?' I said.

'I might have,' he said and winked.

And, on cue, was the sound of a roaring motorbike. A Harley Davidson swung around the corner and into the garage forecourt, past the bouncy castle, the ice cream van, past Brian, past the Irish dancers. And just in front of P. J., it stopped and the rider pulled off his helmet. There, shorter than I had imagined but wearing orange tinted glasses, was local resident and massive celebrity, Bono. Initially there was a shocked hush and then, in a moment a surge of excitement flooded the place. There were even a few screams. The band on the stage started up with 'Unforgettable Fire' and the party took off again, this time rocket-powered.

'Bike needs a bit of work,' Bono said to P. J., after hugging him as though they had known each other forever. 'Will you have a look at it?' There was almost a scuffle between the mechanics as to who would be the one that would have the honour of tinkering with Bono's Harley.

'I always like to keep business local,' Bono was saying to the scrum of fans and local journalists. 'And P. J. is the best mechanic around.'

And I stood there, thinking to myself, I like PR and I might just be good at it, too. Of course, it helps if you are able to reel in one of the biggest singers in the world. But I liked realising that I might have a talent for it. And to think I had forgotten. Maybe it was time to go back to work.

Later, Sheila came up to me and hugged me. 'Thank you, Jo,' she said.

'That's alright.' I was feeling good, satisfied even. I hadn't felt like this for over three years. Being a mother is a different kind of satisfaction. It's so tied up with everything, like love and fear and worry - and a million other different, incredibly powerful feelings - that satisfaction tends to get a bit lost. But with work, I recalled, it was an immediately recognisable emotion. 'I'm just relieved it went well.'

'Listen,' she said. 'I never spoke to you at the time because I didn't know what to say but I wish I had. I didn't want to make it worse for you. But I lost a child.'

Suddenly, all the noise of the day faded into the background and all I could hear was my heart. 'What do you mean?'

'The same thing happened to me. I don't know why she died… the doctor's didn't know. This was over 40 years ago, before Paul Jr was born. She would have been 43 in August, my daughter. 3 August.'

'Oh Sheila,' I said. 'How long… how long did you have her?'

'She died at only thirteen hours old. I held her, but from the moment she was born, it didn't look good. It was a horrible shock.'

'I know.' I laid my hand on her arm. She had tears in her eyes. 'It's the worst, isn't it?'

'"Laura". That's what I called her. Laura,' she said.

'What a beautiful name. I bet she was a beautiful baby too.'

'The loveliest.' She smiled at me. 'The loveliest thing you ever did see. Everyone just said it was just one of those things… it didn't help me because I wanted answers and reasons, just to make sense of it all. I always thought it might have helped. A real answer.'

'Oh Sheila…'

'That's why I left for Alicante. It was ten years on from it all and I still wasn't right. And I had reached the end. I just didn't want to be me anymore. I wanted to be someone else. And so I ran away.'

'To Alicante?'

'It sounds ridiculous, I know.'

'No, not ridiculous in the slightest. I know exactly what that feels like.'

'But I came back. I missed P. J. and Paul Jr and I knew I had to find a way of still being Laura's mam, to learn to live with it, not run away. When it happened to you, your mam told me, and I was going to say something. I wrote you a letter and then thought and thought and I just didn't send it. It was such a terrible thing to have happened and it is something that

I have never got over. I mean, I've got over the shock, I suppose. My little girl… you know? My little girl.'

'I would have liked to have heard from you Sheila,' I said.

She nodded. 'I should have sent the letter but I just didn't want to interfere… or I didn't know what you would have wanted.'

'It's lonely, isn't it, losing a child? The loneliest.'

'Poor P. J.,' she said. 'It hit him really hard. And he didn't feel he had any right to grieve for this little girl we didn't know. People barely spoke of it in those days. Everyone was embarrassed. You know, we went off to hospital and came home with an empty cot.'

'It's still like that now,' I said. 'No one knows what to say.'

'I wondered about you and your husband. Your mother said he'd gone back to live with his father. I wondered, was he finding it difficult?'

'Yeah, you could say that. I mean, we have Harry, so no empty cot. We knew we have to be grateful for Harry but we still miss Oscar so much.'

'Come here,' she said, wrapping me in her arms, her pink hair tickling my nose. 'Okay?'

'Yeah,' I said, wiping my eyes, once she'd let me go. 'Yeah, I'm okay.'

'Laura had the sweetest face. I have a photograph of her. Only one. I have it in a special frame. Laura on one side and Paul Jr on the other. He wasn't so sweet. Face like a potato.'

I laughed. 'Shhh. He'll hear you.' Paul Jr was talking to Ronan in front of the van.

'He's heard me say it enough times. Born with a spud face, but he turned out remarkably handsome. Takes after my side of the family.' She winked. 'But listen, life goes on. It's different, you're changed but it goes on.'

'So they say.'

She smiled at me. 'You're just different. Never the same again.'

'I'm still trying to work out who I am.' I smiled back. 'Thanks Sheila.'

P. J. came to join us, wiping his fingers with an oily rag.

'No, thank you.' Sheila said, as P. J. nodded enthusiastically beside her. 'For today.'

'There's no need,' I said. 'Really. Doing this has given me a few ideas,' I explained. 'It's helped me to get back into things again.' Could I set up my own company? Would I brave it alone? I was thinking, maybe, just maybe, I could.

'There is,' said Sheila. 'I don't know how we can ever repay you.'

'Oh, I have an idea,' said P. J., winking at Sheila. 'I'm working on something right now.'

'Please don't get me anything,' I insisted. 'You truly have done *me* a favour.'

'I hope that Patrick Realta has matured these days,' Sheila said changing the subject. 'He was a wild lad when we were young.'

'I think after forty years he's bound to have grown up a bit.' I was still laughing just as my phone rang.

'You take care, Joanna,' Sheila said. 'And if you need to talk. Ever. Come and see me.' She gave me a conspiratorial smile, one full of encouragement. We are never alone, really, however much we think we are. 'Promise?' she said.

'Thanks Sheila,' I said, as I pressed a button to take the call.

It was the police. Marietta had been arrested.

Chapter fifty

There's a first time in everyone's life when the Guards tell you your mother is in custody. Well, maybe just in mine, but Marietta being in the clink wasn't something I had ever, ever suspected might happen. My mother. Marietta Woulfe. Scion of the South County Dublin business world. Lady Captain of Kilbarton Golf Club. She was sixty two years of age, for feck's sake.

I almost dropped my phone.

'It's Sergeant Finbar Brennan, Pearse Street Garda Station,' the voice on the phone had said. 'We are informing you that your mother, Marietta Woulfe, is being held on suspicion of connection to investment fraud.'

'What? But she was chairing that luncheon thing!' I shrieked, unbecomingly. 'It was for charity!'

The guard ignored me. 'I am passing you now to Mrs Marietta Woulfe.'

Jesus Christ!

'Wait a minute,' I said. 'Could you—' But then there was my mother on the line, sounding very much unlike her usual confident self.

'Oh, Joanna.' She sounded shaky and about a hundred years old, utterly broken.

'Mam?'

There was a strangled noise from the other end of the phone.

'It's okay, Mam,' I tried to soothe. 'I'm coming straight away. We'll sort this out. The guard said investment fraud... what does he mean?'

And then she started crying. Something I had never heard before – even when Dad died, even when I came home without Oscar – and I never wanted to hear again.

'What is it? What have you done?'

'It's not me!' she sobbed. 'It's Patrick!'

'Patrick?'

'Patrick has... oh, Patrick has...' Marietta was gulping and choking for air, through her sobs. 'He's stolen everyone's money and it seems that St Patrick's Condominium was a fecking figment of his fecking imagination!'

'Jesus Christ Mam!' I said. 'I'm on my way.'

Driving in the bus lane, all the way into town, I phoned John on the hands-free.

'Mam,' I explained, 'she's been arrested.'

'What?'

'I don't know the details but I have to go. But it's Patrick. He's a crook. According to Mam, the thing in Florida doesn't exist. Are you okay to collect Harry from crèche?'

'Of course,' he said. 'Let me know any developments, okay? And take care Jo. Give Marietta a hug from me.'

It was 7 p.m. when I arrived at the police station and a guard was at the desk, feet up, dipping chocolate digestives into a mug of tea and doing a Sudoku.

'Marietta Woulfe,' I announced breathlessly, leaning on the desk from running half the length of Pease Street.

He barely raised his eyes or his pencil. 'Down the corridor,' he said, jerking his head.

'Okay. Thanks.' Never having been in a police station before, I was more than scared. What would be in there?

Terrible criminals being held until the morning? Violent drunks ready to attack innocent visitors? I felt like Clarice Starling walking down the corridor but then, slightly disappointingly, the place was very calm and quiet.

Another guard was carrying a tray with a mug of tea and just about to unlock a door with a comedy-sized bunch of keys.

'Hold this for a second,' he said, giving me the key.

'I'm here for Marietta Woulfe,' I said. 'I'm her daughter.'

'I was just bringing her a cuppa,' he said. 'She's in a terrible state, so she is.'

He opened the door and initially I didn't think anyone was in the room as it was quite dark and gloomy, but then I saw a tiny figure sitting on the edge of a bench, her head in her hands.

'Mam?' I said.

'Oh Joanna,' she said, bursting into tears again. 'Oh my God, Jesus, Mary and Joseph and all the Saints, this is truly terrible.' Marietta was not a religious woman and never had been, so this calling on God and the gang proved desperate measures were being reached for.

'Mam,' I said, 'what the hell is going on?'

'I'll leave you to it,' said the guard, setting down the tray. 'Now you listen to me Marietta, you are not to worry, will you promise me that?'

'Thank you Mick,' she said, trying to smile through her sobs, 'you're very good.'

'I put one of my own Club Milks there for ye and all,' said Mick. 'It's my evening treat. Sometimes it's the only thing that gets me to midnight, the thought of my tea break. But you have it tonight.' We were fully aware of his sacrifice. 'Eat that up and you'll feel a thousand times better. Works for me. And all this will be sorted out, I just know it.'

Marietta smiled wanly and he disappeared behind the door.

'Mam,' I said, trying to enunciate through the shock, 'why on earth have you been arrested?'

She tried to speak again but was convulsed by sobs. I had never seen her cry before. She was always so strong, my rock. And now she was crumbling. It was time for me to stand up for her.

I tried a different tack. 'Drink your tea and eat your biscuit,' I said, as though I was speaking to a child. 'And then you can tell me.' So I sat there impatiently while she drank her tea and ate the biscuit. Eventually, mug drained, wrapper scrunched and sobs subsided, she managed to speak.

'I didn't realise anything was wrong until the other day, when he disappeared,' she began. 'Everything had been wonderful... he said that he wanted to spend the rest of his life with me. He said he was going to propose and asked how I felt about moving to Florida with him and... well, I've always wanted to go...'

'Have you?'

'Yes,' she said, a touch frostily. '*Always*. Anyway, he said I could play golf while he looked after his business interests and it would be such an adventure. I just didn't realise that none of it was true.'

She began to cry again.

'Keep talking, Mam,' I ordered.

'Well, I'm trying to piece things together in my mind. And I think it started, this part of it anyway, started two months ago when Patrick asked me if he could use my bank account to store some money given to him for investments. He said everything was tied up with the banks in the US and this way the money could be funnelled into the development much more simply and quickly. He said his bank account already had the maximum amount of money in it.'

'Did that sound plausible to you?'

'At the time it did,' she said. 'I didn't question it. If he said it, I believed him. Why would he lie about such a thing?'

'Really?' I interrupted. 'That doesn't sound dodgy? What bank doesn't accept large deposits?'

'I know!' she wailed. 'I know now! But I believed it, I wanted to believe him.'

'So,' I urged, realising that putting the boot in wasn't going to get us anywhere. 'You had all that money in your account.'

'Well,' she said. 'It was my current account. Nearly €25,000 in that, you know. It was going to be my deposit on a little flat, once I moved out from yours. Or I'd invest it in Florida. Patrick told me that this was a win-win. He said it couldn't fail. In Fort Lauderdale it is, lovely scheme, ideal for retired folk like me, lots of Irish people buying there, he said. And I thought that I could make some money and give it to you and to Harry, you know?'

'Right...'

'So, last week, I saw a bank statement. There was over six hundred thousand euro in there... and I asked Patrick if that was right and he said there was nothing to worry about. Apparently there were real flamingos in the fountains at the development, that's what he said. And sunshine every day. And oranges of course, he said we could have orange juice for breakfast every morning.'

'You can have bloody orange juice for breakfast here as well, Mam!' I shouted, letting my emotions spill over. 'And there's flamingos in the zoo if you are into them that much. No sunshine though. He's got me on the bloody sunshine.'

She ignored me and went on with her story.

'So I thought everything was fine and all I had to do was to make a decision whether to invest myself or not. He said there was no pressure and I had all the time in the world. He said once we were in Florida I could play golf every day.'

'But what of your friends at the Kilbarton?' I said incredulously. 'You like playing with *them*.'

'I know I do,' she said. 'But I would only have been in St Patrick's Condominium for six months of the year, I would have still been here for the other half. I wasn't going to leave you and Harry and the rest of my life. Not properly.'

'Glad to hear it,' I mumbled.

'So, then, on Monday, Patrick disappeared.'

I nodded, lips pursed.

'So, I kept phoning him, his phone was dead. I called hospitals, Garda stations…' She shrugged at the irony. 'Everything I could think of. But it was during the charity lunch earlier that I thought I should just check the account. Make sure the money – the six hundred thousand euro – was still there. I don't know what made me do it, check it, I mean. But my heart actually stopped when I saw it was empty. I was in the middle of the luncheon. We were about to have the Baked Alaska.' She stopped. 'I've made quite fool of myself.'

She smoothed down her trousers and I could see her hands trembling.

'No, you haven't Mam,' I said. 'Don't say that. Anyone would have fallen for his… his charm, especially with all that history between you.' I took her hand and she let me hold it.

'Yes I have!' She looked shell-shocked. 'Six hundred thousand. And then my phone rang and it was the bank, asking about the withdrawal. I could hardly speak, I was so in shock myself. I didn't even think it was possible to take that much money out. All these years he knew I would do anything for him. And he does this to me. *This*. I handed over my money. And Fionnuala and Joan too. After Joan's Charlie passing like that, so suddenly, she wanted to be sensible with his pension. We all thought we were being sensible.'

'Oh, Mam.'

'So the man on the phone, ever so nice he was, asked me if I was still there. And he said that it might be better if this was investigated straight away. And all I said was yes. Yes it should. But I didn't want them to. I still didn't want them to. Because I didn't want Patrick to be investigated.' She tried to smile. 'I didn't want it to be true. It's funny, you know?'

'What is?'

'How you can keep fooling and fooling yourself, even if inside you know the truth. But I shouldn't have let that happen. I shouldn't have gone for all those dinners, the dancing... I shouldn't have done anything.'

'No, Mam... you weren't to know.'

'But I did know. I knew he was a bad egg all those years ago. I knew it. Sheila knew it. We all did. But I was in love. So in love. Still am.'

'I'm so sorry...'

'I was young then. But now? What do they say, there's no greater fool than an old fool.'

'You're not old,' I said. 'Or a fool,' I added quickly.

'I'm both,' she said.

'But why have *you* been arrested?'

'Because I held the money in my account. I am involved. I should have asked questions. I might...' she paused, clearing her throat bravely, 'go to jail.'

'Oh my God,' I said. 'But where is fucking Patrick?'

'Florida, I'm presuming,' she said. 'How could I have persuaded Joan and Fionnuala to invest? Fifteen thousand euro each. They were to get a time-share in one of the apartments. Four weeks in Florida for life. And they can't afford to lose that money.' She began to cry again.

'Oh, Mam,' I said, 'I'm sorry.'

'What's done is done. But what is clear, I can't show my face at the club ever again. I'll have to resign as lady captain, that is, if they haven't sacked me already. The shame,' she said, 'the shame is what I can't bear. He can have my money. He can ruin me, but the shame is something terrible. And Joan and Fionnuala. I have ruined them.'

'Oh Mam…'

'And another thing,' she said, almost angry now. 'He lied to me about being pals with Richard Branson. He's never met him! He told me that when he was drunk. Said he was trying to impress me. And I thought how sweet, him wanting to impress me. But I'll tell you something that impresses me: people who don't lie and don't cheat and don't steal money from my best friends.' And she began to sob so I put my arms around her and patted her on the shoulder. When the sobs subsided a little, I pulled away. There was someone I needed to call.

John answered on the first ring. 'I've been waiting and waiting… what's going on? How's Marietta?'

'Not good,' I admitted. 'She's what is known as a fallen woman.'

'What?'

'She's been done,' I said. 'And undone, which is entirely possible…'

'Jo,' he sighed. 'You're doing it again. The unnecessary drama. Just tell me what happened.'

And so I told him, the whole story, how Marietta had been arrested for aiding and abetting a criminal, and how she had no defence because she said he could put the money in her account.

'So, I'm going to see if I can get her out tonight,' I said. 'She can't stay here.'

'Well, I did a bit of digging around while you've been in there... there's a journo in Galway who's been on Patrick's case. Not enough evidence yet to publish anything but I had a chat with him anyway.

'Paddy *Ryan* has a reputation, you know,' he said. 'And, according to this journalist, he's done this before – many times – but he's managed to get away with it. In fact there are three separate claims of extortion and money laundering against him. But no one can prove it and the witnesses are reluctant to come forward.'

'But why hasn't he been caught? You know, being famous and everything?'

'He takes the wig off.'

'Wig?'

'Yes. It's a wig. He slips it off and he's not Patrick Realta anymore. He's just Paddy Ryan.'

'Oh my God.'

'He's still charming though. Women will still fall for him and that's who he...' he searched for the right word, '*preys* upon. Women, often widows, women who might have a small fortune hidden away, or a rainy day fund, or a couple of thousand they've been saving for a once-in-a-lifetime cruise, or money for the grandchildren, or to put on the horses, whatever. And, you know, he puts on the old Patrick Realta charm. He's known by various names: Fonzie Fitzgerald, Pip O'Hara, Horace Houlihan, John-Paul Pope... this journalist has managed to find complaints about all these different men, all of whom match the same description.'

'The little…' I started, words failing me. 'So, if we know he did it and others know he did it, what happens now?'

'The thing is, people are far more likely to believe the word of someone like Patrick Realta with his silvery tongue.'

'Please don't mention his tongue, I feel nauseous enough as it is,' I said.

'He took advantage of people feeling ashamed about believing him and giving him their life-savings. They don't *want* their families or communities to know and so he gets away with it… so far. Apparently too, he was always promising to pay them back, saying that the money was held up in different bank accounts. And some *were* paid back with money he stole from others. He was just keeping all these balls in the air.'

'And breaking hearts all over the country,' I said. 'What a creep. Listen, I'm going to try to spring Marietta…'

'There you go again,' he said. 'Speaking as if we are in some kind of cop show.' He chuckled, even though nothing at that moment was a laughing matter.

'But she's in the clink,' I said. 'She needs to be sprung.'

He laughed again.

'Anyway,' I said. 'I can't help it. It enlivens ordinary life.'

'You know what, Jo,' he said. 'You enliven ordinary life. You. All on your own.'

But I was too busy thinking about my next move to have time to analyse that particular enigmatica.

'Mick,' I said to the nice guard, after I had rung off from John, 'I really must get Marietta out. I don't think any justice will be served by keeping her in for the night. She is an old, frail woman, whose nerves would be irreparably damaged by a night in jail. Nice as it is, clean, something I was pleasantly surprised by, so congratulations there but…'

'She's already gone,' he said, thumbing in the direction of the main counter. 'She just has to report back here in the morning.'

At the main reception, there was Marietta helping the other guard finish his Sudoku.

'Well,' he was saying, 'I was only doing the 'simples' but you're a dab hand on the 'hards'.'

'Anytime, Anthony,' she said. 'And you say hello to your Dad, will you?' And then she saw me, 'What took you so long?' she said, back to her old self. 'Oh, Joanna, this is Anthony O'Callaghan, his father has a plumbing business and was always one of my best customers. I remember Anthony from when he was this high.' She held up a hand.

'Anto, please,' he insisted. 'You take care Mrs Woulfe,' he said, all smiles.

'Will do, Anto!' She waved as we walked out, before muttering under her breath, 'I bloody well intend to.'

'So, Mam, you must be exhausted. Let's get you home to bed. Maybe a mug of hot milk?'

But Marietta was never one for cosseting and she had spotted my car.

'Interesting parking, Joanna,' she said, 'Personally, I always park *parallel* to the curb. I think you'll find you're far less likely to have a wing mirror knocked off by a joyriding teenage tearaway.'

'Mam!' I hissed, suddenly furious. 'We're in a crisis here and all you can think about is my parking!'

'No,' she said stiffly. 'I hadn't forgotten and thank you Joanna for reminding me.'

It took us until Blackrock before we started speaking again.

Chapter fifty-one

The next morning I went downstairs to find Marietta up, dressed and done, and poring over my laptop.

'What are you doing?' I said.

'Googling,' she said, looking at the screen intently. She took a slurp of black coffee. She had a notebook beside her and was scribbling things down. There were sums, names, arrows pointing this way and that. 'Research,' she said. 'Investigation. This Joanna, is how I'm going to get through this. I can't sit round and feel sorry for myself. I did too much of that yesterday.'

'Mam, you were in custody. Anyone would feel sorry for themselves if they had been wrongfully arrested.' I put the kettle on and rooted around in the dishwasher for my cup.

'Your John has been on to me.'

'He's not *my* John…'

'Anyway, *John* has been on to me and has brought me up to speed on what… that man has been up to. And I am seeing what I can find myself.'

'John updated me last night,' I said. 'Apparently the Guards have investigated a scheme like this before. Patrick's name wasn't actually linked to it then. He's a conman… a conman with ridiculous hair.'

'Ridiculous?' Marietta looked up. 'I thought he had a fine head of hair.'

'Mam, he looked like the love-child of Liberace and the Queen.'

'He did, didn't he?' she admitted. 'What a fool I was.' She turned back to her laptop. 'Bingo!' she said. 'Look what I've just found.' She turned the screen around and there was a small article from the *Galway Advertiser* about a woman who had lost her life-savings. 'Look, she mentions that the man was "very persuasive. He made it seem so real and he kept promising that I would get every penny back". She goes on to say, "he was very handsome with a good set of teeth". That's Patrick, wouldn't you say?' She looked at me, trying to appear pleased, but I could see her eyes weren't feeling it. I was starting to wish I hadn't made that crack about his hair. I wasn't going to laugh her out of this one.

'I couldn't be sure. Handsome?'

'And look here,' she said, a small tear in her eye, but she managed to keep her voice as steady as possible. 'Here, in the *Mayo People*, a woman, who wanted totally anonymity, gave thirty thousand euro to someone who said there was a construction scheme in Florida. Florida! "He," she says, "told me that I'd treble the money. That I couldn't lose. Except I feel that I have lost everything. He reminded me of a singer I once used to go and see when I was young. He reminded me of my past but I now have no future. I'm just so ashamed and I am terrified that my children will discover how silly I've been." The poor woman,' said Marietta. 'I've been silly too.'

'No you haven't Mam. None of you were. We all do foolish things for love. It means that your heart is open. That's a good thing.'

'Is it?' she asked, unconvinced. 'Patrick relied on people being so embarrassed and ashamed that they don't say anything. No one wants their family to know that they were… vulnerable… lonely…' She stopped, her voice faltering, as reality set in once more.

'Oh, Mam.'

'No,' she said, firmly, sounding stronger. 'No. We are not to blame. There is no shame in this. All of us can be taken in.'

'Especially by someone like Patrick Realta,' I said. 'He's quite…' I searched for the right word. 'Persuasive,' I said, just as Marietta said: 'Magnetic.'

'Anyway,' she said. '*I'm* not important right now. I need to make two very difficult phone calls. To Fionnuala and Joan. They've probably heard already on the Kilbarton grapevine.'

The doorbell went. John and Harry. John hugged Marietta while I hugged Harry. And then Marietta led Harry into the kitchen while John pulled on my sleeve to keep me in the hall.

'How're you doing?' he said. 'Bearing up?'

I nodded.

'How's your mother?'

'Being amazing, as always.'

He looked at me. 'Like mother like daughter.'

'What do you mean?'

'Don't make me spell it out…'

'Spell what out?'

'That I, that there's only been—'

'John!' Marietta called from the kitchen. 'Come on in and tell us everything.'

'…You,' finished John. 'Only ever you.' We stood there for a moment looking at each other. 'I miss you Jo,' he said.

'Come on John!' Marietta called again and he turned and I followed him into the kitchen.

'I've got some news from my source in the Gardaí,' he said. 'They've got him. Caught buying a burger meal in Supermacs just outside Dundalk, in the early hours. On his way to Belfast, he was, to catch the first flight to Florida. This was his last big scheme. He was leaving Ireland for good. He'd never have been extradited. He was practically scot-free.'

'Has he admitted anything?' I said, Harry safe in my arms. 'Will everyone get their money back?'

'All his assets have been frozen. As he must have been at 3am. Dressed only in an Ireland soccer top and shorts.'

'Patrick would never be seen dead in such clothes,' said Marietta looking horrified.

'Disguise,' explained John. 'Ditched the wig and the Louis Copeland suit and dressed himself in 100 per cent polyester, bought at midnight from Carrolls on his way out of town. Nearly worked too. Except his perma-tan gave him away. Some guard had nipped in to have a mid-patrol strawberry milkshake, gave him a second look and recognised him, straight off. Said his Mam was crazy about him in the seventies and had a signed photo of him stuck on the kitchen dresser. Said he would have recognised those horse teeth anywhere. They had the flashing blue lights there before you could say fast food.'

'And what about Mam? Is she still implicated?'

'No, there's going to be no charges. They've managed to collate the evidence pretty quickly.'

'But is he okay?' said Marietta. 'They didn't hurt him, did they?'

'No,' said John, shortly. 'He's absolutely fine. Just his freedom and bank account have been curbed. And his wig didn't make it with him. Had to surrender that, along with his belt.'

'Mam,' I said. 'You shouldn't be worrying about him. He's a crook, a conman. He took advantage of you and goodness knows how many other women.'

'I know.' She sighed deeply. 'It's just feelings can't be turned off like a tap. You should know that, Joanna.'

I didn't mean to but I glanced at John when she said that. And he caught me looking. I quickly made myself busy by making tea for everyone and getting breakfast for Harry.

'Will you be alright, Mam?' I said.

'I'll be fine,' she said, 'just going to call Fionnuala and Joan now.' She took a deep breath, straightened her cardigan. 'I can't believe he would do this to me.'

'You weren't to know, Mam,' I said.

'I did know. I knew he was a bad one, all those years ago, but I wouldn't let myself believe it. Fool me once, shame on you. Fool me twice. Shame on me.'

She was a shell of the former Marietta. Gone was her jubilant jauntiness, brought down to earth by Patrick Realta, Showband star and now my nemesis. I would have loved to get my hands on him. She took her watch off, the one he'd given her. 'This'll have to go back,' she said, putting it on the table. 'The fraud squad will be trying to recover what they can.'

'Mam—' I wasn't sure how to broach this. 'I don't think it's real. The diamonds. The gold. I hate to say this. It's R-o-l-e-x. No double-l. I'm almost sure of it.'

She looked at the watch then, the weight of Patrick's shoddiness sinking in, entrenching ever further, and slid it off her small wrist. She went over to the bin under the sink, put her foot on the pedal, dangled the watch above it and let it fall. Clunk. It lay amongst the old tea bags and uneaten pasta.

Chapter fifty-two

After collecting Harry from the crèche, we were now both making Lego constructions on the rug in the sitting room.

'This acting is taking up too much of my time,' I said to him. 'It's only a week more and then I'll be back home, for good. I don't think my future lies on the stage.'

Harry held up his creation for me to admire.

'That's amazing, Harry,' I said. 'But, listen, what if I was to work from home? My own company. PR. I'm thinking of calling it Wilde Woulfe PR. I thought I could make myself a little office. You could still go to Crèche, but it would be nice, wouldn't it? You'd like that, wouldn't you Harry?'

The name Wilde Woulfe PR appealed to me because of Oscar – *my* Oscar – not just the playwright. My Oscar would be a part of it, too. And that, I realised was so important. As Harry and I moved on with our lives, we had to find ways of bringing Oscar with us. Just in subtle ways, that no one else needed to know about.

'I love you Harry,' I said, kissing him now. 'I love you and I am so glad you are here. We're going to be okay, you know that? You and me, we're going to be just fine.'

I had been feeling guilty all this time, guilty for loving Harry. From now on I was just going to love him with all my heart, set my love free. And I could love Oscar too, not just mourn and grieve him but I could love him, outwardly, proudly. That scan picture of the two of them was going on the mantelpiece where anyone could see it.

Marietta appeared at the door, John hovering behind her. 'We're back,' she said.

'So what happened?' I said. 'What's going on?'

'We went to see Patrick,' Marietta said. 'In Bridewell Garda Station. He's been arrested. *Properly* arrested. Unlike me who was *detained* for a short period of time.'

'Jesus Christ!' I spluttered. 'How on earth did you get them to let you see him?'

'I have a few friends in the guards, you know. Francie Phelan's daughter is chief superintendent. When we explained the situation, she said she was more than happy to bend a few rules.'

'But what did you want from him?'

'Bank account details. All of them,' said John. 'The money, basically.'

'And did you get them?'

'Oh yes,' he said laughing. 'Your mother has ways of making men talk.'

'Mam! For God's sake. What did you say to him?'

'Oh, I just told him that I knew about his other dodgy deals…'

'What dodgy deals?'

'I don't know,' she admitted. 'But I just assumed he had others. And on our way out, we passed on everything we learned to Suzanne Phelan.'

'The chief superintendent' John reminded me.

'And your money?'

'Everything's been seized at the moment, but the Guards are hopeful that I'll get it back. And Fionnuala and Joan.' She closed her eyes. 'He's been getting away with it for years. Well, not any longer. I've spoken to Fionnuala and Joan who say they don't blame me. Just him. They say they made the decision and that they won't let money come between us.' She began to cry again. 'I'm so lucky,' she said. 'I've got some good friends.'

The doorbell rang. 'I'll get it,' said John. 'Marietta,' he said. 'You've been amazing. So strong.'

As soon as John had gone, Marietta's face crumpled and she let out a cry of anguish. 'I loved him,' she said. 'I loved that man. All my life I have loved him and this is what he does to me. This is what he does to a woman who has done nothing but love him. I asked him, Joanna,' she said. 'I asked him did he ever love me…'

'Oh, Mam, you shouldn't have…' I had my arm around her.

'And… and…' she sobbed. 'He shook his head. He said he loved me the first time round but this time not so much.' She was crying openly now. 'But I loved *him*,' she said, eyes wide, face streaked with tears. 'And now I am so humiliated, so embarrassed and so hurt. And yet I have to get on with everything again. And I don't know how.'

'You take it one step at a time,' I said. 'That's what you do. I can help you. I'm here.'

'But I'm old, Joanna,' she said. 'I'm old and it's like he has stamped on me and ground me into the pavement. I don't think I have time to ever recover properly.'

'Mam,' I said, sharply. 'You are not old. You are 62. In your prime. Now, come on. You are going to put one foot in front of the other and get your game face on, everything's going to be alright. Let's have a cup of tea before we all go mad.'

'You know what he said, Joanna?' she said, following me into the kitchen. You know what he said when I stood up to leave?'

I shook my head.

'He said, "be seein' ya!"' Her voice was quiet and quavery. 'And he winked at me!' There were tears in her eyes.

'He's abominable. Monstrous.' I began filling up the kettle just to keep my hands steady. 'Will you be alright, Mam?'

She nodded. 'Yes, I will. I should have known this was going to happen. I knew he was a bad 'un all those years ago. Sheila knew it, too. I should have let him go but sometimes the truth is not what you want to hear. Sometimes you shut off your intuition. Chickens come home to roost. My fault. I knew it about him but I just refused to listen.'

She went to leave the room but stopped at the door. 'He's a crook and a liar, I know that, but I wanted to believe him. I chose to believe him because I had fun with him, the most fun I've ever had. Now, I'm going to have a lie down before the play tonight. I can feel a headache coming on.'

'For you,' John said, coming into the kitchen and handing me a box. 'From that *Ronan* person.'

'You mean the man who rescued our son?'

Inside was a stone, a beautiful, smooth pebble, dark with white marble rippling through.

I read the card:

> From Silver Strand, Wexford
> 'We are all in the gutter but some of us are looking at the stars.'
> Don't stop gazing at the heavens,
> Ronan

The pebble was the size of my palm, a pre-Cambrian relic, something that had been eroded and bashed about for millennia, but was still here, still beautiful. Strong. A survivor.

John cleared his throat. 'Marietta asked me to come along tonight,' he said. 'I hope that's okay.'

I nodded. 'I'd better go actually,' I managed. 'I'm going to be late.' I turned to Harry, who was being looked after by my teenage neighbour.

'Goodbye Harry,' I said, scooping him up and whispering in his ear. Holding him gave me stability and a moment to breathe. 'Goodbye my sweet boy.' I kissed him, thanking God for him. 'I love you, my little only-twin. We'll never forget Oscar but I am so glad I have you.'

I grabbed my coat and keys and turned back to wave to John and Harry who were standing at the door, John looking as though he'd never moved out.

'Good luck tonight, thespo!' he said. 'Break a leg!' And the two of us smiled at each other, a smile containing everything that was true and important. Everything that was us.

Chapter fifty-three

After all that, I had no idea how I was going to channel Oscar Wilde and be Gwendolen. Acting seemed to me a ridiculous pursuit, when the rest of life wasn't without its own drama.

David came up to me and shook my hand. 'Opening night, Joanna,' he said, almost giddy. 'It's the most exciting point in any production, those moments before curtain up!'

'Good luck Gwendolen!' Connie said, holding both my hands and kissing me on both cheeks.

There was a lot of good-lucking, and break-a-legging as we changed and made ourselves up and I changed into my costume behind an insufficient curtain. Siobhan was beside me, transforming herself into something quite, quite beautiful.

'Wow!' I gasped. 'You look amazing.'

There was a wolf-whistle behind her. 'My, my, such lovely ladies, aren't we lucky to have such wonder in our midst!' Fergal was loosening his stiff collar. 'I think... it is causing me...' he fell to his knees, '... to lose consciousness... such beauty!' He collapsed in a heap and then in an instant had bounded athletically to his feet, grinning at us both. 'Have you seen your betrothed, *Bobbity*?' he called to Robert who was in his costume too. 'You're a very lucky man!'

'Shut up *Fergus*!' said Robert and carried on talking to David. Siobhan flushed scarlet and began pulling on her plait, as though trying to wear it away. I saw her give Fergal an angry look.

Then David addressed us all. 'I believe in you,' he said, quietly and kindly. 'Right now, you might be thinking that you can't do this. That you shouldn't be up on stage representing the three decades The Seaside Players have been entertaining the community of Dun Laoghaire. I was a young man when I joined the Players. I didn't think I could do it, we were honouring the great Bard… or rather I was *dis*honouring him with my Hamlet.'

He looked around, making eye contact with each of us in turn. 'My first night was a disaster. I was Hamlet. Or so I thought. I had my lines learned, I knew what I had to do in my head. I was technically alright. But I forgot how to act. I went on stage as wooden as a spoon, gazing out into the audience as though I was looking for my Mammy.' He looked over at Connie de Courcey. 'Connie was there that night, weren't you, Connie. Playing Ophelia.'

'It was a long time ago,' she said, smiling.

'You made a beautiful Ophelia,' said David. 'I was a terrible Hamlet. But my failure taught me a great many things. And one thing I know is that this humble troupe, this band of brothers and sisters, our *company* will triumph tonight. You know your lines, you know where to stand and I know you will act, you will *be*, and you will transport our audience to the world of Wilde.'

We cheered and clapped. Of course we could do this. We would do this! We would do it for the Seaside Players. We would do it for Dun Laoghaire. We would do it for Oscar Wilde himself! We all cheered, except for Siobhan and Robert who were urgently and intently whispering on the other side of the kitchenette.

There was a scrape of chair and a rush of air as Robert suddenly left the room.

'First-night nerves, I expect,' said Connie, as Siobhan rushed out after him. Fergal put two feet on the table and lit up a cigarette, casually. But I could see his hand was shaking slightly as he fumbled for his matches.

'Outside, please, Mr Forest,' said David, politely, forcing Fergal to also up and leave.

Whatever was brewing among them wasn't anything I had time to wonder at, because I had to try to keep my own nerves under control. I looked at my watch. Half an hour to go. Nothing to do except get nervous. From behind the curtain, I could see people starting to take their seats. Breath of fresh air, that'd do me good.

In the car park behind the hall, I set a ruminative pace and walked up and down, petrified that I couldn't remember my lines, desperately trying to think of the first line I had to say, hoping that if I remembered that, they would all come to me. First line, I thought, first line… what's my bloody first line?

And then an ice cream van came around the corner, squeezing through the tight passage between the corner of the hall and the shed where the bins were. Ronan. He waved when he saw me, parked the van up against the wall of the shed and jumped out. 'It is so good to see you,' he breathed, after kissing me, his arms around me. 'I've been working all day and you are the only person I want to see. I've missed you.' He smiled at me, his handsome, gorgeous, knee-trembler of a smile. God, he was properly good-looking.

'The pebble,' I said. 'Thank you so much. Much better than boring flowers. Oh God. You haven't bought me flowers?'

'No.' He laughed. 'I wanted something a bit longer lasting. Something to remember me by.'

'Why? Are you going somewhere?'

'No, well… that's what I want to talk to you about. It's just that today I found someone who can run the van for me here in Dublin and do deliveries. I'm needed more in the production side of things, down in Wexford, and I can do marketing and strategising from there. I've got to move the business on. It makes sense. And Fergal gave his notice in to his landlord and so, not only am I homeless but my house is practically ready back home and so...' He took a strand of my hair in his hand and played with it, loosely. 'Well, it's just all come together today...'

What was he trying to say? And if he said what I thought he might, how would I feel? What *did* I feel for Ronan, this handsome hero? Friendship, something more? Something long-lasting?

From the open window, I could hear Piers calling my name. Was this my last chance for romance and love and companionship? If I didn't take this chance was I destined to spend the rest of my life alone, no one to hear my paltry amount of correct answers on *Mastermind*, no one to make me a cup of tea, no one to ask to put the immersion on when I was on my way home? No one to talk to?

'What time is it?' I said, suddenly panicked. 'I've got to go.'

'Listen, Jo,' he said, urgently. 'I have something to say. It's just that ever since I met you, I can't stop thinking about you. I like you. I *really* like you. And I thought that you, me and Harry, well, we could all go to Wexford and live there. Okay, I know that sounds crazy but it just seems like the most right and proper thing to do. It might be good for you, after everything you've been through. It's beautiful and calm in Wexford and the people are nice. Much nicer than Dublin folk...' He smiled as I playfully hit him on the arm. 'No road rage or traffic jams. And the sun *always* shines there. Everyone knows that.' His eyes were fixed on mine.

'Ronan—'

'It's just that I have never felt this way, and you're something different. You're interesting and fascinating and you need someone who… who loves you, someone to take care of you and Harry. And, well, if you'd have me, I'd like to apply for the position. I know you said you weren't ready, but I didn't want to leave without at least *trying* to persuade you to come with me.'

'Ronan—'

'No, don't say anything. Hear me out. You've had this terrible time and maybe it's right for you and Harry to leave Dublin and go somewhere new, with me… *someone* new.' He took my hand in his. 'I promise you,' he said. 'I won't let you down.'

'The sun *always* shines in Wexford?'

'Always. And the birds sing more sweetly and the blackberries in the lanes are syrupy, and the hawthorn is covered in flowers and the cows actually wag their tails. And being there is like a balm, wherever you go, whoever you meet. It's the most healing place in the world. And I know I am biased, but I think it would help you. I just know it would do you and Harry good. The three of us together. We could have a big adventure in my small house. And every night the three of us could lie on our backs under the Milky Way and count the stars.'

'It sounds beautiful.' And it did. A new start, a fresh beginning, away from all the rollercoaster drama of life. Harry could grow up on a farm and the two of us could become freckly and happy, living on ice cream. We'd become experts on birds and trees and how to live well. The good life.

'I wondered if you might feel the same way?' he said, his eyes following my face. 'About me. I thought that perhaps you might or rather, I hoped you might… oh, I'm rambling now but what I'm saying is that I can't stop thinking about you and I want us to be together. Properly.'

Oh God. Ronan, lovely Ronan.

But I knew very clearly I wasn't going to go to Wexford, despite the sunshine and the cows and the hawthorn bushes and blackberries and the road rage-less people.

I took a breath. 'Ronan,' I said. 'I think you are amazing. I really do. But I can't. I'm going to stay here. Me and Harry. You see—'

'It's John, isn't it?'

It was. John was the person I loved, I knew that now so clearly. He was the man I wanted to hold my hand, to have Saturday morning croissants with. The person I wanted to keep a tally of right answers with on *Mastermind*. He was my soulmate, the man I wanted in my life, by my side, for ever and ever. He was the one I wanted to talk about Harry to – and to remember Oscar with. And if I couldn't be in a relationship with him, I was more than happy on my own. Turning down this immensely flattering invitation for a life of solitude was a risk I was going to have to take. Because I was starting to like my life and everything I was. From my amateur (emphasis on the amateur) dramatics, to my new friends, to being able to watch the big Sunday night drama uninterrupted, to having the time and the space to just be me. It was actually going well now. I knew I could do this thing called life all on my own. And the future did not look bleak or lonely. And I had a double bed all to myself. That was priceless.

'Yes, it's John,' I nodded. 'Always. I'm so sorry.'

'Maybe us Forest boys are incurable romantics. We always fall for women who don't feel the same way.'

'Well, there's something wrong with women, then, not you,' I said. 'Definitely not you. The world needs more incurable romantics.'

Here was the sweetest and kindest person I had ever met and I was letting him walk out of my life. Ronan may not be my future but he'd played a crucial part in my life. He'd helped me recover myself, something I thought had gone forever. For that, I was eternally grateful.

'I've loved meeting you Jo,' he said, taking my hand and squeezing it. 'And Harry. He's a lovely little boy. Can I come and see him tomorrow? Give him one last go in the van?'

'You've helped me, more than you will ever know. You were there when I needed someone. And thank you for listening to me about Oscar. You have a real gift for… what is it? Empathy, that's it. Thank you for that. Not everyone has it but you do.'

'Well, you have my number. Any time you need a friend.' He gently broke into song: '*You just call out my name and you know where ever I am, I'll come running, to see you again.*'

'What would you be without James Taylor?'

'Inarticulate,' he laughed but, when he smiled at me, I could feel my tears well up again.

'Thank you for rescuing Harry, too,' I said. 'I'll never forget that day, feeling so scared and then seeing the cavalry in an ice cream van. Oh and Puffball.'

He laughed. 'Poodles and toddlers. Some kind of superhero I am.'

'You are *exactly* like a superhero,' I said. 'In the ice cream-mobile, rescuing and saving people. You *are* FroRo.'

He smiled then. 'I like it,' he said. 'I'll take that.' He took my hand and put it to his lips. 'Look after yourself, alright.' He looked straight into my eyes. 'You take care.'

'I will. You too. Are you staying for the play?'

'I wouldn't miss it.' He smiled, waved and began to walk away.

Ronan wasn't just a superhero, he'd been my guardian angel. He had arrived just when I needed someone and had helped me move on to the next stage. I don't know if anyone else would have been able to do that.

But suddenly all I could think of was John, my John. I had missed him so much. He was the man I wanted, the love of my life, the father of my children.

I tried to focus on the play – what *was* my first line? – trying to reel my thoughts back in, but everything began crowding me. John and Marietta must be taking their seats by now. How I wished I was there with them, instead of in a car park, ridiculously dressed and on the verge of tears.

Chapter fifty-four

'I was getting worried,' said Piers, when I got back to the little kitchen. He was in full-Lady Bracknell: hat, gown, rouge, massive bustle. 'Everything alright?'

'Fine,' I smiled at him, panicked at the thought of the play. First line, what's my first line? 'Absolutely great!' My brain was blank as I tried desperately to remember anything.

Robert walked in and spotted Siobhan. 'There you are!' he said. 'I've just settled Mam in her seat. She's asking to see you.'

'I'll go and say hello later,' said Siobhan, wearily. Fergal had moved to sit beside me, he was almost humming like a generator, full of tightly-coiled energy. 'Is she okay?'

'She's up to her eyes in wedding coddle,' he said. 'Just finished another batch. It's in Tupperware in the freezer, so that's good. And Mam says she knows you can't eat it, you being a vegetarian, so she said she'd make you a few cheese sandwiches. I'll pick up some vac-pack cheddar from work. They'll keep you going on the day. Isn't that nice of her?'

'Yes.' Siobhan nodded, defeated. 'Really nice.'

'What's wrong with you now?' he said. 'Why the face like a cold cup of tea? At least Mam *cares* about the wedding. You're acting like you've gone off the idea!'

'Leave her alone,' jumped in Fergal. 'Don't stress everyone out just before we go on stage.'

'You!' hissed Robert. 'Stop your sniffing around and keep that nose well out of it. This is between me and my fiancée.'

Fergal stood up, grinning maddeningly, but there was anger bubbling beneath, glittering and almost dangerous. '*Bobert,*

Bobert,' he said. 'Just go on stage and say your lines, there's a good boy.'

'She's my fiancée,' he said. 'This is between her and me.'

'Well, maybe don't start on her in front of us. Or, better idea, don't start on her at all.'

Robert glared at him before turning to Siobhan, and changing his tone. 'We'll talk later, okay my sweet?' He swept out of the room, giving Fergal another hard stare before slamming the door shut. This did not bode well for our troupe.

Siobhan buried her face in her hands and I could see Piers talking to her in a low voice.

'Okay Fergal?' I said. 'Ready?'

'Always ready, my dear Joanna,' he said, unabashed. 'Always ready for action.'

Piers stood up and spoke to all of us. 'We're going to do this, aren't we? We've worked so hard. On stage we leave our lives behind and we become different people.' We all nodded. Yes, yes, we could do this. 'For Oscar!' said Piers.

'For Oscar!' we called back. And inside I thought of my own Oscar. For Oscar, I repeated. For Oscar. And then Connie appeared, checking we were in our positions and David gave us all hand-shakes and wished us the 'spirit and guile of Mr Wilde'.

Chapter fifty-five

Fergal and Robert were first on and they took their places on stage. The rest of us waited in the wings, breath bated, aware of the audience on the other side of the curtain, the talking, the coughing, and the rustling of sweet packets… I steadied my nerves by thinking of Harry, imagining I was holding his hand and I had to be calm for him. And Oscar. I had to be calm for Oscar.

And the next thing we knew the curtain was swept aside and we were on! From the first moment, it was a mess. Robert and Fergal hissed their lines at each other; there was no ease between them. It was as though they had a score to settle, their enmity palpable for all to see. They were meant to be Edwardian gentlemen, hiding behind social mores and manners, but there were no manners here. At one point, Piers Byrne whispered in my ear, 'what the fuck is going on?'

Shrugging, I pretended not to have the foggiest and hoped to God that they would sort it out, everything would be okay and we would turn the thing around. But it wasn't just them, it was all of us. When it was the turn of me and Piers to enter the stage, my first line came out slightly shaky and I immediately forgot the next one. Then, just as I began to panic, I landed on it and spluttered it out. Even Piers Byrne, as Lady Bracknell, usually perfect in every way, slipped on something and nearly entered the stage flat on his face. Instead he managed to catch himself and entered by running on ridiculously fast, hopping from foot to foot. He brought himself up to full height and regained his Bracknell demeanour within seconds, but it was too late as the audience were in hysterics already.

And then, from the wings, I stood watching Fergal as Jack and Siobhan as Cecily, hoping that all would be well. But Siobhan was no longer the brilliant young actress we had seen in rehearsal, she stumbled over lines, couldn't look Fergal in the eye and seemed disorientated and panicked. Robert, standing beside me, had his fists clenched, his jaw set hard. He stared at Fergal and Siobhan on stage, menacingly.

Even Connie made a mistake, coming on at the wrong time and leaving again just as quickly when she realised her error. The laughter from the audience was in all the wrong places. There was something awry about the show or rather around the energy between us as a cast. We were not in the same groove. After all our rehearsals, the bonhomie, the camaraderie, it was as though we had been lumped together. The colour visibly drained from David's face as the true horror of our performance dawned. The emphasis was on 'am' rather than 'dram'.

Despite our lovely costumes and Connie's clipboard of positions and stage directions, we were awful. I forgot another line and gaped like a fish until Piers Byrne hissed it to me. Fergal, as Jack, now seemed nervous and jittery. Not his usual smooth self. He walked into the fireplace at one point thinking it was the door and actually ate the cucumber sandwiches which were for the opening scene. Siobhan seemed on the verge of tears the whole time, she couldn't say her lines with any kind of expression. Piers himself tripped over his long skirts and swore louder and more foul-mouthed than I have ever heard before. As quickly as he fell out of character, he fell back in. 'I'm so terribly sorry,' he said, in his Lady Bracknell voice.

It was a shambles. And then I heard someone call out: 'this is rubbish!' And everyone laughed at that. 'Oscar'll be spinning in Pere Lachaise!' some other wag shouted out. And then some of the audience began leaving, they were getting up and putting on coats. Jesus. Could this be the worst production of *The Importance of Being Earnest* ever? Could that be its legacy?

The second half was even worse, if that was possible, than the first. We were all terrible. Frederick and George caught the failure disease and began hopping around like rabbits, rushing through the stage, panic in their eyes. We lurched through it all like drunks at a wedding, trying to carry on and wondering, hopelessly, if it might be saved. I could feel sweat break out all over my body as I fought the instinct to run home and hibernate for life. When it came to Piers' 'handbag' line, the audience shouted it out in unison, all in varying degrees of pompous superiority, which made everyone collapse in helpless laughter all the more.

Finally, we got to the last scene. It was the scene where Fergal had to stand by the velvet curtains, which hung on either side of the large painted window. One of the tassels got attached to the back of his jacket and when he went to move away, the whole of the back wall came crashing down on top of him, the rest of us running for cover, Fergal's head sticking out the plasterboard. I've never seen people actually rolling in the aisles before and one man was on his knees slapping the floor. Tears were pouring from people's eyes, some almost begging us to stop because they couldn't breathe.

And then Robert lost it. 'This is all your fucking fault,' he shouted at Fergal and he pulled his fist back and plunged it into Fergal's face. Fergal staggered backwards clutching his cheek and then lunged at Robert, grabbing him in some kind of head-lock, while trying to kick him at the same time. The two of them wrestled, Giant Haystacks-style, on the stage.

The audience cheered, whooping and laughing and clapping. Us 'actors' stood stupefied on stage while Piers tried to pull Fergal off Robert. The sight of Lady Bracknell breaking up a fight finished the audience off, leaving some in serious need of oxygen. Surely someone would have a heart-attack? Finally David wrestled with the ropes and managed to bring down the curtain. All we could hear was the laughing and gasps of breath from the audience and then cheers and cheers and shouts of 'encore!'

*

Afterwards, in the tea room, we tried to pick up the pieces of our broken dreams and eviscerated dignity. Fergal and Robert were battered and bloody, they looked most ashamed. Siobhan was standing away from them, refusing to make eye contact with anyone. My hands were shaking, my make-up shimmered on my sweaty face.

'What happened out there?' I said. 'How did it all go so wrong?'

No one answered. It was as though we had all experienced some great trauma. David returned from the stage, where he'd spoken to the audience. He was ashen-faced, as though he had seen the ghost of Oscar Wilde himself.

Connie dug around in the back of a cupboard and produced a dusty bottle of cognac. She poured us all extremely large measures and David necked his in one. We followed his lead.

'I shouldn't,' said Piers. 'I've been on the dry for ten years.'

'Tea for you,' said Connie. 'Extra sugar.'

He stood up, still dressed as Lady B, but with his wig and hat pulled off. He looked monstrous. 'And tea it will be. For fuck's sake. I have never needed a drink more in my life and I have to stick with tea.' He threw a venomous look at Fergal, as though it was all his fault.

'Gather round, everyone, gather round,' said David, wiping his mouth with his hand, having taken another swig of the brandy. 'Now,' he said, 'tonight was the worst piece of theatre I have ever been involved in, that much is true. It was an embarrassment, an indignity, a travesty, no less, and something our dear compatriot and genius, Mr Wilde, does not deserve, indeed could never have dreamt of, that his wonderful play could be turned into such a…' he paused, trying to find the perfect bon mot. 'Such a pile of postulating awfulness.'

We hung our heads in shame. David sloshed out another serving of brandy and swigged it back. The colour began to return to his cheeks. 'However,' he continued. 'It is, as dear Oscar, would be the first to agree, only a play. Without darkness, there is no light. Oscar himself saw the grime which lay beyond the stage door, he saw that there is no such thing as true goodness. We are humans, after all. And tonight, the Seaside Players were human. And I think Oscar would have been satisfied as a man who knew the realities of death, a man born into a world traumatised by famine. We can't imagine the poverty and suffering he would have seen on the streets of Dublin. And London, too, would have had its share. He may have written about the drawing rooms of society, but he knew of the human condition. He knew something about the human spirit. This was a man who was persecuted for his love, for his innate goodness.'

317

We were all silenced, thinking of Oscar all alone in Reading Gaol. But David was only warming to his theme.

'When real life, when the outside world, when passions and affairs of the heart are brought on stage, then things can go wrong. Very wrong indeed. Tonight, it seems, from what I can see, real life refused to be silenced. We attempted to take our audience on a journey. But in that we failed. I tried to give everyone their money back but every single person refused, most of them saying that it was one of the best nights out they have ever had. One man said, and I quote, 'it was fecking great craic', another said he hopes we will be that funny next time. So,' he finished, 'no one died. Thankfully. We will learn and the Seaside Players will rise again. The curtain comes down on this production but we will reconvene in September. More brandy anyone? Let's drink to Oscar.' We raised our glasses.

'To Oscar!' we said, feeling a little more cheered.

'To being human!'

'To being human!' we echoed.

Siobhan had been sitting behind Frederick and George and she pushed through them. All eyes in the room turned to her and a hush fell. 'This is all my fault,' she said. 'And it's time I took responsibility. Robert,' she said, in a small voice. 'I don't want to marry you. I am so sorry but I feel so trapped.' Her voice grew stronger. 'I am twenty five and I want to go to drama school. All you want is a house and babies and so I can turn into your Mam—'

'What's wrong with that?' Robert's neck was turning red, his jaw straining. 'My Mam loves her life. What's wrong with turning into Mam?'

'There's nothing wrong with it, if that's what you want. But it's not what *I* want. I shouldn't have agreed to marry you, but I didn't know at the time what else I wanted. But now I do.'

She looked at him, tears in her eyes, pleading with him to understand. 'I want to get the fuck out of this place and *do things.*'

'Like what?' Robert, poor Robert, was having difficulty imagining life beyond Dun Laoghaire.

'Like everything!' Siobhan roughly untied her plaited hair and combed her fingers through it so it hung over her shoulders. She shook her head, as if to be free, and untucked her beaded turquoise necklace, the one which was meant to have come from a cracker but now its origins were so obvious - from Fergal, with the money he borrowed off Ronan. 'Like travel,' she continued, 'like seeing things, doing things, saying things... *feeling things.*' She glanced at Fergal, who was just standing there, his body suspended of all movement, as though his whole life was on hold.

'Feel what?' said Robert, his eyes now glistening. He had seen her glance and his eyelids had developed a twitch.

'Love.' She spoke quietly again. 'Passion. Excitement. I want to feel *life* within my belly...'

'You want a baby?'

'No! Jesus, Rob!'

'Well, then what the feck do you want?'

'I want to leave. I want to go to London. I've been offered a place in drama school there. Rada. I auditioned at Easter when I went to stay with my sister.'

'What?'

'Sorry Rob.'

'Sorry?' He said. 'You're sorry? We're trying to buy a house, we've been saving every last penny for a deposit and for the wedding. I've been doing overtime just for us... I've spent every minute of the last five years thinking of you, working for you, for our future, and you say 'sorry'. And you're off to *drama school.*' He put on a silly voice. '*In London.*'

'Sorry,' she said again.

'What's Mam going to say, eh?'

'I don't give a fuck what your Mam is going to say. She's one of the most passive aggressive, controlling people I've ever met. She won't even call me by my name, for God's sake. She calls me Sarah. Says it's nicer. And she knows I'm a vegetarian but makes sure the fridge is full of those horrible pork pies and those disgusting sausages… and she's always got some dead animal hanging around. Last week it was pig's trotters boiling away for hours. The week before it was tongue.' She looked revolted. 'Real, *proper* tongue.' She looked around for support from all of us.

'She says you'll grow out of it…'

'But I won't!' Siobhan was crying now. 'I won't grow out of it! I like being a vegetarian. It's me, the real me. It's important to *me.*'

'Mam's going to be so embarrassed,' Robert said, shaking his head at the thought. 'And I'm only trying to my best for you. Mam has been nothing but kind to you. She treats you like the daughter she never had.'

'She doesn't,' protested Siobhan. 'She told me the other day that I was putting on weight and would never fit into my wedding dress.'

'Yes, but she's just being careful. I mean, we can't exactly buy another dress, can we? Waste that perfectly good one. I mean you're only going to wear it once, aren't you? There's no point in spending any actual money on it, is there? I'm just trying to be sensible. One of us has to be.'

'Yes, but that dress is not me. And anyway it's way too big. Your Mam is wrong. She's just trying to be mean to me.'

'Siobhan!' Robert was shocked. 'Mam would no sooner be mean to you than she would miss Bingo.'

'Rob—'

'No, Siobhan,' he said. 'We are going to get married, you are going to wear that dress and you will look beautiful because that is the kind of thing that is important to ladies. Apparently. And the wedding will not make a dent in our savings. Because the important thing is saving for our house, isn't it. The wedding is just one day, our marriage is for life.'

He looked around at all of is, expecting us to nod and agree with this, in his eyes, uncontroversial piece of wisdom. But Siobhan, who I thought had been wilting again, suddenly pulled herself up tall.

'Rob, listen!' She commanded. And then he looked at her, as though for the first time, this young passionate woman who couldn't face a future devoid of passion and adventure, who wasn't ever again going to settle for okay. Her blonde hair over her shoulders, her body standing squarely, her eyes blazing, she looked as though she had been set on fire. When you stop saying no to things and you allow the notion of possibilities into your life it can be the most exciting thing in the world. I felt like cheering. 'Listen to me. I'm not just going to drama school but I've also fallen in love. Properly.'

Robert looked agog as Fergal stepped towards Siobhan and took her hand.

'What do you mean?' said Robert, confused. 'Not *him*, Siobhan. Not him! Not the biggest tosser this side of the Liffey.'

'We're in love,' said Fergal. 'Sorry Robert but I love her and she loves me. We're going to London together.' He squeezed Siobhan's hand, reassuringly.

'Everyone's so fecking sorry aren't they?' said Robert. 'I knew it, I knew it. But I thought you were just flirting with her, I didn't realise that you…' he looked at Siobhan, searching her face for an answer, something to tell him that she was making a mistake, that their relationship could be saved. 'I didn't realise you felt the same.'

'It just happened,' she said. 'And we knew it was wrong, but I didn't know what to do. It was so hard to make the decision to be brave and put what I wanted first. All my life I have been falling into line, doing what everyone else wanted. Being the good girl…'

Robert snorted at this. 'Well, it says something about your mental state that you would choose someone who wears ladies' scarves and who hasn't seen the inside of a barber in a decade. Day manager at Superbuy Dun Laoghaire, that's me, one day *general* manager. Maybe, in the future, if I work hard enough, manager of the Leinster region.' At this his voice broke, tears springing to his eyes. 'You are fooling yourself, Siobhan. You are making a terrible decision. You'll regret this.'

This shouldn't have been the best performance of the night, I thought to myself, as the cast and crew of *The Importance of Being Earnest* watched the unfolding drama, but it was. Poor Robert's life was imploding, two people in love were grabbing their chance at happiness, compounded the feeling that life and love were seldom simple. If only our audience had seen this act, we might have had a better reception.

'Well,' said Robert, finally. 'You are going to have to bloody well tell my Mam, because I'm not.'

'Fine,' said Siobhan. 'I'll go and find her now.'

David stepped in, to bring the final act to a close. 'Boys,' he said, to Fergal and Robert, 'why don't you shake hands. All's fair in love and war, as the great bard of Stratford said. Enmity is the brother of resentment, forgiveness the sister of love.'

Fergal held out his hand to Robert and Robert came right up to him and for a moment I thought he was going to shake it, but he swung at him again. This time however, Fergal ducked and Robert's fist flew through the air. 'Bastard!' Robert yelled, trapped now by Frederick and George who had him by either arm. 'Fucking bastard!'

'I'm sorry,' cried Siobhan. 'I'm sorry for everything. It's all my fault. If I hadn't been so stupid then none of this would have happened.' And she started to sob.

'Don't you worry,' said Connie, putting her arm around Siobhan and pulling her close. 'Sometimes the most compelling drama is that in our own lives. We've all been there. Nothing can compete with real life.'

'Does this mean we have to cancel the wedding?' said Robert.

'Cancel what?' said Siobhan. 'There's nothing to cancel!'

'There's all that coddle in the freezer,' he said. 'We'll be eating it for years!'

'I'm sorry Rob,' said Siobhan. 'I'm so sorry.'

'Listen, I'll forgive you and we can forget all this happened,' said Robert, wriggling from the tight hold of Frederick and George. 'We'll just carry on as normal. And we'll never talk of it again. Mam says there's a job going in the dry cleaners. Nice place to work, she says. Easy work. Just a pair of comfortable shoes and you'd be fine. You get a lunchbreak and everything. We'll just pretend nothing ever happened.' He was breathing heavily, trying to rein himself in. 'Please, Munchkins.' His voice cracked. But Siobhan wasn't for reining in.

'But it did happen,' she said, breaking free of Connie. 'It *did* happen. And I am going.' Fergal moved towards her and took her hand again. 'We are going,' she began to sob. 'We are going to London.' She leaned her face against Fergal's shoulder as he gently kissed the top of her head. 'And we're so happy! So happy!' Her sobs echoed around the room while Fergal tenderly held her. 'I love him,' she managed. 'I love Fergal. So much, so, so much.'

'It won't last, you know,' Robert said, his eyes shining with tears, 'it won't be a happy ending. Mark my words.'

'I feel alive when I'm with him,' she said quietly. 'I feel like I'm the best me I could be.'

'Sorry Robert,' said Fergal. 'We really are so sorry to hurt you, but it's for the best. Siobhan wasn't for you and you weren't for her. You'll find someone. I know you will. You're a good man, Robert. But take it from me, sometimes the person who think is the love of your life, just isn't. But Siobhan is mine. And I hope I am hers. I'm certainly going to try to live up to her expectations.'

'Oh fuck off,' said Robert and left the room, leaving David to run after him. But Fergal and Siobhan remained, huddled together in the centre. They may not have been sure of the ending but their adventure was just about to start. Next stop London.

Chapter fifty-six

Outside, in the car park, I could see Marietta and John waiting for me, but first I wanted to see Ronan who was leaning against the van.

'Hello,' I said. 'Well, that went well, didn't it?'

He laughed. 'I thought it was brilliant. It's like life… perfectly imperfect.'

'With the emphasis on the imperfect.'

'Perfection is overrated. Life lesson number one.' He smiled. 'It's not goodbye, you know. We don't have to not see each other again. I'll send you a postcard from Gorey.'

'Do that. Will you?'

'I'm just waiting for Fergal. I'm driving him and Siobhan to the ferry. All their bags are in the back of the van. They're leaving for London tonight.'

We hugged, hard.

'Thank you Ronan. I'll miss you.'

'Me too.'

I turned and walked back to Marietta and John. They had both been watching me and Ronan intently.

'Sorry about that,' I said. 'I just wanted to say goodbye to Ronan. He's leaving for Wexford. He's been a good friend.'

'And he rescued Harry, let's not forget that,' said Marietta.

'Absolutely,' said John.

We watched as Fergal and Siobhan appeared, holding hands, Siobhan tear-streaked, Fergal's jaw set, they stepped up into the van. Ronan started the engine and they rolled away, into the night. I waved to them but I'm not sure if they saw me.

'So, what did you think of the show?' I asked. 'Good, eh?'

'Possibly the funniest thing I have ever seen,' said John. 'I thought I was going to die laughing. The two of us did, didn't we Marietta?' He began to laugh again.

'Just the tonic,' agreed Marietta. 'Remember that bit when that man punched the other…' The rest of her sentence was lost to her hooting. I looked at the two of them, bonded, united in mirth and merriment. And at my expense.

'Glad to have provided such entertainment for you,' I said drily. But it only made them laugh more. 'Oh God,' I said, realising this was something I couldn't fight. 'We just kind of imploded. I want to emigrate or disappear.'

But John was still going on. 'And when Lady Bracknell got involved and tried to beat the other one with the handbag…' he howled. 'That was priceless. In my opinion,' he said. 'Oscar Wilde would have been laughing harder than anyone.'

'Can we forget about it, please?' I said.

'But then, when the little guy with the red hair skidded on the cucumber sandwich, I thought I was going to have a heart-attack.' He wiped his tears away.

'And I thought you were depressed, John. You seem to be most buoyant.'

David appeared.

'Ah, Joanna,' he said. 'Is this your family?'

'Yes,' I said. 'Well, this is John… my… uh…and this is my mother, Marietta.'

'Oh!' he said, doing a double-take when he saw Marietta. 'Enchanted,' he said. 'We've met before, I think, when Joanna was at school. But it seems as though the years have been nothing to you, Mrs Woulfe.'

'Thank you so much,' she said. 'And may I say what a fine performance it was this evening. We really enjoyed it. You must have put in so much work. I am just sorry it was ever so slightly marred by the antics of the younger generation.'

'Well, if you can't be foolish when you're young, when can you be?' David said, twinkling at her.

'When you are old?' said Marietta coquettishly and they both laughed at their shared joke. John raised his eye brows at me.

'Are you coming Mam?' I said, desperately longing for a cup of tea and my bed. I didn't even have the energy to talk to John, my head was so full of the performance and the showdown between Siobhan, Robert and Fergal. We watched John cycle off and Marietta drove us home.

'It really was terrible, wasn't it Mam?' I said in the car.

'Yes,' she said, 'it really was.'

'Oh God,' I said. 'I'll never live it down.'

'Nonsense,' she said. 'If I can show my face in public after Patrick Realta humiliation, you can show your face after this.'

She was right. It put things into perspective, rather. I had never admired my mother more than after seeing how she dusted herself down and got on with things. I still had a lot to learn.

Life-lifters

- Brand-new pyjamas

- Clean sheets on bed

- Drinking tea in bed when Harry is still asleep

- Knowing that he will wake up and I will see him again

Chapter fifty-seven

The next morning, in town, I was on Grafton Street trying to find something that would signal my new identity at Wilde Woulfe PR. I didn't want to look corporate and the thought of squeezing my body into a tight waistband did not appeal. There had to be a middle-ground. Half tracksuit bottoms, half work-appropriate attire. I was on the hunt for the impossible.

A crowd of people drew my attention and I squeezed through to the front. And there was a heavily pregnant woman, dressed as Mary, mother of Jesus. I'd seen that outfit before. A queue of people came up to the woman one by one and placed their hands on their belly. One man had his ear to it, and was nodding as though he could hear the baby talking. The woman had her eyes closed, as though she was meditating. People were crying as they walked away, shaking their heads at the profundity of the moment. It was Coco.

In front of her was a pile of leaflets. 'Mother' it said, by Coco Crawley, winner of the Constable Prize, currently represented by the Gold Gallery.

> The notion of woman as mother has been commodified, objectified and ultimately patronised because of fear. The fear of men. Men fear our power. The power we have over life. They tremble at the thought of our might, our strength, our energy. We are the givers of life. We are the souls of the world.
> We take our power back.

I am Mother. Hear me roar.

I joined the queue and edged along and when it was my turn to put my hands on Coco's belly, she opened one eye.

'Hello Jo,' she said.

'Coco.'

'Are you annoyed with me about Nicole?'

'Yes.'

'We didn't think that she'd be so hurt. Kristof always said she was so cool about things.'

'But how can you be doing all this female empowerment stuff if you walk over someone's marriage? It doesn't fit, Coco. It's not cool.'

Both her eyes were now open. 'But Nicole's alright. She had her own show – *my* territory, you might say. Am I complaining? And it was amazing. It got so many write-ups. Marina Abramovich said she was "moved" by it, Taylor Tourniquet said he was "deeply changed" although into what we can only imagine but that's Taylor for you. But the thing in, Nicole got something out of it, didn't she? It's not all bad. Jo, don't look at me like that. Okay, I am sorry. I was wrong. But it was a mistake, alright? Not the baby, the baby wasn't a mistake, but thinking that Nicole would be cool about it. *That* was a mistake. But we are all fallible.' We looked at each other, my hands still on her belly. She nodded. 'Life is messy, though' she said. 'There's no formula. It's visceral. You've got to agree with that.'

'That's one way of putting it. Or you could say there are some messes that are avoidable.'

'Okay, I was wrong,' she said. 'And I am sorry. Really sorry. Nicole didn't deserve it, but I wasn't thinking about her. I was just thinking about me. I do that sometimes. A lot, actually. It's just a thing I do, think about what I need and want and I don't take into consideration other people's *feelings*. I've been accused of being insensitive before, you know.'

'Really? I am surprised.'

'The baby's kicking, can you feel it?' Coco slid my hand across her belly, warm and swollen with new life. Now, that *was* moving.

'I should go.' I took my hands away and stood back but Coco put her own hands on my head, like a pope blessing a child. The crowd behind us burst into applause. When I looked around, some people had tears in their eyes and their mouths open. There was a sense that they believed something deep and momentous was going on.

'Forgive me Jo,' she said. 'I know not what I do! Ah, go on. Please?' She opened her eyes wide into a sweet face that even Puffball couldn't pull off.

'Do you ever learn from your mistakes?'

'Never!' she said. 'Anyway you've given me a new idea for a piece. Two women, one man,' said Coco, eyes shining. 'A baby. I'm thinking blood on the walls, on the floor, blood pouring from the ceiling... blood signifying life, the female body. Tate Modern would definitely commission it. I'm thinking Turbine Hall, a huge effigy of bleeding and weeping woman. What do you think?'

'It's a blockbuster waiting to happen.'

'Thanks Jo.' She smiled.

'Good luck Coco, with everything,' I said. 'I hope it all goes well.'

'Do you mean that?'

'Of course.' And I did, of course I did. There was a baby on the way, a new life. Nicole would be alright, I was sure of it. As long as she stayed away from Kristof and Coco.

Coco raised her arms, Christ-like, and faced the sky, eyes tightly closed again, as if drawing in the sun's energy, to the hushed awe from the crowd. Stepping away from her, I was nearly knocked off my feet by the next in line, one of Coco's bustling and over-excited fans, who quickly flung her arms around her belly and fell to her knees, in prostration.

I looked back at Coco and she gave me a wave, while simultaneously patting the super fan in benediction.

Chapter fifty-eight

The next morning, Brenda, Sheila's sister, hired Wilde Woulfe PR to mark the salon reboot. She had just spent a fortune in turning her slightly-shabby hairdressers into something sleeker and smarter and now wanted to tell the world. Well, Dun Laoghaire at least.

'How much?' she enquired, her leather trousers creaking.

I gulped, invisibly, worried that my prices were too high especially after I'd done the work at the garage for free. 'Five hundred euro,' I said. 'Plus VAT.'

She didn't blink. Instead, she looked pleased. Maybe I should have asked for more. But no matter. Wilde Woulfe PR had its first customer. We shook hands on the deal while Brenda studied my eyebrows.

'We could do something about them, you know?'

'What's wrong with them?'

'Ageing,' she said. 'You need a total reshape, colour and condition.'

'On my eyebrows?'

She shrugged. 'That's entry-level. There's no end to brows these days. It's a minefield.'

As I walked out, I felt a surge of excitement. And it wasn't the promise of reinvigorated brows, it was the commission. I had a job, my own company.

'What do you think Oscar?' I said out loud, making a woman pushing a buggy look at me. 'I'm doing okay, aren't I sweetheart?'

I hadn't spoken to him in ages, but that was okay. Everything was going to be just fine. As I drove home, I thought about the fact that I had spent too long wishing it all hadn't happened, almost as though Oscar should never have existed, because his death had brought me so much pain. I loved him and I missed him and that was horrible, but the thought of him not ever having existed brought far more pain. He had stayed as long as he could and I had been so lucky to have met him and held him. I would love him forever.

At my house, I parked on the road. Behind me I heard a voice.

'Jo!' It was Nicole, stepping out of her car, which was full of bags and boxes. 'I've been waiting for you. I wanted to say goodbye. I handed in my notice at school and I'm off to Sydney for a month, maybe two. My brother says I can stay as long as I like.'

'Oh my God…'

'Just need a break, from the whole thing. Need to get myself back together again. It's been so difficult being married to Kristof. I need to see if I'm still in here somewhere.'

'I know the feeling exactly. Don't stay away for too long, will you?'

'I won't. Did you hear the baby was born yesterday?'

'But I saw Coco in town, she was performing.'

'Jesús.'

'That's the baby's *name*?'

Nicole actually laughed. 'Yes, *Jesús*.'

'That's brilliant.'

'Isn't it just? She went into labour *on* Grafton Street, apparently. She wanted to give birth there but they made her get into an ambulance – kicking and screaming – and brought her to the hospital.'

'How do you know all this?'

'Kristof was there at the birth, live texting me all the way through. But Coco had already phoned me, from the ambulance.'

'Really?'

'She said she was sorry and that although she lives her life beyond, as she put it, the narrow societal constraints, she realises that she hurt me.'

'What did you say?'

'I wished her well. There was one line – one line! – in all of those self-help books which stayed with me. *So Your Man's a Prick What Do You Do Now?* recommended that you hold onto your dignity at any expense. So I did. So the books weren't all bad,' she said. 'Just *mostly* bad. I said, that I hoped everything would be okay and good luck in the future.'

'What did she say?'

'Well, she yelped in pain, but I think it was just a contraction. So I've left them to it. And do you know what? I don't care. It came to me to just get out of here for a while. I phoned Thomas and booked my flight all in the space of half an hour and started packing. All I need are flip-flops anyway. I feel released from it all, from them. It was like a prison that situation. I couldn't breathe. Anyway, I actually feel pleased for Coco, you know? A lovely boy.'

I nodded. 'There's nothing like them.'

Nicole and I smiled at each other.

'Time for tea before the flight?' I said.

'Will *you* be okay?' she said, looking at me. 'I'm so sorry that I didn't come to the play last night.'

'You had other things going on. Anyway, I'm glad you didn't. It was a shambles.'

She laughed. 'Oh dear.'

And then I laughed, too. 'It's David, our director I feel awful for. He put so much work into it and we were all terrible. It just kind of snowballed. I'll tell you all about it when you come back. When I've had time to process it.' She smiled. 'It's not forever, is it?' I said, suddenly worried. 'You will be coming back, won't you?'

'Of course! Dublin's my home and even though the weather is appalling, I wouldn't want to live anywhere else. Thomas is constantly homesick. He's asked me to bring some Tayto crisps, some Barry's tea and a Dairy Milk. I don't think he cares about seeing me, just as long as I have some treats from home.' She sighed. 'You know, one day I will wonder what I saw in Kristof… I'm not there yet, but I know I'll remember what a massive idiot I was once married to.'

'Yes you will,' I said confidently.

'What about John?'

I shrugged. 'I've been too busy making a fool of myself in amateur dramatics to think about him.' But we both knew this was a lie.

'Jo,' she said. 'I have a huge favour to ask you.'

'What is it?' I said.

'One second…' she said and left the room, going to her car.

She returned carrying a little box, with a handle. There was a wire window on the front of it and inside was Puffball.

'Would you take him?' she said. 'I know it's a big ask, but he wouldn't be happy at my Mam's. She's not a dog-person and hates mud and paw prints and the whole thing would freak her out. I was thinking – *hoping* – that you might take him. Would you?'

While I hesitated, she babbled on.

'I don't know what else to do. And you love dogs…'

I nodded.

'And you love Puffball.'

That was true. I nodded again.

'And Harry loves him,' she went on. 'And there are no allergy worries or anything.'

'Yes—'

'And he's very sweet…'

'True.'

She smiled the Nicole-smile of old, which gave me even more confidence that one day she would be able to move on from Kristof and Coco and everything that had happened. Life *was* about collecting experiences, however awful, and learning how to carry them with you, without them dragging you down. With Oscar, I knew that I would rather have had one day with him and a lifetime of heartbreak than nothing at all. And life, I was learning, was about holding steady during the down times. Developing your sea legs ready for the next swell.

'So, what do you think?' She held up the dog carrier.

'I don't know…' But I could feel myself breaking.

'And you're at home all day and you can work from home and take him out for walks. You know, when you are running your hotshot PR company…'

'Wilde Woulfe PR.'

'Yes, and you have your dog at your feet. That's living the dream, my friend, living the dream.'

'If you're a dog person.'

'Right.' She laughed. And it was so good to see her laugh.

I opened up the little door of the carrier and took Puffball out. He snuggled up to me and licked my arm.

'Of course,' I said, realising that there was never any question of me saying no and Puffball was exactly the new addition myself and Harry needed. 'We'd love him, Harry and me.'

'Oh would you?' She had tears in her eyes again. 'I've been so worried about him, thinking how miserable he would be with my Mam. He wouldn't be allowed up on the sofa and she'd probably make him wear special socks around the house.'

'Oh Nicole,' I said, suddenly getting a pang. 'I'm going to miss you.'

'And I'm going to miss you,' she said. 'I should have listened to you when you told me the situation with Kristoff and Coco was impossible. You've been such a great friend.'

'Hardly!' I said. 'I've been so preoccupied with my own life.'

We walked outside and I waved Puffball's paw at her.

'I'll miss you both,' she said. 'You and the Puffmeister. But especially you.' She smiled at me and we hugged.

She kissed Puffball's head. 'Thanks for everything, Puffball,' she said. 'I'm sorry I can't stick around but you have a new owner now, and she's going to be far nicer than me. Goodbye Jo,' she said and hugged me again, harder this time.

'Bye, Nicole,' I said, trying and failing not to cry, the two of us, standing in the street crying our eyes out and then me waving a dog's paw at a car disappearing around a corner, tears pouring down my face.

As I walked back inside, I felt as though things were becoming normal again. Not crying in the street, of course, or having to say goodbye to my best friend. They were awful. But *feeling* things again. Not being numb and shut off, feeling like you are in a bubble floating slightly apart from the rest of the human race. I belonged on earth again.

Chapter fifty-nine

The sound of a rattling engine and a beepity-beep of a car horn, brought me outside again.

It was the yolky-yellow VW campervan from the garage, the one P. J. had been tinkering with. And there he was in the front seat, Sheila following him in their car, both waving at me. The engine rattled as though there was a canteen of cutlery inside. Which, being a campervan, there might well be.

'You got it going, did you?' I said, walking down the path to meet them. The campervan gleamed in the sunlight. Sheila parked just behind it and they both got out. 'It's looking amazing, P. J. You've done a great job.'

'She's a beauty alright. Those engines were made to last. You'd get across to Europe in her in no time. You'd get as far as you wished.'

'You would, yes, I'm sure you would,' I agreed, slightly puzzled now as he and Sheila were both grinning at me and seemed overly delighted with themselves. They looked at each other and P. J. nodded at Sheila encouragingly.

'It's your thank you,' said Sheila. 'For what you did. We thought that, when you want to get away, you could head off in the van. You and Harry.'

'What?'

P. J. dangled the keys. 'She's yours, if you'll take her,' he said. 'Her engine is sound as a pound. She won't give you a moment's trouble. You could take her to Outer Mongolia if you wanted to.'

'I'm not sure…'

'And I have the insides clean and beautiful,' said Sheila. 'New upholstery, fridge and cooker. All perfect.'

'I can't—'

'And curtains made by me,' she went on. 'And the seats turn into a bed.'

'I don't know…'

'Take a look,' said P. J., pressing the keys in my hand. He slid the side doors open and I looked inside. There was a small table, a tiny kitchen area. It was clean and shiny, like a miniature home. And suddenly I could see myself, Harry and Puffball driving around in it. The freedom it represented was suddenly intoxicating. Life was not something that should make you feel trapped, ever. You were always free. But you had to allow yourself to be free.

'It's a bit of a strange thank you,' said P. J., suddenly looking unsure. 'Maybe you are not the campervanning type.'

'But we talked about it and we thought we were right to think you were…' said Sheila, also looking worried.

'No,' I said. 'I am. I *am* the campervanning type. I didn't think I was, but now I can't think of anything nicer to be. I am definitely a campervanner. It's gorgeous. I love it.'

'So, you'll take her?' said P. J., smiling at Sheila. 'Not that you'll need it, but I'm throwing in free services for life.'

'I'd… I'd love to. I couldn't think of a nicer present.' And I couldn't. Except for all the things in the world that money couldn't buy.

'We've been racking our brains trying to come up with a good thank you,' said Sheila. 'Business is going great since the open day, all thanks to you. We've had Bono back in *twice* with his different motors. And Fixup aren't doing well. There are rumours it might close. Your Locals For Local campaign seems to be working, too. Rav's DIY has joined, then there's Brian's

Café, Mary and Gerard in the shop and Brenda's salon. They're all on board.'

'We're sharing advertising costs and clearing out the space in front of the shops, planting hanging baskets,' said P. J. 'The council are getting involved as well with the new paving and paying for the plants.'

'That's great,' I said. 'I'm so pleased.'

'How's Marietta,' she said. 'I heard about… you know…'

'She's bearing up remarkably well, considering.'

'He was always a bad egg, that man. Thought more of his own backside than anyone else. I warned her, I warned her, all those years ago… and she wouldn't listen.'

I shrugged. 'Would you have listened, if it was you?'

'Probably not. But I'll give her a call. I'll see her at Joan's daughter's wedding too, no doubt. I promise not to mention that Paddy Realta. I'd love to give him a piece of my mind, though! Now see you later, Joanna. And you take care of yourself. Okay?'

*

Sitting behind the wheel, the engine didn't so much roar but rattled into life. Ahead of me was the open road and all I had to do was start going. First stop, Harry's crèche. It felt strange at first, as I inched through the streets, the engine rattling away. Puffball sat on the front seat, looking out of the window and at one point he crept over and curled up on my lap.

By the time we arrived I was triumphant, I parked the van, my mind full of the things we could do. Suddenly, by being the possessor of a VW van, I was a different person, footloose, fancy-free, flowers in my hair, free-range. Harry was going to love it. Some of the other mums and dads on pick up duty were looking over admiringly. One dad called out: 'Off to a festival, are you?'

'Electric Picnic,' I said, winking. 'We're not too old, are we?'

The dad laughed. 'I'm too tired for it, that's my problem,' he said.

Harry raced towards me. 'What do you think, sweetheart?' I said. 'Look, we can go anywhere, now. We can travel the world!'

But the only thing he said was, 'is there room for my Lego?' He seemed a little subdued.

'Yes, of course, we can keep a box of it under the seats. You'll have to be strapped in at the front but, when we stop, it's just like a little house.' I showed him the cupboards and the little fridge and he pulled across the curtains.

'Don't you like it Harry?'

He shrugged and mumbled something. I bent down to hear him clearly. 'Do you think Oscar will come?' he said, in a tiny voice. 'In the van. I don't want to leave him behind.'

I knelt down, catching my breath, my face close to his. 'What do you mean?'

'When we leave. In the van.' His big eyes were full of worry. 'Oscar's in our house. He mightn't be able to come with us.'

'That's what I've been worried about, myself, Harry. I was worried that we would leave him behind but I know now that we won't. Wherever we go, Oscar will come with us. We can do whatever we like and go all over and he'll be there. We won't leave him behind. Ever.' I took one of Harry's hands and kissed it. 'You see, Harry, he's in our hearts. Yours and mine. And Daddy's. And Granny's and everyone else who loves us. They love Oscar too. And,' I said, placing his small hand on his heart, 'he's in there, the place where you love people. So wherever we go, Oscar comes.'

He listened to me. 'Promise?'

'I promise.'

The three of us, Harry, myself and Puffball, all sat in the front of the van. I could see why Ronan liked his van so much. It was fun up here, looking out. It felt like freedom. Next stop Uzbekistan, by way of Timbuktu.

Chapter sixty

Once, years and years ago, John and I went for a walk out to the Poolbeg lighthouse. It stretches out about a mile into Dublin Bay, on a wall of big blocks of granite, mined and hewn by the Victorians. It was early evening and there were lots of people out there, dog walkers, and couples. And us. Talking. And laughing. And being in love.

Anyway, the clouds gathered quite quickly and we, lost in conversation and love, didn't notice. Everyone else scurried down the long wall back to their cars but we carried on walking in the other direction, out to sea. We had to reach the lighthouse. You couldn't come to the Bull Wall and go home without being up close and personal with a bit of Victorian engineering.

And then, the rain came, suddenly, like someone had tipped a bucket on our heads. A very big bucket and neither of us being the types to own waterproof clothing or anything remotely practical, we got saturated. We may as well have taken a dip in the sea and the shock of the shower made us stop what we were saying and just look at each other, mouths open in surprise. Then we laughed.

'We're the only ones here!' said John.

'Where's everyone gone?' I said.

'Back to their cars,' said John. 'Being sensible.'

We held hands and stood there for a moment or two, watching the sea being topped up with rain and then half-ran, half skidded back to the car. We felt like the only people left in the world. And there was something lonely about it – we had each other, yes, but it was like there was no one else left, almost apocalyptic. And that's how I felt about Oscar.

It was such a shock, you know, what happened, and so sudden. We just weren't prepared for it. It was like a cloudburst, when you go for a walk and there you are, all vulnerable and exposed but you don't realise you are exposed, because it's a nice day. Except, from nowhere, the heavens open and there's no place to hide, and you get drenched. You're all on your own while everyone else is home and dry.

Chapter sixty-one

John's mouth fell open when he saw the campervan pulling up. He had been sitting on our front step, waiting for us.

'Joanna Woulfe,' he said, 'you always were full of surprises.' He picked Harry up and held him in his arms.

'Didn't you know I could drive a campervan?' I said. 'A thank you present from P. J. and Sheila.'

He and Harry poked their heads through the window to look inside. 'It's gorgeous.' He laughed. 'Really beautiful. What do you think, Har? Mummy and I went in one of these, not as nice, mind, for our honeymoon. Remember Jo?'

'I remember.' Driving through vineyards and fields of sunflowers, eating cheese three times a day and feeling so happy I could have burst. 'How could I forget?'

'I haven't.' He held my gaze.

Harry tugged on John's sleeve. 'Mummy says it's our moving home and we can take it whatever we want. I am going to bring Lego and my brudder.'

'Your brother?'

'Mummy says he can come with us in our hearts.'

I felt the tears spring in my eyes and I looked away.

'Listen Jo—'

'John—'

'You go first.'

'No you.'

'I just want… I mean…'

'Do you fancy a trip to Brittas Bay?' I butted in. 'Give the van a run along the coast?' Suddenly I wanted more than anything in the world for everything to be normal. No big conversations, no confusing signals, no agonising puzzling over body-language or hidden meanings. I just wanted the three of us to head off in the campervan. To just be free of all the worry and the sadness, just for one afternoon. 'What do you think? We can make tea in there as well.'

'Ah, now I can see why you like it so much.'

'So, are you coming?'

'I can't think of anything I'd rather do, than be with you and Harry.'

'That's great, good. I'm glad.' We stood there, slightly awkwardly before I began to move into the house to pick up a few bits and pieces.

'Jo'

'Yes?' I turned around.

'I've missed you.'

'Have you?'

'So much.' He looked at me. 'Life is horrible without you. And I'm sorry for everything. For being the world's worst husband, the most terrible friend and a truly dreadful father. To walk out on you... I just can't believe I did it.'

'It's alright.'

'No it isn't. I'll never forgive myself.'

'Well, I do.'

'You do?'

I hadn't realised until now that I did forgive him totally and utterly. It was so easy. Because, really, there wasn't anything to forgive. We are all human and none of us are perfect – especially not me – and to live is, sometimes, to suffer. And suffering and sadness makes us behave in ways that we would never do in times of happiness. 'I forgive you. If you'll forgive me.'

347

'I forgive you.' He smiled at me. 'Anyway, you haven't done anything. You are beyond reproach.'

'If only.'

He smiled and shrugged his shoulders. 'We can go through a checklist later and see who is best behaved and therefore wins.'

'I've missed you John,' I said. 'It's not fun watching *Mastermind* without you.'

'And I can't watch the news without wanting to hear what you would say about every story. I miss your running commentaries.'

'I'm that bad?'

'You're that bad.' He laughed. 'Look,' he said. 'I really am so sorry about everything. I wish I'd never moved out. It was such a stupid thing to do. I knew it the moment I closed the door behind me. To walk away from my family, like that. I'm such a coward.'

'No,' I said. 'I understand. There's no manual for handling grief, we just have to find our own way.'

'I love you, Jo. I never stopped loving you. I missed you every moment. And I had to watch as Ronan was hanging around and you seemed so smitten with him. I had no right to say anything or to feel anything, but I did. I felt so jealous.'

'Ronan's been really important. He's been there...'

'And I haven't... and I wish I had. I wish I could be again?' He looked at me. 'Joanna,' he said. 'I love you. So much.'

He waited for me to speak. And all I could hear was the sound of us breathing. There was nothing else. Just us. And all I wanted was him, I wanted us to work, I wanted a future with him, my best friend, my life partner, my love. The father of my two sons. John.

I nodded. 'I love you, John. Always and forever.'

He grinned suddenly, all angst and worry wiped away by his beautiful smile. He took my hand and kissed it. 'Oh, Jo, I love you so much, so much!' And then we kissed and it was so right, better than anything else, so real and right and exactly the way kissing is meant to feel. 'I love you and I've missed you and I promise nothing like that will ever happen again,' he said, when we pulled apart. 'We won't stop talking to each other, no matter what. Deal?'

'Deal.' We smiled at each other.

'I'm sorry I was so angry with you.' I said. 'I see that now. That I blamed you. It was so unfair.'

He kissed my fingertips. 'It was part of your trying to deal with it—'

'But it wasn't fair on you.'

'But understandable, though, under the circumstances.'

'But *you* didn't blame me.'

'No, but I shut down, though. Neither of us is covered in glory, but what happened, happened. It was too awful to deal with. Losing Oscar, coping with another child.'

'It was. But the one thing I shouldn't have done is blame you.'

He shrugged. 'Maybe it helped you, to think that it someone's fault. Maybe that made sense of it for you.'

'Sorry.'

I'm sorry, Oscar, for blaming your Dad. You love him too, don't you, Oscar. You love him like I love him? There was no answer but I didn't need one. I was sure of the truth. John held my hand tightly.

'By the way,' I said, 'this is Puffball, *our* new dog.'

He smiled at me. 'It moves?' he said. 'I thought it was a cushion.'

'Well, he's *our* cushion.'

'I like being ours again.'

'Me too.' And as we smiled at each other. Inside I had this strangest of feelings, a warmth of happiness, butterflies of excitement. Us… this is what I wanted. We were complete and whole, the four of us. Oscar may not be with us physically but he felt very real and very present. We'd always be a family of four.

'John,' I said. 'If you're moving back in, we're going to have to get a bigger bed. I've got used to the extra space. I don't know if I can compromise on that, anymore.'

'I wouldn't dream of asking you to compromise on personal space,' he grinned. 'Anything else?'

'BBC costumes dramas,' I said. 'Will you not make sunny comments when they're on and allow me to enjoy them in peace?'

'Random but doable,' he said. 'Any other demands?'

'That's all for now but if I think of any, I'll get back to you.'

'I'm all ears,' he said. And he pulled me close to him and kissed the top of my head. 'Anything for the love of my life.'

Chapter sixty-two

John, Harry, Puffball and I, strapped ourselves in, fired up the rattly engine and headed off. The world stretched out before us. First stop Brittas Bay... who knew where next?

You fancy it, Oscar? You coming too? I thought to myself. Thanks for listening to me, sweetheart. Thanks for being there.

We stopped off for milk and tea bags, bottled water and cake, all of us sure and content that this was all you needed in life: tea, cake and the people you love.

The beach spread out like a golden carpet, sand and grass under our feet, the sea breeze blowing, mingling with all the love and kindness and memories that were in the air.

Harry ran off down the beach unable to stop himself from hurtling and rolling, as though he had been kept locked in a darkened room all his life. Puffball bounced off with him and the two of them ran about together.

'I've been doing a lot of thinking,' said John, sitting down beside me on the rug beside the van, on the edge of the dunes, the golden sands stretching for miles and miles.

'Really?' I said. 'That sounds dangerous.'

'I know,' he laughed. 'My brain is worn out. But I want to try and explain a bit more, so you understand that it won't happen again, my leaving. That you can trust me. I had a breakdown, I suppose. My engine wouldn't go, it was dead,' he said. 'Losing Oscar...' He stopped. 'I know you don't want to hear this. You went through it too. I just felt I couldn't add to everything you were going through. I couldn't be another burden, the husband who couldn't handle things, the man who couldn't be a good father, the person who was cracking up. I just had to get away. Leave you. I couldn't articulate it at the time because I didn't quite know what was going on.'

I stayed very still and quiet, waiting for him to continue. He reached for my hand, tentatively.

'I just felt that I couldn't breathe,' he said, quietly. 'I began having panic attacks, on the train in the morning on my way to work. I would arrive at the station and have to stand at the side, to get away from all the commuters. And then in work, I had to go the bathroom during the day to calm myself down. I began to get worried. Really worried.'

I was watching him and listening. 'Why didn't you tell me?'

'You were so busy,' he said. 'And you had your own thing going on. I couldn't burden you with my feelings. And there I was falling apart, just when you needed me. I felt ashamed.'

'Ashamed?'

'And embarrassed.'

'Oh John—'

'I fell apart,' he said. 'I fell apart. But I felt if I didn't do something, if I didn't get out, away from the family, I would bring you down with me. And I couldn't let that happen.'

We looked at each other.

'I love you Jo,' he said. 'I love you. Always have, always will. I have let you down. Badly. I just felt so useless, that I was failing you, you and Harry. And Oscar, too. It probably sounds crazy but I felt I was failing *him*.'

'It doesn't…'

'What?' he said.

'Sound crazy. I think of Oscar all the time. He's a real person…'

'Of course he is. Was. Is.' He put his face in his hands. 'It's so hard, isn't it? It's so hard to make it real, to put it into words, to show the world what you are feeling when you don't quite know yourself.'

'When a baby dies you're expected to just get on with things, act as though they never existed, that you only have one child, when in fact you have two.' I said.

'That's it…'

'So,' I said, firmly. 'I've decided that when anyone asks how many children I have, I'm going to say two.'

'Okay. I'll do the same. Is that a deal?'

Instead of shaking my hand, he put it to his lips and lightly and gently kissed it. A kiss that was full of heartbreak and memories and sorrow but also so full of love and the future.

'Joanna Woulfe,' he said. 'I love you. I love everything about you. I love your tiny nose, your huge brain, your kindness and your sweetness. You make me laugh. And I don't want my life to be without you for a single second longer. I am going to spend the next few decades making it all up to you. I won't let you down.'

'Decades. Make it centuries.'

'Centuries then,' he said. 'I love you, Jo. I love you with all my heart. You and Harry… and Oscar… are everything to me. I can't believe I came so close to losing you. My Joanna. Still intriguing and forever beautiful.'

I looked away, out to sea, to where Harry was making a mound of sand, Puffball keeping guard. And then I turned back and saw the man I loved, whose smile I wanted to see every morning, whose face I had never got tired of. There was the hand I wanted to hold, the body I wanted next to mine.

'Life sometimes gets in the way,' I said. 'It's so hard to keep a steady pace when boulders and rocks are being thrown at you. But John,' I said. 'You're not to do anything like that again, you hear me? Breakdowns and all other stresses are to be talked about. We are a team. Okay?'

'Okay,' he said, smiling. 'We are a team. And you're the captain.'

'Now, you're talking. But you can be co-captain sometimes.'

'Okay Captain, tea?' he said. 'I'll boil the kettle.'

'Oh, I get it now. It's the van you want, isn't it? Not me.'

'I can't pretend that it isn't an added incentive,' he said. 'I've wanted one of these things all my life. But Joanna Woulfe, I would want you even if you came with no van.'

'I'm honoured,' I said.

'No,' he said. 'I am.'

And we kissed as though we'd never been apart, as though we were still on honeymoon, in our campervan trundling through the South of France. And then John made tea and while I sliced the lemon drizzle, I looked at him, my husband, and thought: I love you. I love you for everything you are, and everything that has happened. And our lovely son, our Harry, and our other son who died, our Oscar. I thought how lucky I was, to have these people in my life. How lucky I was to be alive. And I was going to make the most of every single moment.

John looked up from pouring the tea, as though he was thinking the same thing. He smiled at me, a deep, beautiful smile, the kind that stays with you and seeps deeply into your soul, filling you with love and wellbeing. Like the one that day on the cricket pitch in college, the night we met, the smile he used to be so liberal with he was in danger of wearing it out. And there was I thinking he had. Thankfully I was wrong.

John handed me my mug and we kissed and kissed and kissed again on that beach in Brittas. And it was a kiss that meant home and love and connection and partnership. We held hands and looked into each other's eyes, both of us emotional from everything we had been through.

Harry and Puffball joined us for the tea and cake, Harry drinking apple juice, Puffball water out of a mug, lapping away, nose right in.

I love my boys. Oscar and Harry. I love them both, in different ways but I love them equally, fiercely and forever. I loved them from the moment I saw the first scan picture of the two of them swimming around inside me, and then, as they got bigger, the way they seemed nestled together, brothers in arms, peas in a pod.

'Here, John,' I said. 'Harry. Time for a toast.'

They held up their vessels expectantly.

'Here's to us, our family,' I said. 'All of us today. And here's to absent members.'

'To absent members,' echoed John. 'Oscar,' he explained to Harry. 'She means Oscar.'

'He's in my heart, Daddy,' said Harry.

'He's in mine too,' said John, tears rushing to his eyes, causing mine to fill rapidly as well. But for the very first time, the tears weren't about sadness for Oscar and I didn't feel guilty, or struck by grief. I felt grateful... my tears were for everything I had. All of it. Harry, John, and for the tiny life I had once held in my hands for one day, for my mayfly baby. It was more than many mothers have with their babies, and even though we missed him and wished he was here with us, I had held him and kissed him and that counts for so much. So, so much.

'How's Marietta holding up?' said John.

'She's going out with David from the Seaside Players,' I said. 'Off to see *Juno and the Paycock* at the Abbey tonight.'

'We should never give up,' said John, 'should we? Never give up on love… because it's the best thing there is.' He reached for my hand.

'The only thing.'

'And my brudder Oscar,' said Harry. 'I love him.'

'We all do,' I said, smiling at him. 'Now… who's for more cake?' And we ate slices straight out of our hands and we listened to Harry telling us about sandcastles and seagulls, stones and splashing.

Thank you Oscar, I said to myself, thank you for staying as long as you did. My mayfly baby. Thank you. I am so thankful I got to meet you. And my heart felt fuller than I could have ever imagined, full of John, Harry and Oscar. The loves of my life.

Life-lifters

- My yellow campervan

- Harry's smile (how could have I left that one out?)

- My two boys – I love them so much

- My framed scan picture of Oscar and Harry on the mantelpiece

Epilogue

John moved back in with Jo and Harry the next day and the two of them promised faithfully to never stop being a team ever again. In fact, they headed off to Aix-en-Provence for a long weekend, leaving Marietta in charge of Harry, where they spent their days cycling through little villages and talking about *everything*. They spent a great deal of time laughing as well. And drinking too much red wine from local vineyards. And eating more fromage than is healthy.

Marietta found a small flat just down the road from Jo, John, Harry and Puffball with a sea-view and steps straight onto the promenade, ideal for elbow-pumping power walks. The Kilbarton golf club held a vote and it was unanimously decided that she should definitely and absolutely *not* step down from her position as lady captain. Marietta had tears in her eyes when the result was read out and later declared she had been hugged so much she was a size smaller. She also continued *stepping out* with David Donnelly from the Seaside Players, enjoying more theatre trips and fish and chips on the pier. On one occasion she brought him to the driving range to practice his swing. The theatre trips were, they both agreed, far more successful.

Patrick Realta was sent to prison for eight years. Some of the money was recovered and he was named and shamed on national media and many of the women who he swindled felt finally able to tell their stories on *Liveline* and other phone-in programmes and in local and national newspapers. Photographs of Patrick, wigless and toothless (his dentures had been lost in the Dundalk Supermacs while resisting arrest) were circulated widely. However, he didn't remain a broken man for long. He struck up a correspondence with another of his old fans who had seen him on the news. They are, she claims, in an exclusive in a tabloid newspaper, engaged to be married. As soon, that is, as he is released.

Joan's daughter, Kate, had a wonderful wedding with everything going off swimmingly. Joan decided on fuchsia in the end and was flanked by her two best friends, Marietta Woulfe and Fionnuala Fahy, both looking equally glamorous. The three old friends drank champagne all day and at midnight, they were discovered dancing in the moonlight, barefoot and on the grass, as the band played on.

Jo has some new and pretty prestigious customers at Woulfe PR. Decco has sent on some of his smaller clients which she has taken on. All are pleased with her creativity and her personal touch. She works from home; her lap warmed by Puffball, her hands by endless cups of tea, and she can raid the kitchen for custard creams whenever she wants. Best of all she gets to pick Harry up from school every day.

These days, Harry will only eat jam sandwiches for his lunch and remains best friends with Xavier. But he hasn't forgotten about Oscar. Sometimes Jo can hear him talking to him as he plays Lego. This, she has been assured by the child psychologist she called in a panic, is A Good Thing.

Nicole went to Sydney and stayed for three months, returning browner, happier and able to surf. She was last seen heading off to Lahinch to take an advanced course at Murph's Surf. Real life, she keeps saying, will restart once her savings run out. She and Paul Jr have been spotted holding hands during evening walks along the strand.

Ronan's business has gone from strength to strength, and FroRo, now stocked in the country's trendiest cafes and shops, has been given a Gold Award in the *That's Yummy!* food awards. A lovely young woman called Sunny, who runs her own artisan bakery in Gorey, has come into his life after they met at the local farmer's market and she is now pregnant with their baby. If it's a boy, Ronan wants to call him Fergal.

Fergal and Siobhan sent a postcard to Ronan with a picture of the Queen on it. 'Greetings from London,' wrote Fergal. 'Life is going wonderfully well. Hope yours is too.' He and Siobhan are coming home to Wexford for Christmas. Fergal managed to get a small speaking role in *Casualty* and stole the scene. The producers are talking about making him a regular.

When Coco's house became too small for Coco, Jesús and Kristof, Kristof moved into his office at the Gold Gallery and he and Coco realised that they were not to be. Kristof is now seeing Paola, a Brazilian artist while Coco and Jesús moved to New York for the duration of her most recent MOMA show, which involved her and Jesús sitting on a rug playing with bricks. It was called Mother and Child. It has been nominated for the Constable Prize.

Jo's campervan sits on the drive all week until Friday night when Jo, John and Harry pack up and head off. They went all the way to Donegal last weekend and are thinking of returning to France in the summer. Harry is being lured there by the thought of crepes and hot chocolate, Jo just wants to spend a couple of weeks with her two favourite people in the world – John and Harry. And of course, Oscar will be there with them, in all their hearts.

We hope you enjoyed this book!

Siân O'Gorman's next book is coming in spring 2018

More addictive fiction from Aria:

 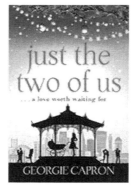 

Find out more
http://headofzeus.com/books/isbn/9781784978259

Find out more
http://headofzeus.com/books/isbn/9781786693341

Find out more
http://headofzeus.com/books/isbn/9781784977009

Acknowledgments

Thank you to my wonderful agent Ger Nichol and to the brilliant team at Aria and Head of Zeus, especially Caroline Ridding, Yasemin Turan and Nia Beynon. Also to my friends Zoë Fitzgerald, Cliona Dempsey and Mike Shaughnessy and, as always, to Sadhbh O'Gorman, Jason Tann and to my favourite person in the world, Ruby O'Herlihy.

About Siân O'Gorman

SIÂN O'GORMAN was born in Ireland, is an RTÉ radio producer and lives in the seaside suburb of Dalkey, Dublin with her seven nearly-eight-year-old daughter, Ruby.

Find me on Twitter
https://twitter.com/msogorman

Also by Siân O'Gorman

Find out more
http://headofzeus.com/books/isbn/9781784979560

Visit Aria now
http://www.ariafiction.com

Preview

Read on for a preview of *Friends Like Us:*

Is it ever too late to take charge and live your life on your terms?

Life for school friends, Melissa, Steph and Eilis, hasn't quite worked out the way they once imagined it might. Melissa may be professionally successful but inside she's a mess of insecurities.

Steph is lonely and lost, balancing the fragile threads of family life and walking on eggshells around her philandering husband and angry teenage daughter.

Finally, Eilis, a hardworking A&E doctor, utterly exhausted by the daily pressures of work and going through the motions with her long-term partner Rob. It's crunch time for all the friends…

A light-hearted and emotional novel about family, friendship and coming to terms with your past.

Can't wait? Buy it here now!
http://www.headofzeus.com/isbn/9781784979560

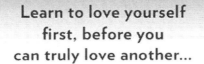

Learn to love yourself
first, before you
can truly love another...

Friends Like Us

SIÂN O'GORMAN

1

Melissa

Of course the crash was her fault. Melissa wasn't concentrating on the road when she whammed into the back of a Mercedes, as she was too busy having an out-of-body experience, thinking about herself; this woman who should have been all grown-up but was as unsorted as a tube of Smarties.

She was driving along the Grand Canal in Dublin, had just arrived back in the city after an unsuccessful weekend in Paris. It was a busy road at the best of times, filled with the usual battered and beaten up vehicles, the odd articulated lorry, the cyclists who only look up to raise two fingers to traffic that skims too close.

And there was Melissa in her orange Beetle thinking about Alistair and the fact he had just given her the old heave-ho. In the airport. After a weekend in Paris. So that was nice, wasn't it? At the age of thirty-eight, shouldn't she have achieved a little bit more, relationship wise?

But what was really bothering her wasn't just the fact that she had been dumped – again – but because she had persisted in pursuing a relationship which had, if she was entirely honest, lacked lustre from the very beginning.

I *should* have children, she thought, buckets of them. Mr Perfect in the corner, smiling, as one child smears Nutella on the sofa, while the other saws away tunelessly on a violin. Isn't that what women should have? Isn't that what we're told life should look like?

But there was no getting away from it; Melissa had had a truly *terrible* weekend, the *least* romantic since her school leavers' do when Tony Tierney puked all over her dress and she walked home crying and covered in vomit. However, being an imaginative type, she preferred to think the weekend's failure was because poor old Alistair had been under the weather and not at his sparkling best. But, come to think of it, she had never seen him at his sparkling best. Maybe he didn't have one.

Flu, Alistair had muttered darkly – and kept re-tucking his scarf, sniffling and snuffling throughout the weekend. She had managed to steer him away from Molly Malone's near the Champs Elysée and instead they ate in a restaurant in the Marais. However, he complained about the steak (too bloody), refused to be amused by the grumpiness of the waiters and blew his nose in the napkin. Crimes on the lower end of the scale and ones Melissa had been certainly determined to overlook.

She remained stoic. Remember Stalingrad, she had kept thinking. It was colder then, surely, and they were hungrier. But although she may not have been *actually* freezing her arse off in a Russian winter in 1943 and fearing for her life, those soldiers at least didn't have to put up with the snufflings of Alistair. Amazingly, he was able to reach out for his pint of lager and shiveringly bring the vessel to his blue lips. Undeterred, she threw back the red wine and the whole weekend became not a romantic cliché but an alcoholic blur.

You can't have it all, she had thought, consoling herself. And it is *Paris*; he's ill and no one can help that. Maybe she just had to try harder, be funnier, nicer, attractiver. With a little helping of Florence Nightingale on the side.

Okay, so it may not have been a success but even if he was a slight hypochondriac, she hadn't *actually expected him to finish with her. At the airport.* They were heading through arrivals, both pulling their little wheelie cases, him still snuffling and she smiling winningly, hoping he would say he had had a lovely time, but instead there was silence from Alistair. Well, apart from the sniffing and the sneezing.

'How are you feeling now?' she said, trying to prompt a response. 'Glad to be home?'

'Going to go straight to bed,' he mumbled. 'Sleep this thing off.' She wondered if he was confusing a hangover with flu. Whatever it was, he was in Garbo-mode.

'Good idea,' she said, masking devastation. 'You do that.' An awkward silence hung in the frozen air. And then she realized her smile was full of hope and desperation but she knew how transparently pathetic she was so instead tried to look frowny and concerned. And, crucially, grown-up.

'Melissa... listen.' He dropped his voice. 'Listen, um...' A taxi had pulled up... it was as if he had actually planned the swift getaway.

She realized, finally, that he was going to finish with her and that his shortcomings were in fact hers and that she was the unlovable one. Please say something nice to me, she inwardly pleaded. Just *want* me again. Just like me. Please *like* me.

'Melissa, it was a fun weekend.' (It hadn't been. They both knew that.) 'But I... I don't really feel able to have anything serious at the moment. I'm so sorry...'

She was motionless, heart thumping now, blood coursing around her brain, sirens going off. She was being dumped.

You'd think she would have got used to it by now. Searing pain that soon numbed to a throb, the pulsations of which were a reminder of her own essential unloveableness. This was how her life was meant to be, a catalogue of failed flings.

'Melissa, are you okay?' He was looking around now for the taxi.

'Of course,' she said. 'Totally. I agree, I'm so glad you said it. I've really enjoyed our time together.'

He looked hugely relieved. 'Thanks. I mean you are great and everything but you know…' Ah, there it was, the taxi! He swung his case into its open boot.

'I know.' She smiled again, this time to show what an incredible sport she was.

She waved bravely as the taxi sped off. Was that him waving from the window? She couldn't quite see. And had he promised the driver extra to vroom away as though on a heist? Regardless, she was left alone.

This was how it always played out: the ascent as she was desired, and then the drop, an ignominious free-fall through the air. However attractive she was, she was no girlfriend material. Not the marrying kind; she was too weird, too needy, bordering on neurotic. It never took long, usually around three months for them to realize… and Alistair had got out in a record-breaking two months.

There was nothing else she could do except to recover her little orange Beetle from the car park and start driving home, allowing the shame and humiliation to embed itself. No one knows, she thought, as tears streamed down her face, no one knows who I am. I am nothing, no one, worthless.

Other people found relationships easy but Melissa found them torturous. It was always full-on and then over. Keeping her deep unloveableness a secret was taking a strain.

Never again, she thought. No more. A life of spinsterhood loomed. Well, anything had to be better than watching a man blow his nose on a napkin.

And now, here she was, wending her weary, woeful way home along the Grand Canal and about to crash into a Mercedes.

A swan flapping its wings gave her a jolt, granting Melissa a look in his beaky, beady face, as if to say, *who do you thing ye are? Gallivanting again? Well, you've only yourself to blame.*

She saw the bumper of the Mercedes whizz towards her; the swan having a good gawp. 'You were right!' she wanted to shout. 'You were right. I do have only myself to blame. It's all my fault. All of this. Everything!'

In the very short journey from uncrashed to crashed, she heard the screeching of her own brakes (her body had gone into action, as least it wasn't letting her down), and then the terrible crunch, the breaking of glass and the sound of her head hitting the steering wheel. A nice Mercedes, she imagined, would have air bags. An old Beetle wouldn't. And didn't.

Her head against the wheel, Melissa wondered what to do before she heard voices and someone trying to help her out. She staggered, stunned and blinking, out of the car, resting on the arm of an old man, who in different circumstances, would have been leaning on her.

'Terrible traffic,' he was saying. 'There's always accidents along the canal. Too many cars. I always walk into town this way and I say to meself that it's a miracle there aren't more prangs or pile-ups. That's what I always say.'

He led her to the wall alongside the canal. Bloody hell, she thought. Jesus Christ. I've just been in an accident. The dizziness was beginning to clear and she looked around. Her head was hurting but she was, she realized, still alive.

'Now, love, are you all right? No broken bones?' said the man. 'Everything in perfect working order?'

'Just a broken heart,' she said, unable to resist the temptation of the drama.

The old man laughed. 'Oh, now,' he said. 'Lovely woman like you. Surely not?'

She managed to smile so as not to scare him off entirely. She put her hand to her head and felt it carefully. A huge lump was forming underneath, bubbling Vesuvius-like. But it was her car she was most worried about. She noticed two men had managed to push it up onto the pavement, its bonnet buckled and forced open, bumper hanging off.

And people – passers-by, good Samaritans? – were helping the Mercedes driver out of the other car, a blonde woman, expensive highlights glinting in the rare late-afternoon winter sunlight.

Oh God, Melissa knew this type. Better just hand over her life savings to pay for the dent in the back of the Mercedes. Although it looked perfect, well *perfect enough*, apart from that teeny-tiny-titchy *scrape*. The woman looked perfect enough too, with her swishy blonde hair. Melissa looked away, still shaky and not quite ready to face the inevitable confrontation, and began rifling in her bag for her phone. She wanted to call Cormac. He'd be nice to her.

She was aware of the woman coming towards her and Melissa braced herself. 'I'm so sorry,' she blurted out, looking up into the sun. 'It was all my fault. I just wasn't concentrating.'

The other woman was open-mouthed, 'Melissa!' She was laughing now. 'Oh sweet Jesus, Melissa!'

'Steph! Oh my God, Steph!'

It *was* Steph, looking exactly the same since they'd last seen each other. Blonder, perhaps, her straight hair in a long bob, her face the same, just slightly older, perhaps, minimal make-up. Polished, groomed, she was working the glorious trinity of the jeans-Converse-Breton just like any other thirty-something mother, but on her, it was smarter, newer, *and expensive.*

Melissa managed to stand up and the two hugged each other for so long it turned into a kind of dance as they began to rock together. The crowd gave a cheer and there was even a round of applause.

Steph, her old, old, old friend. How sweet the vagaries of life. Who said that? Someone, anyway. Oh. She felt strange and had to sit down again.

Once upon a time, Melissa and Steph were inseparable. School friends and then friends into their twenties when something happened – life? – and they drifted. Like a swan on the old canal, especially the type of swan who predicted bad luck… or in this case, maybe the swan was a signifier of good luck. Drifting back into each other's lives again. Or rather *crashing* back in.

'I don't believe it!' Melissa said. 'We haven't seen each other in years and then this happens.'

'Of all the backsides in all the world, you had to run into mine.' Steph was still smiling and Melissa grinned back, but she felt embarrassed. Here was Steph, all gleamy and glowy, and there was she, dusty and dishevelled. She pushed her hand through her brown hair that refused to either lie straight or curl. She was wearing an outfit (skirt and ankle boots) that had been meant for Paris, but now, in Dublin, seemed over the top and ridiculous. She'd plastered herself in make-up too, full foundation, the works, and she felt like a drag queen that hadn't mastered the act of dressing like a woman.

But Steph was still smiling, seemingly not noticing or caring that her old friend was a mess.

'So, what do we do now?' Melissa asked. 'You know about this…' she gestured to their cars. She actually wanted to get herself home and changed and into something more like her. She was feeling a bit ridiculous in her Parisienne non-chic and, she was thinking that maybe they could meet up again later, once she had her jeans and trainers on again. But Steph didn't seem to notice what she was wearing and was too busy thinking about sorting out the car situation which, Melissa had to agree, was the more pertinent of the tasks.

'Well, I think mine is driveable,' said Steph. 'But we can always get yours towed. We'll get it sorted.'

And Steph did, even though the accident was technically Melissa's fault, Steph took charge and phoned a garage to arrange for them to pick up the Beetle while the crowd, slightly disappointed that there wasn't any blood or more carnage, dispersed, leaving them alone.

'You're white as a sheet, Mel,' Steph said. 'And you're shaking.'

Melissa could feel her teeth chattering as though she was Bugs Bunny eating an invisible carrot. She suddenly felt terrible, as if she was going to be sick.

'I think Melissa, that we'd better get you to hospital,' said Steph. 'Get you checked out.'

Melissa began to shake her head, no, which, she soon realized, was exactly the wrong thing to do.

'Come on, we'll go down to Vincent's… to A&E, just to be on the safe side.'

Melissa could only nod and allowed Steph to lead her to the car. She lay back in the seats and immediately felt better. It had to be admitted, what the Beetle gained in cuteness and character, it lacked in the comfort department that the Mercedes had in spades.

They pulled out into the traffic and made their slow progress along the canal. Melissa looked at Steph as she indicated and smiled at the drivers who let them out. She hadn't changed at all, same old Steph. One of life's good people, the kind of person you wanted on your side.

'I've just had a thought!' said Steph suddenly. 'Eilis!'

'Oh my God, yes!' They both laughed. 'Imagine!' said Melissa. 'She could be there, you know?' Eilis was their old school friend, part of their tribe of three. She was a consultant, as far as they knew, at the A&E in Vincent's hospital. 'Ouch!' Melissa pressed both her hands to her head. 'Shouldn't have laughed. That hurts. Major headache.'

'You poor thing,' said Steph, glancing over. 'You must have given it a huge whack. I hope they test you for whiplash too.'

'I hope they won't think I'm wasting their time,' said Melissa. 'You know, when they have really ill people to deal with.'

'You are meant to go to A&E after a car crash,' said Steph. 'You could be walking around with a head injury otherwise. No, of course we are not wasting their time.' There was silence between them for a moment.

'Are you... are you still in contact?' Steph said. 'You know, friends? With Eilis?' For a moment, Steph looked so vulnerable, so easy to hurt; it was a look that Melissa had never seen before. It's true, she realised slowly, people don't *stay* the same, even if they look the same and behave the same. Life always, always changes us. Something had happened to Steph which had made her insecure, or scared. It was hard to tell but Melissa had never seen that look in her eyes before. She was always so together, so happy. And then she had married Rick and she disappeared into wifedom and motherhood, as so many do. Melissa had been sad about it but she had her own life, other friends. It had seemed a natural parting. Melissa was single – still! – and marrieds socialize with other marrieds, and singles with their own kind and never the twain, et cetera.

'It's just that I lost contact with Eilis,' Steph was saying, 'as well as you, but you two probably still hang out…?'

'Not for a long time,' said Melissa. 'Not for ages. Years. D'you think she still works there?'

'I don't know… we can ask.' Steph was looking normal, again, almost relieved. She glanced over at her. 'It's good to see you, Mel.'

'It's good to see you too.' It was, it really was. 'So how is everyone? Rick? Rachel?'

She waited for Steph to say that they were fine, everything was wonderful, Rick grand, work going well, and Rachel was brilliant, or what mothers usually say about their lovely children. But instead there was silence. Melissa looked over and saw tears rolling down Steph's face.

'Steph?' she asked.

'Don't mind me. Must be shock. God, accidents always take it out of you.' She wiped her eyes with the sleeve of her cashmere cardigan. 'Stephanie!' said Steph to herself. 'Stop crying!' She tried to laugh. 'I think I just need a cup of tea. Six sugars. That kind of thing. They're fine, though, Rick and Rachel, before you worry. Both hale and hearty.'

Melissa was suddenly aware that something was wrong with Steph and after having to deal with her own mother all her life, she was highly sensitised to other people's moods, their inner feelings. It's partly what made her such a good journalist but also it made life difficult because you couldn't shake others off, their emotions were always so tangible to Melissa.

'By the way, you make it sound like you have lots of accidents,' said Melissa, trying to make her laugh, bring some light into the car again and give her space to recover herself.

They parked in the car park and began to walk to A&E.

'I feel silly now,' said Melissa. 'I'm sure I'm all right. No brain damage.' She was looking carefully at Steph, who still hadn't really stopped crying, her eyes still filling up with tears. What was *wrong* with her? 'Well, apart from the usual.' But Steph didn't seem to be listening, she was miles away.

They went straight to reception and found two seats in the waiting area.

'Steph,' said Melissa. 'I'm so sorry to have caused all this trouble. You know, the accident. And now I'm taking up all your time, having to sit here for hours…'

'But Melissa,' said Steph, still tearful, 'I've nothing else to be doing… and I've thought about contacting you so many times over the last ten years… or however long it's been… and then it gets too long and then you feel awkward and then you don't think that the person would want to see you and then you literally bump into me. If I was a cosmic person, which as you know I'm not, but if I was, then I would say that you were meant to crash into me.'

'Or maybe it was just an accident.'

'Or maybe it was just an accident. A lucky accident.'

They grinned at each other and Steph took a huge breath. 'Right, I think I'm myself again. Let's see if I can get a cup of tea for us out of the machine. Keep your expectations low.' They sat together, comfortably, chatting away, drinking tea, and it could have been ten years ago, twenty years ago, that old easiness between them had returned. It had just been dormant, ready to spring into life again.

Back home, later that evening, concussion dealt with by machine-tea, Melissa dialled Cormac, her go-to person, her fail-safe, never-let-you-down, best friend.

'Busy?' she said, trying not to sound plaintive. 'Fancy some company?'

'Who are you suggesting?' He sounded suspicious. 'Myself and Rolo are about to sit down to watch Supervet. So, it'd better be good.' Rolo was his spaniel; bouncier than a squash ball and sweeter, believed Melissa, than an actual Rolo.

'Me?' she said.

'Really?' Cormac sounded exaggeratedly surprised. 'I thought you and Basil were currently shagging on the top of the Eiffel Tower.' He paused. 'You're *not*, are you?'

Basil was his deliberately-wrong name for Alistair. He always did this with all of Melissa's flings, pretended not to know their name.

'*Alistair.*' They had been through this routine many times since Melissa began seeing the afore-mentioned. 'And no, we are not *currently* shagging up the Eiffel Tower.' This time it was Melissa who paused. 'It's too cold.'

'Amateurs,' said Cormac. 'Why do I keep forgetting his name? Maybe it's because he is just so *forgettable.*'

'Anyway, we're not seeing each other anymore,' she said airily.

'Come round,' he said, suddenly. 'Kettle is going on now and I am tearing open the Mr Kiplings with my teeth.' There was a rustling sound and the phone went dead.

2

Steph

They had been in the same class since they were twelve… and as the rest of the girls formed twosomes, threesomes, and foursomes, they too found their own group. They complemented each other, they were all easy to be with and there were never the fallings-out, the promiscuity that infected the others in their year. They were all only children, as well, which gave them a different feeling, they needed each other; in a way, they were surrogate sisters.

Steph was always quietly sure of herself. Life, she believed was going to be all right. Her own parents were normal, which is more than she would have said at the time for most of the girls at the Abbey. Nuala and Joe, her parents, never let her down, did anything embarrassing, were just perpetually loving and permanently kind. She knew, even then, how lucky she was.

For Eilis, it had been different, not so easy. Her mother was ill while they were at school, for all of their teenage years, she was dying, Eilis her carer. Eilis was quiet, hard-working and never quite let on how difficult it was for her watching her mother fading away. Steph always believed that she and Melissa gave Eilis her few chances to be a normal teenager.

And Melissa? Who knew what had been going on there, at Beach Court, but it was obvious that Melissa just wanted to get away from it as much as possible, hiding it all with her cleverness and her wit.

Eilis hadn't been on duty that evening they had turned up in A&E, but they scribbled a note, making the woman, Theresa, behind the desk, give it to her.

'Tell her it's us,' said Melissa, who was acting almost giddy after the accident. 'I think sense has either been knocked in or out of me.'

It was another doctor who checked Melissa out, performing all the tests: the biro-following trick, the walking in a straight line, touching her nose with her finger. Steph and Melissa were nearly in hysterics by the end and Steph had (almost) been sorry when Melissa was pronounced perfectly well and they would go their separate ways again.

But the Beetle hadn't fared quite so well. Steph called the garage and was told it would have to stay in for a whole week. Steph said her insurance would cover it.

'Isn't that illegal?' asked Melissa. 'Lying about whose fault the accident was.'

'But perhaps it was me,' insisted Steph. 'I was on my phone, I wasn't concentrating, you know, stopping and starting in the traffic. Let me, please Melissa?' she said. 'Rick's just had some obscene bonus. Divorce. It's very lucrative.'

'Lawyers…' Melissa shook her head.

'I know… I know…' said Steph. 'It's not like they are saving lives…'

'Just tidying them up,' said Melissa.

'Life's great de-clutterers, lawyers.' Steph shrugged. 'So, as a result, I can pay. And I would like to, please?'

She always felt a bit guilty about Rick's money, his obscene pay-check which she felt she didn't deserve. She wanted to earn her own money, not spend his. They weren't a team, he wasn't earning on behalf of them, and if she felt she could pay for Melissa, it made her feel a bit better about it all, at least the money was helping someone else. It also explained the large cheques Steph wrote to various homeless charities and women's refuges.

She was thinking about Melissa, the following day, when she was tidying up, putting things back in their rightful places, cushions, remotes, glasses, mugs, books. The detritus of a home. But it wasn't really a home, was it? Not for her. Hopefully, it was for Rachel, but not for Steph. A home is somewhere you feel safe, but Steph was living with a bully, a man who was quick to anger and who wasn't afraid to push her around. Literally.

When she was pregnant with Rachel, he grabbed her arm behind her back. She'd been reading a pregnancy book at the time and was engrossed in thoughts of maternal love and wondering how to get babies to sleep and hadn't heard what he had said. So, when she felt him twist her arm, she was too surprised and shocked to react and it was over so quickly that the next morning, she wondered if it had actually happened. Although, he brought her breakfast in bed... which was quite unlike him.

'Bit drunk last night,' he said, standing there, in the doorway, tray in both hands. She wondered if he was trying to apologize.

If only she had done something about it then, gone to her parents, refused to live with someone like that. So she had often thought over the years, in a way, *she* was to blame. There was nothing stopping her from leaving, really, was there? But she had chosen not to, and now this was the bed she had made for herself, her own doing and therefore she couldn't complain.

And this is how she lived her life: walking on broken glass.

Even with Rachel, she couldn't say the right thing any longer. Everything caused Rachel, who was now sixteen-going-on-stroppy, to bite her head off. And there was nothing left that she was good at, nothing. Once she might have thought she was a good mother, but that talent had fallen by the wayside. And she used to be a good friend, was she able to at least be that?

But having seen Melissa again, she felt a lift in her heart. Normally, she felt so leaden, so weighed down, as though there was an actual physical pressure on her shoulders, but today she walked a little taller, a little brighter, feeling, weirdly, a little less alone. Steph felt good; she could almost remember the person she once was, the person she was before she met Rick, before she got married. Almost.

Her parents made marriage look so easy, they were a real team. Nuala was the ideas-person, the one holding the reins, and Joe was happy to be along for the ride, one which had now lasted forty-three years.

Whatever Nuala pursued, Joe would be there, her cheerful companion in life, and now on all the retiree trips they seemed to go on – to gardens across the country with the 'Grey Green-fingers', to France for the 'Francophiles over Fifty' group and to the mountains, on the first Sunday of every month, with the Wicklow Wanderers.

Behind every great woman was a man like Joe. It was he who made sure that the book for Nuala's reading group was put aside for her in the library. It was he who took the Dart into town to buy the Prussian Blue from the art shop now she had taken up oil painting. And, even now, he made her a cup of tea, put two shortbreads on a saucer and a flower plucked freshly from the garden into a vase and carried them to her at seven a.m. (He'd only ever missed one day that Steph could remember – when Nuala had gone into hospital to have her gall bladder removed. That day, instead, he had made a flask and transported the entire ritual.)

Steph never failed to marvel at how two people could be so right for each other, and silently and lovingly cursed them for making it look so easy, especially when it was so hard for Steph and Rick.

Rick loved Rachel, of course he did, but it was obvious he no longer loved Steph. If he ever did. And she hadn't loved him for years, there was something mean about him, a darkness and a *rage*, which made life a daily trial.

He had always done exactly what he wanted. He worked, he drank, he socialised, he *womanised*. And she had long suspected that something was going on with Miriam, her next-door neighbour and (former) friend. Miriam was always friendly, always flirtatious, but then, imperceptibly, something changed. There were the little things, like quick glances between Miriam and Rick, or sometimes it was the fact that they didn't look at each other at all. And suddenly it was all rather *perceptible.*

She had no proof, nothing. Except she knew it. If she accused him, he would only call her mad and she would look such a fool. But she knew it, she did! Being the weak person she thought she was though, Steph continued socializing with Miriam and her husband, Hugh, smiling when required, and running the house and looking after Rachel. Inside, she was wallowing in failure instead of going mad and all-Edward Scissorhandsy on his suits. And while Rick sprang up the career ladder, Steph felt she had nothing to show for her life. She used to be ambitious, the girl most likely, until life upended everything and she had achieved absolutely nothing.

And why, oh why, did she have to lose it in front of Melissa yesterday? She normally kept all her feelings buttoned up, but it was just seeing Melissa again, just being around her and remembering the girls they used to be, and the tears just came and wouldn't stop. And Melissa was her usual brilliant self, allowing her to cry and being utterly normal and unfreaked out about it.

And what about Eilis? Would she get the note, would she call? Steph had left both their mobile numbers, asking if Eilis would meet them next week. There was something Steph was hoping to rope Melissa and Eilis into and it was something that might bond them together again.

One of the old nuns at school had called her name when she was dropping Rachel off at school earlier. Sister Attracta, unbelievably still alive and now some kind of honorary nun, wafted around the Abbey looking increasingly wizened but rejuvenated by her the task of organizing each year's reunion. 'Stephanie Sheridan,' she'd called, using Steph's maiden name (another thing, apart from her independence, that she shouldn't have relinquished). 'I wonder, my dear, if you would like to help with this year's reunion. It is your twentieth.'

Normally, Steph would have run a mile from such an event, but Sister Attracta had ways of making you agree. The big night wasn't until December and was to be held in the Shelbourne Hotel, which was a far cry from their leaving do which was held in the school hall, draughty and miserable, with the nuns beadily managing the consumption of orange squash. Steph remembered having a bottle of vodka confiscated and so the orange squash had remained unadulterated.

Would Steph be able to look after all the invitations? asked Sister Attracta in a tone that would not countenance a negative response. *All* she had to do was track down each of the one hundred or so girls in their year and invite them to revisit their school days and their past.

Steph immediately thought of Melissa and Eilis. *She* would if *they* would. She was going to ask them when they met next week, and this, she had begun to think, begun to hope, was a way of them being the way they were, the three of them against the world, a gang. She hoped they would say yes, she didn't know what she would do if they didn't want things to be the same. She hadn't realized how much she had missed them, and she hadn't realized how much she needed them.

Tidying some newspapers, she found Rick's mobile, left over from last night. She was amazed he would leave this hanging around. He normally had the thing permanently in his hand or pocket. Quickly, she dropped it on to the rug and, aided by a sharp kick, its new home was among the dark and the dust. Steph had been engaging in this subtle form of domestic terrorism for quite some time now. It was strangely satisfying.

And then, she spotted Rick's keys on the hall table. Would hiding them be too much? Probably. Don't push it, Steph, she thought. Keys could be tucked behind a cushion or slipped into a drawer another day. The phone was enough for now and she didn't want Rick suspecting he was living with a domestic terrorist, he might get angry and that really defeated the feeling of satisfaction.

She looked at herself in the mirror. This is me, she thought. I'm thirty-eight and what do I have to show for nearly four decades on this planet? What exactly have I *done*? Except turn into a wreaker of domestic acts of terror. The temptation to cackle maniacally was overwhelming. The secret, she realized, was staying on the right side of madness. But she was like a beginner, wobbling on the tightrope.

She heard a beep from his phone from beneath the sofa. She paused, in mid-air, and suddenly she knew she had to see what that text was. Normally, she would never check his messages but she was feeling slightly reckless, the old Steph wouldn't have been afraid of anything and after seeing Melissa again, she could feel something of her younger and more daring self stir.

She fished it out and looked at the screen. Immediately, she wished her younger self had stayed where she was.

Missing you.

And the name of the sender? Angeline. His junior from work.

She scrolled back from the text and read as many as she could, her heart beating wildly, trying to take it all in.

They went back months and months as far as she could tell. Texts from Angeline saying she missed him, texts from Rick saying he wanted her. Arrangements to meet, times and venues, hotel rooms, bars and restaurants, passion, sex, desire. It was all there, an affair in text form.

If she was a braver woman, she thought, she would smash Rick's collection of horrible crystal whiskey glasses or flush his phone down the toilet. But she wasn't brave, not anymore, she was scared of what he would do. Even if she held the moral high ground she never, never, had the upper hand. He was always in charge and in control.

And Steph had met Angeline… how old could she be? Not thirty, anyway. Could she be mid-twenties? Twenty-five? What an utter bastard Rick was.

Managing to keep her anger on simmer, she dropped the phone back under the sofa. And, suddenly, she thought of something else, something else she needed to know. On the sideboard, in the hall, were letters from the credit card company. Normally, she left them to Rick, but this time she opened the envelope and scanned the rows and rows of transactions.

She spotted her own transactions: Rachel's new school coat, Steph's facial, paying for Melissa's car. And then something caught her eye.

Netaporter – €365.

She had often looked at the website, imagining outfits she might wear if she had dates to go on or weekends away. But her life never demanded a cocktail dress, and she had no idea that Rick had heard of the website. He certainly didn't buy her anything expensive and glamorous. Rick had never bought *her* anything like that. It was dated last month. And then more, a few days later, all in London. Selfridges. And the Wolseley, a Claridges bar bill and a room in The Connaught. They came to thousands and thousands of pounds. And she remembered that one of the texts specifically mentioned the bar in Claridges.

She checked the dates; the weekend he went to London to meet clients. But if that was a business trip, she was Rumpole of the Bailey. She then had a thought and went on Facebook and searched for Angeline Barrow. Birthdate? Last month. So it was a birthday weekend away. It had to be. Angeline was 29 years old. Steph shook her head. What was he thinking? Steph felt disempowered, dehumanised, worthless. Someone else was worth his time, his energy and she was nothing. She should have been used to it, but each time she was faced with his utter disregard for her and their family life, it was a new shock, a fresh wound.

Somehow she managed to get her coat, bag and keys and drive to the Dundrum shopping centre, and she did what she always did when subtle domestic terrorism did not quell her feelings of utter powerlessness. She went shoplifting. It was far more soothing than eating cakes, she thought, or drinking alcohol. The high was so much higher.

3

Eilis

Aching feet, damp patches under her arms and, sticky-up hair. For an A&E consultant, this was what was called getting off lightly, the mere physical manifestations of a night shift and it didn't do you much good to dwell too long on the emotional toll. Eilis McCarthy knew dwelling on anything didn't get you anywhere. She was half-way through a night shift and it was 4am but in the parallel universe of hospital life, the time didn't matter, you didn't care. It was a case of getting to the end, whenever and wherever that was.

But in all these years, the nightmarish whirl of a shift on the A&E ward never ceased in its power to shock. And then, suddenly, like some terrifying fairground ride, it was over and you would be deposited on terra normal, legs shaking and eyes blinking in the sunlight, the throb of it all jingling and jangling in your brain.

And all those patients, the old, the dying, the strokes, the beaten-up women, the bizarre domestic accidents – all those *stories* – they didn't just float off and disappear. You couldn't just forget about them and carry on with your day. Well, Eilis couldn't, anyway.

She would go home and try to do some gardening or gaze in the fridge for something to eat or be brushing her teeth and then she would realize she had totally stopped, frozen at the memory of the person who, just hours earlier, was fighting for life. They were men and women at their lowest, at their most vulnerable. Helpless, inadequately clothed, often alone, and Eilis would have stitched them up, made assessments, talked to them, soothed them, dispensed drugs, and then she was expected to just walk away. And then there were those who didn't make it, the ones who couldn't be soothed and medicalized back to full health, the ones who they couldn't help, couldn't save. It was them, the ones who had lost the fight, that were the worst, those were the faces that most haunted her waking moment.

Maybe she should have gone in for paediatrics. But that was heart-breaking, too, wasn't it? Worse, maybe. Or… maybe she should never have done medicine. But it was all her mother wanted for her.

The kettle in the little kitchen of the staff room in A&E was a slow-boiler and even if you tried not to watch it impatiently, it still took ages. But she persisted as she was suddenly desperate for the comfort of a hot mug of tea and a proper read of the note she had skimmed. And maybe a biscuit. Eilis rooted around in the tin hoping for one that wasn't soft or half-chewed.

She was thin and pale, the result of a diet of biscuits and not enough sleep. She was petite and pretty, her hair was cut pixie-style, but she spent most of her life avoiding mirrors so as not to be reminded of the dark circles under her eyes, and anyway, what could she do about it? Unlike practically every other workplace in the world, a hospital was one place where your physical appearance was of absolutely no consequence, thankfully.

The note had been written by Steph and Melissa. She had scanned it quickly, when Theresa had given it to her, but she wanted a chance to read it properly, to take it all in. The thought of Melissa and Steph – her friends! – made her feel that fresh air was being breathed into her life, something wonderful was there for her, if she wanted it.

And she did. She hadn't realised just how much until she saw Steph's handwriting. 'It's us,' the note had said. 'Here to see you. We miss you and want you to join us next week for drinks. Steph and Melissa.'

But what would they think of her? Would they see through her, realize how insular, how introverted she had become? And what would she say about Rob?

She and Rob had been together since they were first years… so twenty years ago now. But she wasn't sure if what she had with Rob was *normal*? They hadn't had sex since… since probably around the last time she had seen Steph and Melissa. No, that was taking it a bit far. But probably six months or so. Long enough anyway. Too long. When were you officially flatmates? What was the cut-off point? Six months? A year?

She and Rob were both doctors, so it was inevitable and entirely un-ironic that their relationship should be clinical. He was a consultant but had had the sense not to specialize in A&E, the front line. He was besuited and officed and led a far more civilised professional life than Eilis. He liked everything just so: his life, his home and his partner. He didn't go in for emotion or mess. Their small cottage was like something you might see in an interiors magazine, where if you left a mug on the table, it all felt wrong and weird. Their kitchen cupboards didn't even have handles, so you had to jab and stab at them, just to try and get them to open. Sometimes Eilis wondered just what was so wrong with handles. But these kind of things mattered to Rob… and it didn't really to her, so she went along with it.

Rob spent his evenings perched on their stylish but incongruously uncomfortable sofa. Supposedly a place to relax, it made you feel like you were waiting for your annual smear test. It wasn't what you wanted in a sofa; that much was sure. But Rob loved it and was happy to balance on its edge.

Their whole house was a bit like that, Eilis thought. Rob didn't even like cushions or rugs. The headboard on their bed had a piece of wood jutting out that caught Eilis on the back of the head. Every time. And even the tea towels were too nice to use. Eilis had her own secret supply of mugs that Rob said he *could not, would not* drink out of. If it didn't emanate from Scandinavia, then it wasn't worth having. He had also sharpened up his appearance lately but isn't that what happens when the forties loom, you either up your game or let things slide. He *was* more muscular these days and his hair was trendier. It was quite a shock when he came home with it, such a departure from the normal hair he had before… But he looked good. And very different from the Rob she had met all those years ago, when they were first years doing medicine in Trinity College.

He had dressed beyond his years in those days, blazer and smart trousers, hair cut in a style only a Granny would love. But now… he exuded that look of the lean, sporty type. Not the kind of man Eilis ever thought she would end up with and not the kind who she would have thought would have gone for her. But he had and there they were. A couple, uncoupled.

It didn't help that she felt surrounded by death. There was the hospital, of course, part of the job. Sometimes she felt like the last person left in the castle which was being besieged by faceless people with swords. She kept having to swing around and fight off the next one. But it was also her mother, who had died in her last year at school. She felt almost embarrassed that she was still, she felt, in grieving, even twenty years on. She still felt like that eighteen year old who lost her mother, she still carried the pain around carefully so as not to dislodge it. She couldn't, hadn't, told anyone about it as no one would understand her inability to move on.

But at least now she had Steph and Eilis… at least she had her friends back, after all that time. They hadn't given up on her.

She was desperate to phone Steph straight away, and say wild horses wouldn't keep her from meeting next week. She had missed the two of them as well and that making new friends like them had turned out to be impossible. She almost skipped out of the tea room, ready to get on with the shift and get home.

'Right, I need to talk to you.' A man in his early forties, wearing a checked shirt and sleeves rolled up, was marching straight up to her. Handsome, she couldn't help noticing. 'Yes,' she said, smiling warily.

'Are you a doctor?' He spoke angrily.

'Yes… but…'

'My mother has been waiting for more than eight hours. I just can't believe that this situation exists in this country. My mother… my mother is out there. Stroke… we think. Who knows? Not anyone in this bloody hospital! She's eighty-five, but no one has bothered to ask her that. No one has asked any questions yet because not a single doctor has examined her…'

'I'm sorry,' she said, thinking how worried he looked, wrung out. 'We are…'

'Listen,' he interrupted. 'I know you're up to your eyes, but when are you going to see her?'

'One of the nurses will have…'

'Do you think that is enough?' he said, speaking more quietly. 'Do you think that it is okay for an eighty-five-year-old woman to be left sitting on a plastic chair for eight hours? She's been given the once-over and that's all. Is it because she's old? Not worth saving? Are you all happy with that?'

'No… but… there's a system here…' She tried to speak kindly to him, to soothe, to calm.

He rolled his eyes. 'A system? There's a better system in any kindergarten. Bedlam this is. Proper bedlam.'

'I am sorry,' said Eilis. 'We are working as hard as we can.' This is the line that they all trotted out, something they have been told to use to keep anxious or angry relatives at bay while they get on with the job of looking after patients. But she was well aware of the flimsiness of the line, the lack of satisfaction it gave the relative who was only trying to help someone they loved. She thought of her own mother and how she would feel if she had been sitting on a chair for eight hours. 'We'll get to her as soon as possible. I promise.'

'Really?' He raised his eyebrow. For a moment, he looked away, his mouth taut with the pressure of the situation, the fight he was having to get his mother off a chair and into a bed.

'I'm sorry,' she said again. 'We will…'

He shook his head, as if to say he couldn't talk about it anymore and suddenly she was struck by him, this handsome man, with blue eyes, and she was struck by his humanity, his fight for his mother. She was touched and moved by him. And when he pushed his hair back, she noticed his hands; strong and tanned, even in this Irish winter. She was suddenly disarmed and didn't know what to say.

'I know it's not your fault,' he began and walked off back to the waiting room.

'We'll look after your mother, don't worry,' she managed to say.

Leaning against a trolley (thankfully patient-less) was Becca, one of the staff nurses, laughing with Bogdan, the porter.

'Everything all right, doctor?' called Bogdan.

'Jaysus, Eils,' said Becca. 'I thought he was going to have a coronary. In the right place, though, eh?'

Eilis didn't answer but instead walked to the nurses' station and took a moment to calm herself. 'Theresa,' she then said, 'there's a woman in the waiting area, she's eighty-five and she may have had a stroke. Could you check on why she hasn't been seen yet. Will you find out?'

'Certainly, doctor.'

Becca came up and sat down beside Theresa, swinging a 360 in the chair.

'Jaysus,' she said. 'I'd do him.'

'Bogdan?'

'No, that total ride. The one with the gorgeous ass. Mr Shouty.'

'Oh him?' Eilis dismissed it. She had a teenager with a broken leg who was just back from x-ray, a man who had been beaten up and needed stitches, and another man who had stumbled down the ladder of his loft and had fallen onto his back on his landing. She needed to assess him straight away.

'I wouldn't mind him shouting me into bed,' said Becca.

Bogdan overheard her. 'You've got to have more self-respect, Becca,' he said. 'Shouting is not good from man to woman.'

'It all depends,' shrieked Becca. 'If you get my meaning!'

Eilis left Becca laughing away and Bogdan shaking his head, puzzled. It was going to be a long night, she felt the note in her pocket, though, and remembered she had something, she had two friends who wanted to see her. And she felt something she hadn't felt in years: excitement.

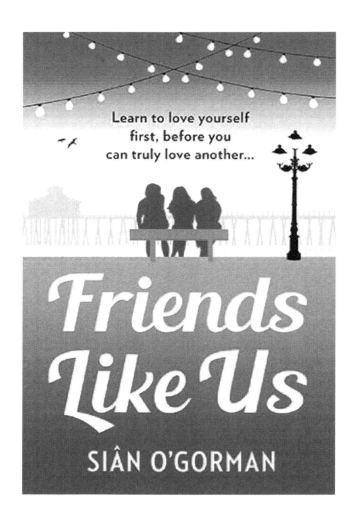

Buy it now
http://www.headofzeus.com/isbn/9781784979560

Become an Aria Addict

Aria is the new digital-first fiction imprint from Head of Zeus.

It's Aria's ambition to discover and publish tomorrow's superstars, targeting fiction addicts and readers keen to discover new and exciting authors.

Aria will publish a variety of genres under the commercial fiction umbrella such as women's fiction, crime, thrillers, historical fiction, saga and erotica.

So, whether you're a budding writer looking for a publisher or an avid reader looking for something to escape with – Aria will have something for you.

Get in touch: aria@headofzeus.com

Become an Aria Addict
http://www.ariafiction.com

Find us on Twitter
https://twitter.com/Aria_Fiction

Find us on Facebook
http://www.facebook.com/ariafiction

Find us on BookGrail
http://www.bookgrail.com/store/aria/

Addictive Fiction

First published in the United Kingdom in 2017 by Aria, an imprint of Head of Zeus Ltd

9 7 5 3 1 2 4 6 8

A CIP catalogue record for this book is available from the British Library.

ISBN (E) 9781784979577

Aria
c/o Head of Zeus
First Floor East
5–8 Hardwick Street
London EC1R 4RG

www.ariafiction.com